Elizabeth Falconer lives in Gloucestershire and spends part of the year in the south of France. *The Counter-Tenor's Daughter* is her third novel; her first two novels, *The Golden Year* and *The Love of Women*, are also published by Black Swan.

Also by Elizabeth Falconer

THE GOLDEN YEAR
THE LOVE OF WOMEN

and published by Black Swan

The Counter-Tenor's Daughter

Elizabeth Falconer

BLACK SWAN

THE COUNTER-TENOR'S DAUGHTER
A BLACK SWAN BOOK : 0 552 99624 6

First publication in Great Britain

PRINTING HISTORY
Black Swan edition published 1997

Set in 11/13pt Linotype Melior by
County Typesetters, Margate, Kent

Black Swan Books are published by Transworld Publishers Ltd,
61–63 Uxbridge Road, London W5 5SA,
in Australia by Transworld Publishers (Australia) Pty Ltd,
15–25 Helles Avenue, Moorebank, NSW 2170
and in New Zealand by Transworld Publishers (NZ) Ltd,
3 William Pickering Drive, Albany, Auckland.

Reproduced, printed and bound in Great Britain by
Cox & Wyman Ltd, Reading, Berks.

For my father

Do I carry the moon in my pocket?
Robert Browning
'Master Hugues of Saxe-Gotha'

Chapter One

Dido Partridge drove her small hired car along a narrow rutted track until it petered out altogether, forcing her to abandon her car and continue her journey on foot. Taking her bag from the rear seat and locking the car, she stood for a few hesitant moments, awed by the solitude of the surrounding groves of tall, unpruned olives, their majestic silence shattered by the shrill persistent cacophany of a million cicadas concealed within their branches. Well, she thought, I've come this far, I might as well try and find the place. She began to look around more carefully and discovered that a goat-track continued where the road had ceased to exist. After consulting her map again, and judging the position of the sun, she decided that the track appeared to be going in the right direction – westwards. Right, she said to herself, I'll give it a go.

Under the shade of the olives, the air was cooler and sweet with the soothing smell of thyme, bruised under the feet of browsing goats. She followed the track for about twenty minutes, until suddenly she saw what she had been looking for, the little monastery of Myrtiótissa, white-washed and dazzling against the blue Ionian sky. Close to the gates she found the half-hidden entrance to the cliff path that would take her down to a beach, a hundred metres below. Shading her eyes with her hand, she looked down through the cypresses, twisted olive trees and myrtle bushes that grew out of the cliff-face, to the sea far below. The water was an incredibly clear emerald-green, pierced by long lines of refracted light undulating beneath its glassy surface. She began to descend the steep, rocky and vertiginous cliff-path that seemed suspended in the air above the water so far below.

Keeping her eyes firmly on the narrow path, Dido picked her way carefully through the rocks and prickly shrubs that threatened to obliterate the track, clinging to the branches of the small, scrubby trees that grew out of the sheer rocky cliff-face beside her. Presently she became aware of the great looming green presence of the sea on her other side and allowed herself to stop for a moment and look down at the narrow, rock-enclosed strip of golden sand below. Bathed in the warm glow of the afternoon sun, the tiny, empty beach seemed to hold out its arms in welcome and Dido congratulated herself on her enterprise in finding such a place and her courage in overcoming her fear of the terrifying means of getting there. Drawing several deep breaths, she negotiated the last few metres of the treacherous path and stepped onto the soft yellow sand. She looked back up at the high, vertical limestone cliff, quite unable to distinguish the path down which she had descended. A strong sense of isolation enveloped her like a great lonely wave, the palpable silence of the place broken only by the sharp, barely audible twittering of birds hidden in the vegetation and the soft hiss of the small, foam-flecked waves that broke gently on the shore.

Dido took off her sandals and walked along the water's edge, her feet cooled and caressed by the shallow waves. As she drew near the tall, jagged rock that rose into the air at the end of the beach, she saw that the sea had worn away its base into small natural pools, full of crystal-clear sea water, and inhabited by minute pink transparent fish, trapped by the receding tide. It was early October and the sea itself was warm enough for swimming, but the pools were even warmer as she discovered when she sat down on the ledge and trailed her hand in the water. She glanced round the cove and up at the cliff to make sure that she was still alone, then took off her clothes and slipped into the pool. The warm water closed over her like a benison and she lay on her back, eyes closed, arms and legs weightless, feeling her short dark hair floating like weed around her head. The leathery grey-green leaves of the stunted olive tree which grew out of the cliff-face immediately above her head threw dappled shadows on her face, and through the submerged perforated rock face, she could hear the distant echoing boom of the sea. Gently lulled by the rise and fall of the ocean, she listened to the rhythmic pulse of the marine universe, and felt herself part of it.

For a long time she remained where she was, relaxed and half asleep, her mind wandering, sliding away in scraps of half-remembered episodes, some happy, some ridiculous, some unreal. She saw Maria, her mother, in her dressing-room at La Scala, being laced into her costume for *Tosca,* with the faithful little Signor Pernice hovering in the background, scolded by Maria's dresser Mabel, who had travelled everywhere with them. Luigi Pernice had been a singer himself, a counter-tenor, and he too had travelled the world giving recitals and making recordings, particularly of baroque music. In his own estimation, his greatest achievement had been his interpretation of a contemporary role, that of the Fairy King Oberon, in Britten's *A Midsummer Night's Dream*, an opera he had adored, and in her dreams Dido frequently heard snatches of the counter-tenor's beautiful, unearthly arias. Although she had always understood that Luigi

11

was her father, Dido had for some unexplained reason always called him Signor Pernice, and it was not until after his death when she was sixteen that she had been able to persuade her mother to allow her to change her name to Partridge. Half-sadly, Dido smiled at the memory of the volatile, kind little man so dwarfed by the massive bulk of Maria Corning, his more famous spouse. Her smile faded as she remembered the extravagant and prolonged grief of her bereaved mother after his death. The light had gone out of her life and she had followed Luigi to the grave two years later, leaving her daughter to make her own way in the world as best she could. The only world Dido knew was the theatre, and since she had no talent, much less any ambition to perform, she had started at the bottom in the movie business, as a messenger. She had graduated to continuity girl and eventually worked her way up to production assistant, her present occupation.

Suddenly, a bird flew noisily out of the myrtle bushes above Dido's head. Startled, she sat up, then scrambled out of the pool and ran along the sand to get dry. She pulled on her shorts and sat on the warm rocks, watching the sun falling slowly down the sky towards the horizon. I'd better not be too long, she thought, and put on her crumpled T-shirt. It'll be dark in an hour; I must get back to Koulari. Climbing back to the monastery seemed a good deal easier than coming down, and in half an hour she was back in her car and heading towards the north coast of the island, driving slowly through silvery olive groves punctuated by soaring clumps of dark cypresses. She put on her headlights as a warning to the elderly shepherdesses tending their long-legged flocks and the old men riding sideways on tottering little donkeys who seemed to materialize like phantoms in the middle of the road right in front of her. She inched her way through them nervously, terrified of the prospect of an accident.

When she got back to Koulari, Dido found that the tables were already laid for dinner on the terrace overlooking the sea. She went up to her room, brushed her hair and changed into trousers and a sweater, for the evening air was quite cool and a breeze blew off the sea. It was only eight o'clock, but she felt quite hungry, so she went down to the bar, ordered an ouzo and asked Spiros what was for supper. They went through this small ritual every night, but so late in the season the dinner was always the same, a salad of feta cheese and olives, grilled fish with lemon and some kind of very sweet pastry or ice-cream. Dido ate rather early for the local custom and Spiros kindly allowed her this eccentricity; the bulk of his clientèle, village people and the odd foreign resident arrived between nine and half-past, and rarely left before midnight. She had chosen the taverna because it had been described as quiet and family-run, small and friendly, and this had proved to be an accurate description. She went out to the terrace with her drink and sitting down at her table, looked across the darkening sea to the coast of Albania, brooding and mysterious, its few distant points of light suggesting the presence of humanity but nothing more.

Dido had been on the island for five days, and now for the first time she allowed herself to think about her reason for coming. Sipping her drink, she considered quite calmly, even dispassionately, the question of Jacob. They had met twelve years ago when they were both working on the same movie, a remake of *Lorna Doone*. She remembered their first real conversation, other than on the set.

'Dido, can I have a word?' he had said, sitting down

next to her during the lunch-break, and offering a paper cup of red wine. 'Have you got your notes?'

'Of course, by all means,' she had replied, slightly flustered at the unexpected attention from the assistant director. 'They're right here.' She had extracted her clipboard from her briefcase and laid it on the table.

'Could you just check for me? Was Lorna wearing a necklace in Scene 14?'

'Let's see,' said Dido, 'that was a wrap on Monday, wasn't it?' She had taken a file from her briefcase and leafed through the pages until she found the date and that day's schedule. 'Yes, she was. Blue dress, cream lace fichu, glass necklace, black boots, hair tied back with black ribbon.'

'Exactly the same as today?'

'Absolutely.' Dido closed the file.

'Great. I had the weirdest feeling that something about her was different.'

Dido had looked at him severely. 'Don't you think I would have spotted it, if that was the case?'

'Yes, of course you would. Sorry. No question, Dido, you're shit-hot at your job.'

'Well, good. I do my best.'

'Cheers.' He had raised his paper cup, smiling, mocking her.

Dido had looked at him and noticed for the first time that his eyes were not the same colour. One was a mottled greenish-brown, the other grey. He had a marked squint, which gave the disconcerting impression that he was looking past one's shoulder at someone else, undoubtedly more interesting. His straight hair, brown and rather greasy, flopped over his forehead. He needs a haircut she thought, taking a sip of her wine. 'I'd better not have too much of this,' she had remarked primly, 'or I probably won't be quite so shit-hot at my job this afternoon.'

After that they became quite friendly and he sometimes took her with him for a drink with the actors
after the day's work. A couple of times he took her to
the theatre, and it was after one of these nights out that
he drove her home.

'Where do you live?'

'It's down Lots Road.'

He drove along the Embankment and Cheyne Walk
and turned into Lots Road. 'Where now?'

'Down the bottom. It's on the river – Chelsea Harbour.'

'Are there flats there?'

'It's not a flat. It's a barge.'

'Really? What fun.'

They parked the car and he insisted on seeing her to
her door, crossing the slippery ridged gangplank and
picking his way through the massed pots of plants
on the deck. Dido went down the wooden steps,
unlocked the narrow door and switched on the lights.
Fascinated, Jacob followed her. *The Maid of Wapping*
had been the London base of the Pernice family for all
of Dido's life, and had been practically the only
bequest from her parents. Her mother had not sung
again after the death of Luigi but had nevertheless
managed to get through very large sums of money
during her remaining years. A pension for Mabel, the
taxman and death duties had swallowed up most of
the residue but Dido was extremely grateful that at
least the stout old barge continued to be her home and
she cherished it, along with the bizarre memories of
her incredible parents.

The major part of the barge was a large, low-
ceilinged sitting-room or studio, with wide windows
just above water-level. Through the windows could be
seen the nocturnal wavering reflections of the lights of
other boats, and several hostile-looking gulls roosting
on the water nearby peered through the glass in an

aggrieved manner. In the spaces between the windows were built-in bookcases and the long room was dominated by a large Godin stove, enamelled dark blue, with a shiny black flue disappearing through the ceiling. In front of the stove, which shed its warmth through the room with comforting efficiency was a wide, well-worn, slightly collapsing sofa, covered in honey-coloured corduroy and heaped with piles of tapestry cushions, the work of Signor Pernice. Dido often thought of him, stitching away in the dressing-room while her mother poured out her soul to enraptured audiences all over the world, and he and Mabel waited patiently to cherish her at the end of each performance. Behind the stove stood a grand piano, black and important, full of the personality of her mother. Indeed, the top of the now-closed instrument was crowded with many large silver-framed photographs of her, celebrating the high points of her glorious career. There was also a rather smaller one of her father, as Oberon.

'Good heavens!' Jacob crossed the room and picked up one of the photographs. 'Did you know Maria Corning?'

'Yes,' said Dido, 'she was my mother.'

'Aha!' He put down the photo and looked at her, as if for the first time. 'So that explains the name?'

'Dido? Yes, she was singing the role when I was conceived, evidently.'

'Any brothers or sisters?'

'No, just me.'

She showed him the very small galley kitchen, and put on the kettle to make some coffee. Then she slid back the panel that concealed the bunk-bed she had used as a child, with her dolls and teddy-bears still piled on the pillows.

'And where did the divine Maria sleep?'

'Here.' Dido opened a secret door, part of a *trompe-l'oeil* panel behind the piano, depicting a Grinling Gibbons carving of musical instruments. She led the way into the large double-bedroom that she still thought of as her mother's, although she had been dead for six years. It had been a long time before Dido had persuaded herself to put away the florid bed-hangings and quilt, and redecorate the room in the simple, much quieter style that she herself preferred. As it was, the offending satin had been carefully folded and packed away in a trunk, along with some of her mother's gorgeous costumes.

'Was it like this in her day?'

'No.'

'I thought not.' He laughed, and so did Dido.

'I loved her, you know,' she said, feeling as though she had betrayed her parents by her laughter.

'Of course you did, silly child,' said Jacob. 'It doesn't mean you have to be a clone of her, does it?'

'No, I suppose not.'

Jacob Kroll had at that time been living in a service flat in Dolphin Square which he did not particularly like but had neither the time nor inclination to look for something more appealing. The grandson of Jewish refugees from Germany in the Thirties, he had been brought up in New York. A strong compulsion to return to his European roots, coupled with an equally strong desire to escape from his highly Orthodox family had brought him first to Oxford and thence into the movie business. He recognized that part of his dislike of his flat stemmed from its bleakness and lack of comfort. In spite of his need to escape from his background, he missed the warmth of his family, the cooking and the jokes. Dido's barge seemed to him to offer the possibility of some of these desirable attributes. He spent more and more time there; it began to feel like home to him. He knew that Dido was in love with him, most women were. He was fond of her, and his relationship with her formed a useful protection from the young actresses who sought his favours. A few skilfully dropped hints concerning his 'wife' were usually enough to terminate an affair that was dead and buried as far as he was concerned. As for Dido, she had been flattered that Jacob, advancing so rapidly in the business, should consider sharing his life with so mere a mortal as a continuity girl.

So he had moved into *The Maid of Wapping*, and they had been rather happy together. Dido had been twenty-six years old at the time and he had brought much-needed excitement and humour into her life. She was dazzled by his success, his wit and his looks. She loved his tall slender body, his long floppy hair and even the squint in his grey eye, though he had now taken to wearing heavy horn-rimmed spectacles which partially concealed this defect.

It had not been very long before Dido's 'friends' began to hint that Jacob was not faithful to her, that he had the reputation of sleeping with the leading ladies in his movies. Dido was not stupid, she understood the casual liaisons that tended to blossom during the making of a film, and she chose to ignore both the warnings and the quite probable affairs. Jacob never embarrassed her and seemed happy in their relationship. They had much in common, were friends as well as lovers and on balance she had considered their ten-year-old domestic partnership a success. Latterly, however, their career obligations had separated them for increasingly long periods, so that they were able to be together only rarely.

Thinking about it now, Dido realized that it had been rather absurd of her to react with such dismay and shock when she had arrived home four days ahead of schedule, due to the smooth and rapid completion of the documentary on which she had been working in Scotland. She had not phoned to announce her coming, intending it to be a surprise. She had taken a taxi from the airport, shopped for food and wine in Chelsea, bought flowers from a street vendor and taken another taxi to *The Maid of Wapping*. She had unlocked her door and gone in, carrying her shopping and her suitcase into the studio. The room smelt of cigarette smoke and she left the door open, surprised. Jacob never smoked, and neither did she. She arranged the flowers in a glass jar and put them on the piano. Then she put the food and the champagne in the fridge, and went to the bedroom to unpack, wash and change her clothes. Immediately she noticed the smell of an unknown scent, not her own and not Jake's. She frowned, beginning to feel extremely nervous, as though she were an intruder in her own home. She opened the wardrobe and saw a pink silk dressing-gown hanging behind the door. With sudden fury, she ripped it off the hook and threw it on the floor, grinding the heel of her boot into it. She crossed to the bed, threw back the covers and almost triumphantly saw at once the black smudges of mascara on her own pillow, and then the long red hair on the sheet. Revolted, she put her hand over her mouth, ran quickly to the bathroom and leaned over the basin, retching painfully. She turned on the tap, swilled round the basin and bathed her face in the cold water, then stood for a moment, shaking, leaning against the porcelain bowl. Reaching for a towel, she stumbled against the laundry basket and saw that it contained Jake's black silk pyjama bottoms, bought on a trip to Rome, and a pair of shell-pink satin knickers, cut high in the Brazilian style and edged with lace. Numb with shock, she sat on the edge of the bath and dried her face. Into her mind quite clearly came the expression *in flagrante*, and a half-hysterical laugh rose like a bubble in her throat, but died before the sound emerged. She stood up and walked firmly back to the bedroom, pulled up the bedcovers, and emptied her suitcase onto the floor. She quickly repacked the case with all the summer clothes, T-shirts, shorts, swimming things she could lay her hands on easily, then telephoned reservations at Heathrow. 'I want a flight to Corfu, please,' she had said calmly.

'Tonight, madam?'

'If possible, yes.'

'Let's have a look.' There was a pause and then the man spoke again. 'I can't do you direct until tomorrow, but I could do you Rome this evening and on to Corfu in the morning. How would that suit?'

'Fine. I'll do that.'

'Right, madam. It's Club Class, I'm afraid, is that OK?'

'That's OK,' said Dido. She gave him the details of her credit card and arranged to pick up the tickets at the airport. Then she telephoned for a taxi, and while she waited for it to arrive she had returned to the bedroom, picked up the in^{...}der's dressing-gown from the floor and pulling several alien pieces of clothing from their hangers in the wardrobe had stuffed them into their owner's elegant Louis Vuitton overnight bag. She went out onto the deck and threw the bag into the river, where it bobbed along on the water for a short distance and presently sank with a satisfying display of bubbles. Then the taxi had arrived, and Dido had picked up her suitcase, her passport and her bag, locked the door and left *The Maid of Wapping* without looking back.

When she arrived in Corfu the following day she took a cab into town to the offices of a villa company she had read about and they arranged for her to stay at the taverna at Koulari, organized a hire-car and some currency for her and gave her a number to ring in case she needed help. Exhausted and tense, she had driven out to Koulari, gone straight to bed and slept for six hours. When she woke it was dark, and she had taken a shower, changed and gone down to dine on the terrace, just as she was doing now. What have I done? she asked herself sadly. Have I burned my boats, or what?

Spiros came out with the feta salad and a small jug of Corfo and laid them carefully on the table, pouring the wine. She ate her salad hungrily, with the delicious coarse local bread, and drank a glass of wine, chilled, light and undemanding. The main course was grilled swordfish, and tonight Spiros brought a small round bowl of hot golden potato chips, perfectly fried and smelling delicious. He laid the bowl on the table as if it were a special treat for a child, and she thanked him, smiling. She did not have the heart to tell him that she never ate chips. In the event she did eat them, all of them, and Spiros showed his wife the empty bowl and they exchanged pleased smiles. They thought their guest painfully thin, and very sad. She never ate the sweet honey-filled cakes they usually brought at the end of the meal, so tonight Spiros brought a dish of ripe black figs, and put them on the table with Dido's coffee.

As she drank the strong, sweet black coffee and ate some of the figs she gazed across the bay at the mysterious Albanian coast, and up at the star-sprinkled sky above and thought that if she had to be so miserable, this was as good a place as any in which to be unhappy. The thought that no one she knew had the faintest idea where she was gave her an odd feeling of comfort. Like a hermit-crab, she had withdrawn into her shell and would remain there until she had sorted herself out.

Spiros approached and offered her more coffee. 'A Metaxa, perhaps?'

'Thanks, Spiros, that would be great.'

He returned with the glass of brandy just as a small flotilla of fishing boats came slowly round the headland from the next bay, the big lamps on their prows sending their powerful white beams into the deep water as they headed along the rocky coast for a night's fishing.

'Spiros,' said Dido, 'would it be possible for me to go out in one of those boats one night? I'd really love to go, it must be fantastic.'

'I will ask Vassili, my brother. He has a boat and a lamp.' He looked at her, doubtful, concerned. 'It can be rough, and cold. You will get wet, you understand?'

Dido laughed. 'Don't worry about that. I'm quite tough, as a matter of fact. I can swim, too.' Spiros, who, like so many of the islanders could not swim himself, looked suitably impressed at this confident assertion, and promised to speak to Vassili in the morning.

Guy Porteous lived in a simple, single-storey Greek house, situated in a magnificent grove of ancient olive trees, and perched above a small, pebbly beach, looking across the blue waters of the bay to Albania. From the sea, the house presented a totally incongruous appearance, the roof of the long terrace being adorned with a peculiar chalet-style fretwork fascia-board of dark brown wood, lending the building the unlikely and extremely foreign appearance of a stretched cuckoo-clock. In spite of this architectural eccentricity, Guy had decided to buy the house because it was cheap and exactly suited his requirements, all the rooms being more or less on one level.

The shape and layout of his house had been crucial to Guy's choice in view of the fact that he was seriously disabled, the result of a childhood accident which had left him with paralyzed legs. He was unable to walk without leg-irons and sticks, but was stubbornly determined not to use a wheelchair unless it became absolutely necessary. This massive disability had not affected his career in the English judiciary until he reached the age of forty-five, when his failure to find a wife to share his life had begun to get to him. He had become increasingly lonely, disillusioned and self-pitying and had begun to drink more than his useless legs could handle, with disastrous results. With alarming frequency he had fallen down the steps of his club, often re-breaking his legs in the process, necessitating a spell in hospital, or more usually, the humiliation of being taken home and put to bed by his driver. After several such painful and sometimes extremely public episodes, the powers-that-be had suggested early retirement on health grounds, and he had reluctantly accepted the offer. He knew that there was no question of a refusal; the alternative would have been the sack.

It had not taken him long to reject the idea of spending his retirement at Inniscarragh, his family home in Ireland. This was partly on account of its dampness and cold, which badly affected his damaged legs, but equally because of the oppressive atmosphere that filled him with depression, even a kind of horror, whenever he entered the house. It was filled with the ghosts of the past; sad reminders of his parents' sudden and untimely death, and of his own childhood loneliness and pain. Most of all, in every room, in the courtyard and stables, even in the surrounding woodlands, he could hear the sharp voice of his older sister, Lavinia, scornful, critical, hectoring and angry. Uncle James, who had looked after the place on his behalf since his parents' death, seemed quite incapable of standing up to her, and Guy himself rarely challenged her in any way. As a small boy, sixteen years her junior, he had thought her beautiful and clever and had wished himself more like her. In the intervening years, she seemed to him to become increasingly domineering and unkind; his admiration had gradually turned to fear and dislike, and ultimately to a cold indifference. Keeping out of her way seemed the most appropriate way of avoiding confrontation, and when she bombarded him with her opinionated letters, which were more like orders, concerning the proper management of his estate, he took the coward's way out and communicated with her through the family lawyers.

Guy had sold his London house and decided to retire to Corfu. He had spent many holidays on the island and hoped that there he would find the affordable house, plus the help and uncritical acceptance so necessary to his well-being. Heleni and Vassili lived in the small cottage in the olive grove, and between them cared for him and his house, his car, his donkey and his boat. After four years on the island, Guy was approaching fifty with little enthusiasm but a resigned fatalistic acceptance of his lot. His black hair was sprinkled with grey. His face was deeply tanned and bore the lines of suffering and bitterness. His nose was long and narrow, an Irish nose, and his deepset eyes beneath strong black brows were a surprising dark blue, the colour of the deepest sea.

Now he lay in his big comfortable bed and watched the sun coming up over the Albanian mountains, swathed in early mist, their contours etched in shades of pearly grey. Through his open window he could see the sky beginning to grow pink along the mountain crests. The sea, only a few kilometres wide between the mainland and the island at that point, gradually became visible, luminous, bright behind a foreground of dark cypresses, soaring like black pencils into the dawn sky. Then, exactly on cue, the ferry from Italy emerged from behind the dark screen of the cypresses and chugged like a toy across the smooth waters, heading slowly towards the harbour at Corfu Town. Guy smiled, pleased that he had been awake to observe this small daily ritual, and watched the ferry out of sight. Then, picking up his book again, he turned the pages with his long brown bony fingers until he had found his place.

During the last four years, he had studied Greek, both ancient and demotic, hard and seriously as a means of preventing his brain from becoming totally destroyed by sun and alcohol, and was now reading the great classical works over and over again, with increasing gratitude and pleasure. Sometimes after dinner he sat on his terrace, listening to Scarlatti or Schubert. But from time to time, if he felt more than usually depressed, he would wallow in Mahler, with a decanter of brandy on the low table beside him, and as he drank himself into a state of mellow and occasionally belligerent intoxication, he would boom out great chunks of the *Odyssey*, which reverberated across the silvery waters of the cove. Then Vassili would look at Heleni as they ate their supper in their cottage, and they would laugh. When the noisy recitation and the music stopped, to be superseded by violent curses, Vassili would have to run through the olive grove in the moonlight to help Guy to bed. 'Legless,' Guy would say, 'is a very apt description of my predicament, Vassili.' And Vassili, laughing, would agree that this was indeed the case.

By eight o'clock Guy had fallen asleep again, and the warm early sun was streaming through his windows.

He woke to the sound of Heleni, out on the terrace, laying his breakfast table, and calling bossy instructions to Vassili down on the shore. He sat up, and supporting himself on one of his strong, muscular arms, he lifted his dead, wasted legs over the edge of the bed with the other. Then he buckled on his hated, uncomfortable leg-irons, took hold of his two rubber-tipped sticks, carefully levered himself up onto his legs and walked to the bathroom. Returning to the bedroom, he sat down on a hard chair and put on the cotton trousers and polo-shirt laid out by Vassili the night before, then made his laborious way to the long, book-lined sitting-room and out on to the terrace, shouting to Heleni that he was ready for breakfast. He propped himself against the wooden balustrade and looked down at Vassili as he fussed around the brightly-painted boat, bobbing at its jetty in the little cove below. He appeared to be fixing on the lamp they used for night-fishing, and Guy smiled indulgently. Vassili loved to fish and they all enjoyed the free meals that were frequently the result of such trips. Sometimes Guy went along for the fun of it, but only in calm weather. The idea of death by drowning held no appeal for him at all. When he felt he had had enough of life, he had already worked out the method of his exit, and a watery grave did not form part of his plan.

Heleni appeared with the breakfast tray and put the coffee-pot on the table, with the customary bowl of yoghurt. Guy thanked her, clumped over to the table and sat down, letting his sticks fall with a crash to the floor. Heleni poured his coffee, then picked up the sticks, looking severely at him as she hooked them over the arm of his chair.

'Sorry,' said Guy.

'*Típota,*' she replied. 'You're welcome.' But the message from her black eyes, like sloes in her heroic olive-skinned face was clear: 'Don't do it again!' She picked up the tray and departed, with a twitch of her heavy black skirt. Guy grinned at her retreating back, and poured some honey over his yoghurt. He ate the yoghurt with pleasure, the slightly charred toast with less enthusiasm and drank the strong black coffee. Then he heard the grunts of Vassili ascending the narrow goat-track from the beach, and in a moment he appeared, carrying an untidy bundle of brown fishing net hung with lead weights.

'Bloody thing is torn; a rock has snagged it. Heleni will mend it.' He dropped the offending bundle on the floor, where it lay, smelling faintly of fish.

'I wouldn't count on it,' said Guy, and offered Vassili his tin of roll-up cigarettes.

'Oh.' Vassili laughed and took a cigarette. 'It's one of those days, is it? Anyway, I got a couple of mullet, she'll like that.' He opened his sea-stained old bag and showed Guy the two large pink fish, their beautiful scales iridescent, their eyes still bright. Guy admired the mullet, looking forward to lunch.

Vassili sat down and took a deep drag of his cigarette. He looked across the table at Guy, silently debating whether or not to tell him of Spiros's request that they should take one of his guests night-fishing with the lamp and harpoons. In all the time he and Heleni had looked after Guy, he could not remember a woman coming to the house. Once his old Uncle James had come and they had all enjoyed his visit, but he had not come again and Vassili often wondered whether Guy was terribly lonely. He appeared to be happy enough living out his quiet existence with them, content with his books and his music, riding his donkey through the olives with Vassili in attendance, going out in the boat in fine weather. Occasionally they drove into town to visit a bookshop or to watch

27

cricket, and for these excursions Vassili insisted that the hated wheelchair be used, berating Guy for being too sensitive on the subject. 'No one will be looking at you anyway,' he said. But the handsome crippled man, helpless as a child in a buggy, hiding under a panama hat and wearing dark glasses, attracted immediate sympathetic glances. He knew it, and so did Vassili. Thus the trips into town were not very frequent.

Guy's one great and daily pleasure was swimming. Vassili, with the help of Spiros during one winter, had excavated a small pool at the side of the house, and lined it with concrete. The pool was filled from the garden hose, and emptied by means of a simple bath plug, connected to a long French drain which carried the stale water to the sea. Every morning Vassili threw in a few chlorine tablets, but every three or four weeks the pool got too warm and became cloudy. It then had to be emptied, scrubbed out and refilled, a process taking two days. At the narrow end of the pool, Vassili had constructed a series of wide shallow steps so that Guy could get in and out of the water comparatively easily. A large black inner tube floated on the water, attached to a long rope tied to a metal ring let into the concrete. Guy could sit in this and read without too much effort, though sometimes he actually lay without support on the water, his useless legs floating, so that for a time he looked, and even felt almost like a normal man.

Vassili cleared his throat. 'Spiros has a guest at the taverna, a lady.'

'Oh?'

'He is asking, can we take her night-fishing? She sees the boats go out at night; she wants to go.'

'What do *you* think, Vassili?'

'It's not for me to think. It's for you to say. It's your boat.'

28

'What's she like? Is she old, young?'

'It's hard to say. Maybe middle-age, not old, not young. I don't know, she is not a Greek.'

'Is she pretty?'

'Not *pretty*, no. She is very, very thin. But she has nice face; she is dark hair, dark eyes. But thin, very thin. Spiros says she is very quiet lady, no trouble.'

'Well,' said Guy, 'why not? It would make a change from our usual routine, wouldn't it?' He looked at Vassili and smiled, but his eyes were apprehensive.

Vassili began to regret passing on Spiros's request, and immediately back-tracked. 'There's no need if you don't want to, Mr Guy. Spiros can ask someone else, no problem.'

'No,' said Guy. 'Tell Spiros we'll take her, OK?'

'OK. Tonight, then?'

'Why not?'

Chapter Two

Joshua Wickham cycled from his workplace to his house on Strand-on-the-Green, as he did every evening. He left the office as early as possible to get home in time for Max's bath, give him his supper and read him a story, before settling him for the night. Max was five, and they had been living in London for nearly a year, Josh's contract in Prague having come to an end. He had been fortunate to get another job in London, and very lucky to find the large, shabby house on the river. After a family conference, his mother Anna had sold her small house in Church Street and divided the proceeds between Josh and his sister Olivia, enabling him to afford the down-payment on his new house, taking out an enormous mortgage on the rest. In order to service the loan, he had converted the top floor into two studio flats for letting, and himself lived on the ground and first floors with his wife Nastassia and their small son Max. The tenants were comparatively young, like himself, and were friends, or friends of friends. One of them, Ruth, was an architect in the same practice as Josh and she had recently become the pivotal person in Max's life, taking the place of his mother when she was away from home, an increasingly frequent occurrence.

Nastassia was a tall cool blonde Czech, with eyes like iced blue vodka. She and Josh had married when she was eighteen and he twenty-three and their baby boy had been born a year later, though not exactly welcomed by his mother. For Nastassia, marriage to Josh had meant one thing, a passport to a better life and much greater opportunity. Once in London, she had had little difficulty in establishing a career in modelling, and was beginning to be offered work in TV commercials. She had worked hard at English, was highly disciplined in matters of diet and exercise and relentless in the pursuit of her career. She also earned a good deal of money, though she was secretive about this and did not think that contributing to the household was any of her business. She spent a lot of money on clothes and cosmetics, had a stockbroker to take care of various funds, and sent a cheque to her mother in Prague every month.

As Josh rode his bicycle down Thames Road he saw Ruth's blue VW beetle parked by the garden entrance to the house, and sighed with relief. She had got home in time to release the sitter, who had her own family to cook supper for and resented being kept later than the agreed time. He walked down the alleyway between the houses, leading to the towpath and the riverside. Pushing his bike, he observed the yellow 'Mermaid' rose dangling over the high brick garden wall to his right. The wonderfully pungent smell of the river floated towards him, trapped within the narrow confines of the alley. Reaching the towpath, he paused for a moment, and watched the brown tide swirling past, as the willows on Oliver's Island dipped their drooping branches into the water, and a long black barge chugged past in mid-stream, its engines labouring against the tide. Josh chained his bike to the railings of his house and went up the steps. He unlocked the front door with his latchkey and went in. He hung up his parka and glanced up the stairwell with resignation as *The Ride of the Valkyrie* boomed from the attic studio, the home of Robert, a journalist and opera buff. It was his night off, so if Robert felt like a Wagner night, that was what the whole house, and the neighbours got.

Josh crossed the hall to the kitchen and went in, closing the door behind him. He found Max and Ruth sitting at the big, scrubbed table, playing a card game.

'SNAP!' shrieked Max, leaping about and waving his arms over his head. 'I've won! I've won!' He looked at his father, his dark eyes brilliant beneath pale silky hair, his mother's hair. 'Hi, Dad.'

'Hello, darling.' Josh picked up his son, hugging him to his chest and kissing the top of his head. 'Thanks, Ruth, you're brilliant. How is it that you always manage to get home first? I didn't see you leave early.'

Ruth smiled, and stacked the cards neatly, putting them in their box. 'I had a site visit in Mortlake. It was quite efficiently run for a change, so I was able to get away pretty early.'

'Stay to supper?'

'Yes, if you'll allow me to cook it.'

'Why not?' agreed Josh. 'What's in the fridge?'

'Not a lot, as a matter of fact.' Ruth got up and went to the fridge. She took out a bottle of milk and poured some into a saucepan. 'I got some stuff at lunchtime. Steak, is that all right?'

'Very all right,' said Josh, smiling at her. 'You're an angel.'

'Well, I felt like a bit of good red meat myself.' She glanced at Josh. 'Will Nastassia be coming?'

'I don't expect so, she's in Venice for a shoot, or was, on Tuesday.'

'What about you, Max? Sausages? Baked beans?'

'Can I have tomato ketchup?' said Max.

'You can,' said his father.

'And mustard?'

'If you like.'

'Right,' said Ruth, laughing. 'Up you go and have

32

your bath, it'll be on the table in ten minutes.'

Josh and Max departed and Ruth remained where she was, listening to the water rushing into the bath immediately above her head, and the laughter and screams of excitement as Josh pursued his small son round the adjoining bedroom, endeavouring to divest him of his clothes. Peace reigned for a moment, and quiet voices, then a loud thump and a roar of rage. 'MAX! DON'T DO THAT! Look what you've done! Naughty BOY! I'm all WET!' Delighted laughter from Max, then Josh's voice again. 'NO, Max, I mean it! DON'T do it again, do you hear me?'

Ruth smiled, got up from the table, took the sausages and steak from the fridge and put two sausages under the grill. She opened a small can of beans and emptied them into a saucepan. Then she opened the door that led to the long narrow back garden, and walked down to the herb-bed. She picked some parsley and some mint and returned to the kitchen, passing Max's yellow plastic slide and his sand-pit, and observing with regret the worn, scuffed grass beneath her feet.

Jacob Kroll drove his brand-new BMW along the M4 towards London, and *The Maid of Wapping.* It was a fine evening and he drove with the hood down, enjoying the breeze in his hair and the envious glances of other drivers. It was now more than a week since he had arrived home to find that Dido had packed a case and decamped without so much as a word, either of condemnation or explanation. Arriving at the barge with Julie in tow and realizing at once that Dido had caught him out had been a bad moment. He was not in the habit of making major blunders of that sort; in fact, he had never taken a girl there before, and as sure as shit would think twice before doing so again. In the meantime, where the hell was Dido now, the stupid cow? She knows I love her, he told himself self-righteously, what more does she want? It's bloody inconvenient, not knowing; it's extremely inconsiderate of her.

He parked his car in the usual place, closing the electrically operated roof and windows, and sat for a while, his senses soothed by the exquisite smell of the new leather seats. Then he got out of the car, took his briefcase from the boot and aimed the remote-control, causing the car to lock itself with a satisfying clunk. He ran his fingers through his wind-blown hair, walked across the road, negotiated the gangplank of *The Maid of Wapping* and let himself in with his latchkey, half-hoping to find Dido back home and preparing something delicious for dinner, her sense of humour restored. He had felt a bit guilty when he had discovered her celebratory champagne and food in the fridge. He had considered briefly sharing it with Julie, but took her out to dinner instead, after she had packed what remained of her things into two supermarket bags. Before going out, he had sprayed the entire place with pine air freshener. It was the least he could do he felt, in case Dido came back, but his feelings of guilt did not prevent him from taking Julie to *The Ivy*. A working-supper he had planned to say, if by any chance paparazzi were to crawl out of the woodwork. In the event, the dinner had not been a success. Julie was furious at the loss of her clothes and suitcase, and found the substitute plastic bags humiliating. She left in a taxi after the starter, pleading a headache.

The barge was silent and empty. Jacob sighed, dropped his briefcase on the sofa and went to the fridge in search of vodka and tonic. Apart from drink, the fridge was pretty bare but in any case he felt extremely disinclined to cook for himself. I'll go out later, he thought, as he poured his drink. He slammed the fridge door, turned on the television and flung himself down on the sofa to watch the *Channel 4 News.* A commercial break was in progress and he watched the screen carefully, observing not for the first time the high-quality filming, the brilliance of the camera-work, the terrific sharpness of the images and the beautiful colour. It's all about money, he thought; if only one could do stuff like that in features. He took a deep swig of his drink, and a new ad, one he had not seen before, filled the screen. A tall, very slender girl walked away from the camera, wearing a white shirt, black palazzo pants and a long, billowing scarlet chiffon scarf. She turned, the camera zoomed in on her profile, and the brilliantly red scarf and the girl's long, pale blond hair blew in a graceful curve away from her face, held on a rush of air from a wind-machine. She turned to face the camera, and looked straight into the lens with a faint, aloof smile. Her eyes were enormous, an icy pale-blue, fringed with black lashes. She lit up the screen.

'Jesus!' exclaimed Jacob, sitting up. 'That could be her!'

The commercial ended, he turned off the sound and lay down on the sofa, staring at the ceiling. For some time now, he had been seeking an unknown actress to play the female lead in his production of *The Lost Domaine,* a new adaptation of Alain-Fournier's famous novel, *Le Grand Meaulnes.* Most of the pre-production work had already been done; screenplay approved, finance organized, a good cast assembled, costumes hired or in the process of being made, and a marvellous crumbling eighteenth-century house in Ireland leased for the location filming. The only difficulty had been finding the right girl for the key role of Yvonne. The part did not seem to Jacob to require much in the way of technical acting experience.

Rather, it needed a special kind of passive, but incandescent youthful perfection, and the capacity to project an emotion merely by thinking and feeling it, with very little need for words. Now at last he thought he might have found the perfect girl. Of course, he had yet to hear her voice, but he was not seriously worried about that, he was sure that she had enormous potential, properly directed. Tomorrow, he would get the casting director to track her down and arrange an audition. Already he could visualize the scenes in which she appeared, in the costumes already designed and waiting to be made; they were perfect for her and she for them, he knew. He finished his drink, took a shower and put on a clean silk shirt and a cashmere sweater. He picked up the phone and called a nearby restaurant he often used, to book a table.

'Table for two, Mr Kroll?'

'No, just me, tonight.'

As Jacob drove slowly up the King's Road towards the restaurant, he felt entirely happy to be alone, already at work in his head, planning every move, every close-up as the characters of *The Lost Domaine* passed like so many exquisite puppets before his mind's eye. All these people would become, at least for the duration of the filming, more real and much more important to him than what is normally thought of as 'real life'. To Jacob, 'real life', with its attendant domesticity, home, insurance, pension funds and the like had no appeal and seemed deeply irrelevant, and *The Maid of Wapping* became, for the time being, merely a place to rest and marshall one's forces for the next day's work. In his heart, he felt far more alive and at home in the artificial world of movie-making, where his emotional involvement with the story and characters was total, vivid and intense. At the conclusion of each day, 'real life', especially home-life seemed rather dull and boring by comparison. As for Dido, he barely gave her a thought during such creative periods. Nonetheless, it was irritating of her to piss off at a time like this, just when he most needed her to be there to protect him, if and when things began to get out of hand.

James Porteous ate his solitary breakfast on the vast, filthy kitchen table at Inniscarragh, sharing his leathery toast with two African grey parrots that were his constant and only companions. Their large wire cage, thickly bespattered with their malodorous droppings occupied the major part of the draining board, but the birds were confined behind bars and covered by a threadbare Indian shawl only when James was in bed, or had gone shopping. In normal circumstances they accompanied him everywhere, perching on his shoulders or on the back of his chair, if he happened to be reading or watching his ancient black-and-white television in the library.

James had long since ceased to worry about the condition of the huge, rambling house with its cold damp high-ceilinged rooms. The purchase of oil for the antiquated central-heating system was now out of the question, and he could not even afford to employ anyone to cut wood, much less buy it in for the many yawningly empty, soot-smelling fireplaces. He had lived in the place for forty-seven years now, since the tragic deaths in a plane crash of his older brother and sister-in-law. Giles had left nothing to the heir, his little son Guy, except the house and its land, which had at that time been well-farmed and produced an adequate income to maintain Inniscarragh properly, as well as supporting the family. The still-unmarried James had reluctantly taken over as guardian to the two-year-old Guy and his much older sister, Lavinia, then aged eighteen. James, whose personal inclinations tended to be of the indoor variety, had not managed the land as efficiently as his brother before him, but he had nevertheless done his limited best for the children. At her insistence, he had sent Lavinia to university to read economics, and had sent Guy first to a good prep school and then to Eton. From school, Guy had gone on to Oxford, reading law. James had always felt a good deal closer to Guy than to Lavinia, who had seemed to him a difficult, hostile and resentful girl. It was no surprise to him that she had remained unmarried, in spite of her successful career in London, and subsequent retirement in the largest of the gardeners' cottages at Inniscarragh. Their paths rarely crossed, by silent mutual agreement.

As for Guy, James's dreams were still haunted by the memory of the ten-year-old boy, unconscious, pinned to the ground by the overturned tractor, his face deathly pale, his thin crushed legs oozing blood into the wet grassy earth, as James and three of his farm-workers struggled to lift the heavy machine off the child's shattered body. James had had Guy flown to London for specialist treatment, and Guy himself had fought like a lion to get back on his legs, with limited success, but James could never forgive himself for an accident that should have been prevented, as Lavinia never ceased to remind him. After Guy's early retirement to Corfu, he had invited his old uncle to visit him, which James had done with a good deal of pleasure, envying Guy the beauty and simplicity of his way of life and the devotion of Vassili and Heleni.

Now eighty-five, bony, malnourished and increasingly impoverished, James looked at the envelope containing his bank statement with disfavour. He was perfectly aware of the contents and slid it unopened into the drawer of the table. 'Just as well the film people are coming,' he said to the parrots, sweeping crumbs onto the floor and getting up to add his plate and cup to the tottering pile in the sink. 'That'll fix the bloody shits.'

'BLOODY SHITS!' shrieked one of the parrots.

'Shits,' whispered the other hoarsely, and clawed her way up the outside of the cage with her curved grey beak.

Lavinia Porteous glanced up from her well-polished satinwood writing table when she heard the erratic sound of the engine of James's elderly Daimler in the lane, and thought for a moment that he was going to stop at her gate. She hoped fervently that he would not, and relaxed, shaking her head with irritated relief as the car spluttered on towards the main road, and presumably the town. Stupid old fool, she thought, why doesn't he get the timing fixed? She signed her letter with her neat scholar's hand: L.D. Porteous. She folded the thick cream paper with precision and slid it into the matching envelope, addressing and stamping it, ready for the postman. She closed her leather-bound blotter and replaced it in its drawer, with her address book and writing materials. Then she rose from her chair and walked from her elegant sitting-room with its pretty chintz Colefax and Fowler furnishings and faint smell of Culpeper's pot-pourri, to her small black-and-white tiled hall, furnished with a Strawberry Hill Gothic hall table and chairs of ebonized wood. The walls and staircase were painted in an approved National Trust cream and hung with a valuable set of Hogarth prints, in gilded frames. On the hall floor a small but exquisite Persian runner basked in the soft light that fell in a half-hearted, watery shaft through the glazed front door. Lavinia opened the door and put her letter in the lidded wooden box that was screwed to the wall next to her polished brass doorbell. The postman, well-trained in her ways, would collect it when he left her mail and newspaper.

Now that James had gone to town, Lavinia decided to take a walk up to the house and see what further neglect of her family home she could uncover. She locked the front door, put on a raincoat and covered her iron-grey hair with a tweed fishing hat. She chose a stout walking stick from the stand and went into the kitchen to rouse Fritz, her dachshund, asleep in his basket by the Rayburn. Upstairs, she could hear Mrs O'Reilly thumping about with the vacuum cleaner, hitting the skirting-boards. Frowning, Lavinia considered reminding her to do the ironing, but decided against it. She called sharply to Fritz, who woke with a neurotic start, and they left the cottage by the garden door. In her walled Italian garden, formerly the gardener's kitchen garden and once brimming with vegetables, pig-pens and rabbit-hutches, Lavinia now grew roses and clematis climbing through the espaliered fruit trees that clothed the mellow rose-pink brick walls. On either side of a central gravel path, small box-edged beds were planted with hardy geraniums in pale colours, massed around neatly clipped obelisks of Irish yew. The gravel path ran down to a wooden gate in the garden wall, newly-painted Mouse's Ear grey and opening into the park surrounding Inniscarragh. Here, Fritz was able to have a pee; he knew better than to do it in the Italian garden.

Across a grass paddock, kept mown by her own gardener, was a small, rushy, weed-choked lake edged with clumps of overgrown azaleas. On the other side of the lake stood two great stands of deciduous woodland, separated by a narrow, worm-eaten *chinoiserie* bridge, spanning the stream which fed the lake. Behind the bridge, and visible through the gap in the trees, stood Inniscarragh, tall, calm and mist-grey in the watery morning sunlight, its Georgian windows with their narrow white glazing-bars spaced in harmonious symmetry along the beautiful façade of the house. As she gazed at its frail perfection, Lavinia's heart swelled with emotion. She was filled with the familiar sensation, a mixture of huge injustice and impotent anger that occupied the major part of her waking thoughts, and the bitter disappointment that the house should have come to Guy, merely because of his sex, instead of to herself, the first-born. Quite apart from the aspect of sexual discrimination, she knew very well that she would have made a much better job of managing the estate than James had done on Guy's behalf, especially as her brother had never shown any great interest in the place anyway. She was quite confident that she would not have had to sell off most of the land and allow the house to crumble, as James had done, the stupid, drunken old fool. She had spoken to the family lawyers about throwing James out, installing herself and possibly building a golf course in a distant part of the estate, maybe even converting the stables for holiday lettings. The lawyers had promised to pass on her suggestions to Guy, and in due course she had received a letter from them informing her that Guy had no wish to drive his uncle from his home, and reminding Lavinia that she was a guest in his, Guy's, cottage. She had flushed with anger and humiliation at this insolent message from her younger brother, and her mind had flown back to that day, thirty-nine years ago when she and Guy had been walking the dogs along the edge of Burke's Wood. They had found the tractor parked by the field gate, the driver having evidently gone home for his dinner at noon. 'Wouldn't you like to have a go, Guy?' she had suggested.

The ten-year-old Guy had worshipped his sister, so elegant in her London clothes, so beautiful and clever, with her green Irish eyes and thick black hair like their mother's. At twenty-six she had been tall, sharp-tongued and bewitching, but scornful of any kind of frailty or cowardice. In the winter vacation she rode to hounds on one of the two remaining hunters, wearing her mother's habit and jumping the huge fences with enormous boldness and resolution, while Guy did his best to emulate her on his scruffy Welsh cob, though rarely succeeding. Always anxious to impress her in any way he could, he had scrambled up onto the tractor and turned the key, the engine springing into life with an exhilarating roar.

'Off you go then!' cried Lavinia, laughing.

Guy had driven the tractor bumpily along the edge of the field as far as the high hedgerow, and stopped.

'Turn round, twit!' shouted Lavinia.

He had looked apprehensively up at the deeply sloping bank at his right hand side, where the meadow fell sharply down towards the hedge. 'It's too steep,' he had called back, annoyed with himself for having driven into the corner, leaving himself no room to manoeuvre.

'Don't be daft! That's what tractors are for! Just turn the wheel right round and drive in a circle. Go on, Guy, don't be such a sissy!'

So Guy had restarted the engine and turned the wheel. Slowly, the tractor had begun to climb up the slope, the big wheels digging into the soft, rain-sodden earth. Up and round he went, higher and higher, while his heart pounded with fear, his palms sweating, slipping on the shiny black steering-wheel.

'That's it,' called Lavinia, 'you're doing fine!'

Then, as it reached the top of the high bank, the tractor began to tip, at first very slowly it had seemed to Guy, and then gathering speed, as a terrified scream rose in his throat and he made a feeble, desperate attempt to jump clear of the toppling machine. He had hit the ground with a sickening thud, then watched with helpless horror as the tractor fell on top of him, pinning his legs to the ground, while the smell of diesel pouring from the tank filled the air, and blackness engulfed his mind.

Lavinia remembered perfectly clearly how she had run along the hedgerow towards the fallen tractor with her young brother trapped underneath it. She had knelt beside him, stared at his chalk-white face, his sweaty black hair plastered on his forehead, his closed eyes. His pale lips had been slightly parted and he appeared not to be breathing. Kneeling there in the soft, wet earth, her heart had filled with a glorious excitement, and the knowledge that justice had been done and that she was at last the rightful heir of Inniscarragh. She got to her feet and ran back to the house in a convincing state of great agitation, weeping hysterically, to raise the alarm and get help for the child who had robbed her of her patrimony and now lay dead.

But Guy had not been dead, and James and three of his farm-workers had brought ropes and raised the tractor. Carefully, prising Guy's splintered limbs from the blood-soaked ground as gently as he could, James had gathered up the unconscious child and carried him tenderly back to Inniscarragh in his arms, his smashed legs dangling like a rag doll's, bloody and useless. As he lay on the kitchen table, half-conscious as they waited for the ambulance, Guy had become aware of his sister standing beside him, her eyes glittering, unnaturally brilliant. 'Sorry, Lav,' he had whispered, trying to focus his clouded, pain-filled eyes on her face.

43

'Never mind, old chap,' she had replied. 'Better luck next time.'

The ambulance had arrived and Uncle James had gone with Guy to the hospital, but Lavinia had remained behind at Inniscarragh. Agitated, filled with conflicting emotions, partly shame and partly extreme anger and disappointment at the failure of her plan, she had called the dogs and walked swiftly towards the woods, in an attempt to make sense of her feelings. Had she really meant to cause her brother's death? Lavinia was nothing if not brutally honest, and her answer had been swift and truthful. Yes, she had. Would she try again? Probably not; that might arouse suspicions. With any luck, Guy's injuries would be serious and permanent, and even if they failed to remove him from her path, they would almost certainly ruin his life. Rather shocked at her own thoughts, Lavinia had stopped in her tracks and stared at the ground, frowning. Did she *really* hate Guy so intensely as to wish him dead? She had turned and stared back through the trees towards Inniscarragh, pearly grey, magical in the soft afternoon light. Tears had filled her eyes, tears of love for her dead parents and her home, and tears of chagrin that the place did not belong to herself, but to her ten-year-old brother, a stupid little schoolboy. Yes, she had told herself, I do wish him dead.

Lavinia had returned to London before Guy's release from hospital. For some months they had not seen each other, but her love of Inniscarragh drew her back time and again, and she was frequently there during Guy's school holidays. She had found it difficult to conceal her feelings of revulsion and hostility towards him, and rarely missed an opportunity to make a malicious reference to his lack of mobility. Equally, she poured continual scorn on her uncle's

attempts to preserve the house and farm the surrounding land, which he did with depressing lack of
success.

Now, nearly forty years on, she walked round the
edge of the lake, and mourned the disgraceful state of
the rush-clogged water, remembering its former glory
in her parents' time. She crossed the crumbling
Chinese bridge and walked towards the house. Inniscarragh was one of the very few things that Lavinia had
ever felt deeply passionate about in her entire life, and
now as each succeeding week brought fresh evidence
of the irreversible destruction of the fabric and the
inexorable returning to nature of what remained of
the land of her forebears, she cast around incessantly
in her mind for some means of saving it. She could not
understand how Guy could simply stand back and
allow it all to rot away. Even if he hated the place,
surely he must be concerned that his inheritance was
losing its value, the money dripping away with each
passing year, each passing day, in fact.

She walked along the terrace, peering in at the tall
windows, checking out the familiar details of each
beautiful room; the delicate hand-painted Chinese
wallpaper in the drawing-room with its paeonies and
birds in soft blues, pinks and greens; the great crystal
chandelier over the long dining-room table, now
covered with a dust-sheet, dirty white against the dark-
red brocade covered walls. Each room contained its
treasures, and each brought a fresh stab of pain to
Lavinia's elderly and resentful heart. Why did I come
back here? she asked herself. I would have been much
happier staying on in Hampstead, with my friends, the
shops, exhibitions, the theatre, a much more civilized
and interesting life. But on her retirement from her
senior post in a London merchant bank, with its
excellent pension scheme, Lavinia had let her little

house for ten years and returned to live at Inniscarragh as though pulled by a magnet to her old home, energized by some ill-thought-out but nonetheless powerful urge to save it from its present dire situation.

Chapter Three

Guy sat on his terrace after dinner, drinking his coffee and looking out for Vassili's boat which should be appearing round the headland at any time, bringing the young woman who wished to go night-fishing. The heat had gone out of the day and a slight breeze blew off the sea, so that Guy was quite glad of his sweater. He hoped that the wind would not get up and spoil the trip but the water in the bay was glassy-calm and reflected the stars that were already appearing in the darkening sky above. The waning moon would not rise till late at night, so with any luck the conditions for fishing with the lamp should be perfect.

On the table in front of him lay a canvas satchel containing a small corked bottle of oil, a flask of brandy and a half-used packet of rolling tobacco for Vassili. His sticks rested on the table in readiness for the short descent to the cove, and Nansi the donkey, already saddled, was tied to the post at the foot of the terrace steps, waiting patiently, resting his rear hooves, changing feet every few minutes. Presently the boat appeared, coming slowly round the rocks at the end of the cove, blackly silhouetted against the starlit water, its outboard motor's gentle putter-putter just audible as it came slowly across the bay. The lamp was already screwed on to the prow of the boat, though not yet lit, and Vassili sat in the stern, his hand on the tiller, his shipped oars sticking out behind him. The guest, looking very small, was sitting in the prow, surrounded by baskets and other fishing gear. Vassili approached the small wooden jetty on the beach below the house and cut the engine. He jumped out onto the jetty and tied up the boat, then ran up the path to the terrace, leaving the stranger on board.

Guy reached for his sticks and levered himself onto his feet, balancing himself carefully as Vassili arrived at his side. 'The bag, Vassili,' he said. 'Don't forget the bag.' Vassili picked up the satchel and slung it round his neck, and they walked to the top of the steps. Here Guy allowed Vassili to slide an arm under his shoulders and help him down the stairs to the waiting Nansi. Then, with a swift strong heave he lifted Guy into the saddle and they began the descent to the beach. Nansi, docile and well-versed in the procedure was led by Vassili to the end of the jetty, where Guy slid off into Vassili's arms and was lowered carefully into the boat, and into the special folding seat which supported his back.

Guy looked at the visitor, sitting quietly in the prow, waiting for her to speak. 'How do you do?' he said rather formally. 'My name is Guy Porteous.'

'Dido Partridge.' She smiled, showing even white teeth in her tanned face. 'It's so kind of you to let me come out with you. I've been watching the boats going out in the evening, nearly every night. They look so beautiful with the lamps lit, like glow-worms on the sea.'

'It's true, they do look beautiful, but sometimes you can see real glow-worms, in the olive groves.'

'Really?' said Dido. 'That must be lovely.'

'It is.'

Vassili tilted the outboard motor out of the water and stood in the middle of the boat. He picked up an oar and pushed off from the jetty, allowing the boat to float into deeper water, then he began to row, with a smooth rolling forward motion so that the vessel moved silently over the water, barely breaking the surface. As they progressed slowly towards the other side of the little bay, Dido watched the glowing lamps of other boats fishing far away, close to the jagged outline of Albania. I must remember this always, she said to herself. Drawing near to the rocks, Vassili handed an oar to Guy, then scrambled into the prow to light the lamp, while Dido did her best to get out of his way.

'Come and sit at this end,' said Guy.

She made her way carefully towards him, trying not to rock the boat, and sat down on a tarry bundle of nets. Vassili lit the lamp and at once the hidden underwater world was brilliantly revealed in the circle of incandescent white light, a magical submarine universe of fretted rocky caves and lagoons, forests of gently waving fronds of pink and green seaweed, and darting shoals of blue and silver fish, tiny and transparent. Dido gazed over the side of the softly rocking boat, entranced by the enchanted groves and canyons and the dark, mysterious entrances to deeper caves, through which squadrons of fish, striped black-and-white, popped back and forth erratically, changing direction in one swift corporate movement as if responding to a single urgent signal.

Vassili made his way back to the centre of the boat and began to row carefully along the edge of the rocks, the circular movement of his oars propelling the boat slowly forward. Guy, sitting on the side nearest the rocks, kept a sharp watch as they approached a large projecting slab of greenish rock, worn away underneath to leave a sheltered hiding place for fish.

'Shall we try for octopus?' Vassili slowed the boat to a standstill and quietly shipped the oars.

'Why not?' Guy tied a small bundle of bright green knitting wool to a piece of nylon line attached to the end of a long wooden pole fitted with a savage-looking hook, then lowered it gently into the water, trailing the green lure slowly to and fro in front of the long crevice of rock. For a few minutes nothing happened, then Vassili spoke in a whisper. 'There he is. Look, he comes out.' Dido, slightly repelled but fascinated all the same, looked over the side and saw the long slender anaemic-looking tentacle taking exploratory dabs at the bait. Guy moved the wool further away from the octopus's hiding place, and presently another tentacle appeared, followed by the domed albino head of the creature, hypnotized by the lure.

'Hold tight,' said Guy, and he slid the hooked pole under the hood of the octopus and gave it a great heave. 'Got it!' he cried, laughing. 'Right, Vassili, you take over now.' Vassili grabbed the pole firmly in both hands and quickly pulled the quarry to the surface. He dumped the writhing mass into the bottom of the boat, killed it with a spear, and then bundled the corpse into a lidded basket, where its tentacles could still be heard trying to grip the sides with their suckers, making an unpleasant noise like tearing off strips of parcel tape. Dido, shocked, looked nervously at the lid of the basket.

'OK?' asked Guy.

Dido looked at him, and gave a shaky laugh. 'Yes, I'm OK, just surprised.'

'It's a terrific delicacy for the Greeks,' said Guy, smiling. 'Isn't it, Vassili?'

'Number one. Heleni will be glad.'

The commotion of landing the octopus had agitated the water, making it difficult to see the bottom, so Guy undid his bag and took out the bottle of oil, handing it to Vassili, who went up into the prow. He dipped a piece of twine into the oil and sprinkled a few drops onto the water, which immediately cleared and became calm and still again, as if by magic.

Guy unscrewed his flask of brandy and handed it to Dido. 'A small swig would be appropriate, I think,' he said.

'Thank you, I could do with it.' She took a mouthful of brandy and the neat alcohol ran down her throat like fire. She swallowed hard, coughed and laughed, handing back the flask.

Guy took a drink himself, passed the flask to Vassili, then turned to Dido. 'Have you had enough, or shall we go on?'

'Go on, of course.'

'Good.'

Vassili resumed his rowing and they headed towards the rocks nearer to the channel, where he said they should find mullet and squid. Guy kept watch on one side and Dido on the other. After four or five minutes she saw several large pink fish grazing on the tiny minnows, threading their way through a waving forest of weeds anchored to the sandy bottom by large pebbles. Quietly, she turned her head towards Guy. 'Over here, I think,' she whispered, and her heart began to thump again.

'Vassili,' said Guy, and silently Vassili shipped the oars, picked up his harpoon and stood poised like a statue as the boat floated in the direction indicated by Dido's pointing finger. Very slowly, he lowered the long harpoon, then struck swiftly and in a moment the handsome fish, neatly skewered through the middle, lay in the bottom of the boat, flapping and gasping. Vassili pulled out the harpoon, despatched it with a sharp blow to the head and put it into another basket.

'Well spotted,' said Guy. 'It's a good fish, your first catch.'

'Thanks.' Dido laughed. 'But I didn't really catch it, did I?'

'You wish to try?' asked Vassili.

'Could I?'

Vassili let the boat drift for a few metres, allowing the surface of the water to clear, and showed her how to hold the harpoon. 'Strike when I say,' he ordered.

'Over this side,' said Guy quietly, and Dido moved carefully to the other side and stared intently into the water, one hand gripping the gunwale, the other holding the harpoon raised in readiness.

'Do you see him?' Vassili pointed, and suddenly she saw the fish. It hovered close to the sandy bottom, its fins scarcely moving, half-hidden in a clump of pink and brown floating weed.

'Yes, I see him,' she whispered, gripping hard on the harpoon and taking aim.

'Now!'

She struck with all her strength and to her astonishment the harpoon pierced the fish just behind the head and it thrashed around in agony and terror. 'Oh, God! What have I done?' she cried. 'Poor thing, how awful!'

'Look out, you'll lose it!' Guy took the harpoon from her and with a swift accurate twist of his strong wrists, he flicked it out of the water and into the bottom of the boat.

'Is very good,' said Vassili, removing the harpoon and killing the fish. 'Is *bourdétto*; you don't often get them around here.'

'Beginner's luck,' said Dido, feeling foolish after fumbling her catch.

'You did very well. You'll enjoy it, done in oil with red peppers, won't she, Vassili?'

'She will,' said Vassili, who would have liked to take it home to Heleni himself. Still, she would be pleased with the octopus, no doubt.

They had been out for a couple of hours and it was beginning to get quite cold. 'Let's work our way back now,' said Guy, and Vassili began to row towards the jetty, skirting the rocky ledges as he went, and spearing another mullet and several cuttlefish on the way. The thin yellow sickle of the moon was rising over the Albanian mountains as they tied up at the jetty. Vassili ran quickly to fetch the patiently waiting Nansi, and with the efficiency of long practice he got Guy out of the boat and into the saddle.

Guy looked down at Dido, still sitting in the boat. 'Riding for the disabled,' he said, and laughed. 'Come up to the house for a drink before you go.'

'A cup of tea would be great, thank you.'

'A cup of tea it is.' Guy turned the donkey round and headed for the terrace, with Vassili close behind. Dido scrambled out of the boat and followed them up the steps and onto the terrace, where Guy steadied himself, getting his balance on his sticks.

'I bring up the fish and put Nansi in his stable,' said Vassili. 'I wait in the boat for when you are ready to go back to the taverna, is OK?'

'Fine,' said Dido. 'Thank you very much.'

'If you really want tea, we must go to the kitchen.' Guy began to walk awkwardly but quite quickly across the terrace. A table lamp had been switched on in readiness for his return, and Dido glanced swiftly round the room, observing the book-lined walls beneath the high timbered ceiling, its closely packed joists painted a deep terracotta, overlaid with a patina of woodsmoke, cobwebs and dust. The floor was paved with concrete slabs, unpolished and without rugs. A wide open fireplace faced the terrace windows, with burnished steel firedogs waiting to receive the logs and compressed, dried cakes of olive detritus that burned there in the winter, after the last drop of oil had been extracted from the olive harvest. In front of the fireplace was a long, low sofa, covered in heavy, string-coloured cotton, with sheepskin rugs thrown over the back. To one side of the fire was a comfortable chair, made of moulded plywood with soft, black leather cushions. It had a matching leg-rest and Dido recognized it immediately for what it was, a classic Charles Eames design. Behind the sofa was a long table, stacked with books and magazines, and lit by a tall, handsome steel lamp with a dark-green glass shade. Beside the leather chair was an Edwardian wickerwork trolley with wheels like those of a child's perambulator, and this useful piece of furniture carried more books and writing materials and, on the lower shelf, bottles and glasses. On the other side of the chair was a small table with an adjustable reading lamp and a telephone.

Guy led the way to the kitchen, through a bead-curtained arch at the far end of the sitting-room. It was a long and narrow room, whitewashed, with cupboards recessed into the thickness of the walls along one side, their doors painted a bright cobalt blue. On the opposite side a stone sink, a bottled-gas cooker and a battered noisy fridge were ranged beneath three windows, their frames painted to match the cupboard doors, their sills crowded with pots of herbs and bright pink petunias, and looking down through the olives to the sea. In the centre of the room was a kitchen table that looked as if it might have been made from olive wood, surrounded by local rush-bottomed chairs. In the centre of the table stood a dark-blue jug, containing a bunch of late-flowering roses.

Guy pulled out a chair and lowered himself care-fully into it. 'Let's see,' he said, looking rather vaguely at the cupboards, 'I wonder where Heleni hides the tea?'

'Don't worry, I'm sure I can find it.' Dido filled the kettle and lit the gas under it, then opened the blue cupboards until she had found the teabags and a couple of stoneware mugs. She went to the fridge for some milk.

'Are you sure you don't want something a bit stronger?' Guy looked at her, as she poured the boiling water over the teabags.

'No, but I expect you probably do. Shall I get you something?'

'Would you? It's on the trolley thing in the sitting-room; brandy, please.'

'Do you want ice or anything?' she asked, coming back with the bottle.

'No, just a slug in the tea will be fine.'

She poured the brandy into his mug. 'Perhaps I will have just a drop in mine too. It's a nice idea.'

'Good,' he said. 'Purely medicinal, of course.'

She laughed, and sat down on the other side of the table. She took a sip of her drink. Quite suddenly, a feeling of constraint seemed to manifest itself, now that they were no longer in the darkness of the night, with Vassili as a buffer between them. Dido, not particularly socially adept at the best of times, felt awkward and rather shy of the damaged man sitting across the table, silently drinking his tea. At last she put down her mug, raised her eyes and tried to look steadily at him, at his tanned face, his long rather saturnine nose, his grey-streaked black hair and strongly-marked eyebrows emphasizing unexpected dark-blue eyes. He looked sympathetically back at her, for once not feeling irritated or resentful of the unspoken embarrassment in the face of his handicap. Poor thing, he thought, she doesn't know how to handle this at all. He smiled at her. 'It's the legs, isn't it?' he said gently. 'You don't know what to say?'

'No! Er, I mean, yes,' she stammered. 'I don't know. I'm sorry, I don't know what to say, you're quite right.'

She looked at him, her cheeks red with mortification. 'I'm so sorry, I'm being stupid.'

'It's perfectly all right. There's nothing to be sorry about. Would it help if I told you how it happened?'

'Not if you'd rather not talk about it.'

'I would quite like to talk about it,' said Guy, rather surprising himself, for usually it was the very last subject he ever wished to discuss.

'OK.' She smiled at him timidly.

She looks so young, and somehow vulnerable, he said to himself. I wonder what brings her here, all alone? Then he began to tell her about the accident, the many operations in London, the realization and partial acceptance of his disability and his long fight to lead a normal working life. Having got thus far, he poured another shot of brandy into his cup and told her the circumstances of his early retirement. 'So here I am, and lucky to have Vassili and Heleni.'

Dido looked at him, her eyes serious and dark. 'What a bloody thing to happen, what rotten luck. Do your legs hurt a lot? Do you get much pain?'

'Yes, sometimes, especially if the weather is wet and cold. Otherwise it's just frustrating to be so comparatively helpless, to depend so much on others.'

'I think you manage very well.'

'Do you?'

'Yes, I do.' Dido looked at her watch. 'It's late, I mustn't keep Vassili hanging about.' She stood up, preparing to leave.

'Come to lunch tomorrow, and we'll eat the *bourdétto*?'

'I will, thank you.'

'Goodnight, Dido.'

'Goodnight, Guy, and thanks for the fishing.'

Later, lying in bed, wakeful but unusually relaxed, Guy stared at the blue-painted ceiling of his otherwise white bedroom, listening to the owls hooting in the olive grove and the faint slosh of the sea on the pebbles of his little cove. He thought about Dido. She's just like a wren he said to himself; small, brown, bright-eyed but curiously depressed. There's a sadness about her, I wonder why? He did not regret having told her so much about his own tragedy; on the contrary, it was as if by telling her he had begun to rid himself of a little of his bitterness and anger. The surprising thing was that it had felt quite comfortable to speak so freely on such a short acquaintance. Well, he thought, I don't suppose she'll be here for much longer. It's a question of ships that pass in the night, isn't it? He stretched out his hand and switched off the lamp, closed his eyes and slept.

Just after noon, Dido got into her car and drove along the coast road to the next bay and took the track through the olive groves to Guy's house. The road was steep and winding and she changed down and proceeded with caution. Through the tall, twisted and venerable trees came the occasional glimpse of the sea, and she slowed to a halt while an elderly woman wearing the traditional white wimple, with an apron over her black skirt, shepherded her small flock of sheep away from the track, smiling and waving cheerfully at Dido as she passed. Then, rounding the last bend, she saw below her the group of buildings that formed Guy's property, recognizing the long, low house at the water's edge, with its sun-bleached Roman-tiled roof half-hidden by the trees. Dido stopped the car, and looked down at the peaceful scene. To the side of the house, and shaded by a vine-covered trellis, the small egg-shaped swimming pool looked cool and inviting, its bottom freckled with shifting spots of sunlight, and she could see Guy himself sitting in a deckchair under the trellis, reading. To her left, and set a few metres back from the track, was a small square whitewashed cottage. A string of washing hung between trees at its side, and chickens scratched by the pots of geraniums at the door. Draped over a bush was a brown fishing net. To the rear of the cottage was a lean-to shelter, Nansi's stable presumably. This must be Vassili's house she said to herself, releasing the handbrake and driving carefully down the steep slope. Through the trees to her right she could just make out another building, narrow and tall, its flaking lime-washed walls pock-marked, the underlying stone green-stained with damp. The disintegrating structure had a crumbling bell-tower, its single bronze bell still suspended from its carved headstock, painted the colour of ox-blood. It must be an old chapel she thought, how lovely. She drove the last few metres and parked the car neatly next to Guy's at the rear of the house. She got out, tipping the seats forward to keep them cool, picked up her basket of swimming things and walked towards the pool.

Guy turned in his chair as she approached, putting down his book and taking off his spectacles. He was wearing swimming trunks and had taken off his leg-irons which lay on the ground at his side. 'Good timing,' he said, 'I was just thinking of having a swim. Have you brought your things?'

'I have.' Dido held up her basket. 'Where can I change?'

'Easiest in the house, isn't it? Go in through the kitchen door and Heleni will show you.'

In the kitchen, Dido introduced herself to Heleni, who was cutting up large red bell-peppers. She put down her knife, gave Dido a dark, appraising look, then smiled and took her through the sitting-room to a small bedroom at the far end of the house. There Dido changed into her bathing-suit, picked up her towel and left the room on silent bare feet. On her way back to the sitting-room she caught a glimpse through its open door of Guy's room, with its pale-blue painted ceiling, big white bed and windows open to the sea. Feeling slightly intimidated by Heleni, she did not go back to the kitchen but went out through the French windows to the terrace, and stood for a moment looking out at the breathtaking view. She felt as though she could remain glued to the spot and look at it forever, and never become bored with it. No wonder he chooses to live here, she thought. She went down the terrace steps and found the path that led round the end of the house to the pool.

Guy was already in the water, paddling himself round the pool on his inflated inner-tube. She paused by the spare deck-chair, spreading her towel and brushing the bits of dust and twig from her feet before walking down the shallow steps into the water and swimming across to the other side of the pool, where she climbed up the metal ladder and sat on the edge, the water running in rivulets down her brown body. 'It's lovely,' she said, 'but a lot colder than the sea, isn't it?'

'It's just been filled from our spring, that's why. When the sun is really hot the water gets like consommé, warm and green, and we have to drain it and refill it. Or rather, Vassili does. It's rather a bore, it takes two days to fill.'

'But you can always swim in the sea?'

'True, but that's much more of a hassle for me, it's hardly worth the effort, and I'm quite a deadweight for poor old Vassili.'

'He seems mighty strong to me,' said Dido.

'I suppose he is.'

Dido slid back into the cool water and swam twice round the pool, then back to the steps where she rested

59

her head on the second step and let herself float on her back. Guy paddled slowly across the pool and came to rest at her side, easing himself out of the inner-tube and floating on his stomach, his fingertips touching the step below, his legs drifting behind him, brown, bent and wasted.

Dido's eyes were closed, her face turned towards the sun. Guy thought that she looked relaxed and rather sleepy, but still rather sad. He saw that she had blue shadows under her eyes. 'Did we stay out too long last night?' he asked. 'Was it too tiring for you?'

'Good heavens, no.' Dido opened her eyes and looked at him. 'Why do you ask? Do I look tired?'

'Not exactly. But you look sort of weary, preoccupied.'

'Do I?'

'Yes, you do.'

He smiled at her so kindly and sympathetically that a lump rose in her throat and she sat up abruptly and crouched on the step, folding her arms round her knees in a protective manner. She rested her chin on her knees and looked at Guy severely, regaining her composure. 'If you must know, I *am* weary and I *am* preoccupied, as you put it. But I am trying to dismiss it from my mind, to forget about everything, just have a holiday.'

'And are you succeeding?'

'No, not very well.' She sounded so cross that Guy laughed, and Dido laughed too, in spite of herself.

Heleni came towards them through the trees. 'Lunch is ready in a half-hour. I have put the drinks on the terrace, is your wish?'

'Fine,' said Guy. 'Thank you, Heleni. Ask Vassili to come and give me a hand, will you?'

Assuming that Guy would prefer to get dressed without an audience, Dido got out of the pool at once. 'I'll go in and change,' she said. 'I don't want to sit about in wet things. I'll only be a few minutes.' She picked up her towel and ran round the house, wrapping the towel around her. She regained the terrace and retraced her steps to the spare bedroom. She closed the door, stripped off her wet suit and dried herself. She sat down at the small plain wooden dressing-table and looked at herself in the spotty mirror as she blotted her wet hair on the towel. She took a comb from her basket, parted her hair in the middle and then carefully combed it straight down, so that the thick fringe rested on her eyebrows and the rest fell evenly all round, just below the level of her earlobes. I suppose that's one thing that's not a problem, she thought, my stupid hair. Deliberately not hurrying, in order to give Vassili plenty of time to get Guy settled on the terrace, she sat for a few moments looking at her reflection in the mirror. At least I've managed to get a nice even tan she said to herself, but he's quite right, I do look tired, in spite of that. She looked at her thin brown arms and felt her ribs, clearly visible under the skin beneath her small breasts. God, I'm a wreck she thought, I must try and put on some weight. I look like a skeleton. Fleetingly, she thought of Jacob and was shocked and angered by his capacity to undermine her self-confidence and her health to such an extent, and despising herself for being feeble-minded enough to allow it. She put on her khaki shorts and the fresh white T-shirt she had brought with her, slipped her feet into her brown leather sandals, hung the damp towel over the back of a chair and left the room. Hearing the sound of voices and the chink of bottles and glasses, she made her way to the terrace.

'There you are,' said Guy. 'What about a drink?'

'Thanks, I'd love an ouzo.'

'Would you really? I'm amazed.'

'Why?'

61

'Oh, because it's a very Greek drink, I suppose. You know, the hard stuff.'

'Really? I just like the taste, that's all.' Dido sat down on one of the long bamboo chairs with canvas-covered cushions that furnished the terrace. She took the proffered glass of ouzo.

'Water?'

'Yes, please. A lot.'

Guy poured water from a glass jug full of ice-cubes. 'OK?'

'Lovely, thanks.' She sipped the powerful aniseed drink and relaxed, looking around her. A sprawling vine climbed up the wall of the house and scrambled along wires fixed under the roof of the terrace, fronted by its elaborate wooden filigree fascia-board.

'Mad, isn't it?' said Guy, following her gaze. 'The house was built by a Swiss about a hundred years ago, as far as I can gather. Presumably he imported the woodwork to remind himself of his native land.'

'As a matter of fact, I think it's rather nice. I like it.'

'It's OK from the inside, sitting here. But it does look a bit bizarre from the outside, tacked onto the tiled roof. Just like a dainty Swiss chalet.'

'But you wouldn't change it?'

'No, I wouldn't. I might have done so, when I first came here, but I've got used to it now.' He looked at Dido and smiled. 'One can get used to almost anything, given time.'

'Yes, that's true, but sometimes it's a mistake to accept everything that happens. Some times you have to have the courage to fight back, if something threatens to destroy you.' She looked into her glass, waiting for him to ask the obvious question, rather hoping that he would, but he remained silent. Disconcerted, she looked up and saw him looking at her attentively, waiting. 'Aren't you interested? Don't you want to know?' She sounded put out, defensive.

Poor thing, thought Guy, she's very used to being put down. 'Certainly I do,' he said, 'but only if and when you want to talk about it, OK?'

'OK,' said Dido. 'Sorry.'

'Nothing to be sorry about.'

The rattle of wheels on the tiled floor of the sitting-room announced the arrival of lunch. Heleni appeared in the doorway pushing a trolley, a twin of the one in the sitting-room. On the trolley was a large, dark-green glazed earthenware dish containing the filleted *bourdétto* in a brilliant oily red-pepper sauce. Heleni put the dish and thick white, blue-rimmed plates on the low bamboo table, with knives and forks, salad, the coarse brown bread, a bottle of chilled *corífo* and fresh glasses.

'That looks absolutely wonderful,' said Dido, suddenly feeling ravenous. She smiled at Heleni, who looked pleased.

'*Típota,*' she replied rather shyly and glanced at Guy, as if to remind him that everyone likes to be appreciated sometimes. He smiled at her, saying nothing, and she took away the trolley with her familiar haughty lift of the chin.

Dido looked at Guy, mystified by this curious little display of temperament. 'What was all that about?'

Guy laughed. 'It's just her way. She's got a heart of gold, but if I gave her the slightest encouragement she'd turn into a full-time twenty-four hour nurse. She'd smother me. But I can't affored to lose them; Vassili is literally my legs. I couldn't manage without him.' He handed a spoon and fork to Dido. 'Help yourself, we mustn't let it get cold.'

They ate the *bourdétto*, spicy and delicious, with thick slices of bread and the salad, simply dressed with oil and lemon juice.

'Have some more?'

'I couldn't,' said Dido, putting down her fork. 'That was terrific, but I couldn't eat another thing, really.' She picked up her glass and leaned back against the cushions of her chair, feeling comfortable and well-fed, too well-fed for the present size of her stomach. She looked at Guy, who had refilled his plate and was consuming his second helping with considerable relish. 'You have a good appetite,' she observed, smiling.

'Why not? The pleasures of life aren't exactly thick on the ground, are they? Food, books and booze; they're the best staples as far as I'm concerned.'

'You don't seem to have put on weight, do you?'

'Look who's talking.'

Dido looked away, annoyed with herself for walking into her own trap. She changed the subject. 'On my way down your drive, I saw a building in the trees, with a bell-tower. Is it a chapel?'

'It is, but it's a total ruin, I'm sorry to have to admit. It was here long before the Swiss chap came. I've been meaning to restore it, or at any rate prevent it collapsing, but it'll cost money.' He looked at her, his eyes serious, and frowned. 'I do have to be fairly careful, that's the problem.'

'Don't we all? I'd love to look inside; would you mind?'

'Of course not. I'll take you there later, when we've had a siesta.'

Heleni reappeared with coffee and took away the dishes, pleased that everything had been eaten. Guy and Dido lay in their chairs, and presently she fell asleep, overcome by sun, wine and food, and the late night. She was woken by the rattle of china on the table, as Heleni brought tea in a Victorian silver teapot, with heavy Venetian cups and a dish of lemons. Guy was not in his chair, and Dido lay still for a moment, quietly waking up, collecting her wits, wondering where he had gone. In a few moments, she heard his heavy, dragging footsteps punctuated by the tap of his sticks.

'I knew I had the old boy's monograph somewhere,' he said, lowering himself into his chair, and producing a dog-eared pamphlet from his pocket, six or seven small pages stapled together. 'Chapel of Ayía Aphaía, Corfu.' He handed the pamphlet to Dido. 'There you are, you can read all about it.'

'Thank you, how interesting.' While Guy poured the tea, she read the faded typescript, with some difficulty, since it had obviously been typed on a dodgy machine with several very indistinct or even missing letters. '*A pale blue vaulted ceiling covered in gold stars,*' she read aloud, '*and limestone walls with traces of frescoes depicting the saints.* How marvellous, are they still there?'

'Yes, but only just.'

After tea they went to look at the chapel. By crossing the sitting-room and passing through a door beside the fireplace, Guy was able to avoid the terrace steps, and they walked together slowly along the rough path towards the ruined building, under the cool green shade of the olives. A couple of worn, shallow stone steps led up to the door, which stood slightly ajar, loose on its hinges. Dido pushed open the door and held it open, waiting for Guy as he carefully negotiated the threshold. The little chapel was surprisingly light inside, because a large part of one wall was missing and lay in a heap of broken stone on the floor. The air was very cool, almost cold to the warm, sunburned skin. The place was completely unfurnished, emptied of everything movable. The white walls rose all round them, the faded wall paintings powdery and fragile, their pale pinks, blues and flesh tones barely discernible, the gold-leaf gone from the haloes of the saints. In the central space a rusty erection of metal scaffolding posts had been built to support the dome, and a long rickety-looking ladder made of lashed-together poles led up to a small platform of wooden planks. Dido gazed through this crazy structure at the blue-painted vault high above her head. As the pamphlet had informed her, a pattern of large and luminous golden stars was clearly visible against the blue of the dome, and on the central boss a white dove flew, perpetually on the wing.

'It's beautiful; what a treasure,' said Dido. 'Thank you for letting me see it.'

'Poor little place, there's not much to see now.'

A low stone ledge formed a narrow bench around the walls, originally built for the use of the old and infirm, unable to remain standing throughout the long masses. They sat down on the cool stone, leaning against the wall and taking care to avoid the droppings of the swallows that had nested round the rim of the vault in the spring, and now swooped in and out with their fledglings through the gaping hole.

'Do you see that wooden platform near the top of the scaffolding?'

'Yes.'

'There's a family of owls up there. Look at the ghastly mess on the floor underneath, scruffy things.'

Dido looked and agreed that they did indeed make a terrible mess. 'But I do rather love owls, all the same.'

'So do I,' said Guy. 'I adore them. I listen to them hooting in the night, hunting. A couple of weeks ago one of them flew into my room when I was in bed, reading. He sat calmly on top of the bookcase for quite a while, staring at me with his great yellow eyes, and then flew out again through the window. Their wingspan is huge, their flight absolutely silent, it's quite spooky.'

'What a lovely thing to happen, weren't you thrilled?'

'I was. I wish he would come again.' He turned his head and looked at her, unsmiling. 'I wish *you* would come again, Dido.'

'I will come again, Guy.'

'Stay to dinner tonight?'

Dido laughed. 'That would be very nice, but why don't *you* come and dine with *me* at the taverna?'

'I can't. I never go out.'

'Why not?'

'Because I'll get pissed and fall over and it will all end in tears, that's why not.'

'Don't you have a wheelchair? It must be a fearful bore never going out at all, because of a silly thing like unreliable legs.'

'I have got a chair,' Guy admitted reluctantly, 'but it's only in case I break a leg. I hate using it, it makes me feel old and useless.'

'We'll compromise then,' said Dido firmly. 'You can arrive under your own steam, and depart with a bit of help. How would that be?'

'All right, I suppose, if I must.'

Dido slid her cool hand round Guy's neck and, leaning towards him, kissed his cheek. 'Good,' she said. 'I'll look forward to seeing you.'

Chapter Four

Nastassia lay in a deep hot bath scented with *Rive Gauche*, her eyes closed, her hair screwed on top of her head, willing her throbbing feet and aching back to stop hurting so badly. She was going to be very late for her dinner date, she knew, but at this precise moment she didn't really care.

It had been a long and difficult day, beginning at half-past five in the morning, when she had submitted to being heavily made up by the make-up artist; very badly, in her own opinion. Nevertheless, she had not expressed her displeasure, there was no point in antagonizing the woman. Then the hairdresser had arrived and had curled, twisted and tortured her long blond hair, building it into a towering confection with copious sprayings of lacquer. The dresser approached with the first garment, a night-gown, a diaphanous affair of chiffon and lace. Nastassia was not wearing a bra, but she had kept her pants on. The dresser slipped the night-gown carefully over her piled up hair, and it slithered over her body in soft folds. The dresser stood back and looked at her, frowning. 'Your pants are showing, you'll have to take them off, sorry.'

Reluctantly, but obediently, Nastassia took off her pants.

'Shit,' said the dresser, 'that's worse. Your pubic hair shows. Why don't you shave, for Christ's sake?' She went to her property box, took out a sordid-looking pink G-string and handed it to Nastassia. 'Put that on,' she said coldly. For a moment, Nastassia considered telling her to get lost, then changed her mind and meekly stepped into the offending article, telling herself that it was important not to get a reputation for being difficult; one had to deal with these same people over and over again. Carefully, she smoked a cigarette while the shot was set up. They were working on the top floor of a *palazzo* in Venice. The building was supposed to be on fire, and Nastassia was to stand on the balcony, looking suitably terrified, while smoke poured through the window behind her. A team of Venetian firemen in their fire-barge was already in position in the canal below, and they had agreed to allow Dave, the photographer, to go up on their hydraulic ladder to take the first shot. When he was in position and had set up the camera to his satisfaction, the dry-ice was activated and two men with tennis racquets began to direct the smoke towards the open window.

'OK, Stassi, come out now,' called Dave.

Nastassia went out through the smoke onto the balcony. 'Now what?' she shouted, her eyes beginning to smart.

'Scream! Wave your arms! Look scared!'

Nastassia raised her arms, spreading her fingers, and shouted 'FIRE!' at the top of her voice.

'That's too much, your tits popped out. Do it again, will you, darling?'

They did the shot several times more until Dave pronounced himself satisfied. Nastassia retired behind the makeshift screen to be changed for the next picture, an action shot of a fireman carrying her down the ladder, while the smoke swirled around them. She was not looking forward to this, not being at all good at heights, but she told herself that she must just close her eyes and not look down. The second night-gown was made of a comparatively opaque satin, which was a relief in view of the fact that she was to be carried over the shoulder of one of the firemen, with the smoke billowing around them. When she had changed, and checked her make-up in the proffered mirror, she stepped out again onto the balcony. 'OK,' she called down to the team below. 'Ready.'

The dry-ice was reactivated and the ladder began its ascent, bringing with it a *pompiere*. The ladder drew level with the balcony, and the fireman grasped the railing and looked at Nastassia, his dark eyes amused, enjoying himself. '*Buongiorno, signorina. I miei ordini sono che lei deve aggiustare il suo corpo sulla mia spalla sinistra, così. Io la tengo sulle ginocchie con il braccio sinistro, così. Poi, la scala scendera. Capisce?*'

Nastassia was unable to understand a single word. She held onto the balcony and shouted down to Dave. 'What's he saying?'

'Drape yourself over his left shoulder, and he will grab you behind the knees with his left arm. OK?'

'OK,' she replied, faintly. She took a deep breath to steady herself, and looked nervously at the *pompiere*.

He gave her a reassuring smile and leaned towards her, holding onto the ladder with his right hand. '*Non si preoccupa, e sicura con me.*' He grasped the railing firmly and Nastassia, petrified with fear but determined to do the job, leaned over his shoulder and slid her arms down his back until she could grab hold of his belt with her fingers. Her eyes were tightly closed, but she could feel the vice-like grip of his arm round her legs. Instinctively, she bent her knees to lessen the chance of slipping through his grasp. 'OK?' he asked. 'OK,' she replied. The ladder began to move slowly downwards.

'Wave your arms! Look scared!' shouted Dave.

Nervously, Nastassia raised one arm.

'That's feeble! Use both arms! And kick your legs a bit, too! Don't forget you're supposed to be scared!'

'I *am* scared,' she whimpered.

'And open your bloody eyes, for God's sake!'

Abandoning any ideas of self-preservation, Nastassia did as she was told. The ladder went up and down a dozen times, until even the *pompiere* began to grow rather red in the face. At last Dave pronounced himself satisfied, and the fireman was permitted to unload her onto the barge, both of them sweating. *'Grazie,'* said Nastassia, and gave her *pompiere* a chaste kiss on the cheek. *'Niente,'* he replied. *'Dopotutto non e esattemente un grosso peso.'*

'Right,' said Dave. 'Now we do the glam shots inside the *palazzo.'*

'Oh God,' said Nastassia, 'the gear is all up there.' She looked up at the balcony.

'Shall we take you up on the ladder?'

'No way,' she replied firmly. 'I'll use the stairs, thanks.'

Four more night-gowns had to be photographed, while she ran barefoot through the beautiful but cold formal rooms of the *palazzo*, or lay on the silken cushions of a gilded eighteenth-century settee, her eyes closed, a frail white manicured hand pressed to her forehead. At last, the shoot was finished and the firemen had departed in their barge, their siren sounding urgently as they returned to base through the crowded canals.

'I'll go up and put my kit on,' Nastassia had said, wearily, and prepared to climb the stairs yet again. Roger, the photographer's assistant, a kind and sympathetic man, had offered to call a gondola to take her back to the hotel. 'Thanks.' Nastassia had smiled at him gratefully. 'You're an angel.'

'Have dinner with me?'

'Thanks, that would be nice.'

Back in the functional, rather poky little hotel suite, the bathwater was beginning to get cold, and she sighed, reluctant to move a muscle. The phone rang in the bedroom. Oh shit, she thought, he's here already. She scrambled out of the bath, wrapped a towel round herself and then ran to the telephone, trying to think of an excuse for not being ready to go out. But it was not Roger. It was Richard, her agent, telling her that she must return to London at once, to have an interview and possibly a screen-test for an important movie. He had made an appointment for her to meet the director, Jacob Kroll, the day after tomorrow. 'Be there,' he said.

'I will,' said Nastassia. 'I'll get the first plane out tomorrow.'

Her tiredness miraculously vanished, Nastassia got dressed, brushed her hair, and went downstairs to go out to dinner with Roger.

Lavinia, peering through her front windows on a damp October morning, observed with considerable distaste the comings and goings of the advance party of the film company. Two enormous pantechnicons, three minibuses and a Range Rover had passed her gate, some of them carelessly driving over the neat mown strip of grass that separated her yew hedge from the main drive to Inniscarragh. The drive, like everything else, was in a poor state of repair and Lavinia pursed her lips angrily, knowing that the constant passage of heavy vehicles could only make its condition worse. Annoyingly, she had had the potholes in front of her cottage filled quite recently, but it was plain to her that it would have to be done again later. She would certainly insist that James paid for the repair. No doubt he would have included such things in his contract, and if he hadn't, that was not her problem. She sat down at her desk and wrote James a stiff, businesslike note to that effect. She signed it, stamped it and put it in her postbox. Then, feeling slightly better for having taken a positive step, she poured herself a large sherry from the Waterford crystal decanter and sat down beside her sweet-smelling log fire to drink it.

In the stable-yard at Inniscarragh, James was showing the location manager, Gavin, the many ancient horse-drawn vehicles that were crammed, covered in dirt and cobwebs, into one of the big Georgian stables, no longer housing the beautiful hunters and carriage-horses of his parents' time.

'These will be really great,' said Gavin enthusiastically. 'Just what we need.' He took copious notes of all the different types of carriages, everything from jaunting-cars to stylish four-wheelers, and one really wonderful early nineteenth-century coach, its great black leather hood cracked and split, but its windows still working and its elegant lamps intact.

'They're a bit tatty, I'm afraid,' said James.

'Doesn't matter, it won't show. This will be a day-for-night scene. We don't actually shoot it at night, but we can make it look as if we have. The carriages are all packed into the yard, like a sort of horse-drawn carpark, waiting to take home the guests at a party in the house.'

'Where are the horses?'

'Search me,' said Gavin, and laughed. 'Look, this is the shooting script. It says here: A courtyard packed with carriages. MEAULNES CLIMBS OVER THE TOPS OF THE PARKED VEHICLES, PUSHES OPEN A WINDOW AND DISAPPEARS THROUGH IT, CLOSING IT BEHIND HIM.'

'Is that all?'

'That's it.'

'Oh,' said James. 'Well, I'm sure it will be most interesting.' In fact, he thought it sounded extremely dull. Fancy dragging out all the old carriages and cleaning them up, just to do that. Still, no doubt there would be a good reason for it.

From one of the pantechnicons, looming like elephants in the sepulchral light of the yard, came a team of young women, wearing denim jeans, baseball caps and heavy black-leather boots, carrying high above their heads clothes hangers on which hung a fantastic array of beautiful Directoire costumes. There were frock-coats with high velvet collars; embroidered silk waistcoats; white frilled shirts with long neckcloths; nets containing dozens of black-leather pumps of the period. One girl carried a single costume at a time, the party frocks of the same era, with velvet bodices and flounced gauzy skirts, frilly pantaloons hanging incongruously below the hem. The girls disappeared through a door in the corner of the yard and climbed the dusty wooden backstairs to the first floor of the house, where a large empty bedroom had been allocated to house the wardrobe department. The room had already been equipped with long portable steel racks on which to hang the costumes. Two wardrobe assistants sat at a small table, checking each costume as it arrived and attaching to it the relevant docket, complete with a polaroid showing the costume and all its accessories and marked with the name of the character, the actor and the scene in which the clothes would be worn.

Another, older woman, the wardrobe mistress, was checking over the working equipment, the sewing machines, the irons and ironing boards and all the schedules and production notes. 'Good job you've got them all up,' she said, peering through the dirty window at the lowering sky. 'It looks like rain to me.'

'Rains all the time in Ireland, so they say,' said one of the girls cheerfully.

'Cold too,' added the other. 'It's about time catering got here; I could murder a coffee.'

'So could I,' said the wardrobe mistress. 'Kitchen's out of bounds, I don't know why. Just as well the pub's only down the road.'

Downstairs James and Gavin walked through the house, followed by the lighting crew, while Gavin checked his schedules and decided which items of furniture should be removed and stored in the old morning-room, and which were to remain. The wide stone-flagged entrance hall was to be stripped and a series of long trestle tables erected, with benches on either side. The tables were to be covered with the coarse cream-linen cloths specified by the designer and set with pewter plates and thick country earthenware. On one side of the tables enough room had to be available for a large troupe of revellers to dance through the room, entering from a corridor and leaving through the main entrance. On the other side a track was to be laid on the floor, to carry the big camera on its dolly for the important tracking shots that were planned for the scene. Overhead, the lighting battens would be suspended above the performance area, and fitted with the appropriate *luminaires*, filtered to give the illusion of candlelight. James sat on a chair and watched with interest while Gavin, the lighting and technical directors and first cameraman took measurements and made copious notes for the lighting plot.

'Right.' Gavin came over to James. 'That's great, it's going to work well. Now we need a small music-room with an old-fashioned piano and a small sofa.' He referred to his notes, and read aloud: 'A door leads to another small room, furnished with a fireplace with a rug in front of it, and five footstools. A small table holds a pile of photograph albums (Props).'

'Follow me,' said James and led the way to his mother's private sitting-room. The shutters were closed and the room was dark. He crossed to the window and opened the shutters, letting in the watery green light from the overgrown garden.

'Good Lord!' exclaimed Gavin. 'It's pretty well perfect, isn't it?' He turned to the lighting manager. 'What do you think?'

'No problems here.'

'Excellent.' Gavin turned to James. 'Leave the shutters open, will you? The set and props people can do their stuff here right away.' He looked at his watch. 'Ten to one, time for lunch. Catering's not here yet, so we'll go to the pub, OK?'

James rather hoped that they would invite him too but they did not, and he made his way through the rapidly dismantling house to the refuge of the kitchen. The two parrots, silenced inside their covered cage, uttered clicks and squawks of welcome when he came through the door and he could hear them climbing up the bars of their prison in confident anticipation of their imminent release. He went to the sink and flicked the shawl off the cage to a volley of abuse or affection, he was never quite sure which. 'Silly old sods,' he said, and unlatched their door. Stiffly, complaining, they sidled out and flew wildly round in a circle, shedding grey feathers and bits of dirty litter and sunflower seeds from their cage all over the kitchen. Finally, they came to rest on the big brass lantern suspended over the table, where they rearranged their ruffled plumage and defaecated extravagantly onto the table below. 'Bloody things,' said James crossly and poured himself a whisky. Then he got the dishcloth from the sink and wiped up the mess.

At five minutes to three Nastassia stepped out of her taxi, paid the driver and looked up at the rather grand entrance to the hotel, and at the equally grand door-man, resplendent in gold-braided brown uniform and top hat with a golden cockade. She drew a deep breath and walked towards the door, smiling at the doorman, who saluted politely as she went confidently through the famous portals. Her agent had been able to give her very little information concerning the nature of the film for which she was about to audition, except that the director was Jacob Kroll, the film was called *The Lost Domaine* and that the female lead, as yet uncast, was a blue-eyed blonde; he thought it was a costume drama. Rather than attempting any kind of period dressing, Nastassia had decided to wear her black-wool Jil Sander pants suit, a white shirt and a black silk tie. She had washed her long fair hair and allowed it to fall naturally over her shoulders. To the casual observer, her face appeared innocent of make-up. In fact, she wore the sheerest film of foundation and blusher, a subtle grey eye-shadow, some delicately applied black mascara and a little transparent lip-gloss. She looked around her, hesitating, then approached the reception desk. Before she reached it, however, a man intercepted her, smiling. He was tall, with floppy brown hair and wore horn-rimmed spec-tacles. 'Nastassia Dušek?'

'Yes.'

'Jacob Kroll.'

'Hello.' They shook hands.

'I have a private sitting-room upstairs, the studio has a permanent suite here.'

The lift took them to the second floor and he led the

way to a pleasant room, furnished in the grand English country-house style. They sat down on a chintz-covered settee, and at once Nastassia noticed the script lying on the coffee table, beside a camcorder and a maroon-coloured briefcase with the initials JK and matching gold clasps. Jacob Kroll picked up the script and opened it, flicking through the pages. 'Do you know the story?' he asked. 'Have you read the original novel – *Le Grand Meaulnes*?'

'No.'

'Good. It's much better that you haven't.' He turned the pages, searching for a particular scene. 'Now, this is a scene where Yvonne – that's you – is walking in the woods with an old lady. They are chatting quietly together, heading towards a landing stage on a river-bank, where they expect to board a pleasure-boat. Behind them, following at a little distance is Meaulnes, a young student who has stumbled into the festivities by accident, but who is nevertheless joining in all the celebrations. Have I lost you?'

'No, I understand.'

'Right. The two women arrive at the landing stage, and as they do so, the girl half turns, stares straight at the unknown young man, slightly worried but intrigued by him, and gives him a look which says: "I don't know you. Who are you? Why are you here? And yet . . . somehow I think perhaps I do know you, don't I?" ' Jacob Kroll put down the script and looked at Nastassia, sitting straight and attentive at the other end of the settee. 'Now,' he said, 'what I would like you to do is to walk across the room to that table, then turn towards me and give me that look. Can you do that?'

'I think so. I will try, anyway.' Nastassia stood up, paused for a moment, her head bent, concentrating her thoughts. She walked away towards the table, turned quite slowly and looked at a point above Jacob's head, a puzzled expression on her face, then transformed it into a half-formed smile of recognition. My God, thought Jacob, she's a natural.

'Excellent,' he said, 'that's exactly right. Now, will you repeat the scene, exactly like that, and I'll record it?'

'OK.' Nastassia sounded very calm, though she was in fact beginning to feel slightly nervous, and could feel her pulse beating urgently in her neck. She returned to the settee, then walked slowly towards the table once more. 'Action,' said Jacob Kroll quietly and she turned, staring straight into the camcorder and reproducing exactly the same look of questioning welcome as before.

'Cut.' Jacob took his finger off the button. He sat down, referring once more to the script. 'I'd like you to memorize this little scene with Meaulnes. Just these four lines, OK? I'll be Meaulnes and read his lines.'

'Right.' Nastassia picked up the script and read the scene to herself several times.

MEAULNES: Please don't go. Stay for a moment.

YVONNE: But I don't even know your name, I don't think we've met.

MEAULNES: I don't know who *you* are, either.

YVONNE: My name is Yvonne de Galais. I'm sorry, I really must go.

'OK?' said Jacob. 'Then we'll run through it a couple of times.' They rehearsed the scene, sitting together on the settee. 'Now, stay right where you are and I'll record it as a close-up. Are you ready?' He raised the camcorder to his eye.

'Ready,' said Nastassia, sitting up as tall and straight as she could, her eyes bright and her cheeks flushed with excitement.

'Action!' They performed the scene. 'Cut! Excellent. We'll do it once more, and this time take it slightly slower, think before you speak.'

They did it twice more, then he went over to the TV set and loaded the tape. 'Let's play it back, shall we?' They watched the short video recording. When it was over, he stopped the tape with the remote control and turned towards her, smiling. 'The part's yours, if you want it.'

'I want it.'

'Good. Of course, we'll have to do a proper screen test. I'll set it up for Friday probably, OK? Then I'll have to clear it with the studio executives, but we're all ready to go, you're exactly the right girl, I don't anticipate any serious opposition from them. After that, the studio will get back to your agent.'

Nastassia looked at Jacob Kroll, at his oddly-coloured eyes with their slightly obsessive stare, behind the heavy spectacles. She observed that he needed a shave, and thought that this was probably deliberate, like the rather greasy brown hair falling over his forehead. She decided that she was going to get on very well with Jacob Kroll and learn a great deal from him.

'Thank you very much, Mr Kroll, I look forward to working with you.'

'Call me Jake.'

'Jake.'

He stood up and took her hand. 'So far, so good, Nastassia. I'll call your agent about the screen test, then the studio will be in touch about the contract. By the way,' he added, almost as an afterthought, 'we'll be shooting for several weeks in Ireland. Is that OK for you?'

'Perfectly,' said Nastassia. 'No problem.'

On the way downstairs, he asked her how it was that

she spoke such excellent English, with virtually no Czech accent.

'It's my husband. He is English. He has a very nice voice.'

'Oh, I see.' Jacob felt curiously sorry that he had asked the question. He laughed. 'Good Lord, I didn't realize that you were married. You look too young to be thinking of marriage, Nastassia.'

She looked at him, her blue eyes serious. 'I *am* too young, Jake. But I needed to get out of Czechoslovakia; to come to England, you understand?'

'Ah,' said Jake, 'I see. Yes, of course I understand.'

Josh and Max walked along the towpath on a mild Sunday afternoon in October. The tide was out and they went down the stone steps to the exposed mudflats, so that Max could throw bits of stale bread to the ducks and gulls that congregated there, searching for worms. Tiring quickly of this, Max turned his attention to his current preferred activity, chucking stones into the water.

While Max threw his stones, his father sat on a step, keeping an eye on him and watching the river traffic passing by, and remembering his own riverside childhood with a deep nostalgia, bordering on sadness. It's so ironic that Nastassia doesn't really want to live here with us, he thought, we could have been so happy here, a real family. She had been working in Ireland for two weeks now. She had phoned a couple of times, sounding cheerful and happy, finding the filming enormously exciting. She asked after Max, but did not want to speak to him, just sent her love. Josh tried very hard to be proud of her success and glad for her, to understand and encourage her ambition, but deep down he knew what he had always known but had never allowed himself to admit, that Nastassia did not love him and never had. She had been barely able to conceal her anger and dismay when she became pregnant. The amazing thing had been her going through with the birth at all. Each day when Josh returned from the office in Prague he expected to discover that she had found an abortionist and had had a termination. His joy at the birth of his little son had overwhelmed him; the child had transformed his life. Just as I once thought Stassi had, he reflected sadly, but it won't be long before she forgets us completely. Thanks be to God, she won't want to take Max from me, I'm pretty sure of that.

'Hello.'

Josh looked up and saw Ruth standing on the towpath above him, a supermarket bag in each hand, smiling as she watched Max chattering to the ducks as he threw his stones. 'Hi,' he said. 'Been shopping?'

'Yes. You needed a few things, and I was going to Sainsburys anyway.'

'Oh,' said Josh rather ungraciously, 'did I? Well, you must let me know what the damage is, won't you?'

'No need to do a major audit.' Ruth spoke quietly. 'There are loads of things you do for me, Josh. See you later, OK?' She continued down the towpath to the house.

Josh sighed. He had what he thought was a perfectly good arrangement with Mrs Maloney, who not only looked after Max, collecting him from school and giving him his tea during the week, but also did Josh's shopping and cleaned his part of the house. Mrs Maloney thought Nastassia the most beautiful creature she had ever seen, was thrilled when she saw her on the telly and was delighted to look after her husband and little boy. Josh had the feeling that Mrs Maloney disapproved of Ruth's increasing presence and influence in Max's life and thought her up to no good with another woman's husband, and sucking up to the child as well. Nevertheless, she was forced to acknowledge that it was good of Ruth to get back from the office in time to allow her to go off-duty at the proper time. Women, thought Josh, they do tend to stir things. As for Ruth, he realized that her feelings for him *were* probably more than simple friendship, but felt helpless in the face of her devotion to Max and her kindness and supportiveness to himself. He liked Ruth, respected her qualities as an architect and was grateful for her sympathy and friendship. But he could see perfectly well which way the wind was blowing, and knew that he should make it clear to her that even if Nastassia did cease to be a part of his life, he could not contemplate for a second the idea of someone else taking her place. The problem, he said to himself, is how to say this to Ruth without hurting her feelings. Poor girl, she means so well, and Max adores her. How could I be such a shit?

The streetlamps came on, one by one. There was a hint of frost in the air, a sharp reminder of approaching winter. Josh got to his feet. 'Come on, old chap,' he called. 'Time we went home.'

'One more throw?'

'OK, just one.'

Max threw his last stone, narrowly missing a duck, which put on a spurt and swam away towards the island, quacking angrily. Then he staggered across the mud in his duffle-coat and blue wellies, his fair hair blown by the wind. In spite of the fact that his dark eyes were Josh's own, the little boy looked exactly like his mother. He climbed the steps to the towpath, holding tightly to the railings. Josh gathered him up and hugged him close to his chest, feeling as though his heart would break. He began to walk back towards his house.

On the steps, they bumped into Robert on his way out. 'Coming to the *Barge* for a quick one, Josh?'

'Thanks, but no thanks,' said Josh. 'I've got this young man to get bathed and fed.'

'Can't you get Ruth to do that?'

'No,' said Josh. 'Sorry, but I can't.'

'Why on earth not? Come on, Josh, you haven't been to the pub for weeks; it'll do you good to get out for a bit. Ruth won't mind, she's crazy about Max. You know that.'

'Yes,' said Josh stiffly, 'I *do* know that, Robert. Thank you for the invitation, but the answer is still no, OK?'

'Oh. Well, sorry if I spoke out of turn, Josh. No offence?'

'Of course not. Have a good time.'

He stood for a few moments, still holding Max in his arms, watching the retreating figure of his friend, his shoulders hunched in his plaid jacket as he walked quickly towards the *City Barge*. Josh pushed open his front door and went into the house, knowing that he had been unnecessarily brusque to Robert, who had only been trying to be friendly, when all was said and done. The kitchen door was slightly ajar, the lights were on and he guessed that Ruth was in there. He took off Max's boots and coat. Then he hung up his own coat and took Max straight upstairs for his bath.

Ruth heard the conversation on the doorstep, then the front door closing, followed by Josh's footsteps on the stairs and the bathwater running overhead. Washing the fruit and vegetables at the sink, she stared unhappily through the window at the darkening garden, wondering what she had done to make Josh so distant and prickly with her. He never spoke about Nastassia, except to Max, and Ruth could only guess at his feelings. Being an intelligent and logical, rather than an intuitive woman, she concluded that he felt betrayed and angry and was missing Nastassia pretty badly. That was understandable; she was, after all, a very beautiful woman. And a total and utter bitch, said Ruth to herself angrily, how *could* she leave her child just like that, for weeks on end?

She dried the fruit and vegetables carefully on kitchen paper and put everything tidily in the appropriate storage units in the fridge. She leaned against the table for a moment, trying to decide whether to start on Max's supper, or just quietly disappear up to her own flat.

Maybe I should go down to the pub and have a drink with Robert, she thought, with a flash of spirit. The telephone began to ring in the hall and Ruth hesitated, unsure whether to answer it or shout up the stairs to Josh. She went into the hall and called up the stairs: 'JOSH! TELEPHONE!' but failed to make him hear. She picked up the phone and gave the number.

'Ruth?' It was Nastassia, sounding far away, and as if she were with a lot of people.

'Hello, Nastassia, how's it going?'

'Wonderful! It's fantastic, I can't tell you, Ruth.'

'Great, good for you,' said Ruth.

'How's Max? And Josh? Is everything OK?'

'Yes, everything's fine. Mrs M is thrilled that you're in a movie, she's told all her friends.'

'Oh, good.' Nastassia laughed, rather self-consciously. 'Is Josh there?'

'He's giving Max his bath just now. Hold on, I'll call him for you.'

'No, it's all right, don't bother him. Just give them my love, will you? Say I'll ring again soon.'

'Yes, of course.'

'Well, goodbye Ruth, it's so kind of you to help with Max. I do appreciate it, you know.'

'It's my pleasure,' said Ruth. 'Goodbye, it was nice talking to you.' She hung up and turned to see Josh and Max descending the stairs together, Max snug in his fleecy blue all-in-one and his Babar slippers.

'Oh,' said Ruth, 'there you are! That was Nastassia, Josh. She sent love to you both.'

Josh stood stock-still on the stairs and looked hard at Ruth. Two angry spots appeared in his cheeks. 'Why the hell didn't you call me?'

'I did. You didn't hear.'

'You didn't try to *make* me hear, did you?'

'I'm sorry, I would have done, but she said not to bother. I think she was in a pub. She'll ring again later. Excuse me, Josh, I'm just on my way out.' She snatched her coat from its hook and left the house without saying goodnight to Max.

Mechanically, Josh gave Max his supper, took him upstairs to bed and read him a story, leaving the door open in case the phone rang. Then he returned to the kitchen, poured himself a glass of wine and waited for the call. He thought about telephoning Nastassia himself, but he had called her at her hotel three times before, and she had always been out. Ringing later was pointless, since the little country hotel did not have phones in the bedrooms, and he knew that Nastassia would not appreciate being dragged out of bed to talk on the phone in a draughty public place late at night. At half-past eleven he heard Robert and Ruth come in and go upstairs. At half-past twelve he gave up his vigil and went to bed himself, taking a look at Max on the way. He had kicked off his covers and lay like a little blue starfish, his long dark lashes resting on the smooth delicate skin of his cheeks, tiny beads of sweat on his upper lip. Josh half-covered his sleeping child and stole from the room. He undressed and took a shower. He lay in his bed, his bed and Nastassia's, and stared blindly at the ceiling. I can't bear this, he said to himself, I can't bear the thought of her never being here, of losing her. The trouble is, said a cold voice in his head, the trouble is, you never really had her, did you?

Chapter Five

Vassili drove Guy to the taverna just before nine o'clock. The sun had long set, but the late evening light still threw a pearly glow over the sea, and distant lights could be seen far across the water, where the profile of the Albanian mountains floated, mysterious and alien against the darkening sky. Strings of cheerful coloured lights were festooned in the prolific vine that grew over the terrace, and each table was lit by a candle in a small tin lantern. The tables were covered in checked plastic cloths and were surrounded by white plastic chairs. So late in the season there were few tourists; only half-a-dozen tables were occupied, and most of the diners appeared to be local people or foreign residents like Guy himself. The evening was cool after the warmth of the day and he had decided to wear a linen jacket. Dido watched him as he made his slow but purposeful way through the tables towards her. One or two people glanced at him as he passed, but Spiros came out of the kitchen to welcome him with a friendly volley of Greek, to which Guy responded with equal warmth.

How handsome he is, and how kind, thought Dido; it's cruel that he should be so disabled. No wonder he keeps himself to himself, it must be horrible to be stared at. She pushed back her chair and stood up as he approached. Transferring his sticks to one hand, he took her outstretched hand with the other and gave it a little shake. 'Here I am,' he said.

'Yes,' said Dido, 'here you are.'

Spiros pulled out the chair opposite Dido's, guiding Guy unobtrusively into it and pushing it up to the table. Dido sat down again, and Spiros gave them the small menu, handwritten in faded purple ink. He brought two small glasses of ouzo, water, a plate of black olives and a small bowl of hot golden chips.

'*Arní souvlákia* is OK today,' he told them, pad in hand, pencil poised.

'Is that the good smell from the charcoal grill?' asked Dido.

'Yes. Is young sheep on skewer with onion and herb, very good.'

'That's what I'll have,' she said. 'Sounds great.'

'It does,' said Guy. 'I'll have the same, thanks.'

'And a jug of our own wine, from the cask?'

'Is that the same red that Vassili gets for me?' asked Guy.

'The same. From my father's vines.'

'Excellent stuff,' said Guy, looking at Dido, waiting for her to decide.

'Yes, of course,' she said. 'Thank you, Spiros, we'll have your wine.'

'And to begin?'

'Some *dolmádes* perhaps?' Dido looked at Guy.

'*Dolmádes* would be fine.'

Spiros departed with their order, delighted that Guy had at last been coaxed from his shell for an evening out, even more delighted that it should be in the company of their quiet, mysterious guest. He stuck their order on the spike over the stove, gave his wife a knowing wink and slid a *bouzoúki* tape into the music centre, keeping the volume low. It was too early in the evening for the full blast of music to be released, to bounce joyfully across the little bay and perhaps lure in a few latecomers to drink and dance.

Guy and Dido drank their ouzo and ate the olives and chips.

'I shall start putting on weight soon,' said Dido. 'I can't resist these sensational chips. Now they know that I like them so much, they bring them nearly every day, they really are kind people.'

'You're right, they are. It's another world, isn't it, compared to England?'

'Don't you miss it at all? London? Your work? Galleries and theatres, things like that?'

'Hardly ever went to the theatre, too difficult. But the work, yes. I do miss that sometimes. And concerts; I used to go to quite a lot of concerts. I do miss that, rather, but I shouldn't complain; I have hundreds of tapes, LPs and CDs.'

Spiros approached with the *dolmádes*, small vine-leaf parcels stuffed with rice and pine-nuts. He put the wine and a basket of bread on the table, with a saucer of lemon wedges. They squeezed lemon over the dark-green parcels and ate them, their appetites sharpened by the night air and the aromatic smells emanating from the kitchen, where Katerina could be seen calmly moving her pregnant bulk between stove and charcoal grill, giving a swift stir here and a confident shake of a frying-pan there.

'Delicious,' said Guy, putting down his fork and pouring wine into their glasses. 'I must get Heleni to do them more often at home.'

'Or come here more often, perhaps?'

Guy smiled at her and raised his glass. 'That would depend, wouldn't it?'

'On what?' asked Dido, taking a sip of her wine.

'On whether there was someone to keep me company.'

'Oh.'

Spiros arrived with the *souvlákia*, sizzling on their

skewers, and accompanied by a tomato salad. They ate slowly and with enjoyment. The lamb was tender, the salad a perfect complement to the meat. By the time they had eaten all the food, the jug of wine was empty. The music was beginning to get a little louder and a few of the tables had been pushed back. Some local young people and a German couple who lived high up in the hills formed a line and began to dance the *syrtáki*. Guy and Dido watched, entertained by the impromptu party atmosphere that seemed to have sprung from nowhere.

'It does look fun, doesn't it? And not really very difficult to learn, probably?'

'It's not,' said Guy. 'I have observed from time to time some fairly inebriated people doing it perfectly.'

'Really?' Dido laughed, and picked up the wine jug. 'Good heavens, it's empty,' she said, sounding surprised. 'Shall we have another?'

'Why not? But I'll probably need help getting to the car if I drink any more.'

'So what?' said Dido.

Spiros brought fruit and a plate of honeycakes.

'Let's not have any more wine,' said Guy. 'Let's have a couple of *metáxas*, shall we?'

Spiros took away the empty plates and brought the brandy, leaving the bottle on the table. 'Coffee in five minutes?' he offered.

'Thanks,' said Dido. She leaned her elbows on the table, feeling relaxed and happy. To please Spiros, she ate a honeycake as she sipped her brandy. She looked at Guy, sitting back in his chair, watching the dancers, and had the comfortable feeling that at this precise moment there was no other place that she would rather be, and no other person that she would prefer to be with. 'You like the *bouzoúki*, Guy?' she said.

He turned his head and looked at her, smiling. 'Yes, I

do. I love it. But there are other tunes and other dances that are more interesting as well as more beautiful than the *syrtáki*. I must ask Vassili when the next village feast is, and take you. They are always happy to welcome strangers and then we might see the *agiriótikos* or the *naftikós*; they're the real Corfiot dances. The *syrtáki* is fun, but it's really only for tourists.'

'It sounds fascinating,' said Dido. 'I'd love to go.'

'I'll talk to Vassili, and we'll arrange it.'

Spiros brought the coffee, and Guy poured more brandy. 'Now my legs definitely won't behave,' he said ruefully, and Dido laughed.

'Dido?'

'Yes?'

'Tell me why you're here.'

Dido drank some coffee, took a swallow of brandy and rested her chin on her hand. She looked seriously at Guy. 'I am here because I returned home unexpectedly and found another woman's mascara on my pillow, her nightdress in my wardrobe and her knickers in my laundry basket.'

'Poor you, how very sordid.'

'Yes, it was.'

'So, what did you do?'

'Well, I packed a bag and telephoned for a flight to Corfu.'

'Just like that? What decisiveness.'

'Yes, but before I left, I threw her expensive tarty underwear and her posh French suitcase into the Thames.'

Guy laughed. 'Good for you; well done. I bet that annoyed her.'

'I hope it did.'

'Did you know her?'

'No. I never really knew who Jake's girls were, though I knew he had them, all the time. People used to tell me about them, especially women. I think they fancied him themselves.'

'Is he so very fanciable?'

'I suppose he must be; he's pretty glamorous.'

'What does he do?'

'Same as me, he works in the movies. The only difference is that I am a lowly production assistant and he is a rather well-known director.'

'I see.' Guy looked sympathetically across the table at Dido. He understood only too clearly how things must have been for her, and how humiliating. He poured more coffee for them both.

'Thank you.' She spoke quietly, without looking at him. 'The trouble is,' she went on, 'I loved him. For all I know, I probably still do, in spite of his obvious lack of commitment to me.' She raised her eyes and saw Guy looking at her thoughtfully, his dark-blue eyes reflecting the small flame in the lantern still burning on the table.

'So, my dear girl, why are you still here?'

'Because I need to make up my mind whether to tell him to go, once and for all, or just ignore it and go on as though nothing had happened, which is what I've been doing for years. You know, the ostrich syndrome.'

'And how long do you expect it will take to reach a decision?'

'I don't know – probably weeks.'

'Oh, good.' Guy laughed, picked up her hand and kissed it. 'Thank God for that. I thought you were about to do a runner, just when we've begun to know each other.' He released her hand, and took a sip of brandy. 'Does that sound more than usually silly?'

'No,' said Dido, smiling. 'It doesn't sound silly at all.'

The music began to get louder, more people arrived and soon there were several lines of dancers crowding the floor. As suddenly as it had begun, the music stopped, the dancers sat down, laughing and hot, and Spiros and Katerina ran about swiftly replenishing drinks. Then above the chatter and laughter came the sound of a soft and beautiful song, with a hauntingly sad melody.

'Isn't that lovely?' said Dido. 'Spiros plays it every night, I never get tired of it.'

'I think it was written by Manos Hadjidakis; either him or Mikis Theodorakis. They were immensely popular in their day; they more or less invented the particular sound of the *bouzoúki* that the world associates with Greece nowadays.'

'Really? And could I buy some tapes?'

'Easily.'

They sat without speaking, drinking their brandy and listening to the music, cocooned in their own silence and thoughts. When the song ended and the buzz of conversation began again, Dido put down her glass and leaned across the table. 'Guy?'

'Mm?'

'Are you doing anything tomorrow?'

'Not particularly, no.'

'Have you ever been to Myrtiótissa?'

'I haven't, no.'

'Could we go there tomorrow; take a picnic?'

'We'd have to get there from the sea; it'd be a pretty long haul in the boat, there and back.' He sounded doubtful.

'Could we not drive across the island, and hire a boat nearby to get to the beach?'

'Good idea. I expect Vassili knows someone at Paleokastritsa, I'll ask him.'

'Can we go, then?'

'Certainly, if that's what you'd like. I'll get Heleni to pack something for lunch, shall I?'

'Wonderful, that's great. Thank you, Guy. How kind you are.'

'Thank *you*, Dido, for a lovely evening, and a lovely day.'

'It was fun, wasn't it?'

'It was. And now comes the moment of truth – getting me to the car without causing an unseemly disturbance.'

As if by a prearranged signal, Spiros and Vassili came across to the table. 'You are ready for going home?' asked Vassili.

'I am.'

The two men linked hands under Guy's legs, he put his arms round their shoulders and they carried him swiftly through the taverna to the carpark. Dido ran after them carrying Guy's sticks. When he was settled in the car, she passed him his sticks, closed the car door and leaned through the open window. 'I'll come to your house about ten, shall I?'

'That'll be fine.'

'Goodnight, Guy. Sleep well.'

'I will. You too, my dear.'

Guy did not sleep particularly well. He lay in his bed, staring out at the starlit sky and thinking about Dido. He thought of her sad little face as she told him about her partner's betrayal of her, and of her own submissiveness in the face of it. The thought of her spending the rest of her life trapped in such an insulting arrangement angered and depressed him. And yet, she did not seem to him to be a woman lacking in courage or spirit, far from it; for all her frailty and smallness she appeared strong, capable and decisive. So I suppose that must mean she loves him, poor girl. It's not just freaks and cripples like me who suffer from the unthinking cruelty of others, he thought. Her kind of situation must be just as demoralizing in its way; in some respects worse. At least I can walk away, metaphorically speaking, when the going gets rough. Presumably she can't, or doesn't want to. He closed his eyes, listening to the owls in the olive grove, and let his mind drift over the events of the day. It was a very long time since he had spent an entire day, as well as most of the previous evening in the company of a woman. Clear pictures came unbidden into his head; Dido leaning over the gunwale of the boat, plunging the harpoon into the *bourdetto*, the brilliant circle of light reflected underneath her slender body. He saw her floating beside him in the pool; sitting close to him in the ruined chapel. He remembered the gentle kiss on the cheek she had given him there, and a long-sublimated sensation stirred within him and he half-smiled, half-groaned. For Christ's sake, not that again he said to himself, please, not that again. God, he thought, I must be very careful not to make a fool of myself, or even worse, of her.

He rearranged his pillows, and presently he fell asleep. Towards dawn he began to dream, a long complicated dream in which he flew high in the blue sky, swam under cool green water, then climbed through his bedroom window and got into bed, where Dido lay naked under the sheet, holding out her arms in welcome. When Guy woke, he was smiling. He remembered the dream quite clearly and found himself filled with an intoxicating feeling of happiness, even a flicker of hope. Then commonsense prevailed, sternly reminding him of his damaged, crippled body, but even this undeniable fact could not entirely destroy his feeling of elation. Allow yourself to be a bit happy, Guy, he said to himself. It's not a crime, after all.

*   *   *

Lavinia sat at her desk, ostensibly writing letters while Mrs O'Reilly cleaned the windows overlooking the drive and gave a running commentary on the comings and goings of the film people. As she did not usually come to work before nine in the morning, she always missed the very early arrival of the cast and crew, so she had changed her hours to the late afternoon for two days a week, informing Miss Porteous that she had to take Paddy to the physiotherapist for his flat feet on those mornings, for the time being. Since she was deeply fascinated by the world of motion pictures and had been from a slip of a girl, she was making a very superior job of all the front windows and taking her time over it, working her way carefully into the corners of each pane of glass. Normally, Lavinia would have absented herself from the sitting-room while cleaning of any kind was in progress, for Mrs O'Reilly was a garrulous woman, mistakenly thinking that Miss Porteous must be awfully lonely, and rarely missed the opportunity of passing the time of day with her, given half a chance.

'Ooh,' said Mrs O'Reilly, 'here comes a real flash car. And if it isn't himself, Jacob Kroll, would you believe?' She watched the car out of sight, then half-turned towards Lavinia, folding her cloth and spraying it with cleaning fluid. 'That's the director, you know, Miss. It's the clever one he is, and good-looking with it.' She sighed, clasping the cloth in both hands, her eyes dreamy. 'Did you ever see his last film, Miss? *The Eccentric Englishman*?'

Lavinia was listening intently, gleaning all the information she could. She, too, was gripped with curiosity and found the visitors rather enthralling, like creatures from another planet. However, she was too proud and too careful of maintaining her superiority over Mrs O'Reilly to allow herself to join in such a vulgar display of adulation, so she merely looked up from her writing-table and gave her cleaner a quelling look. 'No, Mrs O'Reilly, I can't say that I have, I rarely go to the cinema. Have you nearly finished the windows?'

'Yes, Miss, nearly.' Crestfallen, Mrs O'Reilly turned back to the windows and gave a final spirited burst of polishing with a yellow duster. A car passed, a big black chauffeur-driven Daimler. It looked like a limo; a posh hire-car (or even a hearse, God forbid, thought Mrs O'Reilly). In the back seat she caught a glimpse of a beautiful young face, pale, with huge blue eyes, beneath the folded-back brim of a squashy-looking black velvet hat, with a curtain of long fair hair falling over one shoulder. Mrs O'Reilly did not recognize the young lady, but she had no doubt at all that she was the star of the film. She looked forward keenly to the time when she would be able to say to all her friends, with suitable modesty: 'Of course, I saw her before she was famous.'

Nastassia was in her element at Inniscarragh. Wandering through the neglected gardens and cold, atmospheric rooms of the house she had no difficulty at all in imagining that she had been born and had grown up in this romantic place. In spite of her lack of acting experience, she had a quiet confidence and belief in herself that communicated itself to her fellow actors, the crew and the director as the work progressed. That morning they had done the scene in which Yvonne plays the piano, while a little group of children sit on a sofa, listening. Meaulnes appears in the doorway and, leaning against the frame, listens and watches her silently, then withdraws without speaking. Fortunately, Nastassia was able to play very simple piano pieces quite convincingly, in an amateurish manner, which was exactly what Jacob wanted. The boom camera was able to work round her as she played, her long hair coiled into a loose knot, her hands emerging from the frilled lacy cuffs of a starched white high-necked blouse, her feet on the pedals clad in black patent-leather pumps, just visible below the weighted hem of a full black skirt. From her shoulders hung a russet-coloured cloak, of rough frieze. The scene had gone well, and was a wrap before four o'clock.

As she left the set, Jake called her over to look at the video playback. 'Good, isn't it?' he said.

'Is it?' she replied, looking up at him candidly, 'I can't really tell. If you say it is good, I am pleased, of course.' She was gratified at receiving praise from him, for he had not shown her quite the same warmth and admiration on the set as he had at their first meeting. He treated her in exactly the same way as the rest of the cast, with an authoritative, cool professionalism. She smiled at him. 'I am very happy if you are pleased with my work, naturally.'

'Good, that's fine. You're doing very well. Now, I was thinking of driving up to Dublin for dinner, the pub food palls after a while, doesn't it? I thought you might like to come with me?'

'Thank you, Jake. That would be very nice.'

'Half-past six, in the pub carpark?'

'I'll be there.'

Back in her hotel bedroom Nastassia made up her face with care, and put a small box containing travel sizes of all her cosmetics into her capacious soft leather Italian bag. She chose a long grey mohair sweater and black silk leggings, and flung a big aubergine-coloured chenille shawl around her shoulders. She gave herself a long, cool critical look in the narrow wardrobe mirror, then went downstairs, handing her key in at the reception desk. She smiled at the young clerk, already her devoted slave. 'I'm going to Dublin,' she said. 'I might decide to stay the night, so don't worry if I don't come home, will you, Michael?'

'Very well, Miss. Have a nice evening.'

'Thanks, I will.'

In the carpark Jacob was waiting in his BMW. He had put up the hood and was listening to the radio. Nastassia opened the door on the passenger's side and slid into the seat, then swivelling round, put her bag on the back seat.

'Hi,' said Jake, 'you smell very nice.'

Nastassia fastened her seat-belt, then lifted her cool blue eyes to his, with a shy smile. 'This is fun,' she said. 'It's ages since I went out to dinner, it will be a real treat.'

Jacob laughed and releasing the handbrake, drove smoothly out of the carpark and took the road to Dublin.

As she had promised, Dido arrived at Guy's house at ten o'clock to find his car already loaded with a picnic basket, swimming things, fishing harpoons and a bundle of wood, 'to cook the fish, if Vassili manages to catch some.' They set off towards the west coast, taking the minor roads straight up over the ridge of the island, through quiet shady olive groves, glimpsing small hidden hamlets of peasant houses, and once over the summit the occasional sight of the Ionian sea. Slowly, the car dropped down to Paleokastritsa. When they were nearly there, Vassili stopped the car so that Dido could get out and look down at the beautiful coastline, the sea an amazing turquoise blue within a ring of small rock-encircled coves. The rocks, pitted and fretted by millennia of winter batterings from the sea, rose straight up from the water, sheer and majestic, pierced by grottoes and caves. On a larger, wooded promontory stood a Byzantine monastery, white and square, its triple bell-tower with its three great bronze bells sharply etched against the deep green-blue of the sea.

Dido stood on the edge of the road and gazed down at the astonishing scene below. Then she turned and got back into the car. 'I can't think of anything to say that doesn't sound like a travel brochure,' she said.

'It's pretty amazing, isn't it? You can get an even more sensational view from a village about four kilometres further up the mountainside. It's called Lákones. From there you can see the whole of the coastline and even Corfu Town on a clear day. Perhaps we might go there sometime; there's a good taverna to have lunch.'

'Sounds lovely.'

Vassili drove down the hill into Paleokastritsa and parked beside a small quay where several boats were tied up, their owners sitting in the sun smoking, mending their nets and passing the time of day. Vassili got out of the car and went over to one of these groups, greeting old friends, and laughingly refusing urgent invitations to come and have a drink. An animated discussion took place, and a bargain was quickly struck after a bit of haggling on Vassili's part. Money changed hands, and Vassili returned to the car, grinning. 'It's OK, we can take Stavros's boat.'

This turned out to be a large rubber dinghy with an outboard motor. In the season, Stavros was employed by local hotels as a lifeguard to patrol the waters on the look-out for windsurfers and swimmers in trouble. After handshakes all round, the baskets, fishing gear and firewood were carried on board, Stavros and Vassili each gave Guy a shoulder to lean on and he was swiftly installed in the boat. In less than five minutes they were chugging out of the bay and heading south, along the spectacular rocky tree-clad coastline towards Myrtiótissa. The sea was as smooth as silk, a light breeze blew from the west and the boat cut through the water at an exhilarating pace, as if it were enjoying itself.

'How long will it take to get there?' asked Dido.

'About forty minutes, I should think,' said Guy, and in exactly forty minutes Vassili turned into the tiny empty cove, its strip of golden sand basking in the noonday sun, its great sheer myrtle-covered cliffs rising up like a painted backcloth before them. Vassili cut the engine, pulled the screw out of the water, picked up a paddle and began to scull towards the shore. The sudden silence seemed deafening. No sign of human habitation could be seen, the only sound the tiny twitterings of birds hidden in the green thicket. The place seemed spellbound.

'Look out for rocks,' said Vassili, 'we don't want a hole in the bottom.'

Dido hung over the side of the boat, looking carefully around, but the sandy bottom through the pale transparent water was smooth, marked only by the shallow ridges left by the movement of the tides. 'Can't see anything.'

'Good.' Vassili allowed the dinghy to come to rest with a gentle crunch, its prow wedged firmly on the sand, its stern still in the water. Dido picked up the picnic basket and jumping ashore, stowed it under a shady clump of myrtle, close to the cliff. She ran back to the boat as Guy tried to steady himself on his sticks, working out the best way of getting across the fat inflated rubber side of the dinghy.

'Hold on,' said Dido. 'Let me give you a hand, it's too wide.'

'You're right. I'll try something else.' He lowered himself carefully onto the side of the boat, then picked up his legs one by one, swivelling round and lifting them onto the beach. Then, planting his sticks firmly in the sand he stood up triumphantly, walked across the narrow beach, and lowered himself onto a smooth ledge of rock. 'How disappointing,' he said, pulling off his shirt, 'I rather expected a round of applause.' Dido laughed and brought the rest of the stuff, stowing it beside the basket.

'I will try for fish now.' Vassili took Guy's harpoon gun, and pushing the boat off the sand, began to drift slowly along the rocky ledges, steering with his paddle. He disappeared round the tall dark crag that separated Myrtiótissa from the next bay.

Dido sat down on the sand beside Guy, and leaned against him. 'Isn't this heaven?' she said. 'Aren't you glad we came?'

Guy looked down at her smooth dark bell of hair and her sun-burned freckled nose, like a child's. He put his hand gently on her bony brown shoulder. 'Yes,' he said quietly, 'I'm very glad. It's a magical place.'

She looked up at him, smiling. 'I knew you'd like it, in spite of the hassle of getting here.'

'It was worth it.' He looked up at the towering cliff just behind them. 'Did you really come down there? I can't even see a path.'

'I did. I rather surprised myself, as a matter of fact.'

'You must have goat in your genes somewhere.'

'I hope I don't smell like a goat.'

'You don't smell like a goat, Dido. You smell of sun, and clean linen.'

She twisted round and knelt beside him, put her thin arms round his neck and kissed him. 'What a lovely thing to say.'

She kissed him again, and Guy put his arms round her and held her close to him. 'You really must stop kissing me, my love,' he said. 'It's getting to be a habit.'

'Do you want me to stop?'

'No, I don't.' He tightened his arms round her and kissed her and a flood of long-repressed feeling rushed through his body, at once glorious and painful. Reluctantly, he loosened his grip and she rested her cheek against his chest.

'Guy?'

'Mm?'

'Are we falling in love?'

'I hope so.'

She looked at him, her eyes shining. 'I hope so too,' she said. 'Now, what about a swim before lunch?'

'Isn't the sea a bit cold?'

'Yes, but my little pool isn't.' She pointed to the rockpool a few metres away, overhung by its small, shady olive tree. 'Look, there's even a convenient branch so you can swing into the pool.'

'Like an ape?'

'Or like Tarzan?'

Guy laughed. 'Well, you may have a point. At least I won't scratch my bum on that sharp rocky ledge.'

Dido stripped off her clothes, revealing a pale-blue cotton bikini. They crossed the short stretch of sand to the pool and Guy sat down and eased off his shorts. Dido knelt beside him and undid the buckles of the leg irons and took them off. She looked up at Guy. 'You don't mind?'

'No, of course I don't mind,' he replied, surprising himself, for it was true. 'Now comes the crunch,' he said, grabbing the olive branch and letting it take his weight. 'If this bloody thing breaks, Dido, I shall hold you entirely responsible. Come on then, don't just stand there, give me a shove.'

Laughing, Dido gave him a gentle push and he swung towards the middle of the pool and dropped into it, letting go the branch as he made contact with the bottom. He lay there, supporting himself on his elbows and looking up at her, grinning, as she got into the pool beside him. 'What did you think of that? Pretty impressive, don't you think?'

'Brilliant. You could get a job in a circus any day.'

'What, with the freaks in the sideshows? The bearded lady? The two-headed calf?'

Dido knelt beside him in the water and looked at him, her eyes dark and serious. 'I never want to hear you use that word again, Guy. Not ever, do you hear me?'

'I hear you.'

'Promise?'

'Will you kiss me again if I promise?'

'Guy! What a flirt you are!' She held his face in her wet hands and kissed him, then pushed him under the water and lay on top of him, which was quite a surprising sight for Vassili as he came back round the tall rock with his catch. On second thoughts, he was not especially surprised, in fact he was delighted and a broad smile lit up his dark weathered face, revealing his sparkling golden tooth as he made a noisy splash or two to announce his coming, and brought the dinghy up onto the beach. He picked up the baler that he had found in the boat, and which now contained six beautiful small silver fish, and stepped ashore, proudly bringing lunch. He put his catch down in a patch of shade and set about building a small fire, surrounded by a circle of stones.

'Can you imagine anything more idyllic than this?' said Dido. 'A private beach, the most beautiful in the world probably; a warm pool and just-caught fish being cooked over a wood fire for our lunch?'

'It's like the best kind of dream,' said Guy sleepily. 'You don't want it to end.'

She lay in the water beside him, looking up through the shimmering silvery leaves of the olive tree, smelling the faint drift of wood-smoke from Vassili's fire. She felt intensely alive and happy; she had very nearly forgotten how it felt to be so happy. She turned her head and looked at Guy, at his closed eyes, his long nose and his mouth curved in a relaxed smile. 'Does it have to end?' she asked quietly.

He opened his eyes and turned towards her. 'That depends entirely on you, doesn't it? In the meantime, I'm ravenous, aren't you? Let's eat.'

With a good deal of splashing, Dido pulled down the branch so that Guy could get out of the pool. He did this by going hand over hand along the branch until he was over dry land and his feet could touch the ground. Dido slid an arm round him. 'Do you want to put the gear on now, or later when it's time to leave?'

'Later, I think. Why not?'

Vassili, observing them, came swiftly over to support Guy's other side and in a couple of minutes they had settled him comfortably against a smooth rock, and Dido was unpacking Heleni's basket. Bread, wine, cheese, tomatoes and fruit emerged, with plates and glasses, knives and forks.

'Terrific,' said Dido, pouring wine. 'It's just like going to Glyndebourne, isn't it?'

'I think they might take rather a poor view of one grilling fish in their garden, don't you?' said Guy as Vassili lifted the fish from the griddle and put them on the waiting plates.

'I was on location once in India, and we travelled on the trains most of the time. I used to watch the old women in their lovely saris, squatting down in the corridors, brewing tea on their portable charcoal stoves. I thought it very enterprising of them, and no one seemed to object. I've never forgotten it.'

106

After lunch, they lay in the shade, dozing, sometimes chatting, while Vassili took himself off to try for some fish for Heleni.

'Tell me about your childhood,' said Guy, and Dido told him about the long, sometimes boring travels with her mother, and Mabel, and Signor Pernice.

'Who was Signor Pernice?'

'My mother's lover; my father.'

'So why do you call him Signor Pernice?'

'I don't know why. I just always did.'

'So aren't you really Dido Pernice? Ah, I get it. Pernice: partridge. It's a good name for you, it suits you.'

At five o'clock Vassili reappeared and said it was time to make a move. He packed everything into the boat, while Dido helped Guy with his leg-irons. They got him safely on board and headed north as the sun began to drop towards the west. They reached Paleokastritsa just after six, transferred to the car and drove slowly home across the island, through the darkening wooded lanes to Koulari, the fading sky overhead flecked with thin broken clouds, pink-washed by the last rays of the sun. Heleni was preparing dinner in the kitchen, and had already set the table on the terrace for two.

'You'll stay, won't you?' said Guy.

'Do you really want me to? Aren't you tired?'

'I really want you to stay, and I'm not tired at all.'

After dinner they sat on the terrace and watched the boats going out to fish, their white lights floating over the still waters of the channel. The owls hooted in the olive trees and the stars appeared, one by one. At eleven, Dido rose reluctantly to her feet and said that it was late, she must go.

'Why don't you stay? The room is ready.'

'Well, it would be nice not to drive alone in the dark. Thank you, I'd like to stay.'

In her room, Dido undressed and took a shower in the tiny adjoining cubicle. She wrapped herself in the big white bath-towel and thought about how to clean her teeth without a toothbrush. She hesitated, then left her room, went down the corridor, tapped on Guy's door and went in. He was lying against his pillows, his spectacles on, reading. His bedside radio was playing softly.

'Sorry to be a nuisance, Guy, but do you have such a thing as a spare toothbrush?'

'I have. It's in the cabinet in my bathroom. Didn't Heleni put one out for you?'

'I expect she thought I'd bring one.' She went to the bathroom, found the brush and cleaned her teeth. Then she went back into the bedroom.

'Dido?'

'Yes?'

'Stay for a minute?'

'Only for a minute?' Dido smiled and sat on the side of the bed.

'As long as you like, my love.' Guy put down his book and took off his glasses.

'All night?' said Dido.

He held out his arms and she got into the bed beside him, folding herself against him, her body warm against his.

'Dido, my darling, there's something I have to tell you.'

'What?'

'It won't be the missionary position, I'm afraid.'

Dido buried her face in his neck and laughed until he began to laugh too. 'I'd already worked that out for myself,' she said. 'Don't worry, I'm sure we'll manage.'

Chapter Six

Crouched on the top step of the main staircase at Inniscarragh, and half-hidden in the gloom behind the balustrade, James Porteous was watching the filming of a scene in the hall below, refreshing himself from time to time from a bottle of whisky. A great company of extras, most of them recruited locally, were seated at the long row of trestle tables enthusiastically consuming the quantities of real food and bogus wine that had been set before them. They were dressed and made-up to represent ordinary country folk, farmers and their wives, milkmaids, drovers, ploughboys and grooms of the early twentieth century. The tables at which they sat appeared to be candlelit but in fact a battery of supplementary lighting came from the long battens suspended overhead. The Irish extras were acting their heads off and enjoying themselves immensely, making a great clatter with knives and forks as they ate and chatted to each other. The big camera on its dolly moved slowly along the length of the table several times, filming the tracking shots. It all seemed to be taking an extremely long time, and James was beginning to wonder whether the crowd could really go on eating much longer, some of them already looked very red in the face.

'Quiet, please,' said an authoritative voice. 'Now we'll do it with the dancers. Are they ready, Brenda?'

'Yes, they're right here in the passage.'

'Good. OK. Scene fourteen, take one. Clear the frame, please.'

Make-up girls scurried out of sight, the sound and picture cameras were activated and brought up to speed. 'Action!' called the assistant director and the feast began again. Then, from the kitchen passage a group of young people danced into the hall, led by a pretty girl in a velvet bodice and a long, frilled skirt, partnered by a young man wearing a high-collared coat and tight trousers with footstraps. They danced their way along the packed tables, followed by a noisy, jostling crowd in fancy-dress costumes of the Directoire period, pursued by a tall, thin man dressed as a *pierrot*, his chalk-white face slashed by widely grinning reddened lips. On his head he wore a tightly-fitting black skull-cap and his oversized white suit had wide baggy trousers and long, loosely trailing sleeves. He leapt high in the air, arms flailing, covering the ground with huge, elastic strides. After him came a gaggle of little children, half-alarmed by the *pierrot* but giggling nervously and mimicking his manic leaps.

'Cut!'

The actors stopped and trailed back into the corridor, preparing to do the scene all over again. James took a drink from his bottle. He was beginning to be slightly bored and rather wished they would do something more interesting, preferably with a bit of dialogue. It did seem to go on a bit, this endless repetition. He wondered whether anyone would notice if he got up and walked away down the landing to the back stairs, and thence to the sanctuary of the kitchen. Down below, the scene was being set up again and he hesitated, unable to make up his mind whether it would be possible to make a dash for it without drawing attention to himself. He took another swig from his bottle and suddenly, with a small sibilant flurry of subsiding black cloth, someone sat down beside him. Surprised, he looked to his right and saw that the black cloth was in fact a nun's habit, and a snow-white goffered wimple framed a cheerful blue-eyed rosy face.

'Give us a go then,' said the nun in a hoarse, tobacco-roughened whisper. 'I'm parched!'

James wiped the neck of the bottle and handed it to his new companion, who took a long gurgling drink. God almighty, thought James, what a swallow! She handed back the bottle and cuddled up to James, giggling, while he took another good shot himself.

'Clear the frame!' shouted the assistant director. 'Quiet please!' James put an arm round his nun and they watched silently as three times more the action was played out below, taking nips of whisky to fortify themselves, until James put the bottle to his lips and found it to be empty. 'Bugger,' he muttered, 'it's finished.' He looked at the nun, who looked back at him, smiling slightly inanely, bright-eyed, a bit pissed. That goes for me too, he thought. He put the empty bottle carefully behind the big square newel post and turned to his new-found friend. 'Let's go somewhere quieter, shall we?' he whispered. 'I've got another bottle in my room.'

'OK, why not? Which way is it?'

James pointed along the landing and the nun hitched up her habit and began to crawl away from him in the direction he had indicated. Following her, he observed with some interest that she was wearing black under-wear of the satin and lace variety and sheer black stockings and suspenders. I say, he thought, what a little cracker! He caught up with her and when they reached the fourth door on the landing, he put out a restraining hand and nodded towards his bedroom door. 'In here,' he whispered. Once inside the room, they got to their feet rather unsteadily, hot and laughing. The nun looked round James's room with undisguised admiration, while he staggered over to the night-cabinet beside his enormous old four-poster and took from it a partly-consumed bottle of whisky. 'Blimey!' exclaimed the visitor, impressed by the Venetian-red damask hangings of the bed and the gilded corkscrew posts supporting the tester. 'What a knock-out bed! Do you really sleep in it?'

'I do,' said James, unscrewing the bottle, 'and it's bloody uncomfortable, I can tell you.' Recalling the jolly sight of the black underwear, he looked at the nun in a manner that he thought rather roguish, but was in fact nothing more than the leer of a drunken old lecher. 'Want to give it a try?' he offered.

Somewhat to his amazement, the nun at once began to remove her wimple and habit, revealing the greying red hair and the flabby, drooping body of a rapidly ageing woman. She came and sat on the bed beside him, smelling of sweat, cheap scent and whisky. She put her fat, freckled arms round James's neck and began to kiss him in what he thought of as an extremely continental manner. Oh well, he thought, no point in looking a gift-horse in the mouth, is there? I'm no bloody oil-painting myself. After a lot more whisky, some rather silly horseplay and inelegant divesting of each other's remaining clothing, they did eventually succeed in performing a grotesque act of love. At the moment of congress James gave a great shout and fell unconscious, spread-eagled on top of his partner. For a few moments the poor woman thought that James had merely exhausted himself in achieving his orgasm and was having a rest, then it gradually dawned on her that he was in fact dead. With a little cry of horror she pushed him off her, extricating herself with some difficulty from his body. She scrambled from the bed

112

as though it were a nest of vipers and dressed herself with remarkable speed in view of the fact that she was trembling violently from head to foot. She looked in the dark looking-glass and carefully adjusted her wimple, taking deep breaths to steady her nerves. Then she went back to the bed and looked at the pale, naked old body lying so still and cold upon it. Gently, she closed his eyes, adjusted the pillow under his head, and covered him tidily with the sheet and the red damask coverlet. That's a bit better, she thought, he just looks as if he's sleeping now. Poor old sod, what a way to go. For some obscure reason, she made the sign of the cross, then picked up the whisky bottle, slipped it into her capacious pocket and stole from the room, closing the door carefully behind her.

On a Saturday morning in late October Josh woke early and lay listening to the quarrelsome shrieking of gulls on the foreshore and the lonely, mournful hoot of a passing barge. He gazed through the window at the pale grey overcast sky and watched the yellowing willow leaves whirling past, tossed by the stiff westerly wind. No sound came from Max's room next door and Josh decided to let him sleep. He folded his hands beneath his head and stared at the ceiling, dreading the weekend in front of him, dreading the sympathetic glances of his tenants, and most of all dreading the probability of having to be unkind to Ruth, and offending her yet again. Why does she hang on? he asked himself. Why doesn't she just get the message and leave, poor girl? He looked at his watch: five to eight. It'll be five to nine in France, he thought, and then surprised himself by picking up the telephone and dialling his mother's number in Paris.

'*Oui?*'

'Mum?'

'Josh! How are you, darling? Is everything all right?'

'No, Mum, it's bloody all wrong as a matter of fact. I was wondering, could I bring Max and come for the weekend? We could come on the Eurostar and back tomorrow night.'

'Of course you could, darling. The thing is, we're just on our way to Normandy, to Grandpère, why don't you come there? It's ages since he saw you and Max, I'm sure he'd be delighted.'

'Are you quite sure? We wouldn't be in the way?'

'Don't be silly, of course not. Get the first shuttle you can, you could be in St Gilles in time for tea.'

'OK, Mum, thanks; if you're really sure?'

'I'm sure. See you later, darling. Drive carefully.'

'I will.'

Josh put the phone down. Thank God, he thought, I've done something positive. It was surprising how much better he felt; less depressed; almost cheerful. He got out of bed and went to Max's room. The little boy was lying on his pillow, blinking, half-awake.

'Come on, old chap. Time to get up, we're going on a trip.'

'Where to?'

'It's a secret.'

'Oh, good. Will Mummy be there?'

'No, Max, she won't be there. She's still working. But someone else will be waiting for you.'

'Who?'

'You'll see.'

Anna put the phone back on the hook and sat down at the kitchen table again. She picked up her coffee cup and looked at her husband, a slightly anxious frown on her face.

'Trouble?' asked Patrick. 'Something wrong with Josh?'

'Sounds like it, yes. He's bringing Max to St Gilles; he'll be there this afternoon. I'd better ring Philippe and warn him. Or would you, darling, please, while I put the stuff in the dishwasher and check that Tom has packed the right clothes?'

After ten happy years living in the attic apartment of the rickety old mansion on the Quai des Grands-Augustins, Patrick and Anna had come to the reluctant conclusion that the place was too inconveniently planned to be really comfortable for themselves and their ten-year-old son Thomas, with occasional visits from Anna's older children, Josh and Olivia. So when the much bigger apartment below them became available, they had moved into it. This had given them a large, rather impressive salon with wood-panelled walls painted a pale, Gustavian blue and wide deep windows overlooking the Ile de la Cité. The apartment also had a good-sized kitchen, four bedrooms and two bathrooms.

'My goodness!' Anna had exclaimed when they first went to look at it. 'How very grand! Are we moving up in the world, darling? Is it what we really want?' She was a woman of fastidious but simple tastes; the idea of a fashionable, obviously expensive apartment held little appeal for her.

'We don't have to live anywhere at all that you don't feel comfortable with, my love, you know that.'

Anna had looked around the high-ceilinged spacious room again, beginning mentally to furnish it. She crossed to the windows and sat in one of the embrasures, looking out over the river to the island and Notre Dame. 'Well, it *is* very light and airy, and the view *is* even better than upstairs, isn't it?'

'True.' Patrick sat down beside her, observing her with his customary devotion as she wrestled with the problem. The years had been kind to Anna, for in spite

115

of the fact that she had reached the age of fifty and was already a grandmother, she remained much the same as she had been when she had first met Patrick. She had not gained weight, her hair was still dark and glossy and the only signs of ageing were the fine lines at the corners of her luminous dark eyes. Equally, she had not changed in character; she was still the same Anna, intensely private, passionate and totally devoted to her children and her husband. Patrick considered himself the happiest and most fortunate of men.

'And I suppose it would be good not to have the bedrooms and bathrooms split into two separate places, wouldn't it?'

'M'hm.'

'And *very* nice to have a proper big kitchen, not a *coin-cuisine*?'

'Certainly.' Patrick permitted himself a small indulgent smile.

Anna looked at him seriously. 'Just one thing, before we make up our minds?'

'Anything.'

'Could we get Giò to come and take a look, and see whether he could come up with any ideas to make the place a bit less opulent; a bit more like us?'

'Of course; excellent idea.'

Giò, Anna's twin brother, owned an antique shop in the arcades of the Place des Vosges, but now spent the bulk of his time in Souliac, the family home in the Languedoc, where he and their father had been developing a vineyard for some years, growing, harvesting and bottling their own wine. They were now well on their way to achieving the much-coveted *appellation contrôlée*, a matter of enormous importance to them both.

So Anna had telephoned Giò in Souliac, and on his next trip to Paris he had come to look at the proposed

116

new apartment with Anna. 'What do you think, Giò? Don't you think it's too grand, too *haute bourgeoisie* for us? I can't really visualize our pictures and books, tapes and things, against these elegant, blue-painted *boiseries*, can you?'

'No, I can't,' said Giò. 'It's not your style at all.' He walked round the big empty room, considering the problem. He sat down in the window and looked up at the high, ivory-painted ceiling, slightly crazed with age, with bits of the intricate plaster mouldings missing. He looked at the honey-coloured wood-block floor, beautiful with centuries of beeswax and turpentine. 'You know, Anna,' he said, 'it's only the panelling that's the trouble. What if we stripped it, got rid of the blue paint? It's probably the most lovely natural pale pine underneath.'

'Do you really think so?' At once she saw the room as it would be in pale, woody, neutral tones, a perfect foil for all their possessions, especially the many small pieces of gilded carving that were her particular *métier.*

Giò got up and knelt down in a corner of the room, taking a small folding pen-knife from his pocket.

'What are you doing?'

'What do you think? Having a look at the wood.'

'Giò! You mustn't!'

'Nonsense, they'll never see.' He scraped carefully away at a small patch close to the floor. 'Come and look,' he said, glancing up at Anna.

She knelt beside him and looked. Their eyes met. The colour of the wood was perfect, a soft pale silvery beige, hatched with fine white lines where the original undercoat had sunk into the grain of the wood. 'It's beautiful,' she said. 'Thank you, Giò, what a treasure you are. I'd never have thought of doing that by myself.'

Giò had then organized everything for them with his

customary efficiency, getting the panelling stripped, finding some threadbare ancient curtains that fell in soft heaps on the floor. They still had their original wooden rings attached as well as the poles to hang them on. Since Anna was concerned about damaging the panelling with fixing holes, Giò designed and had made a storage system of steel and glass for all the books, tapes, pictures and gilded carvings. The units were suspended from the ceiling on invisible steel wires and bolted to the floor. Within a month they had moved downstairs, and Anna had felt immediately at home, and as if they had lived there forever.

Now Patrick locked the door to the apartment and he, Anna and Thomas descended in the creaky old lift, went out to the car parked in the narrow street behind the building, and drove through the back streets of Paris towards the *périphérique* and the *autoroute* to Normandy.

Josh drove into the farmyard at St Gilles just after five o'clock, tired and hungry, and parked his car beside Patrick's in the open cow-byre. He got out and opened the rear door, releasing Max from his safety harness, then retrieved their overnight bag from the boot.

'Hello, Josh, old chap. How very nice to see you.' Philippe had emerged from the house and now stood rubbing his hands together and smiling, delighted to see his grandson and great-grandson. He bent over and took Max's hand gently. 'You don't remember me, do you, young man?'

Max looked carefully at Philippe, at his snow-white cropped hair, his brown old face, wrinkled like a walnut, his hooked Norman nose. 'No,' he said seriously. 'I don't.'

Philippe and Josh laughed, and Josh put his hand on Philippe's shoulder and kissed him on both cheeks.

'Hello, Grandpère,' he said, 'it's good to be here. I hope we're not making life difficult for Marie-Claude? Too many of us at once?'

'Certainly not. You know Marie-Claude – the more the merrier. Come in and have some tea.' He took Max's hand, while Josh carried the bag and they walked across the yard to the house, the windows sparkling in the horizontal rays of the late afternoon sun as it dropped down the sky. It's red ball shone through the crisp withered leaves of the apple trees in the orchard, some of their abundant golden fruit still clinging to the ancient branches. A rusty iron wheel-barrow stood in the knee-high grass, already loaded with windfalls waiting to be taken to the press.

Philippe led the way to the sitting-room where tea was laid on the round table. Anna and Tom sat on the floor in front of the open fire, roasting chestnuts on a shovel, while Patrick sat in a comfortable armchair, reading *Le Monde*.

'Hello, Mum.' Josh crossed the room, knelt beside his mother and kissed her. 'Hello, Patrick. Hello, menace.' He ruffled the dark curly hair of his half-brother, who looked up at him with blue adoring eyes, his father's eyes.

'Hi,' he said. 'Want a chestnut?'

'Thanks,' said Josh, taking one and burning his fingers. He tossed it from hand to hand until it was cool enough to handle.

'What about me?' said Max loudly. 'I want one, too.' He was tired. His lip trembled. He looked ready to cry.

'Have this one, darling,' said Anna hastily, offering hers.

'No, I don't want *that* one. I want *that* one, Dad's one.'

Josh hesitated, but Max's face was scarlet, his tone belligerent; he capitulated at once. 'Here you are then, it's cool enough now. Look, I'll take off the shell for you.'

'No, *don't* take off the shell, Dad. I can do it myself.'

'OK,' said Josh. 'Here you are.'

'What a stupid little baby,' said Thomas loftily, turning back to the fire.

Max looked at Tom's disapproving back, glanced round at the anxious faces of the others, handed his chestnut back to Josh and went to the door. 'I don't want to be here,' he said, in a small, tight voice. 'I want to go home. I want my mummy.' He reached up, turned the handle of the door and departed.

'Oh dear,' said Anna. 'Poor little boy, he's exhausted. That was pretty unkind of you, Tom.' She got to her feet. 'I'll go after him. You have your tea, Josh. He'll be all right, don't worry.' She took a piece of cake and a mug of milk, and left the room. She found Max standing beside Josh's car, trying to open the door. 'Would you like to help me shut up the ducks, Max?'

Max hesitated. He looked at the cake. He would have liked to have rejected his grandmother's offer, but he was extremely hungry and the ducks sounded quite fun. 'Where are they?'

'Oh, all over the place. They have to be shut up for the night, in case the fox gets them.'

'What happens if the fox gets them?'

'He eats them.'

'Oh. Well, all right, I suppose so, if you can't manage by yourself.'

'Thank you, it's much easier to round them up with two people. They hide in the long grass in the orchard.'

'OK.'

'What about a snack? You must be terribly hungry? Did you have any lunch?'

'Not much – just a sandwich and a Coke. Dad didn't want to stop, except for petrol.' He ate the cake and drank the milk, and left the empty mug on the rear bumper of the car, to pick up later. Then he took Anna's proffered hand and they went to the orchard in search of the ducks.

Patrick sat quietly in his chair, pretending to read his newspaper and trying to gauge the degree of seriousness of Josh's apparent situation. Presumably the problem was Nastassia. Had she left him and their child? Poor Josh, he certainly looked miserable enough for that to be true. With a stab of remembered anguish he thought of the loss of his own first wife so long ago now, nearly forty years, and his heart bled for his young stepson, so like Anna, tall and thin, with the same dark eyes.

Josh swallowed the remains of his cup of tea and looked straight at Patrick, caught his eye and smiled briefly. Patrick returned the smile, folded his paper and stood up. 'We need more logs for this evening,' he said. 'I'll go and get some.'

'I'll come and help,' said Josh.

'So will I.' Thomas threw down his shovel, bored with the chestnuts.

'No, Tom,' Philippe intervened, 'you stay and give me a hand with the tea things, will you? We'll wash them up for Marie-Claude. She'll appreciate a tidy kitchen when she comes to cook the supper, won't she?'

'Oh, *merde*! Must I?'

'Yes, you must. And don't say *merde* unless you have a good and proper reason, please.'

'OK.'

The old man and the boy piled the cups and plates carefully on the big black oval tin tray, and Philippe carried it to the kitchen, followed by Tom with the cakestand.

Josh picked up the log-basket and he and Patrick

121

went out to the barn where the logs were stacked in towering, sweet-smelling tiers. 'Fires already,' said Patrick. 'The days fly past so quickly, don't they? It seems like it was summer only last week.'

'Patrick?'

'Josh?'

'I need to talk.'

'Of course.' Patrick sat down on the chopping block and waited.

'I think Nastassia has left me. Or if she hasn't, she very soon will.'

'Are you sure?'

'Yes, pretty sure.' He explained about the film job in Ireland; how he could hardly ever talk to her on the telephone, much less see her. 'I'm afraid she has got what she was always looking for, a real start in the movies. She doesn't need me any more.'

'And Max?'

'It seems she doesn't need *him*, either.'

'But you do?'

'Of course I do!' cried Josh violently. 'Poor kid, I'm all he's got now. Come to that, he's all I've got.'

'So, do you have any plans, or is it too early for that?' Patrick did his best to sound pragmatic and support- ive, but not too sympathetic, sensing that Josh was pretty near to breaking point. He began to pile logs into the basket and Josh helped him, splitting some of the very big ones with the long-handled axe. 'The trouble is,' he said tiredly, 'I've never really settled down in London: I suppose you don't if things are going badly. I don't have many real friends there, after all those years working in Prague. I have far more close friends, and of course family, in Paris. I thought I might try and get a job and a flat there.'

'And Max?'

'He'd come with me, of course.'

'And the house in London?'

'I thought I'd let Nastassia stay on there for a couple of years. Then, if she wants a divorce, we'd sell it and split the money between us, I suppose.'

'You've already worked it all out, haven't you?'

'It's my logical mind,' said Josh sadly. 'It's obvious, isn't it?'

'Try not to make up your mind in too much of a hurry, Josh. Things might settle down, you know.'

Josh shook his head. 'They won't. Stassi doesn't love me, Patrick, or Max. She never has, not for one single second.'

'Has she said so?'

'She doesn't have to; I just know.'

Patrick looked at his stepson, his eyes full of compassion. 'But I take it you still love her, don't you?'

'Yes, I do,' said Josh quietly. 'And I always will. It's like a terminal illness, isn't it? There's no cure for love.'

'Would you want one?' Patrick took hold of the handle on his side of the basket.

'No, I wouldn't.' Josh looked at Patrick, his dark eyes bright. 'But at least I've got Max; there's a lot of her in him, and I'm thankful for that.'

They walked back across the yard to the house, carrying the load between them. 'There's just one thing,' said Josh, as they approached the kitchen door, 'could you tell Mum for me? I can't tell her myself, or I'll go to pieces. I couldn't handle the sympathy just now, OK?'

'Of course. And Grandpère?'

'Yes, him as well. I'll have to leave straight after lunch tomorrow, so when I've gone might be best?'

'Understood,' said Patrick. 'You're probably right.'

In the kitchen, Marie-Claude and Anna were starting their preparations for dinner, pheasants with Calvados and cream, *à la Normande*, followed by apple tart. Anna sat on a stool at the table, rolling the pastry. She looked up as Josh and Patrick came in with the logs.

'Hello, Marie-Claude,' said Josh. 'How are you?'

'I am in good form, Josh, as always. And you?'

'Fine, thanks,' said Josh, and kissed her on both her soft, downy cheeks.

'What about Max's supper, Josh?' asked Anna. 'What does he usually have?'

'Anything,' said Josh. 'You know, Mum. Sausages. Baked beans. Bacon. An egg; he loves eggs.'

'Fine,' said Anna. 'We'll give him a boiled egg and soldiers, a glass of milk and an apple. How would that be?'

'Perfect.'

'And what time would he like it?'

Josh looked at the kitchen clock: ten to seven. Ten to six English time. 'Whenever,' he said.

'Why don't you give him his bath, and then bring him down here for his supper?'

'OK, Mum. Thanks, I will.'

Josh and Patrick carried the logs through to the sitting-room and found Max, Tom and Philippe playing *Happy Families*, the irony of which was not lost on Patrick.

'Max, have you got Mr Bun the Baker, by any chance?' asked Tom with a sly grin.

Silently, Max handed over the card.

'There, I've won!' said Tom triumphantly, spreading out his cards. 'But you jolly nearly did, Max,' he added quickly, trying to be nice.

'It's a boring game anyway,' replied Max, trying to sound unconcerned, and failing.

'Couldn't agree with you more, Max,' said Philippe swiftly, throwing down his cards. 'Come on, Tom, get out the chessmen. That's a proper game, much more my style.'

Max shot a look of panic to his father, who laughed and gathered him up, hugging him tight. 'Come along, it's time for your bath, old chap. Do you remember it? It's the hugest bath in the world, probably, with enormous shiny brass taps.'

Josh carried his son upstairs, comforted by the smells of cooking emanating from the kitchen, and the ambiance of the old house. Like others before him, he felt soothed by the deep mellow patina of the carved oak staircase, the stiff nineteenth-century portraits of former Halards hanging on the panelling and the fat tick of the longcase clock in the stone-flagged hall.

'Dad,' said Max, his arms clasped tightly round his father's neck, 'Tom says he's my *uncle*. Is that right?'

'Well, he's *my* brother, darling, so he must be, mustn't he?'

'I've got quite a lot of uncles and grannies and things, haven't I?'

'You have,' said Josh. 'Aren't you lucky?'

'I like Anna.'

'So do I.'

Chapter Seven

Three days had passed since James Porteous had so spectacularly departed this world. No one had missed him and he lay, silent and peaceful on his great bed in his cold bedroom, sleeping the deep, uncaring sleep of one whose troubles are over.

In the courtyard, the first cameraman, the second assistant cameraman and Jacob Kroll were trying to figure out the best way of filming the scene in the extremely small dark room in which Meaulnes dresses himself in preparation for the wedding feast.

'It's too small to get a decent frame, Jake. We should do the scene in the studio later, it would be a lot easier.'

'Or we could knock down the exterior wall,' Jake suggested. 'That would only take five minutes.'

'We can't do that without getting permission first, then rebuilding it properly afterwards, all that hassle.'

'OK, we'll get permission, no problem. I'll ask the old man now. Where is he, by the way? I haven't seen him around lately.'

'Dunno – perhaps he's away?'

'Shouldn't think so,' said Jake, 'his car's still in the garage. Send someone to look for him, right away.'

They searched high and low, all over the house and grounds, and eventually the assistant director found James. In fact, the old man made his presence, or rather, the lack of it, felt as soon as the bedroom door was opened. The room was filled with a strange smell, rather sweet, with an underlying note of corruption.

The assistant director ventured further into the room, then caught sight of the motionless figure on the bed. Christ Almighty, he said to himself, the poor old sod's snuffed it! He ran from the room, slamming the door behind him, and raced downstairs and out into the stable-yard, where Jake was waiting impatiently.

'I've found him.' The assistant director sounded breathless and looked green. 'He's dead!'

'He's what?'

'Dead!'

'You're *kidding*?'

'I'm not.'

'For Christ's sake!' exclaimed Jake angrily. 'How bloody inconvenient of him! Now what do we do?'

'Well, we can't knock a hole in the wall . . .' began the second assistant director.

'Bugger the *hole*, you fool. What do we *do*?'

'Oh. Um, well, call the police, I suppose, or get a doctor or something? What about the old bat in the cottage at the gates? Isn't that his niece?'

'Oh, shit,' said Jake. 'This is a real pain in the arse, it's going to wreck the schedule. OK, I suppose I'd better phone the police. It's their job, they can cope.'

The Garda came out from the town, bringing the police doctor with them. After pronouncing James dead, presumably from natural causes, they went through the drawers of the dead man's bureau and found the name of his lawyers in Dublin. The senior partner, an old friend of James's, told them to remove the body to the mortuary and carry out all the necessary procedures, and himself undertook to inform Miss Porteous and to write to the owner in Corfu.

For a moment it crossed Jake's mind to ask the lawyer for permission to knock down the wall. Then some small vestige of propriety reminded him that this was not an appropriate moment for such a request, and he decided against it. In the event, after the ambulance had departed with the body, he ordered the wall to be knocked down anyway. No one will know, he reassured himself, I'll just say he gave permission before he died.

Guy and Dido had spent a happy day in Corfu Town. They had paid a visit to the Church of St Spyrídon and seen the splendid silver coffin of the island's saint, looking at his tiny slippered mummified feet through a glass panel, and admiring the life-sized icons of the saints on the surrounding walls, the painted figures dark with age and smoke but the burnished silver of their haloes shimmering in the gloom. Afterwards, they enjoyed a protracted lunch at a pavement café on the Listón, and spent the rest of the afternoon in a cool bookshop.

The last two weeks had been ones of almost unbearable happiness for Guy. After a couple of days of coming and going between his house and the taverna, Dido, to no one's surprise, had moved in with Guy. He felt like a man reborn, strong, confident and full of well-being. He had ceased to be difficult about using the wheelchair, largely because the sight of the disabled man in the company of an attractive young woman seemed to draw glances of admiration rather than the embarrassed looks of pity he had previously had to endure. Equally, by taking the wheelchair, he and Dido could sometimes go out by themselves in the car, though of course they still needed Vassili for trips in the boat. This state of affairs made Guy feel a great deal more independent. He was of course very dependent on Dido, but somehow it didn't feel like that to him, or to her. Their days were leisurely, long and full of interest; their nights brought unbelievable happiness and fulfilment to them both.

Now they emerged from the bookshop, deciding that it was time to go home. They drove along the coast road towards Koulari, the only other traffic the occasional rackety speeding bus. They turned off the road and into Guy's drive, happy to be home and looking forward to a drink before dinner. On the coffee-table in the sitting-room Heleni had left the mail. Guy flicked through it, and extracted a long envelope with a Dublin postmark. 'I wonder what this is?' He opened the letter and read it, twice. Dido poured the drinks and put Guy's on the table, sitting down on the sofa. Guy looked at her, his eyes dark and troubled.

'What's the matter?'

'It's Uncle James. He's died, dear old man.'

'How sad, I'm so sorry,' said Dido quietly. 'But he must have been really quite old, wasn't he?'

'Yes, he was. The bloody thing is, my love, I'll have to go to Ireland. It's my house, you see. I'll have to go and sort everything out.'

'I'll come with you.'

'Would you really?'

'Of course, what else?'

Guy and Dido arrived in Dublin late at night, tired and extremely hungry in spite of the various packaged meals offered them on the aircraft. It was raining hard and they could see little of the city as their taxi delivered them to their hotel. Here, all was comfort and kindness and food and drink were brought to their suite although the dining-room had been shut for hours. The next morning, after a good hot breakfast, they hired a chauffeur-driven car to take them to Inniscarragh, about two hours drive from the capital. Dido, who had never been to Ireland, found herself quite glad to sit peacefully beside Guy in the comfortable car, watching the rolling green countryside pass by. Guy seemed quiet, preoccupied, and rather depressed. Whether this was on account of the death of his uncle or the fact of being in Ireland again, she could not guess and did not ask. She had never questioned Guy about his past, in case of reopening old wounds, preferring to wait until he chose to talk about it himself. In any case, their recent life together had been so idyllic that neither of them had felt the slightest inclination to rake over the sad or disappointing aspects of their respective former lives.

It was half-past eleven when the car drove through the gates and up to the main entrance of Inniscarragh. 'Goodness, is this it?' said Dido, peering through the car window. She had been expecting some kind of small, pleasant manor house, certainly not this stately pile.

'Wait till you see inside,' said Guy drily.

They got out and Guy negotiated the wide shallow steps to his front door without assistance. The driver extracted the luggage and the wheelchair from the boot.

'Guy,' called Dido, 'are we staying here, or is there a hotel? What about the luggage?'

'There's a pub with rooms, in the village. Hang on a moment will you please, driver? I'll phone for a reservation.' A few minutes later he returned, looking annoyed. 'It's incredible,' he said. 'It appears that every bed in the place is occupied by a member of a film company. Evidently they're filming right here, in the house.'

'Can't see any sign of them,' said Dido, looking round.

'Well, they must be somewhere, I suppose. How very irritating.' He looked at Dido. 'Do you think you can bear to rough it here? It's incredibly squalid, you know.'

'It's OK, we'll manage.' Dido hoped that she sounded positive and cheerful. She turned to the driver. 'Do you think you could help me in with the stuff, please?'

The driver obligingly stacked all the luggage in the hall, took the large tip offered by Guy, gave them both a look of unmistakable commiseration and drove away down the drive, leaving Dido feeling curiously vulnerable without transport. 'What'll we do if we need to shop for food, or go somewhere, Guy? Can we get taxis, do you think?'

'No need, if Uncle James's old Daimler is still going strong. I expect it's in the garage.'

'Great, what fun.'

Guy laughed, feeling better. 'Yes, it is, rather. The old boy had good taste in motors, if in very little else.'

They walked through the formal rooms of the ground floor, starting with the beautiful drawing-room with its eighteenth-century Chinese wallpaper, its threadbare heavy cream silk curtains, lined with palest blue, framing the tall Georgian windows looking out over the long, uncut grass towards the misty lake below. They stood together, gazing out over the ruined, run-down terraces where long ago flowers had bloomed and a descending series of steps had led down to the water. Suddenly, on the far side of the lake, half-hidden in the mist, Dido noticed the film crew. 'Look!' she exclaimed. 'There they are!'

'Who?'

'The film company. Look, they're filming on the other side of the lake. Can't you see them?'

'Oh yes, so they are,' agreed Guy, without much interest.

They continued their tour, inspecting the huge ugly dining-room with its depressing wine-red brocade walls and curtains, its massive crystal chandelier and vast table, covered in an equally vast and dirty dustsheet. 'What a table! It must seat at least twenty?'

'Yes, and often did, in my father's day.'

They looked at the other ground floor rooms, big and small, finally going into the library, which felt warmer than the rest of the house and smelt pleasantly of peat. It also had less enormous windows than the ceremonial rooms and had a door into the ruins of a small overgrown rose-garden, enclosed within a high yew hedge, shaggy with neglect. Lined with books in glass-fronted cases, the room was welcoming, even cosy, and was furnished with a big, sagging brown-leather sofa and armchairs, a beautiful Chippendale desk, and a square table of limed-oak. On the table was a large double lamp, its dark-green sheet-metal shades bordered with a gold-leaf pattern. Books and papers were scattered over the table, with a bottle of whisky and some dirty cut-glass tumblers on a tarnished silver salver. Beside the fireplace, on a small low table, stood an ancient television set.

'This is lovely, Guy. We could be quite comfy here, couldn't we?'

'Where are we going to sleep? On the sofa?'

'Why not? It's big enough, isn't it?' Dido sat down on the sofa, then lay down on it. 'Mm, not bad at all. I must see if I can find some pillows and blankets.'

The door opened and an elderly grey-haired woman in a Burberry entered the room, followed by a small, depressed-looking dachshund. Dido sat up at once, and got to her feet, feeling foolish.

'Guy! You got here then. You took your time, I must say.' The woman looked at Dido. 'Is this your nurse?'

Guy chose to ignore this question. 'Dido,' he said, 'may I introduce my sister, Lavinia? Lavinia, this is Dido Partridge.'

Lavinia stood her ground, and persisted rudely: 'Miss Partridge is your nurse? Presumably you have to have one?'

'Dido is not my nurse, Lavinia, she is a friend. She has very kindly come to help me sort out the mess here.'

'I see.' Lavinia's eyes shot angrily round the room, while she tried to think of something crushing to say to her brother. 'You're not thinking of staying in the house, are you? Wouldn't that be rather basic for Miss Partridge?'

'We don't have any choice in the matter, Lavinia. The pub is jammed with the film people, as I'm sure you're quite aware.'

'I suppose it must be. Mrs O'Reilly did say something to that effect.'

'Unless, of course,' said Guy rather slyly, 'you invite us to stay with you in the cottage?'

'Er, no, I don't think that would be convenient. I'm afraid I'm expecting friends very soon.'

Dido bit the insides of her cheeks to stop herself smiling, but Guy laughed out loud. 'Yes, of course you are, Lavinia. Silly of me to ask, wasn't it?'

'Not at all,' said Lavinia smoothly. 'Under normal circumstances nothing would have given me greater pleasure.' She smiled frostily at her brother, then turned to Dido. 'Perhaps you would like my woman to come over with her daughters and clean the place up for you?'

'Thank you,' said Dido. 'That would be very kind.'

'Well, I must be on my way. Fritz here needs his walk. It gets dark so early now.' Lavinia paused at the door. 'I'll tell Mrs O'Reilly to come and see you this evening; that kitchen is quite revolting, it's nothing short of a health hazard. Those *ghastly* parrots!' She cast her eyes towards the ceiling, gave them a meaningful little smile and departed. They could hear her shouting at the dog in the hall, followed by the slam of the great front door.

'Parrots?' said Dido.

'Yes, parrots,' said Guy wearily. 'Uncle James used to keep them as pets. I'd forgotten all about them. I suppose we ought to go and find them.'

'Guy,' said Dido quickly, 'forget the parrots for the moment. I'm starving, aren't you? We haven't eaten since breakfast. Why don't we see if the car is working and go and buy some food?'

'And drink,' said Guy. 'I don't really fancy poor old Uncle James's whisky, do you? It looks a bit cloudy, doesn't it? As if he took swigs from the bottle.'

'Don't,' said Dido, wincing. She put her arms round Guy's neck and kissed him. 'Come on, let's go out, now.'

Guy led the way through a flower-room to a long glazed passage overlooking the stable-yard behind the house. The yard was empty and Guy noticed that part of an outhouse wall had collapsed and needed rebuilding. The Daimler was in the garage, just as Guy had guessed it would be, and the key was in the ignition. Guy smiled when he saw it. 'Absolutely typical,' he said. They got in, Dido put the car into reverse with some difficulty, then backed the car out of the garage. With not a little nervousness at finding herself at the wheel of such a huge vehicle she drove carefully out of the yard and took the drive to the main road and the village. As they passed Lavinia's cottage Guy observed his sister at the window, spying on them through her curtains. He waved and she withdrew at once. He gave a delighted shout of laughter. 'Silly old cow,' he said, 'she hasn't changed at all.'

'Poor thing,' said Dido mildly, 'perhaps she's lonely.'

'Like hell,' said Guy. 'And if she is, it's her own fault, poisonous woman.'

When they returned with the shopping, they found Mrs O'Reilly in the kitchen, flustered and red-faced, cleaning out the decrepit, rusting fridge. 'It's a proper disgrace, Mr Guy, indeed it is, sir. If I'd known you were coming I'd have been up in a flash. Poor Mr James would never have anyone in the place. Couldn't afford it, he always said, though I'd have done it for love. I would so.'

'Please don't worry about it, Mrs O'Reilly. It's very good of you to come so soon.'

'Well, I couldn't ever not, could I?'

Dido put down her packages on the parrot-stained table and shook Mrs O'Reilly's wet hand. 'Hello, Mrs O'Reilly. I'm Dido.'

'Pleased to meet you, Miss Dido.' Mrs O'Reilly looked anxiously at the shopping. 'Best not put anything down on that table, miss. Will you look at the filth?'

'For a start, I don't think the parrots should really be in the kitchen, do you?' Dido looked at Guy.

'You're probably right. Couldn't they go in the flower-room?'

'Wouldn't they be lonely there, all by themselves?'

'I don't think so. They've got each other, haven't they?' Guy sat down on a kitchen chair. 'I hope they've been fed and given water, Mrs O'Reilly?'

'Indeed they have, sir. My Jimmy's been up here every day to see to them.' She lowered her voice to a suitably sepulchral tone. 'It *was* quite a time before they found the corpse, so the poor birds were well-nigh starving.'

'Do you think Jimmy would care to take them off my hands, Mrs O'Reilly?'

'Sure and he would, sir. He loves those parrots, and they love him.'

'Excellent, that's settled then.'

'In the meantime,' said Dido, 'we'll put them in the flower-room.'

After the parrots had been moved to their new home, Mrs O'Reilly scrubbed the table, cleaned the cracked Belfast sink and disinfected the draining-board, while Dido put away all the shopping in the fridge. The cupboards looked extremely unappealing; she felt sure they harboured mice and probably worse, so she decided not to use them for the moment. The cooker failed to function when she tried to light it, and on investigation it transpired that the gas-bottle was empty, and a spare one was nowhere to be found. 'Right,' she said, determined not to be undermined by this depressing turn of events, 'it'll have to be ham and salad and soda bread for tonight, and we'll get a couple of gas cylinders tomorrow.' Fortunately, the electric kettle was in working order, so they were able to make tea. 'We can even boil eggs in it, for breakfast tomorrow.'

Mrs O'Reilly departed, promising to return tomorrow with her girls and give the place a proper going over. Dido looked around the kitchen, so cold and dreary and now smelling strongly of pine disinfectant and bleach. 'Why don't we light the fire in the library and have supper there? It's a bit grim in here, isn't it?'

'Good idea,' said Guy quietly, 'but wouldn't that be an extra unnecessary job for you? You haven't sat down for hours.' He gazed around him with distaste, aware of depression creeping over him again, and the old familiar feeling of uselessness.

'Certainly not,' said Dido firmly. 'It will be fun. Let's have a picnic in front of the fire. Come on, we'll take the whisky with us. I could use a drink, couldn't you?'

Under the sliding lid of a mahogany box beside the fireplace, she found kindling and slabs of peat. 'Paper?' she asked.

'Here we are.' Guy tore some sheets off a month-old copy of the *Irish Times* and crumpled them into balls. 'Lay the fire straight onto the old ashes; that way the whole heap gets hot right through and should burn all night. That's the theory, anyway.'

After Dido had succeeded in lighting the fire and they had had a couple of whiskies they both felt a good deal more cheerful. She went to the kitchen and returned with the tray loaded with ham, bread, butter, lettuce and some tomatoes. 'Look at the wonderful plates I found,' she said. 'They're Mason's Ironstone, aren't they lovely?'

They ate the food hungrily, their plates on their knees, sitting on the sofa in front of the sweet-smelling peat fire. In the lamplight, the room looked warm and comfortable, and the small blue flames of the peat danced above the glowing red pile of ashes. Dido leant against Guy, and he put his arm round her. 'Tired, my love?'

'Yes, I am. Aren't you?'

'Very.'

'Let's not bother about finding sheets and things tonight,' said Dido. 'Why don't we just sleep as we are?'

'Excellent thinking,' said Guy, 'but I must take off these bloody irons. My legs are killing me.'

'Oh, darling, why didn't you say? I quite forgot.'

'Did you really?'

'Did I really what?'

'Quite forget about my legs?'

Dido looked at Guy, surprised. 'Yes, I did. I haven't

given your legs a single thought all day, isn't that awful?'

'No,' said Guy, 'it's not awful at all, it's terrific. You can have no idea.' He turned her face to his and kissed her gently. 'Nonetheless,' he went on ruefully, 'the sooner I get these irons off, the better I shall feel. I just hope my legs aren't bleeding.'

'Guy!' She leapt off the sofa, pushed up his trouser legs and began to undo the buckles.

'Only joking,' said Guy, and laughed.

'You are rotten! You're winding me up!'

'Do you mind?'

'No, I don't,' said Dido, kneeling on the floor and gently massaging his bruised legs, rubbed by the hard leather straps of the irons. She looked up at him, her eyes full of compassion and love. 'I don't mind anything at all about you, Guy. You should know that by now.'

The next morning, as they sat in the kitchen eating boiled eggs and drinking good strong coffee, they discussed the question of the future of Inniscarragh. 'I'll have to sell it, there's no question of keeping the place,' said Guy. 'It must be a nightmare to run and needs a fortune to maintain it. You only have to look around to see what happens when these places are allowed to deteriorate.' He began to tell her about Lavinia's earlier idea of building a golf course, and converting the stables for letting.

'Is that such a bad idea?'

'I suppose now that Uncle James no longer needs a home it's worth considering. But it would need huge amounts of money to develop such a project, as well as time and energy, wouldn't it?' Guy sounded far from eager to undertake such an enterprise.

'What about simply getting the planning permission?'

138

suggested Dido. 'Then selling it just as it is? The Japanese are mad on golf, aren't they? They'd probably pay a bomb for it, I should imagine.'

'What a brilliant and simple solution that would be; how clever and sensible you are, Dido.'

'It's a shame, though, isn't it? It's such a lovely place, beneath all the grime and rot. One could very easily devote one's whole life to looking after it.'

'But not me, my love, and certainly not you.'

'Well, given the choice, I'd much prefer Corfu.'

'Would you?'

'Yes, I would.'

Guy reached across the table, took her hand and kissed it, just as the kitchen door burst open unceremoniously and Lavinia entered the room, followed by Mrs O'Reilly and two teenage girls bearing brooms, pails and feather-dusters.

'Good morning, Lavinia, and good morning, Mrs O'Reilly.' Guy picked up the coffee-pot and looked at his sister. 'Coffee?'

'No, thanks.' Lavinia peeled off her Burberry in a businesslike way and handed it to Mrs O'Reilly, then sat down opposite Guy, still wearing her green-tweed fishing hat, adorned with a jay's feather. 'Now,' she said bossily, ignoring Dido, 'we should get down to business.'

Before Guy could answer, Dido rose from the table. 'Mrs O'Reilly, could we go upstairs and see what needs doing there? And perhaps the girls could make a start in the library?' Mrs O'Reilly, receiving Dido's message loud and clear, nodded briskly to the two girls and they followed Dido as she left the kitchen, leaving Guy to deal with his sister on his own.

Jacob Kroll drove his car up the main drive to Inniscarragh, and parked at the foot of the steps to the front entrance. He had come to pay his respects to the newly-arrived owner, at the same time assessing how much negotiating skill would be required to bend him to his will. The location filming had already over-run the contract schedule, and further days would be necessary to complete the work. He did not anticipate any difficulties.

He got out of the car and looked around him. There was no one to be seen, except for the crew, far away on the edge of the wood, where the day's shooting was being set up. He had left the scene being rehearsed under the watchful eye of the assistant director, expecting to take over himself in twenty minutes or thereabouts. He tried the door and finding it unlocked, entered the cold, stone-flagged hall. Silence. He opened the drawing-room door and peered in: empty. They'll probably be in the kitchen, he thought, and went down the corridor that led to the green-baize door. He put his ear to the door and heard muffled voices. He turned the handle and went in, smiling his confident smile. 'Sorry to intrude,' he said. 'I've only come to introduce myself and express my sympathy for your recent loss.'

Guy frowned at the tall stranger, wondering who the hell he was, or whether he ought to remember him. Lavinia spoke first. 'Guy, this is Mr Jacob Kroll, the filmmaker presently at work here. Mr Kroll, this is my brother, Guy Porteous.'

'Oh, good Lord, I'd completely forgotten that you people were here,' said Guy. 'How do you do? Take a seat, if you can find a clean one.' Jacob sat down at the end of the long table. 'Incidentally, that hole in the coal-house wall,' Guy went on, looking sternly at the newcomer, 'has it anything to do with your presence here?'

Fleetingly, it crossed Jacob's mind to deny it, then

realized that Miss Porteous might have been snooping around at the time, and replied that, yes, it was, and that the late Mr Porteous had given his permission to make the hole. 'We shall, of course, rebuild it before we leave,' he added.

'Good,' said Guy, eyeing him levelly. 'Make sure it's an invisible repair. I'll give you the name of a good local mason to do the job properly.'

Jake was completely taken aback by the abrasive stance adopted by Guy. He was accustomed to people being flattered and thrilled when he took over their properties, adapting them ruthlessly to suit his particular requirements. Never before had he encountered hostility. He gathered his wits, deciding not to raise the question of an extension to the contract just yet. 'Of course,' he said politely, 'we'll do whatever you wish. Naturally, we would have made good the damage before you got here, but we didn't wish to seem insensitive to the deceased by making unnecessary noise and so forth. That's why we took away all our vehicles and equipment; that's why we're shooting in the woods just now.' He did not add that the bare, leaf-stripped woodland swathed in late-October river mists was at present absolutely perfect for these scenes.

'I'm sure Mr Kroll will deal with everything quite properly.' Lavinia smiled archly at Jacob, and lifted the coffee-pot in an inviting manner. 'Some coffee?'

'Thank you, I'd love some.'

'A cup!' cried Lavinia gaily, lumbering to her feet.

Upstairs, Dido and Mrs O'Reilly were looking at bedrooms and deciding how best to arrange things for their stay in the house. They chose a bed from the nursery to be taken downstairs and made up for Guy in the library, together with a beautiful old Japanese screen to conceal the bed during the day. Mrs O'Reilly,

141

a most amiable and practical woman, also produced a commode, disguised as an elaborately carved oak box. Dido laughed when she saw it. 'He won't use it. He'd rather die than not get to a loo.'

'But it's quite a step to the cloakroom, isn't it, Miss Dido? He might be taken short, the poor man, mightn't he? In the night?'

'OK,' said Dido, 'we'll think about it, shall we?' She decided not to try to explain to Mrs O'Reilly that if taken short, as she put it, Guy would probably go into the rose-garden for a pee.

The two girls took the bed downstairs to the library, and came back for the sheets, blankets and pillows. Thankfully, there were tall airing-cupboards stacked high with beautiful old Irish linen in perfect condition and they had no difficulty in selecting what they needed. 'Best hang them over the bannisters to air for a couple of hours,' said Mrs O'Reilly, who was having a fine time. 'Now, Miss Dido, what about you? We must make you comfortable, mustn't we?' She chose not to ask where Dido had spent the previous night and led the way to a pretty bedroom at the front of the house. It had blue-striped wallpaper, a large half-tester bed, draped in white muslin and a thick honey-coloured carpet on the floor. 'This was Mrs Porteous's room, I'm pretty sure of that,' she said. 'Isn't it nice? It's got its own bathroom, too.' She pointed to a white-painted, panelled door in the corner.

'It's lovely. It'll be perfect, Mrs O'Reilly. Thank you.'

Mrs O'Reilly went off in search of linen for the bed and Dido sat down in a chair for a moment, smiling at herself for indulging Mrs O'Reilly's strict moral code, and happy to oblige her by pretending to sleep there. She got up and crossed the room to the window, glimpsing the lake in the middle distance, half-hidden in the mist. She looked down and saw the BMW parked below, and her heart turned over. She felt sick with surprise, or was it apprehension? It was Jake's car, of that she had no doubt at all. The idea that it might be him filming here had not for a single moment occurred to her. It's simply not possible, she said to herself, it's too much of a coincidence. But such things did happen, of course. Filmmakers like Jacob Kroll and houses like Inniscarragh were not exactly thick on the ground; sooner or later they were pretty well bound to collide in that small, esoteric world. She leaned her forehead against the window-pane, closing her eyes, willing herself to remain calm, telling herself that it was of no consequence, that nothing was changed by Jake's unlooked-for and unwelcome presence.

Mrs O'Reilly came bustling back into the room, her arms loaded with blankets and pillows. She began to strip the bed, preparing to remake it for Dido.

'Excuse me a moment, Mrs O'Reilly,' said Dido. 'I must go downstairs for a few minutes.' She left the room and walked along the landing to the back stairs, without quite knowing what compulsion was taking her to the kitchen, but her instinct telling her that she could not hide her presence at Inniscarragh from Jake for long, or conceal from Guy the fact of who Jake was. There was nothing to be gained by lurking behind doors, waiting for him to go away. She paused at the small narrow door at the foot of the back stairs, listening to the voices in the kitchen. One of them was indeed Jake's. She lifted the latch and went in, closing the door behind her.

Guy turned his head and smiled at her, holding out his hand. 'Dido,' he said. 'Come and meet Mr Kroll, one of the film people. He's just leaving.'

Jacob turned in his chair and stared at her, astonished. '*Dido*? What are *you* doing here?'

143

'Hello, Jake.'

Guy looked swiftly from one to the other, guessing at once the bizarre circumstances of the situation.

'You two know each other?' asked Lavinia, bursting with curiosity.

'Indeed we do,' replied Dido levelly. 'We've known each other for years; we're in the same business.'

Jake said nothing, and stood up, saying that he must get back to work, his mind working furiously. The last thing he wanted just now was a public reconciliation with Dido. His affair with Nastassia was at its peak and the performance he was extracting from her as a result was nothing short of sensational. He could not allow anything to get in the way of that.

With hastily muttered farewells, Jacob Kroll departed, and Lavinia, who had failed to get any sense out of Guy during their little talk and was beginning to feel the need of a glass of sherry anyway, took her leave, promising to return the next day.

Dido sat down opposite Guy. 'You've guessed, haven't you?'

'Yes.'

'Do you mind?'

'Not at all,' said Guy, though he knew that he did, very much indeed. 'Why should I?'

'No reason at all. So that's that.'

'Is it?'

'Yes,' said Dido, taking his hand, 'it is.'

'Really?'

'Really.'

They looked at each other, smiling, happy, relieved.

'Well, good,' said Guy. 'How's Mrs O'Reilly getting on, in the meantime?'

'Splendidly.' She explained about the bed arrangements, but did not mention the commode. 'Guy,' she went on, 'if we're going to spend a bit of time here,

144

oughtn't we to order some oil for the heating and logs for the fires? And we need to get gas bottles so that we can cook properly.'

'Right,' said Guy, 'lead me to the telephone. It's the one thing that hasn't ceased to function, thank God.'

Chapter Eight

It had been a long hard day for Nastassia, and a cold one, too. In the dank chilly woodland in which the scene was set she was finding it difficult to remain radiant and beautiful hour after painstaking hour. In spite of the efforts of her make-up girl with frequent applications of green powder, Nastassia's nose was getting pinker and pinker and her hands were numb with cold. Floods of flattering low lighting from powerful luminaires concealed behind trees lit up the glade like the early rays of the sun, although it was in fact after five on a late autumn afternoon.

'One more time.' Jake sounded tense and irritated. 'Nastassia, please try to relax. It's only one bloody line, after all. Is that too much to ask? *Listen* to Meaulnes' speech; *think* how he must be feeling. Then count to five, look back at him and say your line – *What's the use? What's the use?* OK? Right, clear the frame . . . action!'

For the fifteenth or sixteenth time, Nastassia walked along the path, followed by the leading actor. She listened to his speech, her head bent, trying her best to feel her way into the scene but all she could think about was Jake's cold, sarcastic treatment of her throughout the long day. Meaulnes finished his speech; it was her cue. She counted to five and then looked back and as she did so her eyes filled with involuntary tears of anguish. 'What's the use?' she said, and meant it. 'What's the use?'

'Cut!' said Jake. 'At last! OK, guys, that's a wrap. We'll call it a day.' He turned to Nastassia. 'Good. Well done – better late than never. Do you want a lift back to the pub?'

'Thank you.' Her voice was barely audible. The wardrobe had now been moved to the village hall, so she got into the car in her costume.

Jake drove fast down the lane to the village. 'Anything the matter?'

'I was going to ask you the same question, Jake.'

'What the hell do you mean?'

'You seem so cold and angry. You are humiliating me in front of the crew sometimes.'

'Don't be ridiculous; you're beginning to sound just like a wife, my dear.'

Horrified and stung, Nastassia turned her head away. 'That's the *last* thing I want to be,' she said angrily. 'I don't want to be *anyone's* wife, *ever.*'

'Delighted to hear it,' said Jake, and patted her knee. 'In that case, we might have a future together.'

That night, Dido roasted a duck in the horrible gas cooker, and put potatoes under the rack to cook in the fat and juices that flowed from the bird.

'Smells wonderful,' said Guy, sitting at the table with a glass of wine in front of him. 'I didn't know you were a cook, my love.'

'There are lots of things you don't know about me.' Dido put frozen peas in a pan ready to boil at the last minute. She took a sip of her wine. 'For instance, I know a hell of a lot about making lists; inventories, things like that. You need to make one here, Guy. There's a tremendous amount of valuable stuff lying around. It should all be listed, especially if it's going to be sold before you sell the house and land. The best way would be to hire a PC and a printer, then all the data could be safely stored and print-outs given to the relevant people as necessary.'

Guy looked at Dido with new respect. She had appeared to him to be so small and vulnerable; she was in fact strong-minded and extremely competent. 'You really think it's necessary?'

'I do, and I will do it for you, too, with your assistance over dates, provenance and so on. Mrs O'Reilly can help me, sticking labels on things. And while we're at it, you can choose the things you want to take back to Corfu, and we'll set them aside to be properly packed.'

The duck was delicious, the potatoes sensational, and after dinner Dido made coffee, put the brandy bottle and glasses on the tray and carried it to the library. They sat close together on the leather sofa, soothed by the food and drink, and the warmth of the fire. Guy gazed thoughtfully into its glowing red heart.

'Dido?'

'Mm?'

'I was wondering whether the proximity of Jacob Kroll would oblige you to sleep in my mother's bedroom?'

Dido leaned against him sleepily. 'Do you want me to?'

'Of course I don't.'

'Well, then. Stop worrying about him, Guy. Jake doesn't *own* me, you know.'

'That's true.' He kissed the top of her head. 'Are you really sure?'

'I'm sure.'

Anna sat at her worktable at Quai des Grands-Augustins, regilding the wing of a large baroque wooden angel, destined to be the centrepiece in one of the new galleries of the spectacular glass pyramid at the Louvre. Often, if they did not go to Normandy for the weekend, Patrick and Anna took Tom to the Louvre, a short walk from their *quai* across the Pont Neuf. Sometimes they went to Beaubourg, where the main attraction for Tom was not so much the Centre Pompidou itself, but the constantly changing free spectacle of acrobats, fire-eaters, jugglers, escapologists, musicians and pavement artists that performed daily among the visitors thronging the piazza in front of the huge building. If there happened to be a special children's exhibition they would go and see it, afterwards taking the escalator that climbed the glass walls to the top-floor restaurant to have lunch, and enjoy the spectacular views over Paris.

At this moment, Anna was not thinking about Tom, she was worrying about her first-born son, Josh. After his departure from St Gilles, Patrick had waited until he and Anna had gone to bed to tell her about his conversation with Josh, and the sad news of the failure of his marriage.

'Why didn't he tell me himself, do you think?'

'Because he was afraid of breaking down, poor chap, in the face of your concern for him, and sympathy.'

'But *you* were concerned, and sympathetic?'

'Yes, but you're his mother, that's harder to handle.'

'I see,' Anna had said, though she did not, really. Patrick had taken her in his arms and held her close to him, comforting her with his strength and warmth. 'The good news is that he is thinking of leaving London and moving to Paris, so he'll be nearer to us.'

'And Max? What about him?'

'He'll be coming too, of course. It seems Nastassia doesn't want what she thinks of as the handicap of a child, according to Josh.'

'It's unbelievable, isn't it?'

'Yes, it is, absolutely unbelievable,' said Patrick.

'Josh and Max are lucky to have you, my darling. God knows, we all are.'

'Just the same, I can't help wishing he had confided in me, as well as you.'

'Don't worry about it, sweetheart. He will, in his own good time; you'll see.'

In spite of Patrick's calm reassurance, Anna still felt saddened and a little rejected that Josh had not felt able to come to her first. He was so young when he married, she thought, I wonder why he felt the need for such an early commitment? He'd only just left university; I thought no one married as early as that these days, especially men. She stared through the window across the river to the Ile de la Cité. I wonder whether me leaving him in London when I came here to Paris to live with Patrick had anything to do with it? she asked herself. Maybe he missed me and Olivia more than I realized, even though he *was* with Mum and Dad. Maybe he did feel rather left out and lonely, though I can't remember him giving that impression at the time, at all. Perhaps I was too tied up with Patrick and the new baby to notice. She sighed, cut another piece of gold leaf with her scalpel, then picked it up on her gilder's tip and deftly placed it in position, where it flattened itself onto the damp gesso, as if drawn by a magnet. All the same, she thought, it could have been the reason for him wanting to create a family of his own so soon. Poor Josh, I do wish I could talk to him, help somehow; but I can't until he asks me, I do see that.

At three o'clock Anna put away her tools and left the apartment to fetch Tom from school, a walk of fifteen minutes through the little back streets behind the *quai*. As she approached the school building she could see Tom behind the railings of the playground, rolling around on the dirty asphalt, locked in mortal combat with another boy, who appeared to Anna to be rather larger than her own son. She watched them for a moment through the railings, decided that it was not a serious matter and walked on to join the little group of parents at the gate. Presently, Tom noticed her and came running up, a toggle torn off his duffel coat, his shoelaces undone and his face filthy and scratched. Tall for his age and thin, with thick wild curly dark hair, Tom was the image of Anna's twin brother Giò as a boy, except for his eyes. These were a piercing pale blue, the eyes of Patrick, his father. Anna touched the scratched cheek briefly, but refrained from kissing him. 'Hello, horrible child. I *was* thinking that we might walk over to Place des Vosges and take Giò out to tea, but you look so shambolic that maybe that's not such a wonderful idea.'

Without a word Tom dropped his bag, bent down and tied his shoelaces, took off his coat and gave it a vigorous shake, put it on again, then took from his bag his wire brush and vigorously attacked his unruly hair. He looked at his mother; 'OK now?'

Anna frowned. 'Well, your face still looks pretty awful.' She offered him a tissue and Tom spat on it and tried to clean his face. Anna closed her eyes briefly. 'Give it to me, for heaven's sake.' She took the tissue and did her best to remove the blood and dirt.

'I could have a proper wash in one of the fountains in Place des Vosges, couldn't I?'

'I suppose you could, yes.' Anna shook her head and laughed, dropping the dirty tissue in a waste-bin. 'Come on then, let's go.'

They walked briskly back towards the river, crossing to the islands by the Pont St-Michel, then across the Pont de Sully to the Rive Droite, and through the narrow back streets to the Place des Vosges and Giò's antique shop in one of its beautiful arcades. It was the beginning of November and the leaves were falling fast in the square, the yellow discs like little suns hurled around by the wind before settling in scented golden drifts on the ground, to be swept up by the ubiquitous street-cleaners in their eye-catching light green uniforms, proudly keeping the world's most beautiful city perfectly groomed. Tom especially liked the young men on their green motor-scooters, fitted with green storage tanks and fat vacuum hoses for removing the ordure left by the more ill-disciplined canine residents. He was secretly planning to become a dog-poo man himself, in the fullness of time.

'Go on, then,' said Anna. 'Wash your face.' She walked on slowly as Tom raced across to a fountain, washed his face and hands and raced back to her side, wiping his cold wet hands on his coat.

They found Giò in his shop, going through a pile of correspondence while his assistant, an elegant woman in a designer suit, took notes at his side. As they came in through the thick plate-glass door Giò looked up and smiled. 'This is a nice surprise,' he said, 'on an exceptionally boring afternoon. What brings you here, Anna?'

'We thought we'd take you out to tea?'

'Great idea. Give me two minutes and I'll be with you.'

They walked along the arcade and decided that it was warm enough to sit at an outside table at the small, friendly café-restaurant where Giò often dined when he was in Paris. They ordered tea for themselves, a coke and a huge cream-filled pastry for Tom. Anna looked at her brother with affection, while Giò listened with rapt attention as Tom brought him up to date on the latest smutty schoolboy jokes, laughing obligingly at the appropriate moments and resurrecting one or two old chestnuts from his own youth, which were greeted with delighted gales of laughter by Tom. Darling Giò, thought Anna, he's much more amusing with Tom than we manage to be; there's still a lot of the child in him. It's so nice the way he treats Tom as an equal, doesn't talk down to him, or patronize him. Mind you, Tom needs a bit of suppressing sometimes, he'd be totally out of hand without some pretty strict rules, and spoilt by us all. 'Giò,' she interrupted, 'are you busy this evening?'

'Not especially, why?'

'Patrick's going to be late tonight, he's got a meeting. The thing is, I'm a bit worried about Josh, and I'd like to talk to you about it. Could you come and have supper, do you think?'

'Certainly, I could. About eight?'

'That would be lovely. Thanks, Giò; it's kind of you.'

Back at Grands-Augustins, with Tom ostensibly reading in bed, though actually she suspected playing a game on his Super Nintendo, Anna prepared a meal for herself and Giò. As she cut up tomatoes, olives, basil, garlic and artichoke hearts, intending to fry them very lightly in olive oil and add them to a dish of fresh tagliatelle for the first course, she reflected on what an amazing change had come over her brother since he had gone into the wine business with Robert, their father. For a start, he had gained weight. Gone was the haunted, desperately sad man of five years ago. His tanned, rather beautiful face was unwrinkled, his dark eyes shone, he had regained his youthful enthusiasm for life. Dividing his time between his vines and his shop in Paris, he seemed to be a truly happy man. Anna arranged her prepared vegetables in separate piles on a large white plate, ready for the pan, then took from the fridge two small fillet steaks and dressed them with a little oil and pepper, ready for the grill. To garnish the steaks, she sliced a few flakes of parmesan cheese on her mandoline, and tore a bunch of ròcket into shreds. Then she set the kitchen table with her plain white china, old silver knives and forks and the heavy antique glasses, a present from Giò himself.

Anna's new kitchen was a far cry from the simple row of basic equipment, concealed behind louvred doors, on which she had cooked perfectly happily for ten years, upstairs in the attic studio-apartment. The new kitchen was a good-sized room, decorated in the provençal manner. The walls were completely covered in deeply recessed open shelves, made from solid reclaimed pine, subtly stained and distressed so that the wood glowed as if sunshine fell on it. The shelving had been built in sixty-centimetre wide modules, divided by hefty vertical blocks of pine reaching to the ceiling, each section topped by a graceful ogee-shaped arch. This arrangement had given Anna a generous amount of storage space, and she had arranged her collections of china and glass, her cookbooks and herbs, jars of pasta, couscous, rice, beans and salt, together with bottles of oil and vinegar so that they created a warm and attractive ambiance in which to cook, as well as eat. A small deep square window looked down to the street behind the apartment building, and a terracotta pot stood on the sill, containing a straggly green plant, which Anna was trying to encourage to grow big enough to creep across the ceiling, though without very much success. Beneath the window was a deep sink, with the pine worktops and low-level cupboards ranged on either side. She was opening a bottle of Fleurie as Giò rang the doorbell.

After supper, they took coffee and the rest of the wine into the sitting-room and Anna installed herself on the large, comfortable linen-covered sofa facing the wide windows overlooking the river. Giò stood at the windows for a few moments, fascinated by the beauty of the riverside scene, the floodlit glory of Notre Dame, the barges and the brightly-lit *bateaux lavoirs* cruising past, the red rear-lamps of cars reflected in the rain-washed streets far below. 'You're so lucky, Anna. This is a magical place to live.'

'I know,' she agreed, 'but Place des Vosges is pretty special too, isn't it?'

'Yes, of course it is. It's a question of the grass being greener, isn't it?' He left the window and sat beside her on the sofa. Anna refilled his glass and poured coffee.

'Thanks,' he said, taking the cup. 'Now, what's up with Josh?'

Anna told him about the weekend in Normandy, and her conversation with Patrick after Josh's return to London. 'I can't help feeling a bit sad and hurt that he didn't feel able to talk to me about his problems.'

'I can understand perfectly well why he didn't. You're far too emotional for a situation like that, particularly when your children are being threatened. Your impulse would have been to gather him up and protect him; revert to the mother and child relationship.'

'Do you really think so?' Anna looked thoughtful. 'I do hope you're wrong. You make me sound like an hysterical female.'

'Don't be ridiculous, Anna. I'm not criticizing you, it's just the nature of things with mothers, especially good mothers.'

'I suppose. But why was it less difficult for him to talk to Patrick?'

'Come on, you know very well why. Because Patrick's like a sponge. He listens; says little; doesn't make judgements or take sides. He's just there for you, isn't he?'

Anna sighed. 'You're right, of course.' She drank

some coffee and turned to him again. 'I've been asking myself whether our own childhood without Dad, living all those years in Souliac with just Mum and Honorine, might have made us, you and me, ill-equipped to form good adult relationships ourselves. Me, with a disastrous first marriage; you, not marrying at all? I can't help wondering whether I may have passed on this tendency to my own children.'

Giò laughed and took her hand. 'Darling Anna, you really cannot hold yourself responsible for everything that happens to your children. Each one of us has to struggle through and find his own way, somehow, and each one of us makes mistakes. You should be thankful that you're in a position to help Josh pick up the pieces, if the worst actually happens and if he asks for help. He's not alone, you know. He knows where to come, doesn't he?'

'That's just what Patrick says.'

'Ah, Patrick. The great and the good Patrick.'

'You really loved him, didn't you?'

'I did.'

'Do?'

'No, I love you both equally, and Tom.'

'He's a perfect clone of you, Giò, except for his eyes.'

'Yes,' said Giò quietly, 'he is. It's the great happiness of my life, Anna.'

'Yes, I know, and I'm so glad.' She stretched out a hand and touched his cheek.

They heard Patrick's key in the lock and looked up as he entered the room. He was tired and had a headache, but he smiled when he saw them sitting together, with the very same solemn expression on their identical faces.

'Have you eaten, darling?'

'No.'

'I'll make you an omelette.'

'Stay where you are,' said Giò, getting swiftly to his feet. 'I'll get it.' He picked up the tray and went to the kitchen.

Patrick dropped his briefcase on the floor, took off his jacket, came across to the sofa and kissed Anna.

'Lie down,' she said, 'put your head in my lap. Your head aches, doesn't it?'

He lay down on the sofa, taking off his spectacles and closing his eyes. She stroked his forehead, pressing his temples, his eyes and his cheekbones with her cool strong fingers, then massaging his scalp through his short, silver-grey hair. 'That's wonderful,' he said drowsily. 'It's almost worth having the headache in the first place.'

'Don't go to sleep, darling. Giò will be here with your omelette soon.'

'Mm.'

On the seventh of November James Porteous was laid to rest in the family mausoleum after a short service in the private chapel at Inniscarragh. Only Guy, Lavinia and Dido were present at the funeral, since the family, apart from Guy and his sister was now extinct and James had long since severed all his ties of friendship in the district, either through the deaths of his contemporaries or his own increasing poverty. The priest, an old man himself and suffering from a bad cold refused Guy's half-hearted invitation to come to the house for a cup of tea, as did Lavinia, who took herself off in the direction of her cottage, a strange surreal figure in her heavily-veiled black mourning. 'Silly old bat,' said Guy. 'What does she think she is, royalty?'

'I rather think she does,' agreed Dido as they walked back to the house. 'I suppose she's the last of that generation, isn't she?'

'There but for the grace of God,' said Guy, smiling.

157

'She's only sixteen years older than I am, don't forget.'

'It might just as well be sixty years.' She slipped her hand lightly through his arm, as he leaned on his sticks. 'I can't see you doing the pulling rank thing, ever.'

'I could use a drink,' said Guy, 'couldn't you?'

'I certainly could. Come on, get a move on, can't you?'

'What it is to be plagued by bossy women,' said Guy, and laughed.

Dido, Guy and Mrs O'Reilly had been working hard on the inventory and had already got halfway through the job, with Mrs O'Reilly sticking numbered labels on every item as Guy identified each piece and Dido listed it. Two days after the funeral, a team of surveyors came from Dublin to value the house, land and contents prior to the sale. They spent the entire morning going over the house, taking photographs of the important pieces and dictating into tape-recorders.

Mrs O'Reilly had made a quantity of thick chicken sandwiches and after a break for lunch, Guy took the surveyors outside to go over the outbuildings, gardens and parkland. The film company was nowhere to be seen and was presumably working deep in the woods. After going through the stable-yard, where Guy made a mental note to speak again to Jacob Kroll about the still unrepaired wall, they entered the walled kitchen garden. At once, Guy saw Lavinia at the far end, at the entrance to the derelict vine-house, loading a handcart with the beautiful terracotta garden urns that their grandparents had brought back from Italy so long ago. She was being assisted in this dishonest endeavour by her gardener, Burke.

'Excuse me a moment,' said Guy, and walked as fast as his sticks would permit down the central path to the vine-house. 'What the hell do you think you're doing?' he asked without preamble.

'Saving these pots. I'm sure you have no use for them.'

'Burke,' said Guy, thinking what an apt name the man bore, 'unload these pots at once and put them back where you found them.'

Burke looked apprehensively at Lavinia, uncertain whom to obey.

'*At once!*' roared Guy.

'Sir!' Burke picked up one of the big heavy pots and took it back into the vine-house, at the double.

'How dare you speak to me like that in front of a servant, Guy.' Lavinia was purple with rage and mortification.

'If you behave like a common thief, Lavinia, you must expect to be treated like one if you're caught. I wonder what else you've helped yourself to behind my back?'

Lavinia stared at Guy, bereft of speech for once, her green eyes blazing with undisguised hatred beneath her heavily wrinkled liver-coloured eyelids, while Burke trotted back and forth with the stolen goods, crimson with embarrassment and exertion. When the last pot had been replaced he stood beside the cart, looking anxious.

'Right,' said Guy quietly. 'Take your cart and clear off, Burke, and don't let me catch you here again, understood?'

'Sir!' Burke cast a pained eye at Lavinia, the entire cause of his present discomfort and rattled away with the empty cart.

'Have you quite finished?' Lavinia spoke through gritted teeth, standing her ground.

'Not quite,' replied Guy calmly. 'Get out of here, and don't try that trick again, in case I change my mind about the cottage and give you notice to quit.'

'You wouldn't dare!'

'I bloody well would, Lavinia. It's time you understood that.'

Red-faced, breathing hard, Lavinia would have given a lot to tell Guy that she despised him and thought him a repulsive little cripple, a mockery of a proper man, but her well-developed sense of self-preservation asserted itself. She turned on her heel abruptly and lurched after Burke, contenting herself with a cynical snort.

Poor old Burke, thought Guy; he'll be getting the rough end of her tongue, loathsome woman. He walked slowly back to the little group of surveyors, waiting politely to finish the job.

The lawyers came out to Inniscarragh, bringing an architect with them and took instructions from Guy to apply for planning permission for a change of use of the house and land to a country club and golf course. The architect did not anticipate any difficulties; the house was not a listed building; there was plenty of precedent for that kind of scheme, and if it was going to bring employment to the district, he said, so much the better.

Dido and Guy finished the inventory, the mason from the village duly arrived to mend the wall and Mrs O'Reilly spent a lot of time at the house, cleaning and making life as comfortable for them as she could. Every day she made the beds, brought in logs and peat for the fire and had managed to make the place quite respectable, especially since Jimmy had removed the parrots and they had received a delivery of oil. They now had hot water and even some rather inadequate central heating. What a very neat person Miss Dido is, thought Mrs O'Reilly as she made her carefully rumpled bed each morning. Mr Guy now, he's a different kettle of fish, his bed's a proper haystack. It'll be the poor legs, for sure. They must be enough to try the patience of a saint.

Later in the week Guy received a phone call from the Dublin lawyers, informing him that they had a client who had expressed an interest in looking at Inniscarragh.

'Is he a Japanese, by any chance?' asked Guy, half joking.

'He is, as a matter of fact.'

'Oh.'

They made an appointment for the following day and Guy put the phone down thoughtfully. How extraordinary, he said to himself; it seems Lavinia may not have been so far out in her ideas after all. How very typical of her, always one jump ahead of everyone else.

The next day the lawyers came to Inniscarragh with their client, a small exquisitely dressed man in rimless spectacles, with thick black carefully combed hair, and charmingly diffident manners.

'Carry on,' said Guy, after the introductions were complete. 'Go wherever you wish, please feel free. If you need me, I'll be in the library.'

After the unpleasant confrontation with Lavinia, Guy had asked Dido to include all the garden pots and statuary in the inventory, and she and Mrs O'Reilly were engaged in this task just now, attaching large clearly-marked waterproof labels to everything they could find.

Guy waited in the library, utilizing the time by going through the drawers of the bureau and tearing up quantities of James's old bills and correspondence, ready for burning. After a couple of hours there was a tap on the door and the visitors came into the library. Guy offered them seats. McDonnell, the lawyer, came straight to the point. Subject to the planning permission being obtained, Mr Yakimoto wished to purchase the entire property, lock, stock and barrel.

'What do you mean by lock, stock and barrel?' asked Guy. 'Literally, *everything*?'

'Yes, except those things you wish to retain yourself, for personal reasons.'

The lawyer then mentioned the proposed purchase price, a sum so enormous that Guy had difficulty in concealing his surprise. 'Well,' he said, 'that seems fair. Shall we proceed on that basis?'

'Excellent,' said McDonnell. 'We'll prepare the contracts forthwith.'

The silent Mr Yakimoto stood up and bowed with extreme formality. Guy got to his feet and led the way out to the waiting car. He stood on the steps, watching the shiny black limousine driving slowly away in the late afternoon gloom. Then he went back to the library and sat at his desk for a long time in the deepening dusk. He could not believe that the huge sum of money proposed was really what the place was worth. If the deal came off, it would mean that even after paying off Uncle James's overdraft, the debts and taxes, he would receive a very substantial sum at the end of the day. He felt tired and rather sad; the whole business had been strangely fraught and emotional for him, and half of him felt that he had somehow failed his family by selling out without even making a token attempt to save the place. His legs ached badly from over-use; he longed to be back in Corfu, in his long chair on his shabby old cuckoo-clock terrace with Dido beside him, looking out over the olives to the wide blue sea. Probably wild grey sea by now, he thought morosely, unable to rouse himself from his perversely melancholic mood, and curious feeling of anticlimax.

The door opened and Dido came in with a tray of tea

things. 'Guy!' she exclaimed, 'what on earth are you doing, sitting here in the dark? Are you ill?' She switched on the light, making him blink.

'No, I'm not ill; just rather tired.' He looked at her and smiled. 'I think I sold the house.'

'Good; wonderful. Does that mean we can go home?'

Guy laughed. 'Yes, it does. I suppose we'll have to wait a week or two for the contracts to be exchanged. Then we can go home, my love.'

'Are your legs hurting?'

'Yes, they are, a bit.'

'I thought so. Come on, have some tea, and I'll give them a rub.'

Guy drank his tea, and looked down on Dido's bent dark head as she knelt on the floor, swiftly unbuckled the painful braces and began to massage his bruised sore legs. His heart swelled with gratitude and love. He could no longer consider the prospect of life without her, and longed to say so; but he remained silent, knowing that the commitment must come from Dido herself, that he could not ask her to marry him and spend the rest of his life wondering whether she had married him because she knew he needed her so badly.

Chapter Nine

Nastassia's plane landed at Heathrow, and she looked through her window at the airport buildings, misty through the relentlessly falling rain. She had completed her location shooting but still had the studio work ahead of her, after Jake had returned from Ireland. She had had a happy time shopping in Dublin, finding it necessary to buy an extra suitcase to carry all the lovely new clothes she had bought herself, as well as some pretty Irish sweaters for Max. In addition, she had bought him a large antique Punch and Judy theatre, with a curtained stage on demountable legs, and a complete set of hand-carved puppets, including the policeman, the baby, the crocodile, the string of sausages and the little dog, as well as Punch and Judy. Nastassia remembered with nostalgia the excitement of seeing similar shows as a small girl in Prague, and felt sure that Max would enjoy having one of his own.

The packing case of this toy was large and heavy, and she took a cab all the way from the airport to Strand-on-the-Green, planning to pay the driver to hump the luggage from Thames Road, through the back garden gate to the house. She felt that she had earned the luxury of such an extravagance, but soon, when the publicity machine got going, she knew that the studio would take care of all those things for her, and that all she would have to do would be to smile for the press photographers and journalists, be cooperative and modest, never antagonize them, and always remember how crucial they were to her image.

The cab arrived at her back gate, and she got out, gave the driver ten pounds more than the sum on the clock and asked him to help her with the baggage. He was an elderly, overweight man and normally nothing, not even a financial bribe would dislodge him from his seat, but he was still susceptible to the smile of a beautiful woman, and reluctantly agreed to carry the stuff to the house.

'You're a perfect angel, darling,' said Nastassia, as she followed him down the garden path, carrying only her crocodile dressing-case and handbag.

Through the window, where she was filling the kettle for tea, Ruth saw the little procession approaching. She was so surprised that she almost dropped the heavy kettle. No one had told her that Nastassia was coming home. 'Look, Max,' she said quietly, 'it's Mummy – she's home.'

Max looked up from his colouring book, a fat yellow wax crayon in his hand. 'Did you say Mummy? My mummy?'

'Yes, she's in the garden.'

The back door burst open and the fat cab driver, wheezing with the unaccustomed effort, dropped the two heavy suitcases on the floor with a groan. 'Just the big parcel now, darling?' Nastassia gave him her sweetest smile.

'Yes, Miss. Right away.'

'Poor man, he's not in good shape,' said Nastassia, watching the driver's retreating figure, and taking off her voluminous scarlet cashmere shawl, releasing a delicious cloud of scent. Max, struck dumb, looked at his mother with his huge dark eyes as if he could not believe she was really there, in his kitchen, in person. Somehow, she looked more real when he saw her on the telly. Dad had taped her commercial for him and sometimes he went into the sitting-room to watch it, in case he forgot what she looked like. Now she came round the table, knelt beside his chair and put her arms round him. 'What about a kiss for Mummy?' Max put his arms round her neck and planted a sloppy wet kiss on her cheek, and she laughed and hugged him. 'Did you miss me, darling?'

'Not really,' said Max, untruthfully. 'But Dad did, a bit.'

'Well,' said Nastassia, 'I missed you. Wait till you see your present.'

They went to the kitchen door to look for the driver, but there was no sign of him in the garden, and when Max ran down to the gate, no sign of the taxi in the street. He came running back through the rain. 'He's gone, Mummy! The taxi's gone!'

'Bloody little creep,' said Nastassia. 'He must have driven off with your present, Max, what a bore. Oh well, can't be helped.'

'What was it?' asked Max in a small voice.

'A Punch and Judy show. A lovely antique one, hand-carved.'

'Oh.'

Nastassia looked at her son, sharply; he did not sound particularly disappointed. 'I brought you lots of clothes, too.'

'Oh.'

Ruth poured boiling water into the teapot and set it down on the table, with mugs and the remains of a sticky ginger cake. 'Some tea, Nastassia?' she offered politely, concealing her unworthy pleasure at Max's obvious lack of enthusiasm.

'Oh, hello Ruth,' said Nastassia brightly, 'I sort of didn't see you there.' She sat down, with Max beside her. 'Yes, some tea would be nice. Do you have lemon?'

Bitch, thought Ruth, pouring the tea, and putting

milk in it, slowly and deliberately. 'Oops!' she said. 'Sorry! You said lemon, didn't you? There's one in the fridge if you want it.'

'Doesn't matter, this will do.' Nastassia drank the tea sulkily, and refused cake. Ruth began to regret her bad manners as all three sat in an embarrassed silence. After tea, Nastassia rose from the table, announced her intention of taking her luggage upstairs and asked Max to help her.

'He's too small,' said Ruth firmly, 'I'll help you, of course.'

'Right,' said Nastassia, with a glint of triumph. 'Come on, Max, you can try on your new clothes.'

'OK.'

'And tomorrow we can go to Harrods, and you can choose something for yourself, would that be nice?'

'I have to go to school tomorrow.'

'Oh well, some other time.'

For the rest of the afternoon Nastassia played the part of the perfect mother. Max helped her unpack and put away her clothes, and tried on the Irish sweaters obligingly, though they turned out to be far too small for him. Then they played hide-and-seek all over the house until he was thoroughly over-excited and beginning to be slightly hysterical. Hearing him screaming, Ruth put her head round the kitchen door and shouted above the din. 'It's nearly six o'clock, Max, time for your bath. I'm just getting your supper.'

'OK,' said Nastassia, laughing and hugging her son. 'Enough's enough, come for the bath now.' Peace reigned as she bathed Max and helped him on with his pyjamas and dressing-gown. They came downstairs and Max ate his supper, lasagne, one of his favourite meals. He drank his milk, got down from the table and looked expectantly at his mother. 'Are you going to read me a story?'

'Yes, of course, darling.' She stood up and took his hand. 'Say goodnight to Ruth.'

'Goodnight, Ruth.'

'Goodnight, sweetheart.' Ruth, standing at the sink washing up, did not trust herself to turn round or give him her usual hug. They left the kitchen, banging the door and roaring up the stairs making lion noises.

Fifteen minutes later, Nastassia came down again, a bottle of vodka in her hand. She sat down at the table and poured herself a drink, without offering one to Ruth.

'Are you home for good?' Ruth kept her back to Nastassia, taking a long time cleaning the sink.

'No, of course not. There is still much work to do on *Meaulnes*, and also Jacob Kroll has given me two treatments to read; there are many irons in my fire. Jake thinks I am very soon hot property. Maybe I will go to Hollywood, who knows?' She laughed airily, a false silvery tinkle.

'But what about Max?'

'What about him?'

'Would you be taking him with you, Nastassia?'

'Good grief, no. A child is not helpful for my image. I am only twenty-three. I don't need people to think I am thirty. In the movies, thirty is old, no?'

Ruth turned from the sink, her eyes blazing. 'Nastassia, what kind of a bloody selfish monster are you? Don't you have any idea of how appalling your behaviour is, how much damage you are doing? Josh is out of his mind with grief; his whole world is falling apart, and I can't bear to think about the suffering you are causing your child, poor little boy. You should be ashamed, you cruel bitch!'

Nastassia seemed unmoved by Ruth's outburst and poured herself another drink. 'You always did exaggerate, my dear Ruth,' she said. Her cold blue eyes met

Ruth's, full of cynical mockery. 'But then you're in love with Josh yourself, aren't you, so that explains your attitude, no?'

For a moment Ruth stood there, shaking, her brain paralysed, unable to think of a sufficiently crushing response. Then she gave a choking sob, rushed from the kitchen, snatched her coat from its hook in the hall and wrenched open the front door. At the foot of the steps stood Josh, chaining his bike to the railings. He looked up and saw Ruth struggling into her coat, her face red and streaked with tears.

'Hello,' he said. 'What's up?'

'Nothing.' She brushed past him and walked quickly away down the towpath.

Mystified, Josh frowned and went into the house, hung up his coat and dumped his briefcase. Suddenly, he became aware of a familiar and once-loved scent. He felt the blood drain from his face. He drew a deep breath and went into the kitchen.

'Hello, darling,' said Nastassia, smiling brilliantly. 'What's the problem with that stupid Ruth? Poor girl, she's in love with you, that's it, yes? Don't be worried, I don't mind at all! I don't blame you, you need someone for Max in any case, don't you? She is very suitable, even the same profession, no?'

Josh did his utmost to look steadily at his wife. 'Nastassia,' he said very quietly, as if reasoning with an obtuse child. 'I am not in any way involved with Ruth, you know that perfectly well. She is a good friend, that is all.'

'Oh, come on, Josh, pull the other one. Do you think I am so stupid? In any way, it's not important, I am having an affair myself.'

Josh felt as if the ground were crumbling beneath him. His knees shook, his throat felt tight, he clung to the back of a chair to prevent himself from falling. In spite of the fact that he had been anticipating just such a disaster, he had not realized that the actual event would cause him so much physical pain, nausea and weakness. For a few moments he stood there silently, his bowels dissolving, wishing to die.

'So,' said Nastassia, 'we need to talk, no?' She took a second small glass from the dresser and filled it with vodka. 'You want a drink?'

'Yes, I do, please.' Josh took another long steadying breath and sat down at the table, facing his wife. He drank the vodka at one go and she refilled the glass.

They talked for about an hour, quite calmly, without anger or recrimination. As if they were discussing two other people, they agreed that Nastassia did not love Josh and never had, and felt very little for their child. In his heart Josh recognized that she was telling the simple truth and a cloud of despair descended on him.

Nastassia watched him as sympathetically as her narcissistic nature would permit. She put her hand on his. 'It's not that I wish to marry anyone else, darling. I just need to be free, that's all. I don't need anyone permanent in my life; I'm better on my own. Of course, darling, if you want a quiet divorce, that's OK, I understand.'

Josh stared at her for a long moment. He felt numb; wiped out. He withdrew his hand and finished his drink. Then he told her that he was planning to move to Paris, taking Max with him. 'You can stay here in the house if you wish. The rent from the tenants will take care of the mortgage. After two years, if we decide to divorce, I'll sell the house and split any profit with you.'

'Good,' said Nastassia, 'that seems fair, Josh. But if I wish to keep the house, what then? It's quite convenient, as a London base.'

'In that case, you can buy me out, can't you?' A

shred of courage and self-respect surfaced in Josh's mind and he spoke coldly.

'OK,' she replied coolly. 'I'll be very rich by then; the purchase would be tax effective probably.'

'Then there is the question of Max, Nastassia.'

'What question?'

'I would insist on absolute custody of him.'

'But of course,' she said, 'what else?' She smiled at him, quite kindly. 'Don't worry, I won't make things difficult for you by wanting to see Max. It's better that way, isn't it?'

An uncomfortable mixture of relief and anger flowed like adrenalin through Josh's veins. Relief at not having to get into a custody battle, but anger at how easily she was able to rid herself of her unwanted child. Poor little boy, he thought, what did he do to deserve that?

Nastassia looked at her Cartier watch, a present from Jake. 'Let's go out to dinner, Josh, and celebrate.'

'We can't,' said Josh. 'We haven't got a sitter.'

'What about Ruth?'

'She's out.'

'Oh shit,' said Nastassia. 'How annoying of her. Can't you phone someone?'

'No. I can't.'

'Typical!' She spoke angrily. 'Now you know why it's so bloody impossible for me to live with you, you selfish bastard.'

Josh got up from the table without another word and went upstairs. He sat beside Max's bed for about half an hour, and then went supperless to bed. He lay in the dark, watching the watery reflections from the lamplit river making patterns on the ceiling. He heard footsteps on the stairs as first Robert and then Ruth came home. Around midnight, his door opened and Nastassia came into the room silently, smelling of scent

171

and vodka. He could hear her undressing in the dark, then she slid into the bed beside him. He froze, his eyes closed, feigning sleep. She stroked his back tentatively but he did not respond, and after a few minutes she turned over and went to sleep.

It was the second week in November and rain fell nearly every day at Inniscarragh, making the fallen leaves slippery underfoot so that walking out of doors had become even more of a problem for Guy. Determined not to risk breaking a leg and thereby delaying their return to Corfu, he remained indoors, sorting papers and filling bin-liners with the results of years of incompetent filing. He and Dido had chosen the things they wanted to keep and have shipped to the island. Dido had set aside the ironstone plates and the beautiful Irish linen and Guy decided that he would keep the family Bible, with the births and deaths of his forebears listed in it, adding James's name to the rest. With the Bible, he packed a thick leather album fastened with brass clasps, filled with sepia photographs of wooden-looking people in uncomfortable clothes, apparently on the point of playing tennis or croquet, or, dressed in striped bathing-suits like so many Captain Webbs, preparing to plunge into the lake. There were also many large prints showing winter meets at Inniscarragh, with everyone mounted, elegant in full hunting fig, partaking of stirrup cups. To these bits of family history he added some eighteenth-century miniature portraits and a great many books in sweet-smelling calf bindings. These were in mint condition, barely looked at much less read by former Porteouses. 'Too busy killing things,' said Guy: 'no time for reading.'

They had almost completed the inventory. Guy had half-thought that it had become a pointless exercise, but he was a cautious man and decided to finish the work, in case the deal with Mr Yakimoto fell through and they had to begin all over again. Now, Dido was out in the stables, listing the carriages, the contents of the tack-room, the beautiful Georgian lamps and graceful panelling of the stalls that had housed the hunters in days gone by. In spite of the fact that the last horse had departed long ago, the stalls were still knee-deep in dry but musty-smelling straw, and nets stuffed with hay still hung from the original hooks. The stables were inadequately lit by a couple of naked electric light bulbs and Dido sat on a bale of straw beneath one of them, carefully checking the items on her list and arranging them in the correct order.

A shadow fell across her clipboard and she looked up, startled. Jake stood there, looking down at her. 'Oh, hello,' she said. 'What brings you here?'

'I might ask you the same question, Dido. What the hell are you up to? Where have you been? Why haven't you been in touch?'

'I should have thought the reason was obvious,' she replied crisply. 'Do I have to remind you of the fact that I came home to find the nauseating evidence of your infidelity all over my bedroom?'

'Silly woman. You over-reacted, that's all. You never did before; I never got the feeling that you minded these things particularly.'

'You never left soiled underwear all over my house before, Jake.'

'Well, yes. I'm sorry about that; perhaps it was rather thoughtless.'

'It was worse than thoughtless, Jake, it was fatal. Frankly, I never want to see you again, or be part of your repulsive little games any more.'

'You don't mean that, Dido. At the end of the day, we love each other, don't we?'

'You may think *you* do, but I certainly don't any longer. And since we're on the subject, I want your possessions out of my house as soon as possible.'

'I don't believe you, you're just angry.' He sat down beside her on the bale of straw, and put his arm round her, turning her face to his. 'Come on, let's kiss and make up, darling.'

Dido dropped her clipboard, put her hands on his chest and tried to push him away. 'Please, Jake, go away. Leave me alone.' She turned her head from side to side to avoid his kiss, and as he tightened his grip, pinning her arms to her sides, they rolled off the bale and onto the straw bedding on the floor. He lay on top of her, forcing her mouth open with his and kissing her with all his skill and knowledge of what would arouse her. She bit his tongue as hard as she could, then summoning all her strength, she twisted and turned, struggling to escape from him, raining blows on him with her fists and trying to catch him in the groin with her knee.

'Come on, sweetheart, you know you want to.' He laughed, and seizing both her hands and holding them tightly in one of his, he swiftly pulled down her knickers with the other, and forced himself once more on top of her exhausted body. She lay with her eyes closed, her heart racing, unable to prevent him entering her, while impotent tears of rage and humiliation slid down her temples and into her hair. The episode was violent and quickly over. He lay for a moment, exhausted, then kissed her and withdrew. He stood up, fastening his trousers, and grinned at her triumphantly. 'I was right, wasn't I, my dear Dido? You do love me, you always will.'

When he had gone, Dido lay where she was, too shattered to move, badly bruised and in pain. After a while, suddenly anxious that someone might come into the stable and find her, she sat up, pulled down her skirt and straightened her clothes. She brushed the bits of straw off herself and getting to her feet went to the tackroom in search of a tap. As well as the tap, she found a small cracked mirror hanging from a nail. With her handkerchief she removed the blood from her mouth and bathed her swollen eyes. Then she picked the bits of straw from her hair, and sat for a moment on the groom's bench, carefully checking herself for any further evidence of her ordeal. Then reaction set in and she began to shake, her teeth chattering uncontrollably. Panic, confusion and shame gripped her, though she knew that she had nothing to feel ashamed about. Nevertheless, she did feel ashamed, and dirty. I must have a bath at once, she thought, and wash him off me, then I'll feel better. She went back to the stall, picked up her clipboard and ran quickly back to the kitchen through the rain.

'You're just in time for tea,' said Guy. 'Mrs O'Reilly has brought soda bread and some of her own jam for us, isn't it kind of her?'

'Yes, it is,' said Dido, forcing herself to smile. 'Thank you, Mrs O'Reilly, it does look nice. Look, I'm filthy from the stable, I'll just run up and wash, and change my sweater. Don't wait tea, I won't be a minute.' She put the clipboard on the table and ran upstairs to her room. She turned on the hot tap in the bathroom and tepid water gushed into the huge bath. She tore off her clothes and got into the water, vigorously soaping herself all over and washing her hair, rinsing it in the bathwater. Then she lay in the cooling water for a few moments, making a supreme effort to unwind, and to think rationally.

She thought about Guy, and how much he had come to mean to her; how much he needed her, and how happy they had made each other, even in this present difficult time at Inniscarragh. She longed to tell him about Jake's attack on her, but decided that it would be better not to – there was really nothing to be gained in doing so, except to make herself feel better by talking about it. It could only cause Guy unnecessary pain and anger, and make him even more keenly aware of his own weakness.

She got quickly out of the bath and dried herself vigorously with the thick, rough bath-towel. Then she put on completely fresh clothes, combed her wet hair and ran down to the kitchen.

'You've washed your hair,' said Guy, pouring her tea.

'Yes,' said Dido. 'It smelled of horse.'

By the third week in November the last of the film people had departed and Inniscarragh settled into its habitual late autumn gloom. Mists crept up from the lake, seeping under the doors and through the window frames, leaving a faint smell of putrefaction in the rooms.

'God,' said Guy, 'I'm beginning to hate the place. The sooner I exchange contracts the better I'll feel, before the house actually starts collapsing.' The damp was getting into his bones and his legs ached practically all the time, making him depressed and short-tempered.

'Won't it be cold in the island, Guy?'

'No, but a bit later on it will be. But it's different. Windy sometimes and quite cold, but still a lot of sun, not dreary and endlessly wet, like this bloody place. We'll still be able to sit out on the terrace sometimes and watch the moon rise.'

The next day Guy received a phone call from his lawyers to say that everything was ready for his signature, and they arranged to come out with the documents the following morning. After the lawyers had gone, Guy telephoned a travel agent and booked their flights back to Corfu for the following week. Then they went out in James's old car, to celebrate by having lunch at the pub, each of them privately giving thanks that this rather grim episode in their lives was almost at an end. As they drove through the main gates on their way back to Inniscarragh, Guy's eye fell on Lavinia's cottage, so neat and well-maintained behind its clipped yew hedge. 'Hang on a minute,' he said. 'I'd better tell Lavinia what's happening, I suppose.'

Dido stopped the car and Guy got carefully out. 'Don't wait,' he said. 'I'll walk up to the house.'

'Are you sure?'

'Yes, it's quite dry, for once.'

She drove on and Guy negotiated Lavinia's gate and rang the doorbell. It opened immediately. She must have been on the look-out, he thought, nosy old bag.

'Come in, Guy. To what do I owe the dubious pleasure of a visit from you?'

He ignored this opening gambit and followed her into her warm and chintzy sitting-room, where a log fire burned brightly behind a glass spark-screen. The dachshund Fritz lay on the rug in front of the fire, boiling his brains. Protecting Lavinia did not appear to be part of his brief. Hardly surprising, thought Guy, she's quite capable of looking after herself – probably got a shotgun under her bed. They sat down on either side of the fireplace and Lavinia looked inquiringly at her brother, her eyebrows disappearing into her newly-permed iron-grey hair.

'I have sold Inniscarragh, Lavinia,' said Guy, 'but I have excluded this cottage from the sale. I have arranged with McDonnell to transfer the cottage and its garden to you, with a right of access over the drive.'

Lavinia had observed the comings and goings of the

surveyors and lawyers and had smiled a bitter little smile when she saw the Japanese in his city clothes walking in the grounds with McDonnell. She had guessed pretty accurately what was happening and had already made up her mind that as soon as all the legalities, including those affecting her cottage were completed, she would offer her property to the Japanese consortium and hold out for a very substantial price. In the meantime, she looked down at her heavily-ringed hands as they lay on her grey-tweed lap. 'It's so very tragic,' she said quietly, as if it pained her to speak, 'so sad, to have to sell one's old home, one's family estate, isn't it?'

'Only too thankful to be rid of it,' Guy replied brusquely.

'But *I* am not!' Lavinia stared stonily at her brother, her green eyes angry. 'And if Inniscarragh had come to *me*, Guy, I would never have allowed it to deteriorate in the way it has; it breaks my heart when I look at it, and remember how things were in the old days.'

'But it didn't come to you, did it, Lavinia? Poor Uncle James did his best for us, as I'm sure you're aware.'

'But under a less sexist system, the place *would* have been mine.' Her voice rose as her frustration and jealousy threatened to spill over. 'It very nearly was.'

'What do you mean?'

'What do you think I mean?'

Guy stared at her, reliving all his old admiration and terror of his sister, and his pathetic childish attempts to impress her. In spite of Lavinia's hostility and contemptuous attitude towards him through the years, it had never once occurred to him that she had deliberately tried to bring about the accident that had ruined his life. Now the truth stared him in the face. 'You mean the accident with the tractor, don't you?'

Lavinia laughed, a harsh, triumphant whinny. 'Yes, that's exactly what I mean.'

'It wasn't really an accident, was it, Lavinia?'

'No, it wasn't!' The raw hatred in her eyes left no doubt in Guy's mind that she was speaking the truth. 'I bloody nearly got you that time, little brother. It was the most exciting moment of my life.'

'Yes,' said Guy, 'I can see that it would be, for someone like you.' Sickened, he got unsteadily to his feet, left the room without another word and let himself out of the cottage.

Through the window, Lavinia watched with grim satisfaction as he walked slowly away along the weed-infested drive towards the crumbling house that should by rights have been hers. She watched him out of sight, then turned away to pour herself a glass of sherry and ring for Mrs O'Reilly to bring more logs. But Mrs O'Reilly did not answer the summons; she was up at the house, teaching Dido how to make Colcannon.

After supper, Guy and Dido took their coffee into the library as usual and sat together in front of the peat fire. He had been rather quiet all evening, and she did not ask him why, correctly guessing that the time spent with Lavinia had provoked his mood of depression. Instead, she took his hand in hers. 'Do you remember asking me how long it would take me to find out how I felt about Jake?'

'I do, very well.'

'I know the answer, Guy. I see him now for what he is, a conceited and manipulative man. He never made me feel wanted and happy in the way that you do, and I'm beginning to doubt that I ever really loved him.'

'So what do you intend to do, Dido?' He turned towards her, his heart beating fast.

'Well, I'd rather like to marry you, if you'll have me, Guy.'

'Oh, darling, are you really sure?'

'I'm very sure. I want to spend the rest of my life with you.'

'Till death us do part?'

'Till death us do part, Guy.'

Chapter Ten

One evening Giò telephoned Josh in London and told him about a disused loft he had found for sale in the Bastille district.

'Thank you, Giò. It's kind of you to take so much trouble, but there might be problems.'

'Such as?'

'Well, money for one thing. I'm not selling this place yet, so I have no capital for doing a conversion at the moment. I need a small rented place, preferably close to a nursery school, near enough for Mum to pick up Max for me, without totally wrecking her working day.'

'I see.' The question of Max had not really occurred to Giò. 'Sorry, Josh, I'm a moron. This needs a total rethink, obviously. It's back to the drawing-board.'

Josh laughed. 'You're not a moron at all, Giò. Later on, maybe, a loft would be exactly the sort of thing I'd love to take on. It's just getting things running smoothly for Max that's important at the moment.'

'You're right, of course. Leave it with me, and I'll get back to you. Any news on the job front?'

'Yes. My boss here has been extraordinarily helpful and understanding. He's spoken to two firms of architects in Paris, people he's worked with himself, and I'm coming over for a couple of days next week, for interviews.'

'Lucky chap. You'll be staying with Anna?'

'Yes.'

'Bringing Max?'

'Yes.'

'That's nice, I look forward to seeing you both. In the meantime, I will try and suss out something more suitable for two gentlemen sharing.'

Josh laughed, sounding quite cheerful. 'Thanks, Giò. See you next week, then.'

'*A bientôt,*' said Giò. 'Bye, Josh.'

Josh put down the phone thoughtfully. He's quite right, he said to himself, I *am* lucky. Everyone is doing their best to help me get sorted out, to rebuild my life and Max's. What ungrateful perverseness was it that made him rather wish that they wouldn't try quite so hard? It would be better for me to have to get down to the practicalities without assistance, he thought. That way, I'd be too bloody busy and too bloody tired to think about anything else, especially Stassi. She was, naturally, still sharing their house. She left at five in the morning, picked up by a studio car, and returned, if at all, late at night. Josh had moved into the small spare room, leaving the comfortable double bed for her exclusive use.

He went into the kitchen, empty now and quiet, and made himself cheese on toast. Ruth, thank heaven, had gone out with Robert. Her continued kindness to Max and sad bewildered eyes were a silent reproach to Josh, and he did not enjoy the feeling of being unkind to her, especially as he was quite aware that Ruth was prepared to live with him and Max on any terms he chose. But such a situation, he knew, would be fatal; it was exactly what he had done himself in order to marry Nastassia, so abject had been his love for her. And still is, he thought miserably, swallowing the last hard lump of toast and cheese; probably always will be.

*   *   *

The next day Giò telephoned Anna to ask her about nursery schools in her district.

'There's a very nice one in the same street as Tom's school,' she said. 'Why?'

'I've been apartment-hunting for Josh, and so far I've made a total nonsense.' He told her about the derelict loft in Bastille, and she laughed.

'What a romantic you are, Giò. With Max to look after, as well as a full-time job, he wouldn't have the time, much less the energy to take on something like that.'

'I realize that now,' said Giò ruefully. 'The other rather vital element I left out of my calculations was money.'

'Well, we could always help him in that way, I'm sure.'

'No, I get the feeling he absolutely wouldn't allow that. I think he feels you've done more than enough already.'

'It seems he's not selling his place at present,' said Anna. 'Nastassia's staying on there for the time being.'

'Do you imagine he's hoping for some sort of reconciliation?'

'God knows. He probably doesn't really know himself.'

'Poor Josh.'

'Yes, poor Josh.'

'Well,' said Giò briskly, 'I must get on. I'll draw a little circle round the schools and work round that. Then if I find anything I'll get back to you to come and give it the once-over.'

'You are kind, Giò. I'd come and search with you, but I must get my angel finished, I only have a week left before he's due to be collected.'

'How are you going to get him down the stairs without risking damaging him?'

'With considerable difficulty, I should think,' said Anna. 'They'll probably crate him up and lower him through one of the big front windows to the street.'

'Should be a sight worth seeing; be sure to alert me.'

'I will,' said Anna. 'Talk to you soon.'

Three days later Giò paid a visit to one of his dealers in the Rue Jacob, a quiet, pleasant street hidden behind the Beaux Arts. It housed many antique dealers, as well as several good restaurants and one or two small hotels. He was on the look-out for an Empire console table for one of his clients, and he and this particular colleague often helped each other out in such circumstances, to their mutual advantage. Together they looked through the stock, then went into the storeroom at the rear of the premises, but without finding quite what Giò was looking for. 'Any more upstairs?' He looked up at the ceiling.

'No, this is all. Upstairs is the apartment.'

'Really? I didn't realize that you lived over the shop, like me.'

'I don't. I let it. I am looking for a new tenant now.'

'Really?' said Giò. 'How extraordinary. I know someone who is looking for an apartment. Rue Jacob would be perfect for him.'

'It's very small; only three rooms. How many people would there be?'

'Only two. My nephew and his little boy.'

'A *child*?' Monsieur Petit looked up at the ceiling, with its many hanging chandeliers and lanterns shimmering in the gloom of the showroom and shook his head doubtfully. 'Wouldn't a little boy be noisy? One would hear him running about, no? The chandeliers would shake?'

184

'No, I don't think so,' said Giò. 'He would be at school all day, and in the country at weekends.' This last he had invented on the spur of the moment.

'Oh, well. Perhaps, if he is not at home too much.'

'Could I have a look?'

'Why not?' Monsieur Petit hung his *back in five minutes* card on the door and they went into the street, locking the shop. He unlocked a dark-green painted door immediately to the left and led the way up a steep narrow staircase to the tiny apartment. The sitting-room, about five metres wide and four deep had two windows overlooking the street below, and was furnished with a bizarre assortment of nineteenth-century armchairs upholstered in plum-coloured velours, a large bright Turkish rug and an oval walnut gate-leg table with four bentwood chairs. Rather nasty obelisk-shaped bookcases, empty, were centrally placed on three of the walls. Painted a matt sea-green, they fought bitterly with the armchairs and rug, not to speak of the wallpaper, an art nouveau design in shades of orange and brown.

'My nephew is an architect,' said Giò. 'He might find the decor a little old-fashioned for his taste. You wouldn't object to him bringing his own things?'

'Not at all.' Monsieur Petit grinned ironically. 'I agree, it's hideous like this, but it suits most people well enough. In any event, the terms of the lease would be the same.'

'And they are?'

'Three months, renewable. And three months' notice to quit, on either side. Rent payable in advance, of course.'

'Let's see the rest.'

The rest turned out to be two small square bed-rooms, which looked out through narrow casements to a very small, rather dank yard below. A weak looking, leafless lime tree, too large for the space, was doing its best to grow upright to the light. In one corner was a wooden crate, with a dish containing lettuce leaves on the ground in front of it, and around the grim brick walls of the yard marched a tortoise, its geriatric neck thrust forward in a purposeful manner as it lumbered round its territory.

'Oh look!' exclaimed Giò. 'A tortoise!'

'Yes,' agreed Monsieur Petit. 'That's Bonaparte.'

'Why Bonaparte?'

'Because I found him in the Rue Bonaparte one day, just round the corner from here. He looked as though he'd just done the retreat from Moscow, poor *mec,* so I brought him home with me.'

'Is he friendly?'

'No, not at all. He is rude and ungrateful.' Monsieur Petit laughed his funny croaking laugh. 'He is angry today because I gave him lettuce. He prefers asparagus, but of course, it is out of season.'

The rest of the apartment comprised a small but quite well-equipped kitchen, and an antedeluvian bathroom with a square rust-stained half-bath overhung by a buckled copper geyser fixed to the wall. A round basin on a metal tripod completed the washing arrangements. The lavatory was in the corner at the top of the stairs, an evil-smelling affair concealed behind a curved sliding door painted apple-green with a scattering of hand-painted apple-blossoms decorating the panels.

'Where on earth did you find that?' Giò sounded incredulous.

'Fontainebleau,' said Monsieur Petit drily. 'Where else?'

'It looks as though Giò may have found an apartment for Josh,' said Anna, as she and Patrick ate their supper

186

at the kitchen table. 'He phoned earlier, but I was too busy burnishing my angel to go and look at it with him.'

'Well, we could all go on Sunday, when Josh is here. Wouldn't that be best?'

Anna looked at him, her eyes a little sad. 'I was rather expecting that they would live with us for a while, but Giò seems to have hijacked him, doesn't he?'

Patrick finished eating his excellent *cabillaud à la boulangère* while he considered his response. He put down his fork, and took a sip of wine. 'I think Giò understands only too well how Josh must be feeling just now; hurt, humiliated and betrayed. God knows, the same sort of thing has happened to *him* more times than one cares to remember. Now he is doing his best to protect Josh; not from us, exactly, but from too much sympathy and family solidarity. Josh needs us, but at a distance. The important thing for him is to be incredibly strong and independent for Max's sake. If he came here to us, and they both settled into a routine, it would be only too easy for them to become too comfortable and dependent, especially on you. Don't you think it's vital for Josh that he continues to be the major pivotal point of Max's life, the one sure thing he can rely on, his father? And for that, they have to be on their own, don't they?'

Anna got up and changed the plates. She put salad and cheese on the table and sat down again. 'You're right, of course, I realize that. It's exactly what I would say myself, to someone else in a similar situation.'

'But you're sad, and a bit hurt?'

'Yes, I suppose I am.'

'It'll be all right, you'll see. For a start, you'll probably have to pick up Max from school when you collect Tom, won't you? So you'll see Josh and Max every day, and I expect they'll want to come to St Gilles at weekends sometimes, too.'

'Yes,' said Anna, and smiled at him. 'I expect they will. I hope they will.'

'Be patient, my love. It'll be OK, I promise.'

Guy and Dido flew back to Corfu, arriving on a warm, golden afternoon. Vassili met them at the airport and they drove out to Koulari, overjoyed to be home again and thankful to have left behind the damp, cold and gloom of Inniscarragh.

For the first few days they did very little except sit in the sun, feeling like convalescents. At night, they were able to go to bed together, relaxed and happy, secure in the knowledge that their privacy would not be rudely interrupted at any moment. Sometimes they made love; sometimes they lay quietly, listening to the owls calling in the olives, lulled by the gentle rattle of the pebbles as the sea broke softly on the beach below. 'It's heaven,' said Dido. 'It's like the perfect kind of holiday, except that it's not just a holiday, it's forever.'

For Guy, it was a time of total happiness. He could not quite believe in his enormous good fortune in having Dido not only beside him, but prepared to remain with him always. Occasionally, of its own volition the memory of his last interview with Lavinia entered his mind, reminding him of her cruel confirmation that she had in fact intended to kill him. Looking at his wasted legs, he thought bitterly that she had to all intents and purposes succeeded in wrecking his life, even though she had failed in her attempt at removing him from her path altogether. But then, looking at Dido's sleeping head cradled on his shoulder he reminded himself that under normal circumstances he might never have met her, and perhaps never known such happiness. He would probably have been married for twenty years to a nice dull English girl from the shires, horsy and socially ambitious, and have several hearty children at public schools or even university. Darling Dido, he thought, she doesn't seem to care about my bloody legs, so why should I? He closed his eyes and drifted off to sleep.

After a week of such carefree relaxation, Dido pulled herself together sufficiently to write some necessary letters on Guy's typewriter. She wrote to a firm of lawyers, recommended by Guy, instructing them to arrange the sale of *The Maid of Wapping*. Then she wrote to Jake, enclosing a copy of her letter to the lawyers. She requested that he vacate the barge forthwith, and give the keys to her lawyers. She showed the letters to Guy before posting them.

'So,' he said quietly, handing them back, 'you're burning your boats, literally?'

'Absolutely,' she replied, sliding her arm round his neck, her cheek against his. 'Do you mind?'

'Do I *mind*? Do you have the slightest idea of what you mean to me?'

'Yes,' said Dido, looking at him seriously, 'I think I do.'

When Jacob Kroll received Dido's letter his first reaction was one of disbelief, followed by outrage. Silly little bitch, he thought angrily, who the hell does she think she is? Doesn't she realize how fortunate she is to be the partner of a celebrity like me, someone famous and very rich? Suddenly, an extremely unpleasant thought entered his head. What if Dido was planning to take him to the cleaners, claiming to be his common-law wife? Why had she written to these lawyers? And what was she doing in Corfu, anyway? What was this so-called job with the weirdo Porteous?

Jake had not taken to Guy at all; he thought him cold

and autocratic and was far from impressed by the large sum of money the studio had spent on renting Inniscarragh. I wonder where Dido met him, he asked himself. I'm surprised she'd be prepared to work for such a repulsive little cripple. It did not occur to him for a single second that at that very moment Dido was lying asleep in Guy's arms.

Jake thought about Dido's letter for a few days, on and off, and then spent a boring evening writing to her, a kind and conciliatory letter, expressing his regret at his past mistakes and his hope that everything was not really over between them. He agreed to leave *The Maid of Wapping* at some future date if that was what she wanted, but he thought that a period of calm reflection would be appropriate. It irritated him to have to waste an evening writing all this mealy-mouthed stuff, but he reminded himself that at the end of the day it suited him very well to be attached to Dido, and he was extremely unwilling to lose the protecting veil of her commitment to him. Equally, he was quite appalled at the idea of getting into a legal wrangle with her, with the bad publicity that would doubtless follow. Spiteful little cat, he said to himself, as he put the letter into an envelope and addressed it, I'd like to give her a piece of my mind, or better still, a good bonking. Look how much she enjoyed our little bash in the hay. He laughed at the recollection. She was dying for it; and she even bit me, he remembered. Not many of them do that, it was fun.

Josh and Max went to Paris on the early Eurostar, arriving at the Gard du Nord at 12.23 precisely, and took the Métro to St-Michel. From the station it was a short walk to Quai des Grands-Augustins and they arrived in good time for lunch. Josh's first job interview was at three o'clock that afternoon and Max was to stay with Anna, and go with her to collect Tom from school. The great golden angel rested on the work-table, fully restored and glowing with light. Max gazed at it, his chin resting on the table edge, his dark eyes round with astonishment.

'Don't touch, Max,' said Josh.

Max said nothing, but gave his father a reproving look.

'You're not going to beat this one up, Mum? Distress it?'

Anna smiled. 'No, not this time. There's quite a fashion nowadays for letting new gilding remain as bright and brilliant as it would have been in the first place. I rather like it, myself.'

Josh looked around the beautiful room, at his mother's work, her exquisite small gilded carvings. 'You don't distress your own stuff, either?'

'No, I leave that to time: dirt, dust, pollution.'

'Ah,' said Josh, 'pollution. The great criminal factor of the late twentieth century.'

Anna had prepared quite a light lunch, assuming that Josh would probably be feeling nervous about his interview. She led the way to the kitchen, where the table was already laid with a crisp baguette, several kinds of cheese, butter, salad, *saucisson sec* and a plate of sliced mountain ham. 'What about a drink, Josh?'

'A glass of wine would be great, thanks.'

'And Max? What would you like, darling? Orange juice?' She opened the fridge and took out a pack of juice. Max had fleetingly considered asking for a Coke, but since his grandmother was already pouring the juice into a glass he correctly surmised that this wasn't really an option. 'OK, thanks,' he said, mentally planning to extract a Coke from his father later in the day.

At half-past two Josh left for his interview, carrying

191

his portfolio, and Anna helped Max unpack the overnight bag, stowing their clean shirts and pyjamas in the drawers of the pot-bellied cupboard that stood against one wall of their bedroom. Max took the sponge-bag to the small adjoining bathroom and carefully arranged the toothbrushes in the thick glass tumblers which rested in fat brass rings screwed into the tiles beside the basin. In the bedroom were two single beds covered in blue-and-white quilts, separated by a small night-table carrying a lamp with a shiny dark-green shade. On one of the beds reposed a battered teddy bear. Max looked at it, and then at Anna. 'I brought my own teddy. He's in the case.'

'Oh good,' said Anna. 'I wasn't sure whether you'd have room to bring him, so I thought you might like to borrow my old chap.'

'He must be awfully old, if he was yours?'

Anna laughed. 'He *is* old; very old indeed for a teddy. He was *my* mother's before me, then he was Josh's for a while, and then Tom's.'

'Doesn't Tom want him any more? Is he too big for a teddy now?'

'No, I don't think he is. He pretends to be sometimes, but quite a lot of animals still seem to share his bed with him.'

Max rummaged in the overnight bag and found his teddy. He showed him to Anna.

'What's his name?'

'Dušek.'

'Dušek,' repeated Anna. 'Well, Dušek, I hope you get on with Louis and don't fight.'

'It's Mummy's name,' said Max. 'She called him that so I won't forget her.'

'You won't forget her, darling.' Anna glanced anxiously at Max as he sat on the bed, clutching his bear.

'I *do* forget her, that's the trouble,' he said in a thin little voice. 'She's hardly ever at home now, she's too busy working, all the time. She's in the movies, you know.'

'Haven't you got photos of her?'

'Only one. But I have got a video of when she was on the telly.'

'Well, good, that must be fun. Not everyone's mum is on the telly, after all, are they? You must be proud of her, Max.'

Max looked at her, bright-eyed, feeling rather flattered. 'Yes, I am. She's drop-dead gorgeous. Mrs Maloney says so.'

'Well, Mrs Maloney is quite right,' said Anna. 'She *is* extremely beautiful.' She closed the cupboard door. Even if I could cheerfully throttle her with my bare hands, she added silently to herself.

At three o'clock they left the apartment and went to pick up Tom from school.

'What would you like to do?'

'Let's go and watch the boats go by,' suggested Tom. They walked back to the Pont Neuf and went down the steps to the garden on the tip of the Ile de la Cité, the Square du Vert-Galant. From here one could get a good view of the majestic river boats as they cruised past, their lights blazing in the blue light of a late November afternoon, their deeply throbbing engines reverberating across the water.

'Wow!' exclaimed Max, impressed. 'They're *enormous*, aren't they? Could we go on one?'

'Yes, of course we could,' said Anna, 'but not today. We have to get back to be there when Dad gets home.'

'Dad won't be home for hours yet,' said Tom.

'Not *your* dad, idiot. Max's dad.'

'Oh, you mean *Josh*,' said Tom. 'Why didn't you say so?'

'Josh,' said Max. 'I think I'll call him Josh too.'

'You can't, stupid.'

'Why not? You do.'

'He's my *brother*, dumbo, that's why.'

'That's enough, boys. Come on, let's go and have some tea, shall we?'

They climbed the steps back up to the Pont Neuf and stood by the statue of Henri IV waiting for a gap in the traffic which poured in a relentless torrent across the bridge. 'Right!' Anna grasped the hands of both boys. '*Now*!' They ran across the bridge to the narrow entrance to the Place Dauphine, a small well-concealed square, the bare black branches of its trees silhoutted against the classical façade of the Palais de Justice at the far end. In this little enclave was to be found a favourite haunt of Anna's, Fanny-Tea, where they served a properly made pot of tea as well as the kind of delicious chocolate cake that gladdens the heart of a child.

It was half-past five by the time they got back to Grands-Augustins, to find Josh and Giò sitting on the floor outside the apartment, waiting for them. They stood up as Anna and the boys came out of the lift. 'Good heavens, I didn't expect you to be back yet, Josh. And Giò, too. Where did *you* spring from?'

'I called at Giò's on my way back,' said Josh. 'We're going to take you to see an apartment he's found. It's just round the corner, ten minutes from here.'

'Can I come too?' asked Tom.

'And me?' Max looked worried.

'Yes, of course. We'll all go,' said Anna. 'Come in, let's dump the portfolio and Tom's bag first.' She turned to Giò. 'Where is this apartment, anyway?'

'Rue Jacob.'

'Really? How lovely. I thought it was nearly all antique shops and restaurants there.'

194

'Life is full of surprises.' Giò glanced at his sister. 'Or hadn't you noticed?'

'Now you mention it, yes, I have.' They exchanged the complicit smile of twins. 'Or maybe some people are quite good at locating surprises?'

On the way down in the creaking lift, Anna turned to Josh. 'How did you get on, by the way?'

'Excellently.' Josh looked gratified. 'They seemed impressed with the work I'd done in Prague. They offered me a job.'

'Wonderful! Will you take it? What about the other firm?'

'I'll go and see them, of course, out of courtesy. But I really like the ethos of this practice. The partners are comparatively young or young-thinking, and inno-vative in their approach. The great thing about working in France is that everyone involved, the government, the planners and the architects are all working together with one vision, the enhancement of the quality of life of the whole nation, not just the *grands projets* here in Paris but all over the country as well. Maybe I'm exaggerating, but that's the distinct impression I got from talking to these people today. Politically, they don't use the excuse of the dreaded market forces to further the enrichment of the powerful few, to the disadvantage of the poor and weak, which sadly seems so often to be the case elsewhere. Whatever happened to the ideals of the welfare state, I ask myself?'

This was a pretty long speech for Josh and Anna was touched that his views were still so idealistic, and glad to hear him sounding so enthusiastic about his prob-able new job.

'Sounds right up your street, Josh,' said Giò.

'I think so.'

They walked through the back streets to the Rue Bonaparte, then turned into the Rue Jacob. Monsieur

Petit was busy with a client when they arrived at his shop, but he saw them at once, excused himself and threaded his way through the showroom to give Giò the key to the apartment. 'Go up and have a look,' he said, 'then come and see me.'

'It's pretty poky, I'm afraid,' said Giò, as he led the way up the narrow staircase. 'You'll probably think it's ghastly.'

They looked first at the sitting-room. No one liked to express an opinion, and Giò laughed. 'It's all right. The old boy knows it's awful. He doesn't mind if you redecorate and bring your own furniture.'

'Thank God for that.' Josh sounded relieved. He crossed to the windows and looked down at the street. 'It's a really nice street, quiet but plenty of life. It's just a step to the Marché Buci, isn't it? What do you think, Max?'

'Aren't we going to live with Tom?'

'No, darling, we're not. But you'll see him every day, won't you? And stay with him and Anna till I get back from the office?'

'Where will I sleep?'

They went to inspect the bedrooms, while Anna and Giò remained in the sitting-room, sitting on the hideous and itchy plum velour chairs. 'French bad taste,' said Giò. 'It's the pits.'

Anna laughed and shook her head. 'You're right. I can hardly bear to look at these chairs, much less sit on them,' she said.

Josh and the two boys inspected the kitchen, which they decided could be made quite cosy for two people to cook and eat in, then went to the bedrooms. Max went straight to the window and looked down into the yard. He saw Bonaparte at once. 'Look, Tom,' he said, 'there's a tortoise.'

'Where?' Tom joined Max at the window.

'Down there. Look, he's got a little house.'

'So he has. You are *lucky*, Max. I wish *I* had a tortoise.'

'But he wouldn't be mine, really, would he?'

'Well,' said Josh, coming to look, 'I daresay Monsieur Petit would let you help to look after him, if you asked politely.'

'Do you really think so, Dad?'

'No harm in asking, is there?'

It was the tortoise that was the deciding factor. Suddenly the apartment seemed to Josh to have quite a lot of potential, properly decorated and furnished. He would bring his books, plan-chest and drawing-board from London, and Max's bedroom furniture and toys. He gazed down at the depressed-looking tortoise and gave thanks to some undefined being for his good fortune in finding a congenial job as well as a promising place to live in such a comparatively short time. If only everything in life were as simple as that, he thought sadly.

They looked at the bathroom, and Max was enchanted by the small square bath, with the narrow ledge on which to sit while bathing. Lastly, they inspected the lavatory at the top of the stairs. 'It's terrific,' said Josh. 'I love it, except for the pong, and I daresay we can fix that with an extractor fan. Shouldn't be too difficult.'

They trooped downstairs to the street. Giò locked the door and they went to discuss terms with Monsieur Petit, now alone in his shop. 'So this is the boy,' he said, studying Max carefully. 'What is your name, young man?'

'Max.'

'And what age have you, Max?'

197

'I'm quite old. I'm five. I go to school.'

'Really? I thought you were older. You are tall for your age, I suppose.'

'Monsieur Petit,' interrupted Max. 'The tortoise in the garden, is he yours?'

'Bonaparte? But naturally, he is mine.'

'Do you think, if I come to live here, that I could help you look after him?'

'You mean, clean his house?'

'Yes.'

'It's a deal, my boy. Perhaps, if you do the work conscientiously, we could look for a wife for Bonaparte. She could be yours, no?' He held out his hand.

Wondering briefly what 'conscientiously' meant, Max took the proffered hand and shook it gravely. Clearly, Monsieur Petit was good news. The old man took Anna and the two boys to the yard and left them with Bonaparte, then he returned to the shop to discuss terms with Josh and Giò. 'Do what you like to the place,' he said, adding cautiously, 'within reason, of course. Let me have a list of what furniture you want removed. How soon do you anticipate moving in?'

'As long as it takes to tie up the loose ends in London,' said Josh. 'Say two weeks?'

'Entendu.'

Chapter Eleven

One dark morning Lavinia was woken by an unfamiliar sound some distance from her cottage, and lay for a moment wondering what it could be. It was a high-pitched whining noise, like a mammoth dentist's drill. Suddenly the noise stopped and there was a brief silence, followed immediately by a loud, splintering crash. I don't believe it, she thought, sitting bolt upright in bed, they're cutting down the trees! She got stiffly out of bed and went to the window, pulling back the heavily-lined *toile-de-Jouy* curtain. She stared towards the woods but could see nothing. The excruciating sound of the chain-saw began again and she held her breath, waiting for the crash of falling timber that would follow as surely as day follows night. Stunned, she stood by the window, praying for the work to finish, but it did not, and after five or six trees had hit the ground she gathered her wits and prepared to do battle.

She dressed as quickly as she could, the continuing shriek of the chain-saw like a knife in her soul, then went downstairs. She put on her Barbour jacket and gumboots, rousted Fritz out of his basket and taking a torch, went out through the back garden, heading towards the lake and the woods. It was beginning to get less dark and she located the woodcutters without difficulty, working by the headlights of their Land-rover on the far side of the wood. There were two men, both known to Lavinia, and as she approached the screech of the chain-saw ceased and an ancient balsam poplar hit the ground.

'What do you think you are doing, Geary?'

'Felling the trees, Miss.' Geary touched his cap.

'I can see that, you fool. Who gave you the order to do such a thing?'

'Mr O'Toole, Miss.'

'And who, may I ask, is Mr O'Toole?'

'He's the clerk of the works, Miss.'

'Clerk of the works?' Lavinia frowned. 'What do you mean, clerk of the works? What works? Surely they can't have got planning permission yet?'

'I couldn't be telling you that, Miss. You'll have to speak to Mr O'Toole, Miss.'

'I will.' Lavinia spoke sharply. 'Where will I find him?'

'Up at the house, Miss.'

'Up at the *house*? How can he be up at the house? The sale is not completed yet, to the best of my knowledge.'

'I couldn't be saying, Miss, I'm sure.'

'In the meantime, you must stop this work at once. Do you understand, Geary?'

'Sorry, Miss. I can't oblige you there. It would be Mr O'Toole's say-so, Miss.'

Lavinia did her best to stare him out, summoning all the arrogance of her forebears, but her efforts failed. Geary shuffled his feet, touched his cap, apologized once more, then pulled the cord of his chain-saw, causing it to burst into aggressive life. She turned away angrily and retraced her steps to the cottage, Fritz trotting along dejectedly behind her. She brewed herself some coffee, then made up her face with care. She put on her best Donegal tweed coat, tied her Hermes scarf round her neck and braced herself once more to do battle.

She found William O'Toole in the library, with site

plans spread all over the table and desk. 'Good morning, Miss Porteous,' he said, getting up as she entered the room. 'What can I do for you?'

The man sounds like a tradesman, she thought maliciously; so much for present-day professionals. 'May I ask on whose authority the trees in my wood are being cut down?'

'Mine, since you ask,' he replied mildly. 'Why, is the noise disturbing you? The work will be finished in a couple of days; three, at most.'

'Two or three days!' cried Lavinia, her voice rising. 'Are you felling the entire wood?'

'We are indeed, Miss Porteous. It's necessary, I'm afraid.'

'Why?'

'Many of the trees are over-mature and rather a lot are dangerously rotten. In any case, the land they occupy will be part of the new golf course. It's destined to be the eighteenth hole, and the clubhouse.'

'The clubhouse! Right outside my cottage?'

'I'm afraid so.'

'Does my brother know about this?'

'Mr Porteous gave permission for any preliminary work to be put in hand immediately. At the purchaser's risk, of course.' He leafed through a filing tray and produced a letter from Guy, which confirmed this assertion. Lavinia read the letter, and handed it back coldly. 'But you haven't even got planning consent yet, have you?'

'In all probability, it'll go through on the nod, Miss Porteous.'

Suddenly, Lavinia felt defeated, tired and old. The idea had, of course, occurred to her to write to the Department of the Environment in Dublin in order to oppose Guy's application for planning permission for a change of use for Inniscarragh. On reflection she had realized that if she did such a thing her chances of making a killing out of selling her cottage to the consortium would be greatly reduced, if not completely destroyed. She had therefore refrained from this course of action, in her own interest. Now she felt a curious surge of weakness and misery, as though she were about to be violently ill, or faint, or both. She stretched out an uncertain hand and grasped the back of a chair.

'Are you all right, Miss Porteous? Why don't you sit down for a moment?'

'I am perfectly all right, thank you, Mr O'Toole. You haven't heard the last of this, I can assure you. I shall speak to my brother. Good morning!' She turned on her heel, walked slightly unsteadily to the door and left the room, slamming the door behind her. Fritz, who had been dozing under the table, leapt to his feet and scrambled across the floor in pursuit of his mistress, his sharp little black toenails skittering against the polished boards. He looked up at the brass doorknob with a small anguished whine. William O'Toole got to his feet and let him out. 'Sooner you than me, old chap,' he said, closing the door after the dog and returning to his seat.

That evening Lavinia telephoned Guy. She felt unaccountably nervous as she listened to the far-off ringing tone. Corfu, she thought, what a ridiculous place to live. Like being on holiday all the time. The phone rang and rang and she was about to hang up, when it was answered.

'Porteous.'

'Guy.'

'Lavinia.'

'Guy, I feel you ought to know that these developers are cutting down the trees in the woodland round the lake.'

'Really?'

'Yes, really. It's sheer vandalism, you must stop them at once.'

'It's no longer anything to do with me, Lavinia. Presumably it's necessary to clear the land before they build the golf course.'

'But it's right at the back of my house, Guy. It's wrecking my view.'

'Well, I'm sure if you decide to leave, the developers will be happy to buy the cottage from you.'

'But it's my *home*, Guy.' Surprisingly, Lavinia's voice rose to a petulant whine. 'It's all that's left of our heritage!'

'Sorry, Lavinia, but it's out of my hands now.'

'You're doing this on purpose, to spite me, aren't you, Guy? It will break my heart to leave Inniscarragh, you know that.'

'Then we'll be quits, won't we, Lavinia?'

'What do you mean?'

'You know perfectly well what I mean. And if you don't, then think about it.'

Nastassia lay on the canopied bed with her eyes closed, while the make-up girl blotted the shine off her nose and forehead. She applied yet another layer of powder to the deathly waxen pallor of Nastassia's face, while an assistant adjusted the strips of cotton-wool packed around her hairline. Nastassia was irritated by the cotton-wool; she felt sure that it would spoil the appearance of her 'dead' face in close-up and detract from the beauty of her long fair hair spread over the pillow. A rosary was entwined in her clasped hands as they lay on her breast in an attitude of prayer. She was wearing the dark-blue velvet ball gown, with wide leg-of-mutton sleeves, sprinkled with tiny silver stars. The make-up girl withdrew, the tallow candles on either side of the bed were relit, the lights and cameras were turned on and the cameraman nodded to Jake. 'Action,' said Jake quietly and Nastassia froze, rock solid, doing her considerable best not to breathe for what felt like a very long time. 'Cut,' said Jake. Nastassia took a long breath and opened her eyes.

'OK, Fred?' Jake looked at the cameraman.

'Yeah, fine. Do you want to look?' Jake looked at the close-up through the video-playback. 'Great,' he said. 'That's a wrap.'

The next shot on the schedule was a rather macabre scene involving the carrying of Yvonne's corpse down a narrow twisting staircase, too cramped to permit the transport up or down of the coffin. The actor playing Seurel, Yvonne's faithful friend and devoted admirer, was a slender young man of medium height, who in spite of his twice-weekly training sessions at the gym was having some difficulty in carrying the deadweight of the leading lady down the confines of the purpose-built cutaway staircase. The hot lights blazed and cameras were aimed at them from several angles, and Nastassia did nothing to help him; she was fully occupied in resting her cheek pathetically against his frock-coated chest, taking care to keep her chin as high as she could to avoid the appearance of unattractive lines in her neck. After four or five takes, her task was made even more difficult by the fact that the heat of the lights was making Seurel sweat profusely; dark stains appeared under his high-cut sleeves and he was beginning to smell quite unpleasant. As they inched their way down the stairs Nastassia's right arm hung heavily from the shoulder, causing the blood to flow into her hand, turning it a healthy-looking pink, so that she had to told her arm above her head between takes to restore the pallor of death. She had a crick in her neck and pins and needles in her hand. Oh, do get on, she begged silently.

At the fourteenth attempt, Jake pronounced himself satisfied. 'OK, let's wrap it.' Seurel sat down heavily on the stairs, dropping Nastassia at the same time. She bumped down two or three steps on her bottom before she was able to halt her undignified descent. 'You rotten little shit!' she hissed angrily, through gritted teeth.

'Oh,' said Seurel, scarlet in the face, '*so sorry*! Are you hurt?'

'You did it on purpose!'

'Why would I do that, Nastassia?'

Nastassia tossed her head and ripped the cotton-wool from her hair, handing it silently to the make-up girl. She lifted her heavy velvet skirts and crossed the floor to look at the playback with Jake.

'You really do look very dead, darling,' he said, smiling and putting his arm round her shoulders.

'That awful cotton-wool spoils the shot; it's so hideous, Jake.'

'Got to have it, I'm afraid; it's in the shooting script. Anyway, it emphasizes your deadness. You should thank your stars it's not soaked in phenol, as it would have been in those days, to mask the smell of you decomposing!'

Nastassia pulled a face and shrugged expressively. One day she told herself, when I'm a big bankable star, I shall insist on looking wonderful in every shot. I shall have my own lighting man and my own make-up artist, and I shan't let the director mess me around. In the meantime, since she remained at Jake's mercy, so to speak, she could not yet afford to antagonize him. So when he asked her to dine with him she accepted at once, with her sweetest smile.

They dined at a restaurant on the river at Hammersmith, noted for its delicious Italian country cooking and astronomical prices. Nastassia was quick to observe the presence of one or two famous faces, and was delighted to be seen dining alone with a man who was already himself something of a celebrity. She enjoyed the glances of admiration that came her way, pretending to be unaware of them, but she removed the scarlet cobwebby shetland shawl that covered her head, and shook her long blond mane of hair over her shoulders with a consciously graceful movement.

Jake ordered grilled *polenta* with prosciutto, then partridges stuffed with *cotechino* and a bottle of good Tuscan wine. He did not ask Nastassia whether she was happy with his choice and she did not feel resentful of his dictatorial behaviour; she found it a complete contrast to Josh's treatment of her, his ingratiating attempts to please her, to make her happy. All that he had ever succeeded in doing was irritating her, with his perpetual anxious vulnerability. Nastassia was hungry after the long day's shooting. She had not eaten seriously for three days and she ate everything put in front of her swiftly and with enjoyment. The wine was robust and delicious and she drank her share of the bottle, feeling increasingly relaxed and happy. This is the life, she thought, hard work in the day and dining out somewhere really OK at night.

Jake, too, quite enjoyed his dinner, but his mind dwelt rather uneasily on the disturbing missive he had received that morning in response to his conciliatory letter to Dido. It had been from her lawyers, acknowledging her receipt of his letter but stating firmly that her mind was made up; she wished him to vacate *The Maid of Wapping* by the end of the month. The lawyers added that he should notify them of the time and date of his departure from the barge, in order that they could send a representative to take possession of Miss Pernice's property and receive the keys on her behalf.

This is getting to be a bore, he thought moodily. He could not bring himself to believe that Dido really meant it, that their association was at an end, and with what possible nasty little sting in the tail to come? He was sure the lawyers would be delighted to encourage her along the path to palimony. He tried to feel aggressive and angry, and ready to fight any action she might try to bring against him, but when he allowed himself to think truthfully about his predicament, a sensation completely new to Jake manifested itself, a chill feeling of loneliness, even desolation. It's not so much Dido herself I mind about he told himself, it's *The Maid*. I love that place, so secret, so snug on the water. It's my home, my refuge, I don't want to lose it. He thought of all the relaxed happy years he had spent there, the gentle slap-slap of the water on the hull of the barge, the leisurely meals, and quiet evenings listening to music. Far more than Dido herself had ever done, Jake had loved to listen to the recordings of her mother, Maria, and to a lesser extent, those of her father, the funny little counter-tenor, Luigi Pernice. How could a man who looked like a garden gnome have had such an extraordinary voice, he asked himself? He sighed, remembering a balmy June evening spent listening to Britten's *A Midsummer Night's Dream*, with Luigi singing his favourite role, the strangely moving unearthly beauty of his silvery voice floating over the still oily waters of the midnight river.

Jake found it surprisingly painful to contemplate a future without that secure permanent home, without the quiet affection and understanding of his needs that Dido had always given him. She had been a little like his mother, Jake reluctantly admitted, all-forgiving, patient and kind. A good cook, too. Restaurants do get to be a bore after a while, he told himself, watching Nastassia licking the last scrap of coffee *granita* from a small silver spoon. He ordered coffee and a *grappa*, and asked for the bill.

As they walked to the car Nastassia slipped her hand through Jake's arm. 'Shall I come home with you tonight, darling? Or are you too tired?'

'I'm not too tired, but there's a problem.'

'Oh?'

'Yes. Dido wants me out of *The Maid of Wapping*.'

'But isn't she in Ireland?'

'No. She's in Corfu, with the cripple Porteous.'

'So, what's the problem? She's not *here*, is she?'

'It's possible she may have a private eye on me.'

'Oh, I see. Poor Jake, you're in the same ship as me, a stupid marriage.' Jake did not disabuse her. 'So,' she went on, 'where will you go now?'

'Search me, no time to think about it.'

'You could always rent one of my studios.'

Jake laughed. 'What studios? Are you a woman of property?'

'Yes, I am,' said Nastassia seriously. She told him that she and Josh had decided to separate, that he was moving to Paris, so that the house would be to all intents and purposes hers. 'I have two studios. One of the tenants is a boring up-tight woman architect; I could tell her to leave.' She wrapped her arms round Jake's neck and gazed at him. 'I am slightly longing to go to bed with you, darling. Josh is in Paris for a few days, you could come home with me now if you like. Then you could look at the studio in the morning, no?'

Jake held her close to him, smiling his mocking smile, his eyes obscured by the reflection of a street-lamp on his spectacles. 'Where is your house?'

'Strand-on-the-Green, darling.'

Jake whistled. 'Really? *Very* upmarket. Is your husband rich?'

'No, but his family seems to be, I think.'

They drove to Thames Road, locked up the car and walked down the alleyway to the towpath. A cold moon glittered in the frosty sky and was reflected in the glassy surface of the river, quiet and calm at high tide.

'Terrific spot,' said Jake. 'Where's the house?'

Nastassia turned and pointed. 'Here.'

Jake looked at the tall red-brick Georgian house, its front door up a short flight of stone steps, above the tideline, the whole defended by black-painted iron railing and gate. Well, he said to himself, this'll do very well, until I sort Dido out.

In the morning, on her way downstairs, Ruth ran into Jake as he emerged from the bathroom, wearing nothing but a towel.

'Good morning,' he said politely, and without waiting for a response disappeared into Nastassia's bedroom. Tight-lipped with embarrassment and outrage, Ruth continued downstairs to the hall, catching a glimpse of Nastassia through the half-open kitchen door. She hesitated, then went in. Nastassia was seated at the table, drinking orange juice and reading the movie reviews in the previous week's *Independent on Sunday*. She was wearing a white towelling bathrobe which had fallen open, revealing a good deal of her beautiful breasts.

'Hi,' said Nastassia.

'Who is that man?' Ruth tore her eyes from Nastassia's breasts.

'Well, he's not my brother, Ruth. Though what the fuck has it got to do with you anyway?' She stared at Ruth with cold blue eyes; she did not cover her nakedness.

Ruth flushed angrily. 'I don't care for your tone, Nastassia, and I don't care to see you using Josh's house in this shameless fashion. Haven't you hurt him and poor little Max enough?'

Nastassia laughed. 'Well, you know what you can do, don't you? You can leave. In fact, I was going to give you notice, anyway. I need the studio for a friend.'

'Don't worry; you needn't bother to give me notice, I shall leave at once. I'll have my stuff cleared out by this evening.'

'Brilliant!' said Nastassia. 'That *is* thoughtful of you, Ruth. How kind.'

Ruth stared at her, wrong-footed and deflated. She tried without success to think of a sufficiently stinging retort.

'Needless to say,' Nastassia went on smoothly, 'I shall refund the balance of this month's rent. Let me know what it comes to, won't you?'

'Forget it,' said Ruth. 'Don't insult me more than you have already.' She turned and left the room before her composure deserted her completely. She snatched her coat from its hook and made for the front door, avoiding catching the eye of Nastassia's lover as he descended the stairs. She held the door slightly ajar before shutting it behind her, trying to hear what, if anything, would be said about her. The man spoke first. 'What was all that about?'

'Oh, nothing. It's that stupid woman I told you about. She's a real pain; she's madly in love with Josh, silly cow. Anyway, she doesn't matter, she's leaving tonight.'

'So soon?'

'I'm a fast worker, Jake. Hadn't you noticed?'

Peels of laughter rang in Ruth's ears as she slammed the door. She ran down the steps and along the alleyway to Thames Road, where her VW was parked. In the sanctuary of her car, she waited for her tears to subside, then blew her nose and drove slowly to the office.

On Tuesday evening Josh and Max returned from Paris and bought fish and chips on their way home from Kew Station. Max hugged the warm brown carrier bag to his chest, looking forward to his late supper as they hurried along the moonlit towpath, a light frost making the tarmac sparkle. His little gang of ducks bobbed on the water, quiet and sleepy and Max looked at them wistfully, regretting that he couldn't take them to Paris with him. He looked up at his father. 'It'll be nice looking after Bonaparte, won't it, Dad?'

Josh looked down at him and smiled, guessing what was in Max's mind. 'It'll be very nice, Max. And as soon as we get settled, we must start looking for a friend for him. There are lots of pet shops across the river near the Pont Neuf, quite near Rue Jacob; I expect we'll find one there.'

'Yes,' said Max, his eyes still on his ducks.

'And it'll be fun seeing Tom every day, won't it?'

'Is he *really* my uncle, Dad, or is that just one of his wind-ups?'

'No, it's not a wind-up. He really is your uncle, but it's not a big deal, is it?'

'No, but he is quite bossy, and he speaks awfully good French.'

'That's not *his* fault, Max.'

'Yes, but he does it very fast to annoy me.'

Josh laughed. 'You will yourself quite soon, you'll see.'

Max broke into a trot to keep up with his father. 'He's going to be a dog-poo man when he grows up,' he volunteered.

'A *what*?'

'A dog-poo man. They're really cool. They drive

211

about Paris on special green mobilettes, and they hoover up the dog mess into green storage tanks on the back of the bike.'

'What an ambition,' said Josh, as they climbed the steps of the house. 'I hope you can think of something a bit more challenging for yourself when the time comes, Max.'

Josh unlocked the door and they went in. Max went straight to the kitchen with the fish and chips. Josh, putting down the overnight bag and taking off his coat, heard the sound of the television in the sitting-room and looked through the door. A strange man was lying on the sofa watching *News at Ten*.

'Good evening,' said Josh quietly, in a voice that clearly implied 'and who the hell are you?'

Jacob Kroll looked up, quite unconcerned. 'Oh, hello. You must be the husband.' He remained where he was, his eyes straying back to the screen.

Josh frowned. 'I am "the husband", as you put it. Who, may I ask, are you?'

'Jacob Kroll,' said Jake, as though that made everything perfectly clear.

It did not. The name meant nothing to Josh, and if Nastassia had at some time mentioned it to him, he had long-since forgotten it. 'And?' he said.

'And what?' Jake dragged his eyes from the screen with ill-concealed irritation.

'What are you doing here?'

'I am one of Nastassia's tenants.'

Josh's eyebrows shot up. 'Really? How can that be? Both the studios are already let.'

'One of them became vacant. The architect woman has left. I needed a place; Nastassia has leased it to me.'

'Wasn't that a bit sudden?'

Jake shrugged. 'Was it? I wouldn't know, it was nothing to do with me.'

'Where is Nastassia now?'

'Out. At the gym, I think.'

There seemed nothing to be gained by prolonging the conversation, so Josh withdrew to the kitchen and he and Max sat at the table and ate their supper.

'Where's Mummy?'

'At the gym, it seems.'

'Oh. Who's that in the sitting-room?'

'A new tenant.'

'What, instead of Robert?' asked Max.

'No, instead of Ruth.'

'Has Ruth gone?'

'Yes, Max, I'm afraid she has.'

They put the dishes into the dishwasher in silence and Josh took Max up to bed. He looked dead tired, and drooping.

'Do you want a carry, darling?'

'Yes, please.'

Twenty minutes later Josh came downstairs and found Nastassia in the sitting-room, perched on the arm of the sofa, while Jacob Kroll watched yet another news programme.

'Can I have a word, Nastassia?'

She turned her head, as if surprised to see him. 'Yes, of course, darling.' She followed him to the kitchen.

'What's going on, Stassi? Why has Ruth gone?'

'It was her decision, Josh. I suppose she did not want to stay after you and Max go, don't you think?'

'Why should that make any difference?' said Josh wearily, knowing perfectly well why.

'I am not stupid, Josh. I have always known about Ruth and you.'

'There's nothing to know, Nastassia.'

'Really? Few people would agree with that, my dear. Least of all, Ruth herself, if I understood her meaning.'

Josh poured himself a whisky, said he was tired and

213

was going to bed; there seemed nothing more to say.

'By the way,' Nastassia looked up at him with her great blue eyes, 'Jake wants to rent both the studios, so I've given Robert a month's notice.'

Josh stared at her, feeling helpless, then left the room without comment and went up to the spare room.

He drank the whisky slowly, in bed, turning over in his mind the new situation that was being forced upon him. It did not take him long to realize that without Ruth it was going to be extremely difficult to organize his and Max's life properly. He finished the whisky, got out of bed and went to the bathroom to clean his teeth. Reaching for a glass to rinse his mouth, he noticed for the first time an extra toothmug on the shelf above the basin. It was of dark tortoiseshell marked with the small gold initials 'JK'; it contained a matching toothbrush with real bristles and a tube of American dentifrice. Suddenly, the whole humiliating truth of his situation flooded his being, and a horrible sensation invaded his body, as if his insides were actually dissolving. His hands shook as he wrapped his and Max's toothbrushes and the rest of their bathroom gear in a hand-towel, and took them back to the bedroom. He got stiffly back into bed and lay down, still shaking, cold and frightened, and more miserable than he could have believed possible.

In the morning he woke early and lay staring at the slowly lightening sky, trying to make sense of things, to think of a way of getting through the next two weeks without Ruth's help.

He dropped Max off at his school, then drove to his office. All morning he sat at his drawing-board, trying to work normally, taking telephone calls, sorting out problems with his assistant. At one o'clock he was on his way out to buy a sandwich when his phone rang. It was the senior partner's secretary, asking if he could spare a few moments. He went downstairs to Andrew's room.

'Come in, Josh. Take a seat.'

'Thanks.' Josh sat down in the comfortable black leather chair and waited. He was too tired to think of anything sensible to say, in any case.

'Ruth has been telling me about your problems, Josh.'

Josh looked up, startled. 'Oh, God. Has she really?'

'It's OK. She's only spoken to me. I think she needed a shoulder to cry on, poor girl.'

'Yes. Poor Ruth, it was a shitty thing to happen. Where did she go?'

'To her sister's, I think she said.'

'Oh, good.' In the silence that followed, Josh stared at his feet.

Andrew cleared his throat. 'I had a call from Jean-Luc this morning, Josh. They seem very happy to have you on the team.'

'Yes, they were very kind.' He smiled briefly at Andrew.

'Have you found a flat yet?'

'Yes, it's in Rue Jacob. It's very convenient for Max's school and my mother's apartment.'

'Excellent; well done. Would it help you to leave at once, to forget about the notice? All your work appears to be right up-to-date, the handover should be quite straightforward.'

Josh looked up, relief and gratitude flooding his face. 'Would that be possible?'

'Well, you do have three weeks' leave due, and I'm sure you could use the time to get yourself and your small boy settled in, couldn't you?'

'My God,' said Josh, 'it would be an answer to prayer. Thank you, Andrew, it's exactly what we need. I've been getting more and more frantic trying to figure out how to look after Max by myself, and do my job properly.' He looked at the older man, his eyes slightly ashamed. 'I didn't realize how much I had come to rely on Ruth.'

'Well, she wasn't forced to do it, Josh,' said Andrew quietly. 'It was her own choice after all, wasn't it?'

'I suppose so, but I still feel bad about it.'

'Don't. It's not your fault; these things happen. Come on, let's go and have a farewell drink, shall we?'

In the afternoon Josh packed his personal drawing equipment and reference books into cartons and carried them down to his car. He felt as if a huge unbearable load had been lifted from his shoulders, and as he went round the office saying goodbye to the team he was beginning to feel comparatively cheerful. He left at three o'clock to collect Max from school. In the carpark he met Ruth, returning from a site-meeting.

'I'm so sorry, Josh.'

'Yes, Ruth, so am I.'

The next day Josh was woken by Max getting into bed with him. He looked at his watch: ten to seven. 'Busy day ahead, Max. We're going to Paris.'

'Today?'

'Yes, today. We're going to have a holiday. No school for you, no work for me, isn't that great?'

Max sat up and looked at him. 'Is it for always, Dad? Or will we be coming back?'

'Probably not.'

'What about Mummy?'

'She's staying here.'

'Oh.' Max looked out of the window.

'You can't stay with her, darling,' said Josh gently. 'It would be too difficult to fit your hours in with hers, especially now Ruth's not here. It's much easier in

216

Paris; Anna is there all the time, isn't she? You'll see her tonight. She's expecting us.'

'And Tom,' said Max, brightening a little.

'And Patrick and Giò.'

'And Monsieur Petit and Bonaparte.'

'Right,' said Josh. 'Now, what are you going to take?'

'Everything.'

'OK, let's get moving.'

They went down to the kitchen for breakfast and Josh was, on the whole, relieved to find the other occupants of the house already gone.

When Max had said that he was taking everything, he meant exactly that. Every single book and old broken toy was brought down to the kitchen to be packed in the tea chests that Josh had retrieved from the garden shed. 'Divide the things into two piles, Max. The ones you absolutely have to have right away, and the ones that can come in a few days, with your bedroom furniture and my pictures and books, OK?'

'OK.' A large number of toys, mostly teddies and other animals were set aside to travel with them in the car, and the rest were crammed into the tea chests. Josh packed all Max's clothes as well as his own, and took a lot of bedlinen and towels for good measure, spurred on by anger at Nastassia's betrayal of them both. Cruel bitch, he thought, she couldn't even be bothered to say good-bye to her own child, what kind of a monster is she?

Josh had telephoned a firm of carriers first thing and asked them to send someone to pick up the boxes and the furniture right away, since he could not guarantee anyone being at home if they collected the stuff after he had gone. The doorbell rang just as the last neat label and strong parcel tape had been stuck down. 'Good timing,' said Josh, as he answered the door, 'I've just finished the packing.'

After the men had gone he looked in the fridge and

found eggs and a dried-up lump of cheddar cheese. 'Cheese omelette, Max?'

'All right,' said Max. 'I'll get out the bread, shall I?'

In five minutes they sat together, eating their last meal at that table, in that house, though neither of them mentioned the fact. Then they packed their possessions into the car, leaving just enough space for Max on the rear seat.

'It's a shame I can't sit in the front with you, Dad. There'd be more room for everything then, and I could see a lot more, couldn't I?'

'You could, of course. But you're much safer in the back, old chap. It's the law, anyway.'

Josh parked the car in the back road at Grands-Augustins just before eight o'clock. He looked in the rear mirror. Max, his head lolling sideways against a large yellow camel was fast asleep, his cheeks flushed, his fair hair flopping over his eyebrows. Josh got out of the car and took out the overnight bag, then tried to unfasten Max's harness and lift him out without waking him. But the little boy opened his eyes at once, immediately alert. 'Are we there?'

'Yup, we're here,' said Josh. 'Are you awake enough to carry something?'

'Yes, I can carry Gus and Ted.'

'OK, and I'll bring the cases.'

'What about the other things?'

'I'm going to spread this rug over them and put on the burglar alarm; they'll be all right.'

'Are you really sure?' Max sounded anxious.

'As sure as I can be, darling. Nothing's ever *really* sure, is it?'

'No,' said Max, and Josh immediately regretted his words. 'Come on, I'm ravenous, aren't you? I wonder what Anna's got for supper.'

They went up in the shoggly lift, Max counting the floors, got out at the third floor and rang the bell. They heard Tom's voice behind the door: 'They're here! They're here!' and the sound of running footsteps. The door flew open and Tom burst through, followed by Patrick, who grasped Josh's shoulders and kissed him on both cheeks, causing Josh to have a momentary impulse to dissolve into tears. Instead, he let the bags drop to the ground and returned the hug, laughing, glad to be home.

'Am I allowed to kiss you, too, Max? Or are you too English for that?'

'No,' said Max primly. 'I quite like to be kissed, but not by beards.'

Patrick laughed, picked him up and kissed him, then they went into the apartment, softly lit and with a fire burning in the chimney, imparting a faint whiff of woodsmoke to the calm, beautiful room. How lucky I am to be able to come here, said Josh to himself, to get myself together again, to be able to lean on them for a while; to be loved is what I really mean.

Anna came out of the kitchen, consciously composed and smiling, doing her best to keep the atmosphere normal and light-hearted. 'Supper's ready,' she said, as she and Josh exchanged hugs. 'Did you have a good trip, darling?' She bent down to kiss Max and he held out his arms to be picked up. Carrying Max, she led the way to the kitchen, where candles burned on the long table and the delicious scents of cooking filled the air.

'What's the lovely smell?' said Max.

'*Daube*,' said Anna. 'It's a kind of stew.'

'Doesn't smell like stew to me,' said Max.

Chapter Twelve

Since it was a Sunday, and Heleni's day off, Dido got carefully out of bed without waking Guy, put on jeans and a sweater and went to the kitchen to make breakfast. It had rained in the night and although the air was quite fresh, the sky was a clean pale blue with a few white puffs of cloud scurrying westward, driven by the wind from the mountains of the mainland. The olive trees shimmered in the winter sunlight, new-washed and gleaming, and she decided to take the breakfast tray out onto the terrace. She made coffee, and filled blue bowls with thick yoghurt, then made toast from the coarse wholemeal bread and put a jar of honey on the tray. In January, she said to herself, I'll make bitter orange marmalade; I'd love to do that, I've never had the time till now. She stared through the kitchen window, over the restlessly quivering silvery treetops to the blue sea beyond, flecked with white horses. There are lots of things I'd like to do here, she thought, like making a real garden, like restoring the chapel, and learning to play chess with Guy, maybe even learning Greek. She considered her peripatetic childhood with her parents and Mabel, followed by her strangely narrow experience of adult life, as a continuity girl and then production assistant. Suddenly, she had the feeling that her entire life so far had been spent cooped up indoors, first as a child in the poky airless dressing-rooms of opera houses, trailing round the world in her mother's wake; and then earning her own living on dark cold soundstages, pandering to the requirements of the larger-than-life personalities of the directors and actors who turned a simple script into an elaborate fantasy made manifest. Lately, she had begun to realize what an extremely frustrating way of living and working it had been. With each fresh job, she settled into a new company of players and technicians for three months or so, with the inevitable split-up when the work was completed. Sometimes it had felt curiously like the break-up of a family, and then one had to start all over again, forming new relationships, getting used to the particular idiosyncrasies of a completely different set of characters. Dido remembered with astonishment how irrelevant and without interest the ebb and flow of international events had seemed to the members of such tight-knit groups; they were too busy and too emotionally involved with each other to be distracted by anything outside their own small make-believe world. She had often thought that if a bomb had exploded nearby, no one would have even noticed, much less reacted in any way. How did I stick such a pointless and trivial way of life for so long, she asked herself, when I could have been living in a place like this, with a man like Guy? She picked up the tray and carried it out to the terrace, calling to Guy that breakfast was ready. She set out the bowls of yoghurt, the butter, the honey and the toast and was pouring the coffee as he appeared at the sitting-room door and made his way to the table. 'Why didn't you wake me?' he asked.

'Because you were fast asleep and looked so peaceful. Usually you're awake before me. It was nice to see you sleeping for a change.'

'Oh.' He sat down in his chair. 'I hope I don't snore.'

'You don't snore,' said Dido, and laughed.

Guy drank his coffee, and ate his yoghurt, then turned his attention to the delicately brown pile of toast that Dido had made. 'Don't ever tell her I said so, but you make much better toast than Heleni does,' he said, and spread a thick layer of butter on his second piece.

Dido smiled. 'Do you really think I would?'

'No, of course I don't. Now, what would you like to do today? Shall we go somewhere, have lunch?'

'What about Lákones? The place with the tremendous view?'

'Good idea. It's a perfect day for it, cold and clear. Let's do that.'

They set off just before noon, and Dido drove across the ridge of the island through the lanes, joining the main road to Paleokastritsa, and finally taking the narrow, twisting road that climbed for four kilometres up to Lákones. The surface was tarmac, but full of pot-holes and so tortuous that Dido prayed that they would not meet another car, on its way down. Her prayers were answered and they reached the village without incident. There were few signs of tourism in the main street, though one gnarled old man wearing a black overcoat and a greasy-looking trilby hat, lurked in a doorway strumming on a guitar with a large, angry-looking cockerel perched on the end of the fretboard.

'Good heavens,' said Dido. 'Look at that bird!'

'*Don't* look at it, whatever you do, or he'll try to persuade you to pay to take a photo of him.'

'Oh.'

She drove on slowly, pausing to look through the open doors of an olive press, dark and mysterious, its massive beams and stone troughs silently brooding, awaiting the coming of spring and the olive harvest. Then the troughs would be filled with the ripe olives, the heavy beams would turn the grinding stones

222

and the pressed oil would trickle through a pipe at the base of the trough into underground storage tanks. Even now, a strong rank smell emanated from the sacks of dried olive refuse stacked against the walls of the press, waiting to be sold as winter fuel.

They passed through the village and presently reached their destination, a taverna aptly named *Bella Vista*. They got out of the car and made their way to the terrace perched high above the panorama of the entire bay of Paleokastritsa, divided into separate clover leaf-shaped coves, brilliantly blue against the green-clad rocky shoreline, the myrtles and olives punctuated by occasional clumps of dark soaring cypresses. On a little promontory, jutting out into the blue crystal water, stood the monastery, white, serene and beautiful in its simplicity, its triple bell-tower etched sharply against the dark sea, the three great bronze bells seeming suspended in the clean air. The tiny figure of a monk made his way slowly across a stone-flagged courtyard.

They stood side by side at the parapet, silent as they took in this stunning view. Then Dido turned to Guy, and touched his hand as he leaned on his sticks. 'It's amazing: fabulous. I'm so glad we came, now, when there aren't many people.'

'Yes, it's the best time.'

'Can one visit the monastery?' she asked as they sat down at a table.

'It depends. Sometimes the monks are quite pleased to show you round. Sometimes, it's more difficult; no one seems to be about. I expect it's to do with saints' days and their particular timetable. But there's a very nice little museum, with some lovely old icons, as well as some impressive-looking seashells reputedly found locally, and a few enormous bones. We'll go and have a look on our way back, shall we?'

'Yes, let's.'

The proprietor appeared with a menu, and asked if they would like *astakós,* caught that morning.

'What is it?' asked Dido.

'Salt-water crayfish.'

'Sounds lovely.'

'Right, we'll have it.' Guy ordered the crayfish, with a feta salad to start with, and a bottle of *corífo*.

After they had eaten, they sat drinking their coffee and enjoying the tranquillity of the afternoon and the sensational panorama spread around them. At three o'clock the warmth began to go out of the sun and regretfully they left the *Bella Vista*, and drove down the hill to visit the monastery. An elderly monk, blind but benevolent, showed them the charming small chapel, then the museum and as a special bonus, the neatly tended vegetable garden and the tiny monastery graveyard. Then, evidently tiring of their visit, the old man wished them a safe journey, and vanished through a small door in the garden wall. They made their way back to the carpark, put a contribution in the offertory box prominently displayed, and drove back to Koulari.

When they got home, the sun had fallen behind the mountain and the air was quite cold. Dido put on the kettle and made tea, and brought the tray to the sitting-room. 'I think I'll light the fire,' she said, 'it's really getting colder, isn't it?' She poured Guy's tea, and put it beside him on the wickerwork table. 'And while I'm doing that, why don't you get out the chessmen, Guy? I'd like you to teach me how to play.'

'Would you really?'

'Yes; really. Though I'll probably be moronic at it, so you won't particularly want to play with me very often.'

'Dido,' said Guy seriously, 'the only person I play

224

chess with on Corfu is Greek. He is about eighty-five years old, deaf and with a very poor short-term memory. Because of that, our games are always played at a breakneck pace, which can be exhilarating, but is not exactly the most satisfying way of playing, I have to admit. So, I would be absolutely delighted to teach you, and even more delighted to play with you, I promise.'

'Well, you must tell me if you're bored.'

'I won't be bored.'

Dido lit the fire, using the thin long logs provided by Vassili, and the cakes of crushed olive refuse. The fire burned hot and bright, sending a pleasing shower of sparks up the wide chimney and a comforting warmth into the room. Guy set out the chessmen, and Dido got a stool and sat down opposite him, on her side of the board. He told her the names of the different pieces, how they could be moved, and the object of the game. He watched her as she listened attentively, her lips moving silently as she repeated the names after him: pawn, castle, king, queen, bishop and so on. When he had finished, she looked at him, her eyes bright. 'Is that it?'

'That's it.'

'OK, let's go. Who goes first?'

'You do.'

At Inniscarragh, Lavinia walked in her Italian garden. It was four o'clock in the afternoon and beginning to get dark already. Followed dejectedly by Fritz, she made her way slowly round the labyrinth of box-edged pea-gravel paths. The rows of neatly-clipped yew obelisks shimmered with drops of water after the recent rain and gleamed in the blue crepuscular dusk. The last sodden brown leaves had fallen from the espaliered fruit trees that hugged the rose-red brick walls of the garden and, although there had not yet been a frost of any severity, their naked branches already seemed arthritically locked in the grip of winter. Reaching the bottom of the garden, Lavinia paused by the grey-painted door to the park, but did not open it, still too distressed and outraged by the appalling sight of the devastated woodland on the other side, now an irreversible graveyard of tree stumps.

After the shriek of the chain-saws, each day was now made unbearable by the revving and groaning of the heavy machinery being used to drag the deep-rooted stumps from the ground, and the air was filled with the acrid smoke of the ensuing bonfires. Another machine was being used to dredge the lake, and the evil-smelling sludge was being dumped unceremoniously on top of the crushed and battered azaleas that had previously lined the banks. This act of vandalism was particularly distressing to Lavinia, for she remembered most vividly the planting of those azaleas, all in her mother's favourite shades of pink and orange. They had arrived in the November of Lavinia's fifth year, their big rootballs snugly enclosed in sacking, all ready to be planted in the prepared holes, a spectacular anniversary present from her father to her mother. She recalled minutely the following spring, and the daily walks with her mother to inspect the little pointed green buds as they grew fatter day by day, culminating in the glorious week in which they all burst into heartbreaking bloom and made the woodland glade around the lake a terrestrial heaven. 'Paradise' her mother had called it, in blissful ignorance of the fate that would eventually overtake her special creation. Thank God, thought Lavinia, turning her back on the gate, at least she was spared that, since she had the good sense to die young. The canal that fed the lake was also being dredged, but so far the men had refrained from demolishing the *chinoiserie* bridge. Maybe the dreaded Yakimoto actually *likes* it, she thought sourly, in view of the fact that he's an oriental. She opened the back door and told Fritz to wait while she fetched a towel to wipe his feet. This job done, she ordered him into his basket and went through to the hall, hanging up her coat in the alcove beside the front door. Then she returned to the kitchen to make some tea. While the kettle boiled she looked in the fridge to see what Maeve had left for her evening meal. A plate of cold ham glistened iridescently under a film of plastic wrap, alongside a small dish of thickly-sliced cucumber. On the top of the Raeburn sat a large scrubbed potato, pierced by a metal skewer, waiting to be put in the oven.

Two weeks ago Mrs O'Reilly had given notice, proposing her niece Maeve to take her place. Proudly she had informed Lavinia that she had been offered and had accepted the post of housekeeper up at Inniscarragh, and was being paid a very good retainer while she worked out her notice. Equally proudly, Lavinia told her to leave as soon as she wished, in case Mrs O'Reilly should be under any illusions as to the low esteem in which she was held by her employer. It had not been a wise move, she was well aware, for Maeve was slipshod to a degree, and worse, seemed not to give a tinker's curse one way or the other. Lavinia was forced to refrain from criticizing her in case she too marched up to Inniscarragh and got herself a job. Now, she inspected the potato and observed with distaste the dark stain forming in the hole where the skewer had broken the skin, and knew that when split and opened, the inside of the baked potato woud be black and scarcely fit to eat. She pulled out the skewer and threw the potato in the bin. The kettle boiled and she put a Lapsang Souchong tea bag into a mug, pouring the water over it and stirring it with a teaspoon. When the tea had reached the desired strength, she used the spoon to flick the bag expertly out of the mug and into the sink. This was a habit entirely against her principles but she had become increasingly irritated with emptying the teapot into the sink-tidy, then wrapping the sodden tea leaves in wet newspaper parcels for the bin. Nonetheless, she was conscious of a lowering of her standards, and looked with regret at her pretty Spode cups and saucers.

She took her mug to the sitting-room, put it on a mat on the small round galleried rosewood table beside her chair, and removing the spark-screen, stirred her fire to a blaze. She sat down in her chair, wedging the small tapestry cushion into the small of her aching back and began to drink the tea, inhaling the sharp tarry smell. She looked at the chair on the other side of the fireplace and with a rare flash of imagination saw Guy sitting there on his last visit to her house. In retrospect, although still basically deeply angry with him for not doing more to protect the family property, she was annoyed with herself for having made it clear to Guy that his crippled state had not been entirely accidental. It was not his pain and ruined life that she regretted, more the fact that she had rashly admitted her own murderous intentions towards him, in order to remove him from her path. It was a pity he was born at all, she thought, I'm sure he wasn't really intended. After all, I was sixteen when he was born, horrid little screaming thing. She sighed, and gazed sadly into the fire. Sixteen, she thought, the age of agony and bliss. She remembered the St Stephen's Day meet at Inniscarragh that year, and the hunters being walked round from the stable-yard while she and her father and their house-guests emerged from the ceremonial entrance like royalty, mounting their horses from the stone blocks on either side of the terrace steps. Those were the days, she thought nostalgically, when each guest brought his own groom, two horses, a manservant and a lady's maid; there was no unemployment then. I'm sure they all had great times in the servants' hall – they certainly ate and drank enough, mother used to say. She stared into the flames and heard again the huntsman's horn, saw the close-packed hounds arriving from the kennels, their tails a waving forest, the Inniscarragh hounds with lovely names like Blossom, Fly and Satan, streaming round the corner of the house like a brown and creamy-yellow river, long pink tongues lolling. Her mother had stopped hunting by then and Lavinia wore her old habits, partly for the sake of economy but mostly because the stuff from which they were made was so exquisitely soft, yet strong and supportive, moulded to her figure like a corset, and every stitch done by hand. Her boots and silk topper were her own, the very best to be had, of course. Soft leather gloves and her slim, silver-topped whip completed the outfit, and Lavinia knew herself to be the most beautiful girl in the county, if not in the whole of Ireland, with her glossy black curls and stunning green eyes. Her mother, carrying the baby Guy in her arms had watched enviously from the terrace, recognizing the ghost of her own lost youth in her daughter, as Lavinia wove her way skilfully through the riders, greeting friends, flirting outrageously, on her beautiful black horse with the warning red ribbon tied to his tail.

I should have married Freddy, Lavinia said to herself, replacing her mug on the table. He was a fool, but he was quite good-looking and he was rich, very rich. I know how important that is; *now*, when it's too late. Freddy had been at her side, worshipping and attentive at every meet, every ball, every race-meeting, and had been hers for the taking. But Lavinia's sights had been firmly fixed on another man, an older man, clever and witty and extremely amusing; a friend of her father's, a diplomat, no less. Arthur had been Lavinia's first and only lover and the affair had lasted for two enchanted years, with clandestine meetings in Dublin hotels and snatched moments of joy behind the banks of glossy evergreens spiked with white gardenias that had been in fashion at all the grand country house balls at that time. It had been the high emotional point of Lavinia's life, but when she ceased to laugh, to make jokes and amuse him and instead became serious and intense about their relationship, Arthur, with brutal swiftness, ended the affair. He was, as Lavinia very well knew, a married man and had no intention whatsoever of putting either his marriage or his career at risk.

She never saw him again to speak to, and if they happened to be at the same race-meeting or ball he would vanish like the snow in summer before she had a chance even to say hello or touch his hand. He came with his wife to her parents' funeral and after the interment had paused briefly to offer his condolences to Uncle James and Lavinia as they stood together in the windswept little graveyard. 'We are so sorry, James', he had said, with a cool nod to Lavinia, standing tall and blackly veiled, distant and pale by her uncle's side. Afterwards, at the wake, she had scanned the crowd, hoping to catch sight of him, but he was not there, and presumably had not felt inclined to come.

I was a fool, Lavinia said to herself, as the tight, remembered pain gripped her heart as fiercely as it ever had, and the same bitter scalding tears filled her eyes and slid unchecked down her carefully rouged cheeks. I loved him, the hateful brute; and the real shame of it is that I still do, I always will, even though he wrecked my life just as surely as I wrecked Guy's.

Once he had removed all the hideous wallpaper and paint from the walls of the new apartment, Josh found himself undecided about the kind of atmosphere he wished his new home to have. His own natural inclination was towards a calm austerity but he realized that this would be neither suitable nor desirable for a small boy bereft of his mother. Rather than seek Anna's advice, he turned to Giò for help. Giò, who had held back with an admirable restraint quite alien to his nature, was enchanted to be asked for suggestions, and although it was his busiest time of the year at *Le Patrimoine*, he instructed his assistant to hire another girl for the Christmas season, and threw himself into the furnishing and decorating of Josh's apartment with typical enthusiasm. With all the walls stripped back to the original lime plaster, a pleasing blotched ivory colour, his initial idea was to leave the walls exactly as they were, to cover the floors throughout the apartment with sea-grass and to paint the skirting-boards in a matching colour. The glazing bars of the windows were to be painted ivory, with an egg-shell finish, with the deep reveals of the windows treated in the same way to reflect as much light into the rooms as possible.

'Great,' said Josh. 'I love it.'

'What about furniture? What do you need?'

'We need beds. Well, I do. Max's is on its way from London.'

'OK,' said Giò. 'A bed for you, and a decent big sofa for the sitting-room, plus a proper armchair, I think, don't you?'

'I suppose.'

'What about pictures? Books?'

'They're all at Grands-Augustins,' said Josh. 'Lots of books, lots of pictures; they're still in the packing cases.'

'What kind of pictures are they? Big? Small? Paintings? Prints?'

'They're mostly large black-and-white architectural prints, Piranesi etchings, that sort of thing.'

'The frames?'

'Narrow black ones.'

Into Giò's mind's eye leapt an image of the room, with the walls lime-washed a warm, deep terracotta red and covered in the Piranesi prints, hung close together, their glass reflecting the light from the street. Underneath the prints he saw a large comfortable sofa covered in a quilted paisley fabric in shades of orange, pink and scarlet with a row of matching cushions along the back. He saw concealed uplighters illuminating the pictures and the books, stored in mahogany bookshelves built into the alcoves on either side of the chimney breast. He saw a pale wooden long-case clock, its brass pendulum quietly swinging from side to side behind a round glass window in its bulbous base, its cracked parchment face with black Roman numerals telling not only the time, but revealing the phases of the moon behind small circular windows. He saw big, important lamps on either side of the sofa, modern brass ones, with glossy black shades. Then, going completely over the top, Giò saw a palm tree, almost as tall as the ceiling, its finely cut leaves lit from below by the uplighters, throwing magical shadows all over the ceiling.

Giò hesitated, then began to describe his ideas to Josh, who listened carefully, without interrupting. 'What do you think? Does it all sound totally horrendous to you, Josh?'

Josh smiled. 'No, it doesn't at all. It's not what I would have thought of for myself, but for Max I think it would be terrific; warm, welcoming and fun.' He laughed. 'Especially the palm tree; he'll love that, I know.'

'Well, good,' said Giò, relieved. 'So, what else?'

'Behind the chimney breast is the original fireplace, I'm pretty sure,' said Josh. 'Do you think Monsieur Petit would object to us opening up the chimney? A fire would be nice, or maybe a wood-burning stove?'

'Good idea,' said Giò, 'we'll ask him.'

They decided that the kitchen and the bathroom should be functional, modern and easy to clean, and that they should employ a professional plumber to install the necessary new equipment and to fit an extractor fan in the loo on the landing.

'OK,' said Josh. 'That just leaves the bedrooms.'

'You'll want to arrange your own room, of course. But I'd love to do Max's, with his help, if you'll allow me to.'

'Would you really, Giò? Can you really spare the time? There's so much to do, isn't there? And then soon it'll be Christmas.'

'I *can* spare the time, and nothing would give me greater pleasure.' He looked at Josh. 'Talking of Christmas, do you have any plans?'

'Mum wants us to go with them to Normandy, and then go down to Souliac for the New Year. It's probably the best idea, I suppose. Nice for Max to be with Tom; a lot more fun for him than being on his own with me. What about you? I suppose you're going to Souliac?'

'Well, that was the plan, yes. Olivia and Baz will be there, and I haven't seen either of them for ages. But I've been thinking; Christmas with children is such a special thing, maybe I'll ask Anna if she could squeeze me in too, at St Gilles. Then we could all go south for the *réveillon*, couldn't we?'

'Sounds great,' said Josh, and almost made himself believe it.

The decorating of the apartment had been finished in record time, the furniture found, upholstered and put in place, the bookshelves built and filled with books, the pictures hung. Even the palm tree sat robustly in its Anduze pot, its curved green fronds almost brushing the ceiling. The fireplace had been opened up, the chimney relined and a small wood-burning stove now sent out its comforting warmth, looking as if it had done so for years.

'You're a genius, Giò.' Josh walked round his new home with astonishment.

'I know,' said Giò, smiling. 'Someone has to be, so why not me?'

Max's room, small and white, was already furnished with his own bed and cupboards and was overflowing with his books and toys, but Giò's instinct told him that it was very probably still too much like his original room in London, so he planned a trip with Max to Clignancourt to see what the flea markets had to offer that might appeal to the little boy.

On Saturday morning Josh packed his and Max's clothes, ready for the move that evening to Rue Jacob, and his first night with his son in their new home. Giò and Max had already departed on their expedition to the flea markets, and Josh reflected, not for the first time, on his good ʾrtune in having a family such as his. They're not just generous with their money and possessions, he said to himself, but with their time as well; they really do care about us.

Anna knocked on the door and came in, carrying a pile of freshly-ironed shirts. 'That's the lot, I think,' she said, putting the laundry on the chest, and sitting down on Max's bed.

'Thanks, Mum,' said Josh, picking up the pile of shirts and packing them carefully into a suitcase. 'I don't know what we'd have done without you, all of you.'

'Well, you know what they say, don't you? Family is the one place where you can turn up and they have to let you in.' She laughed.

'Perhaps. But I bet some doors fly open a jolly sight quicker than others.' He glanced at his mother. 'So, when will you and Patrick come and see the apartment? We're almost ready for visitors.'

'Whenever you ask us, darling.'

Josh recognized that this was as near to reproaching him for excluding her from his life that Anna would ever get. But he said nothing, and carefully zipped up Max's grip. He put the bag on the floor and sat down on a chair he remembered from his childhood. He did not look at Anna, but kept his eyes steadfastly on his feet. 'Mum,' he said quietly, 'how did you feel all those years ago when Dad buggered off and left you to bring up me and Olivia all alone? Or is it too long ago to remember it clearly?'

'I remember it as if it were yesterday,' said Anna, 'though it no longer gives me pain to think about it.' She thought for a few moments, frowning, then continued. 'I felt frightened, ill, and in total despair. My brain seemed incapable of functioning at all coherently, and for a long time I clung tenaciously, and very stupidly as it turned out, to the pathetic hope that your father would come back and everything would be all right. Then, after a while, I had to force myself to face the truth and try to get on with life, more than anything because of you two children. As a matter of fact, I was in such a state of mental confusion and grief at the time, that if I hadn't had you and Olly depending absolutely on me, I would very likely have walked into the river.'

'*Really*? You amaze me. You always seemed to me to be so strong, and hardworking and wonderful. I loved our little house and all the glorious altarpieces and putti that lived there with us while you worked your magic on them. You were easily the most important influence in my life at that time.'

It was Anna's turn to be surprised. 'Good heavens, I'm sure I wasn't. I considered you my intellectual superior from quite an early age, in fact.' She laughed, wryly. 'I remember the humiliation when I had to admit that I couldn't even understand your maths prep, much less help you with it.'

'Academic achievements aren't everything, Mum,' said Josh. 'Talent and experience are far more important, and real. Trouble with me is, lack of it. Experience I mean.' He looked up with a rueful smile. 'I suppose I'm getting it now, aren't I?'

'I'm afraid so,' said Anna. 'It's strange how history repeats itself, isn't it? I was only a couple of years older than you are now when Jeffrey left me, and Patrick was even younger when his first wife and their baby were killed, so we've all had early experience of loss and bereavement. It's not just a thing that happens to the elderly, is it?'

Josh said nothing, but his dark eyes were full of pain. He got up abruptly and began to fill the remaining suitcase, his back turned towards her.

Anna went to the door. 'I'll make some coffee,' she said.

'Thanks, Mum. I could use some.'

'Josh?'

'Mm?'

'Promise me something?'

'What?'

'You wouldn't ever think of walking into the river yourself, would you?'

Josh turned towards her and shook his head. 'No, I'd never do that. I'm in the same boat as you were, Mum. I've got Max to look after, haven't I?'

Giò parked his van in a side street near the Métro at Porte de Vanves, and locked it carefully. Then he and Max headed for the flea market, already crammed with bargain hunters turning over the boxes of books, scarves, lace, old records and every kind of relic from the past. Small traders operated from the pavements using makeshift stalls that folded up and disappeared at the end of the day, but there were other more permanent stalls, really little specialist shops selling everything from eighteenth-century chairs to army surplus clothing. Giò and Max looked at the Victorian wax-faced dolls, the piles of lacy bed linen, the Thirties lamps and art deco china and vintage postcards of Paris. The market was noisy, crowded and quite alarming for a small boy. It was also alarming for Giò, who was suddenly gripped with anxiety that he would lose Max in the crush. 'Give me your hand, Max,' he said. 'Let's get out of here; there are too many people.'

It was some years since Giò had last visited the *puces*, and he felt extremely disappointed at how tawdry and tourist-oriented it had become. Gone were the days when you could pick up really collectable things at bargain prices, that was obvious. Oh well, he thought, think again. They went into a small, cosy-looking café and ordered coffee, a coke and *pain au chocolat*. They sat at a table in the window and were served by a pretty girl with a mass of dark, curly hair, wearing a black velvet dress printed with florid red roses. She brought their order, wished them *bon appétit* and retired behind her large espresso machine and glass-fronted counter containing all manner of good things to eat. The room was delightfully decorated with many pictures, and even more glass cases hanging on the walls, containing brilliantly coloured butterflies, exotic stuffed birds from the tropical islands, and even large, sinister-looking sea creatures and ferocious-looking fish, puffed up and covered in sharp spikes. Potted plants, lushly green and heavily scented hung in tasselled baskets from the ceiling, interspersed with silver witch-balls in various sizes. In the centre of the ceiling, where a light fitting would normally have been, hung a remarkable model carousel. Carved from wood and beautifully painted, the creator of this lovely toy had not restricted himself to equipping it with horses only, though there were many of these noble creatures; black, white and grey ones with bared teeth and flaring nostrils, ridden by intrepid jockeys in striped caps and black boots. In addition were several motor cars of the vintage years, including a de Dion Bouton, a Daimler-Benz and a Hispano-Suiza, each car complete with drivers and passengers in dustcoats, caps and goggles, the ladies swathed in veils.

'Look, Giò,' said Max, his dark eyes lighting up with surprise and pleasure when he saw the wondrous thing, gently turning in the warm air of the café.

Giò looked up, following Max's gaze. He gave a small whistle of astonishment.

'Would you like to see the carousel working?' asked the girl, observing their interest.

'We would,' said Giò. 'Thank you.'

The young woman pressed a hidden switch, the carousel's tiny lights came on, and it began to revolve slowly, the horses and cars moving up and down in a stately manner, while the hurdy-gurdy man in the middle played a jolly tune, and his monkey leapt up and down, taking off his little cap and putting it on again. Giò and Max watched the lovely thing revolving, speechless with amazement and pleasure. At last the tune came to an end, the horses and cars came slowly to a halt and the little lights went off, one by one. Max heaved a great sigh, and took a noisy rattling swig of his Coke through the straw. Giò looked at the young woman and thanked her. 'What a pity it's not for sale,' he said.

The girl waved her hands expressively round the room. 'Everything is for sale, *monsieur*,' she said.

'*Everything*?' said Giò.

'Everything except me, *monsieur*,' she replied and laughed, her cheeks pink.

Giò looked at Max, who stared back at him with anxious eyes. Giò smiled. 'What do you think, Max? Would you like it for your room?'

'It must be awfully expensive?'

'Let's ask.'

The girl mentioned a sum that sounded like thousands and thousands of francs to Max, and Giò took out his cheque book. He turned back to Max. 'Anything else, Max, while we're at it? Christmas is coming, after all.'

Max's eyes swept round the room and rested on a case of stuffed ducks. They were ordinary mallards just like the ones at home in London. He hesitated, then looked away and his eye fell on a particularly nasty-looking stuffed snake coiled round a lichen-encrusted tree stump, a sinister bulge in its stomach, presumably the evidence of a recent meal, the entire thing contained in a large glass case. *Brilliant*! said Max to himself, that's *really cool*! I bet that'd stop Tom putting me down. He'll be sick when he sees it; he'll wish it was his. 'I'd like the snake,' he said boldly, looking straight at Giò. 'Please,' he added.

Giò looked astonished. 'Do you *really* want that? Are you sure you wouldn't rather have the humming birds or the butterflies?'

'No,' said Max firmly. 'Snakes are my favourites.'

'OK,' said Giò, doubtfully. 'If you say so.'

They brought the van round to the front of the café, while the carousel was demounted by a young man in black leather, with a gold ring through his nose, who had appeared from the back of the café. He offered to come round to Rue Jacob to wire up the carousel for Max that very evening.

'How kind of you,' said Giò. He took one of his business cards from his Filofax and wrote the address in Rue Jacob on the back of it. The young man took the card. '*Le Patrimoine*,' he said. 'So you are Monsieur Hamilton?'

'That's me.'

'*Monsieur*, it's possible we might do business? Come, I will show you.' He led the way to the back premises, to a workshop filled with every kind of mechanical toy imaginable as well as model theatres, dolls' houses, even a circus with a tight-rope walker floating back and forth over a ring of growling tigers.

'My God,' said Giò. 'Why haven't I heard of you before now? Bring some of these things to my shop tomorrow, I will include them in my Christmas display. As they sell, you can replace them, of course? I will take twenty per cent, is that OK?'

'That's fine, *monsieur*. Thank you very much.'

They arranged that Guillaume, for that was his name, should come to Rue Jacob at six o'clock, and to *Le Patrimoine* at eleven the next day.

'You don't mind Sunday?' said Guillaume.

'I don't mind Sunday when I'm on to a good thing,' said Giò, and they shook hands.

Chapter Thirteen

Jacob Kroll sat on a cold but convenient stone on a bright December morning, contemplating the Erechtheion. He looked at the caryatids supporting the roof of the temple with some emotion, part joy at their continued existence and part enormous admiration for whomever had carved them from stone so long ago. These are real women, he said to himself, with real hips, real thighs and big breasts; wonderful strong necks, too. No wonder they don't have a problem holding up a roof. They're doing just what women are designed to do — supporting their men, bearing their children and sustaining the family; proper wives and mothers, just like mine. An image of his mother, big, rosy-cheeked, smiling, her wavy grey hair screwed into a bun on top of her head, doing her Friday baking in her warm, spice-smelling kitchen filled his mind's eye. She'll be seventy this year, he reminded himself, I must fly over for her birthday. She'll still be taking care of everything, bossing everyone around, I'm sure. He sighed. She's just what I ran away from, he thought, and just what I desperately need now, God dammit. Bloody Dido, why did she have to rock the boat? Why? I don't *need* this kind of situation, that's for sure.

Jacob had arrived in Athens the night before, and had spent the morning making a close examination of the Acropolis, beautiful in the winter sunlight and practically devoid of tourists. He had wandered from monument to monument, taking photographs and rehearsing in his mind how he was going to persuade Dido to stop playing games and come home with him to *The Maid of Wapping*.

He had not told Nastassia of his proposed visit to Corfu, not wishing to complicate that relationship until he deemed the circumstances appropriate, and the timing entirely convenient to himself, of course. No point in letting a bed get cold as long as he might have need of it, he told himself, with a cynical smile. With hindsight, he did not think that it had been absolutely necessary to mislead Nastassia as to his real intentions by going to the lengths of conducting a bogus phone call, booking a mythical flight to New York, ostensibly to attend an important meeting. In the event, she had shown very little interest in his activities anyway, and had merely wished him a good trip. He had had the distinct feeling that she was quite glad to see the back of him for a few days. Women, he thought, you can't really rely on any of them.

He stood up, took a photograph of the beautiful caryatids, snapped the camera shut and zipped it into a pocket of his padded black silk parka. He began to descend the hill, then picked up a cab and drove to a smart restaurant in the Plaka. After lunch he took another taxi to the airport, and caught the next local flight to Corfu, a journey of a little over half an hour.

He checked into a hotel in Corfu Town, hired a car, bought a map of the island, and drove purposefully towards Koulari. He had still not worked out exactly what he intended to say to Dido, except that he wished her to return home with him immediately. He did not speculate beyond that point, but of one thing he was very sure – he had no intention of giving up either Dido or *The Maid of Wapping*, which was after all *his* home as much as hers, without a struggle. If it came to the crunch, he would bloody well marry her and be done with it. He looked at his watch: ten to five. It would be getting dark in an hour's time. Doesn't matter, he thought, I can drive back to the hotel in the dark perfectly easily; one can hardly get lost here, after all. The coast road wound northward, hugging the wooded hillside, with occasional glimpses through the trees of villages at the water's edge, boats bobbing at anchor, the tiled roofs of houses faded pink in the evening light. To his left, soaring high into the sky above the scrub-clad lower slopes Jacob observed the hard barren rocks that formed the majestic, white-domed mountain of Pantokrátor. To his right, across the pearly luminescent sea, he could see the coastline of Albania, blue and mysterious. He stopped the car, turning on the sidelights, and checked the map care-fully. He figured that Koulari must be about six kilometres further on. He drove slowly along the quiet road, on the lookout for a signpost. Suddenly he saw it, faded to the point of illegibility and stuck into a rough pile of stones at the beginning of what looked like a farm track – minor road was too grand a classification for it. He braked and, looking into his rear mirror, indicated right and turned into the track. Realizing that it was practically dark under the thick canopy of olive trees, he switched on his headlights. Cautiously, he rounded a bend and saw that the track was about to divide. He hit the brakes, frowning, and pulling over to the grassy verge, parked the car. What now? He got out, walked up to the junction of the two lanes and looked carefully around. As his eyes became ac-customed to the gloom he saw, below the left-hand track, a small white cottage, with a donkey tied up in a lean-to shack. That can't be it, surely, he said to himself. Then he saw the neatly-painted sign *Porteous* low down in the verge a little further on, and began to walk quietly down the lane. The cottage appeared to be shut up, and he continued on down through the olive grove, looking around for any sign of life. Suddenly, he saw the long low house with its apricot-coloured rooftiles, the sea glimmering beyond. He thought he heard voices, and looking to his right saw the ruined chapel, a wavering yellow light visible through a great hole in its wall. Then the door opened, creaking on its hinges, and Dido came through it, wearing a scarlet sweater and carrying a lantern, followed by Guy Porteous, carefully negotiating the steps with the aid of his sticks. As Jacob watched, Dido stood the lantern on the ground, and put her arms round Guy's neck. He dropped his sticks, held her tightly in his arms and kissed her, for what seemed to Jacob an inordinately long time. Stunned, he crouched down in the undergrowth and watched as they made their way back to the house.

Jacob sat there, paralysed, as the lights appeared in the windows. He felt curiously shocked as well as astonished. He had not for one moment anticipated that Dido's relationship with Porteous should be of a physical nature. Surely, with his handicaps that had to be out of the question? What *had* he been thinking, then? That Dido had taken a job with the guy – secretary, nurse, whatever? It began to dawn on him that there was a lot going on he hadn't bargained for, and most surprisingly a massive surge of jealous rage overwhelmed him. It was an extremely unpleasant feeling, and one he had never before experienced. He took several deep breaths and tried to dismiss such a negative and uncool emotion from his consciousness. After all, he told himself, it was he, Jacob Kroll, who called the sexual shots, wasn't it? Everyone knew that.

The lovely sound of one of Strauss's *Four Last Songs* floated from the house and seemed to hang in the still olive grove. As he listened, Jacob was unable to prevent himself being filled with a self-pitying regret. The music ended, and he got unsteadily to his feet. What now? Should he go down and confront them? He could hear their quiet indistinct voices through the open window, then the chink of glasses and bottles and a burst of laughter. No, he said to himself, I won't go in now, I'm too upset and stressed out, I might make a fool of myself. I'll come back in the morning, when I've had time to think and get my act together.

He retraced his steps to the car, observing a light in the little white cottage as he passed. Through the open door he could see a tall handsome black-haired woman stirring a cooking-pot on the stove. A short swarthy Greek came round the side of the cottage carrying a bundle of brown nets. '*Kali spera*,' said the man and Jacob raised his hand, mumbled something and walked quickly back to the car.

'Vassili says there is a stranger last night,' said Heleni, as she put a fresh pot of coffee on the breakfast table.

'Oh?' said Guy. 'Did he say anything?'

Heleni shook her head. 'I think he is not speaking, no.'

Guy looked at Dido. 'How odd. Who could it be, in the middle of December?'

'Can't imagine. Someone got lost, maybe?'

'Yes, probably. Now, what shall we do today?'

'Well, I thought that perhaps we could begin making a plan for the garden. I was thinking that rather than trying to make the place look English we could maybe dig out a few carefully chosen holes, fill them with good soil and plant cranesbills and artemisias which would flower all summer long and seed themselves among the olives. Does that sound terrible?' Dido looked at Guy anxiously.

'No, it doesn't; it sounds lovely. What about some

245

roses at the foot of the terrace, and perhaps climbing up a few of the very old trees?'

'Wonderful,' said Dido, relieved. 'I thought that you might not want to do anything to spoil the wildness – make it all twee and suburban.'

'No chance of that; it'll be a struggle to keep anything alive in the heat, you'll see.' Guy laughed. 'You make me sound like a real old reactionary, guarding my patch, Dido.'

'It's not that. It's just that I don't want to seem like a philistine.'

'If I were that much of a purist, I wouldn't have built my vulgar little swimming pool, would I?'

'True,' said Dido, 'but thank goodness you did; I love it.'

'So do I.'

After breakfast they began to make a plan of the house and the surrounding land, marking the positions of the olive trees, the pool, the chapel and the various paths as accurately as they could, intending to do a proper measured version at a later date. They sat side by side at the table in the sitting-room, making suggestions and counter-suggestions as to the colours and positioning of the plants, marking the agreed spots with crayons of the appropriate shade. They heard the noise of a car approaching the house, then coming to a halt. 'Did you hear a car?' asked Dido, looking up from her drawing.

'I did. Heleni's in the kitchen, isn't she? She'll see to it.'

But Heleni was not in the kitchen, keeping her usual watchful eye, and in a couple of minutes they heard a heavy footfall on the wooden steps of the terrace, then a tall figure appeared in the open French windows, silhouetted against the sunlit dazzle of the sea and the cold blue winter sky. It was Jacob Kroll.

'Jake!' Dido leapt to her feet, knocking over her chair as she did so. 'What on earth are you doing here?'

'I've come to take you home, Dido.'

'You've *what*?'

'I'm taking you home.'

'Hang on a minute,' said Guy calmly. 'Sit down, Kroll, and explain yourself.'

Jacob took off his parka, draped it over the back of the sofa and leaned against it, folding his arms across his chest. He stared at Guy, his eyes hostile behind his horn-rimmed spectacles. He began to speak in a quiet, unemotional voice. 'Do you have any idea, Porteous, of how long Dido and I have been together? To all intents and purposes, we are married, and I wish us to remain so.'

'But *I* do not!' Dido interrupted, loudly. 'Can't you understand that? God knows, I've said it often enough, why can't you just accept it, Jake? I don't want to live with you any more; our relationship is finished, absolutely. Please go away.'

Jacob looked at Dido levelly, his eyes unnaturally bright. 'It didn't seem like that at Inniscarragh, did it? And that was only a month ago, wasn't it, darling?'

'What do you mean?' said Dido faintly, gripped by a terrible sensation of panic.

'Don't come the innocent with me, Dido. Our jolly little bonk in the stable, sweetheart, that's what I mean. And don't pretend you didn't enjoy yourself; you loved it. It was great, you always did like a bit of the rough.'

The blood drained from Dido's face. 'It was rape, Jake. You know it was.' Her voice sounded strange and little more than a whisper. In anguish, she looked at Guy, her eyes full of tears.

'Dido, is this true?' asked Guy quietly.

'Ha!' shouted Jacob, jumping up. 'I knew it! She didn't tell you about it, did she, Porteous? If it was

247

really *rape*, that's the very first thing she would have done, isn't it?'

'It was rape,' replied Dido flatly. She sounded hopeless, almost past caring. She stared at Guy, who stared back at her, pale, his dark blue eyes full of pain. 'How could you doubt me, Guy?' she said quietly, reproachfully. 'How *could* you?' She walked swiftly out onto the terrace, and stood at the balustrade, looking out to sea, her back turned.

Guy stared after her, his mind in turmoil, full of fear, anger and jealousy. A vivid image of Dido and Kroll making love in the stable invaded his head, and he dug his fingernails into the sweating palms of his clenched fists as hard as he could, trying to regain some kind of control. Since he was unable to stand up and beat Kroll to a pulp as he would have dearly loved to do, nor had a gun to hand with which to kill him, he knew that he must rely exclusively on his intellectual ability to try to overcome the hideous threat that had come so swiftly and insidiously into his life. He looked up at Jacob coldly. 'Sit down, Kroll,' he ordered.

Jacob sat on a chair facing Guy. He guessed that Guy felt both betrayed and angry and was therefore extremely vulnerable. He began to speak, but Guy cut him short. 'Shut up, for Christ's sake, and listen to what *I* have to say.'

'Well, what *do* you have to say?'

'This,' said Guy slowly, his brain working furiously. 'You come here out of the blue, enter my house without an invitation, claiming that Dido is your wife, and that you recently exercised your conjugal rights over her. Is this correct?'

'You got it.'

'Dido, on the other hand, rejects that assertion, insisting that the episode is best described as rape.'

Jacob Kroll laughed. 'Well, she would say that,

248

wouldn't she? My answer to that is: pull the other one. We had a terrific time, we always do. She's an ace little performer in that respect, or don't you know that?'

At that moment Dido marched back into the room and, scarlet with fury, picked up one of Guy's sticks, and brought it down with all her strength across Jacob's back. With a yell, he leapt to his feet and wrenched the stick from her grasp. 'Bloody little cat!' he shouted. 'You could have split my skull!'

'I wish I had, you evil, troublemaking bastard!' She rushed at him again, clawing at his face with her nails. Laughing, he grabbed her hands, pulling her close to him. Tears of rage and humiliation filled her eyes, as she struggled to free herself. 'Let me go, you bullying thug!'

'Let her go, at once, Kroll.' Guy's voice was cold, quiet and authoritative. Jacob released Dido's hands, backed away from her, and put the stick on the table, in front of Guy.

'Sit down, both of you.' Again, Guy spoke with authority, and Jacob sat down once more, smiling superciliously.

Dido, however, chose to remain standing. What's going on here? she asked herself. Is this a court of law, or what? It seems to me that I am on trial here, somehow; that Jake is giving evidence against me, and that Guy is the judge and jury. She glared at Guy, her arms folded belligerently across her chest.

'Please, Dido,' said Guy mildly, 'won't you sit down?'

'Why?'

'So that we can discuss this business sensibly.'

'What business?' Dido's voice rose. 'Picking over the disgusting details of Jake's making me have sex with him, against my will? Which *I* know was *rape*, in plain English, and which *he* says was not. Is that what we're going to discuss? Do you want me to supply some sordid details about *him*, Guy? Is that what you want? Is it? Do you want a blow-by-blow account?'

'No, of course I don't.'

'I see. You're only interested in hearing *his* version, is that it?'

Guy passed his hand across his eyes, confused, trying to think coherently. Then he drew a deep breath, and looked across the table at Jacob Kroll, so cool and confident, leaning back in his chair, his eyes behind the heavy spectacles mocking and without shame. 'It seems obvious,' he said, 'that Dido has three options open to her.' As he spoke, his words sounded legalistic, pompous and unconvincing, even to himself. 'One, she returns to England with you. Two, she remains here with me. Three, she decides to do neither of these things, but rejects us both. In the circumstances, the third option seems to me to be the one she will probably choose.'

Again, Kroll laughed his self-assured, infuriating laugh. 'Do you really believe that? Dido's very domestic, she likes having someone to look after, or hadn't you noticed?'

'Do you mind?' Dido interrupted, angrily. 'Have you both quite finished planning my life for me, in this insulting way?'

Guy ignored this interjection, and continued to look steadily at Jacob Kroll. 'Surely the really important thing in all this should be her happiness, shouldn't it?'

'And what about *my* bloody happiness? And *my* home? You seem unmoved at the idea that I have a strong emotional involvement here, that *I* have rights too. After all, she is my common-law wife, isn't she? I *do* have rights, as a lawyer you must know that.'

'But haven't you constantly made a mockery of this so-called marriage by your infidelity? Is it so surprising that she wishes you out of her life? You haven't exactly brought her happiness, have you?'

'Maybe not, according to your tight-arsed British values, but she sure as hell likes screwing. Can *you* give her that?'

'I don't think that should concern you, Kroll.'

'But it *does* concern me, and it concerns Dido. I don't imagine that you can put on much of a show in that department, can you?'

Jacob Kroll looked insolently across the table at Guy, who stared at his hands, gripping the edge of the table, white-knuckled. Jacob stood up, and put on his parka. He took a letter from his pocket and put it on the table. 'This is for Dido,' he said. He turned towards her. 'Please read it, when you're not so upset.'

Dido turned her head way, refusing to meet his eye.

'I'll be off, then. Goodbye.'

'Get out of my house,' said Guy.

Well satisfied that he had succeeded in sewing undeniable seeds of doubt in Guy's mind, Jacob walked past Dido to the French windows and departed the way he had come, whistling cheerfully. In a moment, the car roared into life and was driven swiftly away up the hill, its wheels spinning on the stony, dry track.

Twisting round in his chair, Guy got unsteadily to his feet and gathered his sticks together. Then, without looking at Dido, he crossed the room to the sofa. He sat down, lifted his legs carefully onto the sofa, and then lay down, his hands clasped behind his head. He stared unseeingly at the terracotta-painted timbers of the ceiling and asked himself a lot of extremely painful questions, to which he could not find any convincing answers. Oh Dido, he said to himself miserably, if it *was* rape why didn't you tell me about it, my dear love? Was it naïve of me to believe that there would never be any secrets between us? Was it? Or did you really make love with him because you wanted to, or even *needed* to, poor girl? Perhaps that bastard Kroll is right, and I really am totally inadequate. He could not trust himself to speak, much less ask Dido whether this was after all the truth of the matter.

The silence in the room became ominously protracted, and pregnant with Dido's anger and frustration. Incredulously, she stared at the back of the sofa, unable to believe that Guy could ignore her in this way, as though she no longer existed for him. She felt cold and numb, though her cheeks were burning. In the kitchen, she could hear Heleni chopping onions, or something, on a board. I wonder how much she heard, or understood? she asked herself, and quailed at the thought of that dark, condemning eye upon her.

Quite suddenly, a mood of stubborn rebellion came upon her, and a cold decisiveness. I'm bloody well not going to stay here and be treated like a criminal, she told herself angrily. I shall clear off; get the hell out of this place; go home. I need to get away; to be on my own again. She crossed the room to the telephone, looked up the number of the airport in the address book, and made a reservation for the next day's flight to London. Then she replaced the telephone in its cradle, made her way to the table, and silently began to gather together the drawings of the projected garden.

'Was that really necessary, Dido?' Guy's voice sounded curiously dull, and distant.

'Was what really necessary?'

'Booking a flight, of course.'

'It's the best thing, isn't it?' She shoved the drawings and crayons roughly into a drawer. 'It's quite obvious that there's no future for me here.'

'Why should you think that?'

'Because it's true. You think I behaved like a whore.'

252

Guy closed his eyes, and sighed. 'I don't think anything of the sort, Dido.'

'Well, you certainly gave that impression.' Dido picked up the letter that Jake had left for her, and tore it into shreds. She carried the pieces to the fireplace and set fire to them with a match. She watched the small blue and yellow flames consuming the thick paper until all that remained was a heap of black flakes, with faint though still legible writing on them. She could read the words: *With my undying love, Jake.* She scattered the ashes with the poker.

There was a light knock on the kitchen door, and Heleni came in. She asked Guy, rather pointedly, whether he wished her to serve lunch.

'Yes, very well,' he said. 'Is that all right for you, Dido? Or would you prefer a drink first?'

'Whatever,' she said. She got to her feet, went to the bedroom and began to pack her things.

The rest of the day passed slowly and silently. The gulf between them seemed to widen, and they could find less and less to say to each other. In spite of his efforts to refute Kroll's claims concerning Dido, and to accept without question her innocence in the whole sordid business, Guy was so full of hurt, dismay and jealousy that he was unable to expunge the shameful images that filled his mind, or to calm himself sufficiently to think rationally. He lay silently on the sofa all afternoon, ostensibly sleeping. Dido, equally silent and angry, finished her packing.

Heleni served their dinner in an uneasy silence, her troubled dark eyes anxious and alarmed as she tried to guess what was happening. She and Vassili had correctly guessed that whatever it was, the stranger was the cause of the trouble. When Guy told Vassili that he was to drive Dido to the airport the following morning, a look of real compassion flowed from one man to the other and Guy turned away brusquely. 'That's all, Vassili,' he said.

'Sir,' replied Vassili, quietly.

At ten o'clock they went to bed, tired and unhappy. For the last time, Dido undid the buckles of the leg-irons and massaged Guy's legs. He thanked her politely and got into bed. He picked up *The Iliad* from the night-table and began to read. Dido went to the bathroom, undressed and washed. For the first time in weeks, she put on a nightdress. She cleaned her teeth and went through to the bedroom. She sat on the foot of the bed. 'Would you rather I slept in the other room, Guy?'

Guy put down his book, and looked at her. 'Not especially, why?'

'I just thought you might prefer it.' She got into bed beside him. He put his free arm round her and began to read again. She turned her head and rested her cheek against the crook of his shoulder, inhaling the familiar salty smell of his skin. What am I doing? she asked herself. I can't be leaving him. I love him; this is mad. Surely we can make it all right again?

'Guy?'

'Mm?'

'Do you think I'm over-reacting, being stupid?'

'In what way?'

'Well, packing my bags and doing a runner as soon as there's a problem.'

Guy had a fleeting urgent impulse to take her in his arms and plead with her to change her mind, and stay with him. Instead, he put down his book and took off his spectacles. 'But this particular problem is a rather fundamental one, isn't it?' he said. 'I can understand that you need time on your own to resolve it, one way or the other.'

Dido opened her eyes and looked at him. 'You think that I'm still attached to Jake, don't you?'

'I think it's possible; even probable, yes.'

'Even when I've told you repeatedly that it's you I love?'

'Even then, Dido. I think you need to be sure.'

'And what about you, Guy? Do you need to be sure?'

'Perhaps I do.' He looked at her sadly. 'You've given me the happiest moments of my life, Dido, but also chaos and uncertainty, and I don't need that.'

Dido closed her eyes, feeling utterly dismayed and increasingly confused and unsure of her feelings. Maybe he's right, she thought, and I *am* on the point of making yet another colossal mistake. She felt deeply wounded that Guy seemed unwilling to make more of an effort to persuade her to stay with him, even though the decision to leave had been hers alone. At the end of the day, he seemed almost anxious for her to be gone, to leave him to rebuild his life in peace. 'Would it have made a difference if I had told you about the rape at the time?' she asked quietly.

There was a long silence, during which Guy struggled to suppress the feelings of rage and jealousy that rushed to the surface, and to answer her question as truthfully and calmly as he could. At last he tightened his arm round her and kissed the top of her head. 'Yes,' he said, 'I expect it would have made a difference. Why didn't you tell me, Dido? Can you remember?'

'I remember very well. In the first place, I didn't want to cause you unnecessary pain. It's not as if you would have been able to rush out and beat him to a pulp, is it?' She looked at him anxiously. 'Sorry, Guy, but you know what I mean, don't you?'

'I know what you mean.'

'And in the second place, it made me realize what a selfish, aggressive brute he can be. He helps himself to women, any woman he fancies, whenever he feels like it.'

'But you responded to him, nevertheless, didn't you?'

'You only have Jake's word for that, Guy. Are you passing judgement on me, by any chance?'

'I'm very sorry, I didn't mean to. I need to know, that's all.'

'Well,' said Dido crisply, bright angry spots appearing in her cheeks, 'perhaps I don't really know myself.'

'Perhaps that's what you still have to find out.'

They spent a wakeful and uneasy night, and in the late morning Vassili drove Dido to the airport. At her request, Guy did not come to see her off. 'I will telephone you as soon as I get to London,' she said, putting her arms round Guy's neck and kissing him. He returned her kiss, but without passion. 'Thank you,' he said, 'that would be kind.'

At the airport, her plane was late and took a long time refuelling and loading. At last the call came to board the aircraft, and the little group of travellers trooped out to the plane, showing their boarding passes at the gate. Dido was relieved to find that she had a window seat, and settled into it, fastening her seat-belt. She closed her eyes, noticing the faint smell of aviation fuel on the air, feeling the warm sun on her hands as it poured through her window. She listened to the roar of the engines as they came to life, one by one. The plane rumbled down the runway, gathered speed and took off, then banked sharply and gaining height, flew across the island. Looking down as they crossed the western coastline, Dido saw that they were passing directly over Myrtiótissa. Her eyes filled with tears, so that all she could see was the blurred, fragmented green of the beautiful sea below.

Chapter Fourteen

Tom and Max were engaged in cleaning out the tortoise house, a laborious and malodorous task. Bonaparte marched round the sooty walls of the yard, followed by his newly-acquired partner, as yet unnamed, since no one was entirely sure of its gender.

'We shall have to wait and see, won't we?' Monsieur Petit had said darkly, somewhat to Max's mystification.

Armed with a scraper, a stiff brush and a bucket of water, the two boys did their best to remove the accumulated hardened muck from the floor of the cage, then swilled water and bleach around it to leave it sweet and clean.

'Trouble is,' said Max, looking worried, 'how to get it dry for them in this weather. They might catch cold, poor things.'

'I don't suppose they like the smell of bleach much, either,' said Tom. 'What about putting down some straw?'

'Good idea. Let's ask Monsieur Petit; he might have some.'

They gathered up their cleaning gear and went into the scullery at the rear of the shop. They rinsed their hands under the tap, picked the worst bits of slimy rubbish off their clothes and made their way to the shop, carefully checking that Monsieur Petit was not engaged with a customer. He was alone.

'Monsieur Petit,' said Max, 'we were wondering, do

you have any straw for the tortoise house? It's awfully damp and cold for them, really.'

'*Arthrose*,' said Tom, looking serious.

Monsieur Petit considered the problem. 'Straw I do not have, no. But maybe something else; one will look.' He led the way to a cupboard at the back of the showroom. Inside were several large cardboard boxes, which, on investigation, were found to contain what appeared to be thick yellow potato crisps, but were in fact made from polystyrene. Monsieur Petit used them to surround frail objects when packing them for his clients. 'This should do,' he said. 'It will make them dry, and also warm, no doubt.'

The two boys looked doubtful. 'Won't they eat them?' asked Tom.

'Do you think Bonaparte is without intelligence?'

'No, of course not.'

'*Alors, on va essayer, n'est-ce pas?*'

The boys took a plastic bag full of the chips out to the yard and spread a good thick layer on the floor of the cage. Then they nailed down the lid, put fresh water and some cabbage stalks into the clean bowls, and returned to the apartment to have tea. They went into the sitting-room where Josh was working at his drawing-board, which he quite often did at weekends. He looked up as they came in, and smiled. 'All done?' he said.

'All done,' said Max.

'Good, I'll put the kettle on.'

The two boys came and stood beside Josh, and inspected his drawing. 'You are clever, Josh,' said Tom. 'I wish I could draw like that.'

'Maybe you will one day, Tom. Who knows?' Josh turned to his son and ruffled his hair, then raised his hand to his nose. 'Max! You smell revolting! You've got tortoise jobs all over your hair, you horrible child.'

'So've I,' said Tom, complacently.

'Go and wash! Or better still, have a bath. And wash your hair, the pair of you, or they won't let you back into the apartment, Tom. Come on, we'll find some clean clothes for you to put on.'

They went to Max's room and Josh tried to find something big enough for Tom to wear. Max turned on the switch of his beautiful carousel and Tom gazed at it as it revolved slowly, its lights flashing, the hurdy-gurdy man playing his little tune, the monkey leaping up and down. He would have dearly loved to own such a thing himself, but he did not permit himself to show too much enthusiasm. 'Nice toy,' he said dismissively, turning away. His eye fell on the glass case containing the snake and he nearly leapt out of his skin. '*Ça alors!*' he squawked involuntarily. 'What's that?'

Max observed with vengeful joy his uncle's discomposure. 'Oh,' he said airily, 'that's Hellebore. Isn't he wicked?'

'Um, yes, great,' said Tom, recovering swiftly. He was astonished. He personally would never have entertained for a moment the idea of having a snake in his own bedroom, stuffed or not.

'Right, chaps,' said Josh, 'these will have to do. I'll lend you one of my sweatshirts, Tom. Max's are all too small.'

They took off the soiled clothes carefully, and Josh dropped them into a plastic supermarket bag to prevent them contaminating the other things in the laundry basket. He turned on the taps of the small square bath. The two boys got in, and sitting side by side on the narrow shelf, began to soap themselves.

'Here,' said Josh, producing a bottle of shampoo. 'Wash your hair; you really stink, the pair of you. Get a move on while I get the tea. And don't splash water on the floor, OK?'

259

'OK.'

'Pooh,' said Tom, lathering Max's hair, 'you *do* stink; you smell like a dead rat.'

'How do you know what a dead rat smells like?' Max wiped the soapy water out of his eyes, blinking at Tom.

'Plenty of dead rats in the Catacombs,' said Tom. 'Loads of them, millions, in fact.'

'What's the Catacombs?'

'Haven't you been?'

'No.'

'It's terrific,' said Tom. 'It's where all the dead people are – eight million of them.'

'*Eight million dead people?*'

'Yes. You go down a stone staircase till you get to an iron door four hundred metres under the ground, and carved in the stone round the door it says: *Stop! Here is the Empire of Death!*' Tom lowered his voice. 'Then the creaking door is slowly opened and you go inside and there are hundreds of creepy cold corridors all lined with bones; millions and trillions of bones all piled up in stacks – arms and legs, hands and feet, and all the skulls in rows, grinning.'

'You're winding me up, Tom,' said Max in a small voice. 'I don't believe you.'

'It's *true*, I promise!'

'And have you really been down there and seen all the bones?'

'Loads of times, it's one of my best treats, though the sewers are pretty good, too. More rats in the sewers. You'd like them, being a snake-fancier yourself, wouldn't you? We'll have to take you next time. Hold the shower for me, Max.'

Max held the shower over Tom's head until the lather was all gone, then they got out of the bath and wrapped themselves in the big towels, warm from the towel-rail.

After tea, Josh and Max walked back with Tom to Grands-Augustins, then they came slowly home together, hand in hand.

That night Max had a terrible nightmare, involving long, dripping stone corridors full of rotting corpses and grinning skulls, intertwined with writhing snakes like Hellebore. Worst of all his own mother, Nastassia, her long hair streaming behind her, was running away from him in her nightie, screaming, while he, Max, tried to keep up with her, shouting as loudly as he could: 'Stop! Here is the Empire of Death!'

'Max! Wake up! Wake up, darling, you're having a bad dream.'

Max's eyes flew open and he leapt into his father's arms and clung to him, sobbing as though his heart would break.

'It's all right, old chap, I'm here,' said Josh, carrying him back to his own bed. 'It was only a dream, you'll be all right in a minute.' Slowly Max recovered, the nightmare faded.

'OK now?'

'OK,' said Max.

'Do you want to go back to bed, or stay here?'

'Stay here.'

'Right, settle down, then.' Josh switched off the light and pulled the duvet over them both.

'Dad?'

'Mm?'

'Do you think Giò would be cross if I asked him if we could take Hellebore back to Monsieur Guillaume and swop him for something else?'

Josh smiled in the dark. 'I'm sure he wouldn't. Had you anything in mind, particularly?'

'Well,' said Max, 'he's got some quite nice ducks.'

'Sounds perfect to me.'

*   *   *

261

Dido lay in her bed, nursing a streaming cold and staring at the telephone on her night-table, willing it to ring. As she had promised, she had phoned Guy as soon as she reached *The Maid of Wapping*. Their conversation had been brief, with awkward pauses. Guy's voice seemed very far away, and so quiet that she could hardly hear him. 'Well, thanks for ringing. I'm glad you've arrived safely, Dido. Take care of yourself.'

'Phone me in a day or two, won't you?'

'Yes. Or you phone me. I'm always here.'

But she had not phoned and neither had he. A stubborn resistance prevented her from making the first move and, quite apart from that, she felt so miserable and ill that she knew that if she heard his voice she would dissolve into tears of loneliness and self-pity, and the entire reason for her being here would remain unresolved. She sat up, shivering in the unheated room, and blew her nose. 'This place is a tip,' she said aloud. 'I must try and get it cleaned up and tidy, it's disgusting.' She got out of bed, took some paracetamol and put on the thickest sweater she could find. She went into the studio and began to fill bin-liners with the rubbish that had accumulated from weeks of neglect. The dishwasher was filled with stuck-on dirty dishes – Jake's dishes. Bloody man, she thought angrily, he's too idle even to turn the thing on. She ran the machine on pre-wash, then turned it back to the beginning of the cycle, loading it with a double quantity of detergent. It throbbed away, exacerbating her headache, while she hoovered the entire place, dusted the furniture and made her bed. She cleaned the bath and basin and put lavatory cleaner in the loo. Her back and legs ached, her throat was increasingly painful, and her nose had become completely blocked. She was beginning to feel really unwell.

God, I'm a mess, she thought, and sat down for a moment. She put a hand to her cheek. It was burning hot. She returned to the studio, poured herself a brandy, sat down on the sofa and drank it slowly. All around her were Jake's possessions; his books, hundreds of them; his tapes and videos; his few good pictures. Feeling slightly better, Dido set about packing his things. A woman of thrifty disposition, she had for years hoarded cardboard cartons, brought back from her local corner shop. Dozens of them lay, flattened, in a neat pile in the broom cupboard. Now she brought them out and reassembled them, one by one, and filled them with everything of Jake's she could find. He had taken quite a lot of his clothes to wherever he was currently staying, but there still remained drawers full of his shirts and sweaters, and many pairs of shoes. She packed everything.

She made a cup of tea and sat down to drink it. She stared at the dreary brown boxes that now filled her room, wondering what to do with them. She considered phoning Jake's agent and asking for his address, then quickly dismissed the idea, in case such an action would reveal to Jake her presence in London, and bring him round to bully her and make a scene. She looked at her watch: six-twenty. I suppose I ought to eat something, she thought, getting reluctantly to her feet. She boiled an egg and ate a slice of toast. She looked in the fridge again, half-hoping to find a piece of cheese or something and her eye fell on a carton of Greek yoghurt. She slammed the fridge door, trying to drive from her mind the memory of the beautiful bowls of yoghurt waiting on the breakfast table at Koulari. She heated some milk, poured it into a mug, and went to bed, worn out, aching and miserable. She took two more paracetamol, and slumped against her pillows, her eyes closed, the hot mug warming her hands. Her mind wandering, half-remembered insubstantial images of childhood floated across her consciousness. Suddenly, and very vividly, she saw herself in a small, overheated room that smelt of Leichner greasepaint. A large mirror was fixed to the wall above a dressing-table, and was surrounded by bright white naked electric light bulbs. Seated before the mirror, her mother was carefully applying black eyeliner in a thick line along her upper eyelids, then painting the inner rim of the lower lids pure white with a fine brush, and adding a bright red dot to the inner corners of her eyes as a final touch. Maria looked critically at her own reflection, pursing her lips and raising her chin in her own particular way, while Mabel took advantage of this break in the proceedings to finish brushing Maria's long black hair. She coiled it up into a fat chignon, pinning it firmly to her head with many strong steel grips. 'You'll need a root job next week, I shouldn't wonder,' she remarked. Maria frowned, but did not reply, and stood up, powdering her freckled bosom with a swansdown puff. The diminutive Mabel, rather buckling under the weight of the heavy, jewel-encrusted costume, held it up so that Maria could thrust her arms into the sleeves, then ran round the back to ease it into position and do up the fastenings that stretched from neck to hem. Mabel would never permit the use of zip-fasteners, knowing well what a display of temperament a jammed one would provoke. Ready for the fray at last, Maria sprayed her throat from an elaborate glass scent-bottle, encased in silver filigree and pumped with a rubber bulb covered in mauve-silk crochet, with a matching silk tassel. A strong smell of TCP accompanied this small but vital routine and seemed an inappropriate perfume to emanate from such an elaborate container. The call-boy pounded on the door. Maria gave herself a last squirt of TCP and headed for the corridor, with Mabel following in her wake, holding up her heavy train.

'*Ciao, cara*,' said Signor Pernice gently, from the depths of his little velvet armchair, and picked up his tapestry again. 'Now, Dido, after me. Once two is two, two twos are four.'

God, thought Dido, and opened her eyes. I'd forgotten all about that. I suppose I must have been about six or seven, I can't really remember. It must have been the tour of Australia; I do remember it was terribly hot. Darling Signor Pernice, he was such a lamb, so dear and kind. He must have been getting on a bit even then. I remember his hair, it seemed dark because of the pomade, but it was quite grey when he'd just washed it, and a bit thin on top. She remembered him giving a concert during a summer festival at Aix, a small slight figure looking more like a bank clerk than an opera singer as he stood on the stage in a circle of blue light. But when he opened his mouth and the exquisite music of Monteverdi poured through the darkened auditorium like a glittering silver comet, one felt the audience hold its breath with pleasure and surprise.

Dido slept badly and woke when it was still dark. She felt cold and stiff but her headache had almost gone. She realized that she hadn't eaten properly for two days and decided that she must do some shopping. She got dressed and made some tea, listening to the news on the radio, with the seasonal warnings about the penalties for drinking and driving. Good heavens, she thought, it's nearly Christmas. How weird; it doesn't feel like it.

In Mr Mehta's corner shop, however, the Christmas spirit was in full swing, with gold and purple tinsel strung along every shelf and an impressive display of ready-made Christmas cakes in the cabinet normally containing pork pies and Indian pastries, samosas and curry puffs. The well-stocked drinks' shelves were also decorated, with large golden cut-out stars and a necklace of gold tinsel round the neck of each bottle. A tray of cooked chipolata sausages on sticks stood on the counter next to the Lottery machine, with a card marked 'Help Yourself. Season's Greetings. Mr and Mrs Mehta.' Dido went slowly round the little shop, and filled her basket with cheese, eggs, bacon, bread, butter, milk and some sliced ham. She also bought a bottle of brandy, some more paracetamol and some cough lozenges. She took the basket to the check-out.

'You are not wanting veg today, Miss Partridge? It is all fresh this morning, very nice. Carrots, potatoes, cabbage?'

'No thanks. Not today, Mr Mehta.'

'Some salad, then? Tomatoes, lettuce? Good for the health, isn't it?'

Dido gave in. 'OK, a few tomatoes, then.'

Mr Mehta weighed out half a kilo of tomatoes for her, and put a bunch of parsley in the bag. 'Compliments of the season,' he said, smiling kindly at her.

'Thank you, Mr Mehta; the same to you, too,' she replied, vaguely wondering whether her greeting was entirely appropriate, and deciding that it probably wasn't but that it didn't really matter, Mr Mehta was not one to take offence.

She carried her shopping back to the barge, standing on the quayside in the early morning light for a few minutes, watching the River Police launch go by, causing the moored boats to bob up and down as its bow-wave reached the riverbank. She watched the launch out of sight as it chugged its way upstream, growing fainter and fainter in the morning mist. What next, Dido? she asked herself. It's time you thought things out. You can't just sit here and rot, and pick up your old life as though nothing has happened, can you? And if you do, bloody Jake will come barging back here whenever it suits him, you know that. Is that why you're here? Is that what you really want? '*No*,' she said aloud, 'I absolutely *don't* want that. I never want to see him again, the bloody bastard.'

A pair of swans sailed silently up and trod water, looking at her sideways with their boot-button black eyes, clicking their beaks, wondering whether Dido was good for some breakfast. She broke off a piece of her fresh loaf and threw it to them, then crossed her gangplank and went below. She made some coffee and toast and ate her breakfast standing up in the kitchen, then sat down on the sofa and looked idly at the newspaper. She had read carefully through an article about the single European currency before she realized that she had not taken in a single word of it. She let the paper fall to the floor and lay down, closing her eyes. Depression flowed over her like a black blanket, and filled every part of her being. What am I doing here, in this cold sad place? she asked herself miserably. Why have I come? What am I trying to prove? Am I trying to punish Guy for his lack of faith in me, for believing everything Jake told him? Why doesn't he call me? If he really loved me, he would. That's all it would take, Guy, her heart cried in silent anguish, one little phone call. Is that too much to ask?

She began to cough and sat up quickly, trying to control the painful spasm. She drank some water and blew her nose, then resolutely got more cardboard boxes from the broom cupboard and began to pack her own books and pictures, and the photographs of her parents. Suddenly, she stopped, realizing that it was highly improbable that she was actually going anywhere. She would remain here and resume her rather mere job, plodding on, paying into her pension fund, going to work and feeding the swans until she was sixty, and then what? She took the big photograph of her mother out of the box and stared at it. There she was, full-blown, laughing and radiant after a performance of *Tosca*, surrounded by excited friends and admirers, with Signor Pernice – Luigi – and Mabel, smiling indulgently in the background. Oh Mabel, thought Dido, where are you now, when I need someone so badly?

She put the photograph back on the piano and thought about Mabel. She must be awfully old now, she said to herself, she's probably in a retirement home for theatricals. Without much conviction, she looked up Mabel's name in the telephone book. 'M. Stibbings, 3 Railway Buildings, E4. That's it!' She hesitated for a moment, and then dialled the number.

'Yes?'

'Mabel?'

'Miss Stibbings, if you don't mind.'

'Mabel, it's me, Dido.'

'Oh. Dido. What can I do for you, dear?'

'Nothing, really,' said Dido. 'I just thought I'd call and see how you are.'

'Can't complain. What about you, then? Still in the movies?'

'Yes.'

'Still at *The Maid*?'

'Yes.'

There was a pause, while both tried to think of something to say. 'You must pop round and see me, when you've got a moment to spare,' said Mabel.

'Yes, of course. I'd love to, sometime.'

'Well, you know where I am, Dido, love. See you, then.'

'See you, Mabel,' said Dido. 'Take care.' She hung up, knowing that the call had been a mistake, that she would not go.

'He is drinking again,' said Vassili, as he and Heleni ate their supper, the table pushed close to the stove and the shutters tightly secured against the cold east wind which rattled through the olives, scattering dry fallen leaves before it.

'I know.' Heleni's dark eyes were sad. 'Half a bottle of whisky since this morning, as well as wine with his dinner, and he has hardly touched the food.'

'I am worried,' said Vassili. 'If he falls and hurts himself, we cannot hear him, in this wind.' He took a last mouthful of *stifado* and wiped the plate clean with a piece of bread. 'I will go down later, and check he is OK.'

Heleni took the plates to the sink and brought two small glasses of thick fig jam, and a jug of cold spring water. She sat down. 'It's all her fault, isn't it?' she said.

'We don't know that, Heleni, do we? She is not an evil woman. She was sad to go, I could see.'

Heleni looked severe. 'So, if it was *he* who told her to go, why is he now so silent, so depressed? Why is he back on the bottle?'

'I don't know.' Vassili looked at his wife anxiously. 'I am afraid for him, Heleni.'

A little later he lit the lantern and went down to the house, through the wildly thrashing olives, the lamp's flame flaring and smoking in the turbulent air, the storm threatening to extinguish it. As he approached the house, he heard snatches of music, loud, booming, aggressive to his ears, and he shook his head. He put the lantern down at the foot of the terrace steps, and went quietly up, intending merely to have a look at Guy, not to disturb him if he was reading and seemed all right. The lights in the sitting-room were on, the thunderous music streamed out of the open French windows. Silently, Vassili approached, and looked in. The room appeared to be empty. The fire still glowed in the hearth, a glass and bottle were on the table beside Guy's leather chair. Vassili's heart began to beat a little faster; he covered his mouth with his hand. Where is he? What has happened? he asked himself, and entered the room. Suddenly the music ceased, the needle lurching across the disc with an agonized shriek, then repeating the same musical phrase over and over again.

'Shit!' said a muffled voice from the depths of the sofa. 'Sod the bloody thing!' A hand appeared, grasping the back of the sofa, then slid off again. 'Bugger it,' said the voice, 'I'm drunk.' Vassili advanced towards the sofa and looked over the back at Guy, lying helplessly on the cushions.

'Vassili!'

'Sir,' said Vassili, frowning crossly, for he had had a bad fright. 'You are ill?'

'Not ill, Vassili,' said Guy, and groaned rather theatrically. 'Pissed would be a more appropriate word for my condition.'

Vassili, wishing that Guy would not express himself quite so pompously when the fit took him, came round to the front of the sofa and removed the needle from the disc. Then he took hold of Guy's hands and pulled him to a sitting position. 'Come on,' he said patiently, 'it's time you were in bed.' He hooked Guy's right arm round his own neck, and putting his left arm round Guy's back, he lifted him to his feet. Erratically, they made their way to the bedroom. Vassili lowered Guy onto the bed, then undressed him and removed the leg-irons. He helped him into his pyjamas and pulling back the covers, manoeuvred him into bed.

'You're as bad as Heleni,' said Guy. 'You treat me like a child.'

'If you behave like a child, you must expect it. What else can we do?'

'You could leave me, couldn't you, if I'm such a bloody nuisance?'

'No,' said Vassili. 'We would never do that.'

'Oh? Why not?'

'It's a pretty good job; we like it. If I did not work for you, I would have to help Spiros all the summer in the taverna. Instead, I can go night-fishing with the lamp, we have our own house, it's OK for us here.'

'Well, good,' said Guy, surprised and rather moved. 'I don't know how I'd manage without you both.'

'OK,' said Vassili. 'I'll shut up the house and go home, if you have everything you need?'

'Just one thing,' said Guy. 'Could you bring the phone through, and plug it in here for me, please?'

Vassili fetched the telephone and plugged it into the jack behind the night-table, carefully leaving the instrument where Guy could easily reach it.

'Thanks,' said Guy. 'Goodnight, Vassili.'

Walking home through the trees, Vassili asked himself why Guy wanted the phone so close to him all the time. It's obvious, he told himself, he is waiting for her to call him, even in the middle of the night. Poor man, perhaps it would have been better if I had never brought her here in the first place. He was OK before she came; lonely, but OK.

Guy lay in his bed, staring at the ceiling, his hands clasped behind his head, and asked himself much the same question. He opened the book on his night-table and took from it the photograph of Dido he was using as a bookmark. She was sitting on the edge of the pool, her feet in the water, the sun shining on her brown shoulders and her smiling face. Oh, Dido my darling, he said to himself, I am missing you so badly. I miss your voice, your laugh, your arms and your mouth. I miss your touch, your gentle cool hands on my bloody useless legs, that torment me during every waking moment and in my sleep as well. He tried to shift his throbbing limbs in an attempt to soothe them by making contact with a cooler part of the sheet. He held the photograph against his heart, as if by doing that he could somehow bring Dido herself back into his bed and into his life, then he propped it against the radio and stared at it. Would it have been better if we'd never met? Would it, darling?

He remembered their first meeting, the magical night-fishing with Vassili, the dinner at the taverna and the day at Myrtiótissa. We were so happy, I suppose it was too good to last. It was probably naïve and foolish of me to hope that it would be forever. He sighed and closed his eyes, and for the first time since Dido's departure, he allowed himself to relive the catastrophic visitation of Jacob Kroll, and his crude revelations concerning himself and Dido at Inniscarragh. Poor Dido, he thought, no wonder she was so angry and upset. With him, for spilling the beans; with me for not immediately treating the whole story as a pack of lies, which is exactly what I should have done. She was right, Kroll's motives were entirely ones of spite, intended to wreck everything for us, and take her back to him. If I'd had more sense, I would have concealed my shock, and kept my stupid jealousy and doubts to myself. I've been an utter fool; I don't blame her in the least for dumping me, poor girl. Oh Dido, my darling, if I'd had a few more lovers before you, perhaps I could have handled the whole thing with a lot more wisdom and poise. But you are my only true love. I'll never love anyone else, either now or in the future, and beyond the grave.

He stared at the telephone, sitting silently on the table beside him. He felt deeply tempted to pick it up, dial Dido's number and tell her what a fool he had been, and ask her to forgive him and come back to him. But then, he thought, if she comes, I'll never know whether it's only because she knows how much I need her. If she decides to come, it has to be because she needs me, too. He kissed the photograph, turned out the light and stared through the uncurtained window. The black sky was thick with stars. The wind had dropped and he could hear his owls hooting to one another in the trees. It seemed to him a sound of unbearable sadness. He closed his eyes, and for the first time since Dido's going, allowed himself the weakness of giving way to his misery. The silent, painful tears slid down the sides of his face and soaked into the pillow beneath his head. Much later, he slept.

Mabel put the phone down, and looked at it thoughtfully, frowning. What was all that in aid of? she said to herself. I haven't had a cheep out of Dido for ten years or more, so whatever's up now? What did she want to ring me for? She shook her head, returned to her seat by the fire and picked up her knitting. Upstairs, her cupboard was full of the skirts and jumpers in rainbow colours knitted by herself over the years, and still worn on a daily basis, but since the price of wool had risen so sharply she could no longer afford to buy it in very large quantities, and now had to restrict herself to the production of berets, table-mats, doilies and the like. At present, she was making a tea-cosy, in purple wool bramble stitch, with a scarlet stripe at the bottom and a matching pom-pom on the top.

It was dark and gloomy in the poky sitting-room at Railway Buildings. The single small Victorian window let in very little light, even in summertime, but Mabel would not permit herself to turn on her lamp until four o'clock. Now, as she worked steadily along her rows of knitting, she wished that she had chosen a lighter colour for her wool, which would have made it a lot easier to see what she was doing. Still, purple was her favourite; she wasn't one for pale colours, so it was no use complaining.

Her little cast-iron grate was stoked to the brim with smokeless fuel, which in her opinion ought to be referred to the Trade Descriptions people, for it was not very smokeless and gave off a nasty acrid smell which made her throat sting and her eyes smart, especially when the wind was in the east. Still, it was better than nothing, and did give off a good blast of warmth to her thin old legs. With care, two shovelfuls could be made to last all day and certainly made the room a bit warmer than the bedroom upstairs, which was like a tomb, damp and freezing cold.

She finished a row, put the work carefully aside and went to the kitchen to make herself a cup of Bovril. Mabel was a great believer in the strength-giving properties of this beverage and drank a good deal of it, as well as a lot of strong Indian tea. During the evening, she drank two double whiskies, one before her supper and one at bedtime. In order to be able to afford the whisky, she bought extremely cheap food, mostly from the barrow-boys in the Cut, and never ate expensive meat. Bacon and pork belly, bread and potatoes were her daily fare. Her ancient gas stove, blackened with decades of baked-on grease, was her only means of cooking. On the rare occasions that she used the oven, it was necessary to drop lighted matches into the hole in the bottom of the oven until it condescended to ignite itself, which it eventually did with a frightening explosion and a blast of hot air. The two gas rings on the hob had long since ceased to operate efficiently. The small one could only manage to produce a ring of very tiny blue flames; the larger one was worse, giving a fiercely flaring yellow flame, which lacked heat and deposited soot on the bottom of her pans. Bloody thing, she thought, as she watched the cold yellow flames licking the base of her buckled aluminium kettle.

She took the mug of Bovril back to the fireside, with a thick slice of Mighty White bread. As she ate the bread and drank the hot savoury drink, she looked affectionately round her room, stuffed with the souvenirs of her working life. The walls were completely covered with the posters and programmes of all Madam's operas, as well as many signed photographs of her at different stages of her career. On the sideboard were her personal props, tastefully displayed – her gloves and fans, a lace fichu, a lovely paste tiara and the little pink satin *bustier* she had worn as *Manon*. Of course, that had been a long time ago, before she got fat and gradually had to give up the younger roles. Poor Madam, thought Mabel, she didn't like that at all. It was having Dido that did it, and no mistake. She was huge after that!

Mabel put half a shovel of nuts on the fire and thought about Signor Pernice and Dido. He was a real duck, she said to herself, remembering him holding the tiny new-born baby girl, his rubbery little face all beaming with joy. He really loved that child, and he loved Madam too, though she gave him plenty of stick, poor chap. She sighed, remembering his sad Italian funeral, the black plumed horses with jingling silver harness, the little coffin in its glass hearse rolling along to the cemetery. At the graveside, Madam, her poor face ugly with grief and tears, had wept noisily and without cease, with Mabel supporting her on one side and Dido, still only a child, on the other. Of course, it had rained.

She had managed to save most of her not very large salary during her years with Madam, so that after her death she had been able to buy her one-up, one-down terrace cottage in Railway Buildings. Dido had been very good about the pension, too, though it couldn't be much, but at least it was something to eke out the pittance she received from the state. All in all, she couldn't really complain. She's a good girl, is Dido, even though she's never bothered to come and see me much, she thought. I suppose it's difficult if you're working, travelling and that. I lost touch with my mum when I was travelling myself; same difference, to be honest. Poor kid, she did sound a bit low, p'raps I'll go and see her tomorrow.

Chapter Fifteen

It was unusually cold and a light covering of snow clothed the countryside as Patrick drove into the courtyard at St Gilles, bringing Josh with him. Anna and the two boys had come down by train a few days earlier, to help Marie-Claude with the Christmas preparations. Patrick parked in the open cow-byre as usual and they got out of the car, just as the boys erupted from the kitchen door and ran joyfully across the yard to greet their fathers.

'Isn't this great?' cried Tom. 'Real proper snow! I hope we get snowed in and have to stay here forever.'

'Me too.' Max clutched Josh round the knees. 'Hello, Dad.'

'Hello, old chap,' said Josh. 'So you like it here, do you?'

'Yes, it's wicked. There's ducks and sheep and goats, and a real pond with fish in.'

'No tortoises?'

'No, no tortoises.'

They got their luggage from the boot, together with some interesting-looking parcels stuffed into plastic bags, and made their way to the house. Josh looked at the shabby old Norman farmhouse, its windows glowing with lamplight against the darkening sky, and thought how safe and permanent it looked. Surrounded by its barns and byres and orchards, it was a kindly, reassuring place, but one which had known more than its share of tragedy in its time, and had survived. More than sixty years *Grandpère* has lived here, Josh said to himself. It's incredible, and amazing; what a star he is.

The kitchen door opened and Anna, wrapped in a long apron, her hands covered with flour, came to meet them. Patrick dropped his bags, folded his arms round his wife, and kissed her.

'Hello, darling,' she said. 'And hello, Josh.'

'Hi,' said Josh. 'Have the boys been a pain?'

'Not at all, we've hardly seen them. Come in, by the fire. You must both be cold and needing a drink.'

In the kitchen, Marie-Claude was preparing the Christmas goose, stuffing it with a mixture of chopped apple, chestnuts, shallots and Calvados. She looked up as the family entered, her old blue eyes alight with pleasure. Now in her late seventies, she had kept house for Dr Halard since the death of his wife nearly forty years ago and remained the linchpin of the household, with undiminished energy and enthusiasm for life. She still kept her own small cottage in the village, and it was a matter of some astonishment to Anna that she found the time to keep both houses in such good order.

'Marie-Claude,' said Patrick, kissing her. '*Ça va?*'

'*Pas mal*,' she replied briskly. 'Where is Giò? Did he not come with you?'

'He'll be along later. He's coming in his own car, so that he can drive down to Souliac for the New Year.'

'Ah, yes, I see.'

They went through to the sitting-room, Anna carrying a plate of warm cheese straws. A fire of apple logs blazed in the wide brick chimney, sending its flickering light and comforting warmth through the old room, illuminating the glass-fronted bookcases, the pictures on the walls, and the big brass lamp on the round table, with its tray of bottles and glasses. Patrick poured drinks for Anna, Josh and himself.

'Cider, boys?'

'Yes, please.'

He poured small glasses of cider, diluting it with a little water. The boys took their glasses and sat down on the rug in front of the fire. Patrick handed round the drinks and sat down himself, stretching out his legs to the blaze. 'Where's Dad?' he asked.

'Fussing over his ewes, I expect,' Anna smiled. 'Since it started snowing he's brought them all into the orchard, and the big barn is all ready, in case we get any early lambs.'

'I helped put the straw down,' said Tom, importantly.

'So did I.'

'Well, you did do a *bit*,' Tom agreed, rather scornfully. 'But you're really too small to be useful, aren't you?'

Max opened his mouth, ready to do battle. 'That's enough, the pair of you,' said Patrick quickly. 'Don't be a bore, Tom. You were small yourself not so long ago, weren't you?' Tom looked unimpressed, and said nothing. He smirked rather superciliously at Max, who gave a snort of suppressed laughter and did the nose-trick into his drink.

'What's the plan for dinner?' asked Josh. 'Is it OK if I have a bath and change, Mum? I can smell the Métro on my jacket.'

'Yes, of course,' said Anna. 'Go ahead. Dinner's not till eight-thirty. I hope that won't be too late for the boys, will it?'

'No!' said the boys together, looking anxious.

'OK,' said Anna. 'But if there's any fighting or silliness, we'll know that you are both too tired and can't handle it, won't we?'

Tom got quickly to his feet. 'Come on, Max. Let's go and find *Grandpère*, shall we?'

'Put on your coats,' Anna called after them. 'It's getting really cold.'

'Well done, Mum,' said Josh, laughing. 'You've got them over a barrel.'

'Not terribly subtle.' Anna smiled at her son. 'But sometimes it works.'

'What about midnight Mass?' asked Patrick. 'Is there one at St Gilles, or is it at another village this year?'

'It's at Ste Anastasie, but there's a family Mass here tomorrow morning, we thought that might be easier.' She looked at Patrick. 'Midnight is a bit late for the children, and for Philippe and Marie-Claude too, don't you think?'

'They're not the only ones. I love going, but it's so hard to stay awake after so much food and drink.'

Anna smiled. 'Good, that settles it; we'll go tomorrow.' She got up and put her glass on the tray. 'I must go and give Marie-Claude a hand. Have your bath, Josh, there's loads of water.'

'Thanks, I will. I'll take the cases up, Patrick. OK?'

In the hall, Josh took the carefully wrapped presents out of the bags and hid them under the wide sweeping sweet-smelling branches of the Christmas tree, which stood in a corner next to the long-case clock, its little coloured lights twinkling, shedding its pine needles in resinous drifts on the threadbare oriental rugs below. Then he picked up the luggage and went upstairs to his bath.

Patrick poured himself another drink and opened one of the casement windows, inhaling deep breaths of the clean outside air. The blazing fire had made the room quite hot, so he decided to leave the window open for a while and returned to his chair. His eyes travelled nostalgically round his parents' much-loved and well-worn room, in the house in which he had been born and would almost certainly die. In ten years or so, he thought, when Tom leaves us, and Dad is either very old indeed or dead, I would be perfectly happy here, alone with Anna. Just the two of us, no meetings, no schedules, no leaving in the morning and coming back dead-tired at night. He looked at Anna's beautiful decorations, hanging over the chimney breast and round the doors and windows; handsome swags of fir, holly and ivy, hung with fat pine cones and red and yellow apples. He smiled, visualizing Anna perched on top of the stepladder, fixing the garlands, her beautiful face serious with concentration. How fortunate I am, he said to himself, and how happy; she has illuminated my life.

'Hi, Patrick!'

Patrick turned and looked round the wing of his chair just in time to see a long, black corduroy-trousered leg come through the open window, followed by a grip, some smartly wrapped parcels, and the rest of Giò.

'Hello, Giò. I didn't hear the car. Why the unusual mode of entry? Is the door locked?'

Giò laughed and retrieved his parcels from the floor, putting them on the table. 'No. I saw you through the window – you looked so peaceful and relaxed. I thought it would be nice to have a five-minute break before throwing myself into the fray.'

'Get yourself a drink, Giò, and sit down. You must be tired. Was it bedlam at the shop?'

'Unbelievable. I don't know where people get the money these days. They seem to go mad, it's really rather appalling to watch them. Rich women are so rapacious – you see their beady little eyes darting round the place, terrified of missing something, or being pipped by someone else.'

'I suppose I'm rather spared that sort of hands-on contact with the market place.' Patrick smiled a little ironically. 'I don't have to sully the hem of my garment in quite the same way as you have to, perhaps, but I do frequently have to fight extremely hard to get my programmes properly financed and that can very often be a dirty business, too. Plenty of stabs in the back in that department, I can tell you. It's not all sweetness and light, by any means.'

'Yeah? I suppose it's the same whatever one does, there's no getting away from it, is there?' Giò poured himself a drink, and sat down on the other side of the fire. 'Anyway, we've left all that behind for the moment, that's the main thing.' Giò looked at his brother-in-law and smiled. 'What did you get for Anna? Or is it a secret?'

'It is, but I'll tell you. I don't know whether you ever saw them, Giò, but when I first knew Anna and stayed with her in London, she was restoring a pair of gilded cherubs.'

'I remember,' said Giò. 'Weren't they sold to a Japanese dealer?'

'That's right. Well, guess what? A few weeks ago I was sent an auctioneer's catalogue, and behold, there were Anna's angels! I remembered how much she had loved them, especially since she was pregnant herself while she was working on them.'

'So, you went to the auction and bought them?'

'I did.'

'How terrific! She'll be knocked out that you recognized them, and remembered.'

'I remember everything about Anna: every single thing, Giò.'

'Of course you do.' Giò took a sip of his drink. 'She's lucky to have you, we all are.'

'I'm so lucky to have *her*,' said Patrick. 'You have no idea.'

'I think I have,' said Giò quietly, 'a very clear idea.'

'Yes,' said Patrick, looking at Giò's face, Anna's face, as he gazed into the rosy embers of the fire, 'of course you do.'

Giò looked up, his eyes bright. 'Have you brought the angels down with you?'

'Yes, I have.' Patrick laughed. 'I've done them up into a very strange-looking parcel, so she can't possibly guess what's inside. Then I told Tom that it was an antique stuffed dog, on the strict understanding that he won't spill the beans. Of course he will have, he won't have been able to resist giving her some pretty enormous clues. I can't wait to see her face when she opens it, and is denied the pleasure of thanking me for such a terrific gift!'

'Patrick, you astonish me!' Giò laughed. 'What a devious old devil you're turning out to be – I never thought you were much of a one for practical jokes, far too straight and serious for that sort of thing.'

'There you are, then. Perhaps I'm lightening up quite a bit in my old age.' Patrick got to his feet and threw another log on the fire. 'Come on, let's go and see if Anna needs help with the table, and get more logs in, shall we?'

In the kitchen, a wonderful smell of slowly-roasting goose was stealing through the room, and a large pan of peeled potatoes stood beside the stove, waiting to go under the goose at the appropriate time.

'There you are, love,' said Anna, embracing her brother. 'I didn't hear you come in.'

'Can we do anything? What about the table?'

'Would you? You're much better at it than I am.'

'Too many cooks,' said Patrick. 'I'll fill up the log baskets.' He went out to the barn. The snow had started to fall again, softly, silently, and he felt the old remembered childhood thrill as he crossed the yard, the snowflakes landing on his nose and eyelashes, and misting his spectacles.

Giò set the table in the dining-room with the best old silver and the thick antique glasses, handed down from generation to generation of Halards. He arranged a garland of ivy, apples, tangerines and nuts along the length of the table, and stuck the twelve tall tallow candles in the brass chandelier that hung above it. The glass and silver sparkled on the deeply polished wood and the fruit glowed in its festoon of ivy, glossy and dark green. Anna came in carrying a tray with the first course, large plates of *fruits de mer*, crabs, langoustines, oysters, mussels and cockles, arranged on beds of seaweed, smelling of the sea. Giò lifted the plates from the tray and put them on the table. 'Wonderful,' he said, inhaling their smell. 'I can hardly wait.'

'I'll bring the rest,' said Anna. 'Run out and round up Philippe and the boys, will you, Giò? I expect they'll all need to wash. And I must go and change, myself.'

Patrick brought in the logs and made up the fires. He got the champagne from the fridge and arranged glasses on the table in the sitting-room. He heard the children come in and thunder upstairs, chased by Giò. Philippe came in and stood before the fire, smiling and rubbing his hands together. 'Boys!' he exclaimed, and laughed. 'Limbs of Satan; I love them.'

'Champagne, Dad?' said Patrick, 'and by the way, *hello*.'

'Oh, sorry, old chap. You've only just come, haven't you? I often think you're already here, when you're not. No, I won't have champagne just yet. I'll have a good slug of Calvados, thanks.'

Patrick poured the Calvados and took it to his father.

'I often wish I *were* here, when I'm not. Happy Christmas, Dad.'

Father and son embraced. 'Happy Christmas, my boy.'

Giò came in, followed by Josh and Max, his face pink and shining with soap. Then came Tom, bringing Marie-Claude, and lastly Anna, looking beautiful in her old red velvet frock. Nothing changes, thank God, thought Patrick, as he poured the fizzy golden wine into the waiting flutes. He picked up the tray and handed it round the company.

'Philippe,' said Anna, taking a glass to her father-in-law, 'you are naughty. You haven't even washed, have you, much less changed?'

'Do you mind?' Philippe's blue eyes were soft with the affection he felt for his daughter-in-law.

'No, I don't,' said Anna, and kissed him. 'Happy Christmas, darling.'

'Tonight is the christening party for Katerina's baby,' said Vassili, putting Guy's mail and papers on the table, and removing his lunch tray, largely untouched.

'Right,' said Guy. 'Tell Heleni not to bother about supper, bread and cheese will be fine.'

'We would like you to come to the party – Katerina will be sad if you don't come and drink the baby's health.'

'That's very kind of her, Vassili, but I don't think so, really.'

'Why not? Are you too proud?'

'No, of course not!'

'I thought you were a friend of my family, as well as my boss.'

'Well, I hope I am. Of course I am.'

'So you will come?'

Guy gave in. He knew it was pointless trying to get

out of it, but he had one last try: 'OK, but if I get drunk and make a fool of myself, won't it rather spoil the occasion?'

Vassili looked at him sternly. 'I expect you could make a particular effort not to do that, until you get home.'

'Yes,' agreed Guy, quietly, 'I expect I could.'

'It is Christmas Eve, after all.'

Guy did not reply. He picked up his mail and began to open it.

At seven o'clock they drove up to the taverna, where the party was already in full swing in the back room behind the terrace, now closed down for the winter. A long trestle table spread with a white embroidered-linen cloth was loaded with bottles of wine and plates of food, and Katerina sat proudly displaying her baby daughter to the relatives and friends who had travelled from distant villages for the ceremony. The women wore their local costume, black and white, sombre but beautiful. The village priest, rosy-cheeked and white-bearded, his greasy stove-pipe hat on his bald head, sat in the place of honour at the head of the table, dispensing blessings to the company and dispatching quantities of wine down his own throat. The heat and noise were overpowering as Guy was manoeuvred skilfully into a seat next to Spiros.

After the usual exchange of greetings, a glass of wine was placed before him. Before he had drunk half of it, Spiros replenished the glass and for four long hours Guy let it sit there untouched, in order to prevent it being instantly refilled. The faces round the table grew redder and redder, the voices louder and louder. Then, as if obeying a silent signal, the women in their black dresses, with white bodices and head-dresses, rose from the table and trooped out onto the empty terrace and formed a ring. The *bouzoúki* and the fiddle struck up and the women performed one of the ancient circular dances, while the younger men took it in turns to improvise in the middle of the circle of slowly-moving women, with ever more athletic leaps and extravagant pirouettes, their heavy boots crashing on the concrete floor. A second circle was formed and the dancing became wilder and noisier, with enthusiastic encouragement from the main party, who pounded the table until the bottles rattled, and clapped their hands in time to the music.

'You are not well today, Mr Guy?' Spiros leaned towards him, his hand to his ear. 'You do not drink or eat?'

'I'm OK, Spiros,' said Guy. 'I have a headache, that's all. It's nothing.'

Vassili appeared and sat in the empty chair on Guy's other side. 'You want for home?'

'I think so, please.'

'Of course. I take you.'

'Thank you.' He turned to Spiros. 'Thank you for inviting me. It's a lovely party. The little girl is fortunate in her family and will have a long and happy life, I'm sure.'

Guy stood up, said goodbye quietly to Katerina, gripped Vassili's shoulder, and they went out to the car. They drove home, Guy got out of the car and Vassili helped him into the house and into his chair.

'Thanks, Vassili. You go back to the party; I'm fine now.'

'We might be late. Do you want to go to bed now?'

'No, not yet. Don't worry, I'm perfectly sober. I can get myself to bed tonight.'

'You are sure?'

'I'm sure.'

Guy leaned back in his comfortable leather chair and listened to the car's engine growing fainter as it climbed

the hill back to the taverna. The house seemed start-
lingly quiet after the noise of the party and for a few
minutes he sat with closed eyes, soothed by the silence.
Then he opened his eyes and looked at the bottle of
whisky on the table beside him and considered having
a drink. Then he looked at the telephone, and decided
against it. It's Christmas Eve, he thought, perhaps she'll
call me. He slid down in the chair and stared at the
phone, willing it to ring.

At midnight, Philippe got up from the table and
opened the window, so that they could hear the
Christmas bells of the little church of St Gilles, floating
over the snow-covered fields and frozen orchards. 'I
think I'll just go out and check on my old ladies,' he
said.

'I'll come with you,' said Anna. 'I could do with a
breath of air.'

It had stopped snowing and the velvety sky was
bright with stars, but a keen north wind blew off the
stiff stubbled fields, as they crunched across the yard
to the big barn.

'Poor old girls,' said Philippe, pulling his woolly cap
firmly over his ears. 'It's always the same, every year.
They choose the worst weather to drop their lambs.
But at least, this is better than rain.'

'Why do you do it, darling?' Anna took Philippe's
arm. 'I should have thought that after all those years of
running round after the patients, the last thing you'd
need is a flock of sheep, and having to be up half the
night when they're lambing.'

'Why do you think I do it?' Philippe looked at Anna,
his blue eyes benign. 'Got to have a reason to get up in
the morning, haven't I?'

He pushed open the big heavy door and they went
into the barn. A small storm-lantern hung above the

door, casting its rays into the gloom of the tall timber-framed building, shining on the massive oak beams and trusses of the roof. Along the walls of the barn Philippe had arranged willow hurdles to form lambing pens, and each space was thickly spread with fresh golden straw. Half a dozen ewes were already installed, and in spite of the cold outside, a heavy smell of sheep and warm straw filled the air. Holding his lantern high above his head, Philippe inspected each of his ewes in turn. They stood patiently in the deep straw, their yellow eyes nervous and alert, their grey ears twitching, chewing abstractedly on twists of hay pulled from the net that hung from a nail above each pen. The barn was filled with the soft sound of munching.

'What about this one?' asked Anna. 'She's lying down.'

'Aha,' said Philippe, coming up and shining his lantern on the ewe, checking the tag on her ear. 'I thought as much, it's number twenty-three. She's always the first, daft old thing.'

They watched her for a few minutes, then her ears flew back, her eyes widened in surprise or fear and her abdomen heaved involuntarily. She uttered a loud aggrieved bleat.

'She's on her way, all right. It won't be long now.' Philippe inspected the rest of his ewes, then went to his veterinary cupboard, and unlocked it. He took out his green rubber apron and put it on, then checked out all the things he might require.

'Is there anything else you'll need?' asked Anna.

'Yes, I need two buckets of really hot water, a bar of yellow soap and some old towels.'

'I'll get them.'

'You're not to carry those heavy buckets, Anna. I forbid it.'

'OK.' She stood on tiptoe and kissed him. 'I'll send Giò or Josh to give you a hand. I'm pretty whacked anyway; I think I need my warm bed.'

'Right. Goodnight, my love, sleep well. Happy Christmas.'

'Happy Christmas.'

Anna went across the starlit yard to the kitchen and found Patrick and Josh putting away the last of the dishes. 'One of the ewes has started,' she said, taking off her coat. 'Where's Giò? Philippe needs two buckets of hot water.'

'He's taking Marie-Claude home,' said Josh. 'Don't worry, I can do it.'

Patrick found the galvanized iron buckets in the wash-place, and they filled them with hot water, topped up from the kettle. Anna put the soap and towels into the pockets of Josh's parka, and he set off across the yard, taking care not to spill the water. He pushed open the barn door with his foot and went in, putting down the buckets and carefully closing the door behind him. Philippe had hung his lantern on a hook and the soft light fell on his white head and green apron, as he leaned over the hurdle, talking quietly to his ewe.

'Where do you want these, *Grandpère*?' Josh approached quietly with his buckets and the penned ewes shifted nervously as he passed.

'Just there, please, Josh. By the cupboard.'

Josh put down the buckets, took the soap and towels out of his pockets, and removed his parka, since it felt surprisingly warm in the barn. He went and stood beside his grandfather and looked at the straining ewe, her head thrust backwards as she did her best to expel her lamb. 'Everything OK?' he asked.

'I hope so,' said Philippe. He got into the pen and knelt beside the ewe, then carefully examined her backside. 'Do you see the feet, Josh?'

Josh leaned over to look, and saw a pair of shiny little black hooves protruding from the ewe.

'Next should come the nose, then the whole head, then a big push and the rest of the lamb's body comes in a rush, and it's all over.' He looked up at Josh, a slight frown on his face. 'Trouble is, the feet have been out for quite a time, the nose should be visible by now.' He climbed out of the pen, rolled up his shirt-sleeves and scrubbed his hands and arms. Then he soaped his right hand and arm copiously, and clambered back into the pen. 'I'm going to have a feel around, the head may be turned backwards, and causing a blockage.' Gently, he slid his hand past the lamb's feet and Josh watched with some astonishment as the old man pushed his hand further inside, eliciting an outraged bleat from the ewe. 'Steady, old girl,' said Philippe. 'Hold her head, Josh. We don't want her standing up. Just as I thought, the head *is* back. Put your weight on her, Josh, and hold her down, while I try and turn the lamb.' Josh, his arm firmly round the ewe's neck, watched as Philippe manipulated the lamb's head, then gently extracted his arm. The ewe gave a vigorous heave and the lamb's head appeared, the nose resting between the two forelegs.

'Well done!' exclaimed Josh. 'That's amazing!'

The ewe struggled to her feet. 'Let her get up,' said Philippe, getting to his own feet as quickly as he could. 'She knows what she's doing now.'

They stood quietly beside her and in a moment the ewe gave a final heave and the rest of the lamb slipped to the straw and lay there motionless. 'Oh, God,' said Josh fearfully. 'Is it dead?'

'No, certainly not.' Philippe knelt down and cleared the cawl from the lamb's face, whereupon it gave a loud bleat, shook its small black head and tried unsuccessfully to stand up. The ewe turned round, sniffed at her lamb, gave a snicker of welcome and began to lick it clean.

'Oh, thank heaven for that!' exclaimed Josh. 'How wonderful!' He sat down on a bale of straw, suddenly extremely moved, and close to tears.

'Keep an eye on her, Josh, while I clean up the mess and take a look at the others. She may have another one in there, one can never be sure. Whether or not, it'll take a few minutes. Whatever you do, don't touch the lamb or try and help in any way, we don't want the ewe rejecting it if she can't recognize its smell.'

Josh sat on his bale and watched as the tiny lamb, still wet from its birth and its mother's thorough cleansing, made repeated efforts to stagger to its feet, its frail legs collapsing uncontrollably as it strove to get its balance. After several abortive attempts, it managed to take a few wobbly steps, then, its nose exploring its mother's flank, finally succeeded in locating a teat, latching on with a vigorous sucking sound, its little tail erect and shaking with joy. Josh smiled tenderly. Well done, baby, he said to himself.

He looked around him, at the medieval majesty of the ancient wooden building, beautiful in the warm glow of the lanterns, at the woolly heads of the other occupants of the maternity ward, at Philippe as he made his unruffled way from pen to pen, tending his flock, just as he had tended his patients for so long. This is what Christmas is really all about, he said to himself. You don't need incense or candles or priests droning on to understand the meaning – it's right here in this barn, with the warmth and smell of the sheep, the hiss of the paraffin lanterns, the bleating of the newborn lambs. A fragile sort of happiness, almost of joy, bloomed inside him, taking him by surprise. The cold painful lump that had for so long occupied the place where his heart should have been, seemed to dissolve and he found that he could now take a deep breath without pain.

'There's another one here, Josh,' called Philippe softly. 'Once one starts, the rest seem to get the message.'

By half-past three, all six ewes had safely lambed, and Philippe and Josh were cleaning up and locking the veterinary chest when the barn door opened and Giò appeared, carrying a tray of mugs. 'I thought you might need some coffee,' he said. They drank the hot coffee, then walked quietly through the orchard with the lantern, to make sure that all was well.

Anna heard the lambing party returning to the house, their boots metallic on the frozen courtyard, their quiet voices clear in the still air. The light from their lantern flickered across her bedroom ceiling through the open casement. She slid out of bed without disturbing Patrick, went to the window and watched as her father-in-law, her brother and her first-born son approached the house. The full moon had set, but the shimmer of hoarfrost and starlight was everywhere; on roofs, on the bare branches of the trees in the orchard and on the ground under the feet of the three men, snug in the warm circle of yellow light they carried with them.

'Pretty good for a night's work.' Anna heard Philippe's voice as he opened the kitchen door beneath her window. 'I wonder what tomorrow will bring?'

'Whatever it brings,' said Josh, 'I'd like to help you again, *Grandpère*, if you'll let me.'

'My dear boy, I'd be only too delighted. You can come and help me with the dipping later on, if you like. That's a real pig of a job.'

'I will,' said Josh. 'I'd love to.'

Anna closed the window, and smiled to herself. Darling Josh, she thought, thank God for that. She got back into bed, and folded herself against the sleeping body of her husband, waking him in the process.

'Anna! You're freezing cold, what on earth are you doing?'

'Getting warm.' She made herself comfortable in the crook of his shoulder. 'Thank you for my stuffed dog,' she said. 'I'm looking forward to him *enormously*.'

'Who told you?'

'Who do you think?'

Patrick laughed, and tightened his arms around her. 'It's not really a stuffed dog, don't worry!'

'I didn't think it was.'

'Oh, didn't you?' He sounded disappointed.

'No. I guessed it was a wind-up.' She smiled in the dark. 'OK. What is it, then? Tell me.'

'Certainly not. You'll have to wait till after Mass, and see, won't you?'

'Will I like it?'

'I'd be quite surprised if you didn't. And it isn't it; it's them.'

Chapter Sixteen

Dido was woken by a sharp tapping at her bedroom window. She opened her eyes and saw the angry faces of two swans, attacking their own reflections in the rain-lashed glass. She felt stiff with cold and rather hung over, but she got out of bed and waved her arms rather ineffectually at the swans, worried that they might break the window. 'Stupid things,' she muttered crossly, and went to the kitchen to make some tea. She stared around her at the mess in the studio while she waited for the kettle to boil. She made the tea and took the mug back to bed. I really must try to pull myself together, and make some sense of this place, she told herself, sipping the scalding tea. First I must tidy up this shambles, then decide what to do with Jake's things. He had not phoned or made any attempt to contact her. I suppose he assumes that I am still in Corfu, she thought. I wonder where he is now, the selfish pig – in some cushy billet, I don't doubt. He's like a cat, he'll aways land on his feet and get to sleep in the best bed, the rat. God, I'm mixing my metaphors she reminded herself, with a bleak smile. 'As if it matters,' she said, putting the empty mug on the night-table. She lay down again, pulling the duvet up to her chin, postponing the moment when she would have to wash and dress and get on with the day.

There was a loud knocking on the door and Dido sat up, her heart in her mouth. God, it's him, she thought wildly, and leapt out of bed. She put on her dressing-gown, and stood uncertainly for a moment, trembling with fright and cold. The knocking began again, insistently, and a muffled voice called '*Dido*? Are you there?' The voice was not Jake's. Frowning, she tightened the belt of her dressing-gown and went to the door. Leaving the chain fastened, she turned the key and opened the door a crack, then peered suspiciously through the narrow gap. Standing on the duckboards, sheltering under an inadequate umbrella, stood a little old woman. She was wearing a purple mac, pink fluorescent gumboots and a red tam-o-shanter pulled over her tight grey curls. She carried a bulging supermarket bag and her nose was blue with cold.

'Mabel!'

'There you are, Dido, and not before time! Open the bleedin' door, for Gawd's sake, it's real brass-monkey weather out 'ere!'

Hastily, Dido undid the chain and Mabel stepped briskly over the threshold, vigorously shaking the umbrella as she did so. She took off her dripping waterproof and Dido hung it on the back of the door. Mabel removed the red tam-o-shanter that matched her knitted two-piece and stuffed it into the pocket of the mac, then, fluffing up her grey curls, she turned to Dido and gave her a bony hug.

'Shall I make some coffee?' said Dido, returning the hug, extremely glad that Mabel had come.

'Rather 'ave tea,' said Mabel. 'Strong, mind. None of your Chinese gnat's pee, Dido.'

'OK.' Dido laughed and put on the kettle.

'Why aren't you dressed, my girl? What you doing, slopping round in a dressing-gown this time o' day? It's nearly twelve o'clock.'

'Is it really?' Dido looked at her watch. 'So it is.'

'What's up, love?'

Dido looked at Mabel, uncertainly. 'Everything's up,

296

Mabel. I seem to be in the process of wrecking my life. Not that it was much of a life anyway, really.' She poured water into the teapot and gave it a good stir. She put milk into the mugs, three sugars in Mabel's, and poured the tea.

Mabel took her mug and looked at it critically. 'It's still gnat's pee, Dido. How do you manage it? You never did learn, did you?'

'No, I never did learn,' whispered Dido, and burst into tears. Alarmed, Mabel put down her mug and took Dido in her arms. 'Come on, old darlin', get a grip, there's a good girl.' She patted Dido's back as if she were a child. 'Lets sit down on the settee. Tell Mabel all about it. You'll feel better then, won't you?' They sat down and Mabel held Dido in her arms and let her have a good cry, regretfully eyeing her mug of tea as it sat cooling on the coffee table. She looked round the room and pursed her lips. It was dirty according to her high standards, freezing cold and littered with cardboard boxes. Is she moving, or what? Mabel asked herself. At last Dido's tears ceased and she sat up, her face blotched, with puffy lips and swollen eyelids.

'Go and put some clothes on, Dido. Right away, while I light the stove and make some more tea. It's like a bleedin' tomb in 'ere, or 'adn't you noticed?'

'Yes, I had noticed.'

'Just couldn't be bothered, then?' said Mabel severely. 'Lazy cow,' she added.

Dido laughed reluctantly, got to her feet and went to the bedroom to put on some warm clothes. When she returned, Mabel had plumped up the cushions on the sofa, stacked the cardboard boxes against one wall, and made some fresh tea, very strong this time. She had also managed to light the stove, which now roared up the flue, its dampers fully extended. It was already beginning to chuck its comforting warmth into the room.

'You'll set the chimney on fire!'

'No chance,' said Mabel. 'Come on now, sit down and tell us all about it.'

Two hours later, Dido stopped talking, blew her nose and looked shyly at Mabel, sitting so silently beside her.

'Well,' said Mabel, after a short pause, 'it's obvious, innit?'

'What is?'

'You love the chap with the dodgy legs, and you've finally given up on that sewer Kroll. It sounds as if you're well shot of 'im, love.'

'It's not quite as simple as that, Mabel.'

'Why isn't it?'

'Well, I've been here nearly a week now, and Guy hasn't once phoned me, or written.'

'So what's stopping you from ringing him? He's on the phone, isn't he?'

'Yes, he's on the phone.'

'So, why don't you ring *him*?'

'Because I'm afraid that the damage is too much for him to take on board; to forgive if you like, though God knows there's nothing to forgive, it wasn't my fault. That's what makes me so angry, and that's really why I can't bring myself to telephone him. How could he believe that liar Jake, even for a moment, when he told him that we'd made love together at Inniscarragh? How *could* he, Mabel, if he really loved me?'

'I expect it was the shock of being told that got to him, love. Poor sod, there wasn't a lot 'e could do about it, was there? Like murdering that cruel bastard? And you didn't hang about yourself, did you? You pushed off before either of you had time to calm down, and get things sorted, didn't you?'

'Yes, you're probably right,' said Dido sadly, 'but there's something else I haven't told you. One of the last things he said was that I had brought chaos and uncertainty into his life and that he doesn't need that.'

'Hoity-toity!' said Mabel. 'He sounds like a right ole woman!'

'He is *not*!' retorted Dido, flushing angrily.

Mabel laughed. 'Well, then,' she said. 'There's your answer, stupid girl.'

It had stopped raining, so they went out to the pub for lunch. Over gin and sausages, they discussed the question of Jake's possessions.

'Where's 'e living?' asked Mabel. 'We could take the stuff round in a taxi, an' dump it there. He'll probably be at work, so you won't even 'ave to see 'im, will you?'

Back at *The Maid*, Dido flicked through the pages of the address book that contained all the regularly-used professional numbers, both her own and Jacob's, then she phoned his agent.

'Mike Crisp, please,' she said to the girl who answered the phone.

'Will you hold a moment? Who's calling, please?'

'It's Dido Partridge.' The cheerful strains of the *Nutcracker* poured into her ear while she waited, then Mike came on the line.

'Hi, Dido? How's tricks, darling? Busy, busy?'

'Frantic, as usual, thanks,' said Dido. 'Just got back from Greece. What's that toad Jake up to, do you know? I need him to sign some stuff.'

Mike laughed. 'I hear he's hanging out with the delicious Nastassia whatsit; or was, the last I heard. Hang on, love, I've got the number somewhere. Right, here it is.' He gave the number.

'Thanks,' said Dido. 'What's the address again? It's probably better if I write first.'

Mike read out the address, told Dido that she was a

good sort, and he wished his wife were more like her. He said goodbye and hung up.

'Strand-on-the-Green,' said Dido. 'Fancy that.'

They called a taxi, piled all the boxes into it and drove out to Strand-on-the-Green. The taxi cruised down Thames Road and stopped at the garden gate bearing the number Mike had given her. There was a row of dustbins against the wall, and Dido asked the driver to help her stack the boxes beside them. She was quite enjoying herself. The task completed, the taxi turned round and took them back to Chelsea Harbour. It was nearly six o'clock. 'Money well spent,' said Dido, handing over the enormous fare and tip.

While Mabel made tea, Dido telephoned Jake's number to inform him that his belongings were stacked in Thames Road, but it was not Jake who answered the phone.

'Hello?' said a soft breathy voice with a slight accent. 'Nastassia?'

'Yes, this is Nastassia. Who is this?'

'It's Dido. You'd better get out to the back road and pick up Jake's belongings, that's if they haven't already been stolen.' She hung up, and turned to Mabel, grinning.

'He's not in, then?' said Mabel, grinning too.

An hour later the phone rang. It was Jake. 'Dido, why didn't you tell me you were back? What the hell do you think you're playing at? My stuff is scattered all over the road, and my tape-deck has been nicked.'

'Good, serves you right,' said Dido. 'I should have done it long ago.' She laughed.

'Come on, darling, be reasonable. You know how much we mean to each other at the end of the day. I need you and *The Maid*, you know I do.'

'Sorry, Jake, you'll just have to put up with it, won't you? You don't have me any more, and you don't have

The Maid, either. If you want to know, I've given her to Mabel, and she's going to live there, on the strict understanding that you never set foot in the place again.'

'You don't mean that!'

'I bloody do.' She put the phone down and looked at Mabel. 'You will, won't you, dearest Mabel?'

'Will what?'

'Live here, and take care of it for me?'

'Yeah,' said Mabel, 'why not? Good idea, you need someone here.' She looked at Dido affectionately. 'Well done,' she said, 'you've cooked 'is bleedin' goose, an' no mistake. That's put paid to him all right.'

'I hope,' said Dido, suddenly feeling terribly tired.

'So,' said Mabel, 'when are you going to phone this Guy, then?'

'I'll phone him this evening, in a minute.'

Mabel, assuming that Dido would prefer to speak to Guy alone, got up and put on her mac. 'I'll nip out to the off-licence for a bottle of scotch, we could do with a drink. It's Christmas Eve, after all, innit?'

'So it is,' said Dido. 'I'd quite forgotten.'

'Then I'll do a nice macaroni cheese for our supper.' Mabel stepped out into the darkness, clicking the door behind her. Dido, her heart beating a little faster, picked up the phone and dialled Guy's number. It rang and rang, but there was no reply. She tried again, twice more. I suppose it is possible that he's out, she thought. It *is* Christmas Eve. She listened to the phone ringing in the empty house so far away, and looked at her watch: twenty-past six, that's twenty-past eight in Corfu. Maybe Vassili has persuaded him to go to a party at the taverna, she said to herself; I'd better try again a bit later.

Lavinia was watching the service of Nine Lessons and Nine Carols on television. A large glass of sherry stood on the occasional table beside her chair, but her customary fire of apple logs seemed reluctant to burn and the room felt much less cosy and comforting without the cheerful blaze. Even Fritz evidently felt the deprivation and had rather pointedly elected to stay in the kitchen, his head wedged against the Rayburn. The week had been a disastrous one. On Monday morning, Maeve had failed to appear, and when Lavinia had enquired of Burke whether there was a problem, he had jerked his head towards Inniscarragh in rather an offhand manner. 'It's up at the house she is now, Miss.' Taken completely by surprise, Lavinia had coloured angrily with disbelief. 'How can she be? She hasn't given notice, she should be here.'

'Is that a fact, Miss?' Burke had looked at her then, his sharp little weasel's face insolent, his tone sarcastic and hostile. 'The pay's very good at the house, Miss. It is indeed. Twice what we're getting here it is, not a word of a lie.' The threat had been unmistakable and Lavinia would have given much to sack him on the spot. But wisdom prevailed and she had retreated to the cottage, to regroup her forces, such as they were. Since that day her logs had been brought in as usual, but they were wet and hardly worth the effort of trying to make them burn; she was well aware that it would be counter-productive to complain.

She stared critically at the face of a small chorister, she supposed of eleven or twelve years of age, listening unmoved as he sang *Lullay, thou little tiny Child*. The pure treble notes of the carol soared high into the vaulting of the college chapel, while the camera dwelt lovingly on the glass-shaded candles illuminating the faces of the choir, then soared up towards the carved wooden angels, blowing their trumpets as they flew so high against the medieval roof.

Perhaps if I'd married silly Freddy I'd have a

grandson like that now, Lavinia thought as the child's face reappeared on the screen. I wouldn't be here in this poky cottage, being insulted by the servants, I'd be in that big house in Connemara, and my sons and daughters would be arriving for Christmas, and it would all be exactly as it used to be at Inniscarragh, only better, because I would be the boss. The carol service came to an end and she switched off the television. Without any real hope she stirred the smouldering logs with the poker; if anything her efforts seemed to make matters worse.

Lavinia gave up and went to the kitchen, wondering what she could find in the way of food. In the fridge, a small turkey occupied pride of place on the middle shelf, its purple thighs studded with the imperfectly plucked quills of its former feathers. She stared at it, appalled at her own stupidity in ordering the thing in the first place. The very idea of cooking it, together with its obligatory accompaniments, filled her with a combination of boredom and dismay. How pointless and idiotic, she thought, to go to all that trouble and then carve one slice and eat it all alone. A slightly hysterical laugh escaped her and was quenched at source, before it could get out of hand. Frowning, she took a plastic packet of cheese from the fridge, and closed the door on the offending bird.

Lavinia made herself a sandwich and took it back to the sitting-room. She poured herself another very large sherry and returned to her seat by the fire, and tried to ignore the fact that it was now completely dead. As she munched her way rather inelegantly through the flaccid bread and cheese, her eyes wandered aimlessly round the room. She counted the Christmas cards on her chimney piece; thirteen, the unlucky number. She herself had sent out thirty. She was not particularly surprised at not receiving more; it was really quite likely that some of the recipients of her cards were now dead. She had not seen or spoken to most of them for years. The annual exchange of greetings had been the only contact. She swallowed the last large lump of her sandwich, easing its downward passage with the remains of her sherry.

Noises of revelry came from the lane outside, and she put her empty glass carefully on the table beside her chair. That'll be the staff going down to the pub, she thought irritably, getting to her feet and crossing to the window. She peered through a crack in the curtains, careful not to be seen. The little company, which appeared to be full of the Christmas spirit already, was walking briskly down the drive in the moonlight, five abreast, heading for the village, no doubt. Their loud cheerful conversation was punctuated with noisy bursts of laughter and outbreaks of singing.

Lavinia pulled the edges of her curtains together with sudden energy. Good, she thought, they're all out. I'll go up and have a look at the house, see what they've been up to. She put on her long winter overcoat and her fur-lined boots and let herself out of her front door without disturbing her odious little dog. Once outside her gate, she fastened the fur collar of her coat round her neck, for the air was sharp with frost, and then turned towards Inniscarragh. She stood for a few moments, looking at the beautiful house that had been the home of so many generations of the Porteous family. The building looked insubstantial, almost ghostly, its many windows glittering in the brilliant cold light of the full moon. Not a single light could be seen from within, the place looked as though it had been empty and abandoned for years. Which, to all intents and purposes, it has, thought Lavinia, and sighed. She thrust her hands deep into her velvet-lined pockets and walked towards the house. She mounted the stone steps to the terrace and approached the ceremonial entrance, the great glass doors looming and tall under the stone portico. She tried the handle and the door opened silently, rather to her surprise. She entered the house, closing the door behind her.

Lavinia looked around at the familiar entrance hall. The furniture and pictures had been removed and the carpet had gone from the wide staircase. Decorators' ladders and trestles stood about the stone floor and pots of paint waited on dustsheet-covered benches, but the air was warm, presumably from central heating, and smelt faintly of old-fashioned distemper. She opened the door to the dining-room and went in quietly, keeping her hand on the knob to prevent the door from closing and shutting her in. Some long-forgotten childish event, some shame-making incident during a meal in this room, had left her with a permanent though undefined dislike of it, even a kind of fear. She looked quickly round. All seemed much as before, except that the long table was shrouded in a new dustcover, blue, which sorted ill with the striped burgundy of the wallpaper. I expect that's coming off anyway, she thought, and no great loss. She left the room and crossed the hall to the Chinese drawing-room, and through that to her mother's little private sitting-room beyond. There, the shutters were open and the small garden outside was brightly lit by the moon, its silvery beams pouring into the room in incandescent pencils of light. The old rosewood piano glowed like a glass of red wine. The instrument was closed, and the silver-framed photographs and books of music had gone from its top. Beside the piano stood her mother's small regency sofa, stripped of its brocade upholstery, the canvas of its lining stark white,

305

with little rust marks where the tacks had been extracted. A tattered piece of grey webbing hung down forlornly under the seat. The pictures had all been removed from the walls, their former positions clearly visible as darker rectangles of unfaded blue-green Victorian wallpaper. Lavinia felt a shock of disbelief. She remembered the walls as always being a very pale linden green, enlivened by the gilt frames of the Victorian watercolours. She shook her head and sat down at the piano, lifting the lid. Cracking her knuckles, she hesitated a moment and then rattled off *The Merry Peasant* with no mistakes. Pleased, she looked at her hands on the keyboard and smiled, remembering the hours spent in that little room, practising, every single day, even Sunday. She had not been a particularly musical child, and had little natural talent, but the enforced drudgery had produced a certain level of competence which had given pleasure to Lavinia's mother, if to no one else. She struck a soft note and then, without really thinking what she was doing began to play *Für Elise* as if for the first time. As her fingers flew over the keys the room seemed filled with the sounds and sensations of her adolescence, of the great country house balls, of girls in white dresses, the smell of gardenias, of satin slippers soaked by early dew, green-stained with grass. The whole of those turbulent years seemed to whirl around her, both painfully and pleasurably. As the last notes faded and her hands were still, she looked up and saw Arthur standing by the fireplace in the moonlight, a gardenia in his buttonhole, his hair slicked back, glossy with brilliantine; his eyes mocking, quizzical. He was holding a little dance-card in his hand. He is going to ask me to dance, she thought, but he put the card in his pocket, made a curt bow towards her, turned on his heel and walked out of the room. Lavinia closed the lid of the piano, put her head down on her arms, and wept.

Weeping was not a very usual or natural thing for Lavinia to indulge in, and after a while she decided to stop, for she felt quite ill and had given herself a headache. I mustn't get caught here anyway, she thought. I must go home and go to bed. She left the house the way she had come, through the front entrance. I won't go down the drive; I might run into them coming back from the pub, she said to herself. She went round the side of the house and followed the path through the wreckage of the old woodland, in order to reach her back garden gate. Prolonged recent rain had made the ground heavy with mud and this stuck tenaciously to her boots, making her passage slow and laborious. The moon had disappeared behind a bank of cloud, making it very difficult for her to see the stumps and roots of trees that still littered the ground. Twice, she tripped and fell, covering her beautiful coat with mud. At last, exhausted and slightly frightened, she reached the *chinoiserie* bridge over the canal and, looking ahead, saw with considerable relief the light in her bedroom. She did not see the hole in the rotten plank as she quickened her step in her anxiety to reach the safety of her cottage. She fell straight through the hole and landed face-down in the icy water below, and must have lost consciousness immediately from the shock. Her heavy coat may have supported her for a while, but her big fur-lined boots filled with water and within five minutes she had sunk without a trace beneath the dark peaty waters, now newly-dredged and deep. All that remained was a row of brown bubbles drifting slowly downstream.

Chapter Seventeen

Giò arrived in Souliac in the late afternoon. He did not park his car in the Place de l'Eglise and go straight to the presbytery, his parents' house. Instead, he drove round the outer lane that encircled the village, and stopped by the door to his own little house, the *remise* at the rear of the courtyard behind the presbytery. Stiff after the long drive, he climbed out of his car and walked down the lane to stretch his legs. The sun had just set but the whole western sky was still vividly scarlet, fading through orange and pink to an intense deep blue overhead. The vineyard that bordered the lane, and belonged to Giò and his father, had already been partly pruned and the stony soil, displaced by the heavy autumn rains, had been carefully harrowed up round each vinestock to protect its base from frost. The hairy black wintry stumps marched in tidy lines across the seventy hectares of their land, and Giò smiled. Good old Dad, he thought, he's fantastic for his age. I've neglected him shamefully lately, fussing over Josh's apartment. I'll try and stay down here for the whole of January, and help him finish the pruning.

He unlocked the door to his house and went in, closing it quietly behind him. The familiar smell of ancient, slightly damp stone filled the air and he sniffed appreciatively. It's like the smell of old churches, he thought; the odour of sanctity. Not that there's much in the way of sanctity about *my* life. All the same, the little building did seem to wrap itself round him like a blessing every time he came back to it. He turned on the heating, then checked that he had logs for his fire, and found a good-sized stack in the space under the stairs, together with kindling and a bucket of coal. He lit the fire, then went to his rather basic kitchen to put on the kettle. While it boiled, he went out to the car and got his bag from the boot and took it upstairs to his bedroom, still furnished with the old battered hospital bed and blue-painted bench and chairs of his childhood. The only change he had made, apart from central heating, was the installation of a half-bathroom, just a basin, shower and loo, squeezed into one corner of the low room, under the roof timbers. He put the bag down on the bench, and crossed the room to open the window and push back the shutters on their creaking hinges, pinning them against the outer wall with their small iron clips. He leaned his elbows on the sill, and looked through the naked branches of the wide, umbrella shaped fig tree to the courtyard below, the scene of so many family summer meals, some happy, some not, that had punctuated his life, from boyhood to the present day. His mother's weathered terracotta pots, filled with box and pittisporum clipped into fat neat balls, were clumped in groups around the high walls, presided over by a lead Virgin, snug in her niche. Nothing has changed, he said to himself, and thank God for it; this place is the linchpin of my life. A small dark shape appeared in the branches of the fig tree, and a slim black cat leapt towards Giò, landing neatly on his folded arms. A hard little head butted itself against his chest, and razor-sharp claws dug into the sleeve of his jacket. 'Watch it, Cat!' he exclaimed, unhooking the cat and tucking it carefully under one arm, while it continued to rub its head vigorously against him, purring ferociously. He closed the window. 'Hell!' he said. 'The kettle! I bet it's boiled dry.' He ran down the stairs, dumped the cat on the sofa and made his tea.

By now the logs were blazing cheerfully in the chimney, and Giò lay down on his long, comfortable sofa in front of it, holding the hot mug of tea between his hands. The cat settled itself on his stomach, still purring ecstatically. 'I suppose you thought I'd done a runner, did you?' The cat opened his almond-shaped green eyes for a second, then closed them again. 'You smell of fish,' said Giò. 'Someone's been spoiling you, haven't they?'

He drank his tea slowly, and looked around his room, calm and beautiful in the flickering firelight. Over the years, he had rescued it from the run-down garage it had originally been. First of all, he had rewired the entire building and installed the necessary plumbing. Then he had employed the village mason to point the crumbling interior stone walls with traditional lime-mortar, rendering them with a thick coat of limestone *chaux*, then skilfully finishing them with a steel trowel to a smooth, natural texture. Giò had left the new work exactly as it was, unpainted and immensely pleasing to the eye. At the far end of the room, he had built a simple but generous chimney-piece, above a traditional fireplace. He had covered the earth floor with plain stone tiles, bedded on sand. At the other end of the room, partly concealed behind the open-tread staircase to the upper floor, he had installed the minimum of kitchen equipment; a counter-top with hob and oven, a sink and a small fridge, the whole lit by strip-lighting concealed in the base of a row of cupboards over the work-top.

The room was furnished with extreme simplicity. The sofa was covered in a soft tobacco-coloured tweed, and had a long refectory table behind it, bearing two beautiful lamps made from Sheffield plate candlesticks, very tall and slender, with plain cream parchment shades. Piles of books and magazines crowded the surface of the table, together with a miniature zinc hip-bath containing the dark-green glossy foliage of a laurel plant, a black wire basket filled with old lead-crystal glasses, together with a bottle of vodka and an English decanter with a silver stopper, containing single malt whisky. In the centre of the table stood a square glass vase. Now empty, this was usually filled with fresh flowers, sometimes wild ones picked from the *garrigue*, occasionally an exotic lily bought in Uzès. Sometimes in August a tight bundle of lavender was jammed into the vase without water, to scent the warm summer air for weeks on end.

It was not a room in which to entertain, or even one to share with anyone else. It was designed to be Giò's alone, a place to withdraw, to be absolutely himself. 'Hello again, Cat,' he said, smoothing its silky head between its ears, 'it's nice to be back.' Especially satisfying was the knowledge that it was quite likely that the smoke from his chimney or the firelight in his window would have been noticed by one or other of his parents, through their windows just across the courtyard. The fact that neither of them would take the slightest notice of his arrival until he chose to declare himself was a matter of enormous importance to him, though neither he nor they ever mentioned it. It's funny, he said to himself, for years I've been chasing after the Holy Grail of happiness, searching for someone to share my life, a permanent partner, but if I'm honest with myself, I'm really happiest on my own.

He thought about the few days he had spent at St Gilles. It had been fun, he had enjoyed himself, but at the centre of his being he knew that he had been alone there. Anna and Patrick, though kind, were a couple, and Josh and Philippe had become a couple, engrossed in their lambing. As for the two boys, they had constantly vanished on secret activities of their own, reappearing only at mealtimes. In the evening, in front of the fire, Giò had made a real effort to amuse them, playing pontoon with them or teaching them card tricks, but they had quickly lost interest, and Giò had become rather bored himself. In the end, he had searched through Philippe's extensive library and borrowed the thickest book he could find – *War and Peace.* Engrossed in the lives of Pierre, André and Natasha, he had made himself comfortable in front of the sitting-room fire and ceased to be the resident clown of the household.

'Are you feeling OK, Giò?' Anna, coming into the room, had looked at him anxiously.

'Yes, of course. I'm fine.'

'Tired?'

'No.'

'Bored?'

'Yes, a bit.'

'I know the feeling.' She had laughed and blown him a kiss. 'As long as you're OK.'

'I'm perfectly OK, but I think I'll push off to Souliac tomorrow. Dad really needs my help.'

'Why not? It'll be bedlam again when we all arrive, won't it? Enjoy a bit of peace while you can.'

Darling Anna, thought Giò, she always knows how I'm feeling. *War and Peace,* on loan from Philippe, was packed in his bag upstairs and he looked forward to finishing it.

In the presbytery kitchen, Domenica poured herself a glass of wine and checked over her list of preparations for the *réveillon* dinner. Tomorrow, Olivia, her granddaughter, would drive to Uzès with Basil, her husband, to collect the barrel of oysters and the brace of fine fat geese ordered at the beginning of December. The champagne was already standing on the cold floor of the cellar, and Domenica's particular contribution to the feast, a cold lemon soufflé, sat on a shelf of the freezer, ready to be defrosted and given its final decoration of whipped cream. The cooking of the geese was to be Robert's affair, and he would stuff them with lemons, bitter oranges and fistfuls of thyme and whole cloves of garlic before roasting them in the bread oven, specially lit for the occasion. Olivia was to help him with the vegetables and sauces that would accompany the festive birds, and Basil was in charge of the making of two kinds of salad. Anna's room was already prepared for her and Patrick, Josh was to go in Giò's old room, and the two boys, thank God, would sleep over at Olivia's cottage.

Feeling slightly sated already at the prospect of eating so much rich food again so soon after Christmas, Domenica got up from the table, opened the fridge door and wondered rather vaguely what there was for supper. That's the trouble with Christmas and New Year, she thought, you don't pay enough attention to all the meals in between. She had a sudden intense longing for a large plate of sweet-smelling thickly-sliced ripe tomatoes, glistening with extra virgin olive oil and fragrant with chopped basil, with a scattering of ripe black olives to add their earth-tasting pungency to the dish, and nothing else except a piece of fresh *pain de campagne* and a glass of wine. Bliss, she thought, the food of summer. She shook her head, remembering Robert's feats of ingenuity in inventing new ways of finishing up the indestructible Christmas turkey, and as recently as yesterday, when she had breathed a sigh of relief, thinking that the dreadful bird was finally finished, its carcase had been turned into bowlfuls of stock, now cramming the shelves of the freezer. She did not doubt that after three months or so of inconvenience, she would grasp the nettle and throw the frozen stock away. Now she gazed helplessly at the shelves of the fridge, which seemed remarkably empty, except for jars of *coulis* of various kinds, half-used, an open packet of designer salad, rather tinged with brown, and a jar of preserved goose. There was also a ham bone with very little ham left on it, and a blue bowl containing three eggs. Unable to think of a brilliant way of dealing with the items on offer, Domenica frowned crossly and closed the fridge door.

Upstairs in the salon, the phone began to ring and then stopped, evidently answered by Robert. Taking her drink with her, she went to the foot of the stairs and listened. She could hear Robert's voice and then his laugh. Then he shouted, 'Darling! It's Anna, for you.'

'Hold on. I'm coming.' She climbed the long stone stairway to the first floor as quickly as her arthritic knees would permit, pulling herself up on the iron railing. She hurried into the salon, where Robert, sitting in his writing chair at the round library table, was still chatting to their daughter.

'Here she is, now. Bye, darling.' Robert handed the phone to Domenica, relinquishing his seat at the same time.

She sat down. 'Hello, sweetheart. Anything wrong?'

'No, Mum, everything's fine. I've just been telling Dad, we've had another heavy snowfall here, and it's been snowing all day.'

'Really? Are you snowed in?'

'Well, no, because Philippe's got four-wheel drive. The thing is, the lambs are arriving thick and fast, and Josh wants to stay here and help Philippe, he really seems to be enjoying himself.'

'Well, that's good, isn't it?'

'Yes, of course, it's very good,' said Anna. 'It's terrific, the answer to prayer.'

There was a pause.

'What you're getting around to saying, is that you're all staying up there with Philippe, instead of coming here for the *réveillon*?'

'Well, it's difficult, Mum. Max wants to be with Josh, and Tom wants to stay with Max. I even have the feeling, though he hasn't said so, that Patrick wants to be here with his father. He's in his late eighties now — you know what I mean, don't you?'

Domenica laughed, her old, harsh braying laugh. 'Come to that, *your* father's in his eighties too, but he doesn't look as if he's ready to pop his clogs just yet!' Robert, sitting beside the fire, listening, though pretending to read a paper, looked up, startled. 'It's all right, darling,' Domenica went on, rather brusquely. 'I quite understand. Don't worry about it, I'm sure we'll manage to have quite a good time without you.'

'I know you will,' said Anna quietly. 'I was really looking forward to spending some time with you, Mum. I feel bad about it too, you know.'

'Do you, darling? Well, that makes two of us. Never mind, later on, perhaps?'

'Yes, of course. Has Giò arrived yet?'

'I don't know.' Domenica turned to Robert. 'Has Giò arrived?'

Robert went to one of the long windows that looked down into the courtyard and across to Giò's *remise*. 'Yes, his light's on.'

'Yes, he's here,' said Domenica into the phone.

'Oh, good. Give him my love, won't you? I'll phone again to wish you *Bonne Année*.'

'Goodbye, darling. Thanks for ringing.'

'Bye, Mum. Thanks for not minding.'

'I do mind,' said Domenica, 'but it's not important,

is it? Love to Patrick.' She put the phone down. 'What a bloody nuisance,' she said. 'How can five of us eat two bloody great fat geese? Not to mention a whole bloody barrel of oysters?'

'Easily,' said Robert, throwing more logs on the fire. 'Cold goose is almost my favourite food, especially with horseradish and the Cumberland sauce we made in the summer. My idea of heaven, we'll have loads of it, what a treat.'

Domenica looked at him in astonishment. 'Do you really mean that, Robert, or are you just saying it to make me feel less cross?'

'I really mean it. All the more for us, for once.'

'Oh, well. If you say so.' She emptied her glass.

'In any case, my love, we *have* got Olly and Baz here, as well as Giò. Quite frankly, I'd really rather have them on their own than the entire mob, especially with those two badly-brought-up little devils.' He looked at his wife, his dark eyes warm in his still-handsome face. 'I'm sure Giò and Anna weren't nearly as tiresome at that age.'

'How the hell would you know?' retorted Domenica rudely. 'You weren't here most of the time, were you?'

'No, I suppose I wasn't.'

'In any case, you're wrong. They were just as bad, if you want to know. All children are horrible.'

'Thus spake the oracle,' remarked Robert drily, and got up from his seat, anxious to avoid an argument. 'What about a refill?'

'Thanks.'

He took her glass and went down to the kitchen. Domenica watched him go. Why am I such a miserable old cow? she asked herself. I really must stop being foul to Robert. No wonder he clears off to the *chai* as often as he can. She got up from the table and sat down on the sofa in front of the fire. I do know why I do it, she thought guiltily. It's because I'm so frightened of losing him, and I know it's got to happen sooner or later. I keep telling myself that we've got years and years in front of us, that it doesn't matter if I treat him badly sometimes, but I know I'm deceiving myself as well as wasting our precious time together. She looked around her beautiful salon, warm and glowing in the firelight and filled with the treasures collected over fifty years. The carved rococo mirrors and gilded picture frames shimmered in the soft light from the alabaster lamp which stood on the table, its yellow circle of light falling on the four Louis XV armchairs, still upholstered in the original fabric, worn to the point of shredding, but nonetheless still incredibly beautiful. Christmas greenery lay along the shelf of the pale stone chimneypiece, and a fir tree stood, as usual, between the two tall windows that overlooked the rear courtyard. It was quite a small one this year, and she had decorated it with real wax candles stuck into the Victorian clip-on holders that had come from Robert's childhood home, along with his rocking-horse and teddy bears. I am a fortunate and happy woman, she told herself severely, staring into the fire, so what is it that makes me so afraid? She sighed, for she knew the reason perfectly well. It's because I believe that this is all there is. I know that when Robert dies, that's it, I won't see him again, ever. And that's what I can't bear to think about; I'm beginning to mourn him even before he's dead. In her mind's eye, she saw quite clearly her mother's house in Aix, so many years ago, and herself opening the door to find a tall dark Englishman, who spoke imperfect French and was looking for a lodging. She had known at once that she would never love anyone else, and neither had she. Darling Robert, she said to herself. I bet he doesn't waste his precious time fretting about the possibility of losing *me*; I don't suppose he's given it a single thought, sensible chap.

Giò opened his eyes and looked at his watch: seven-twenty. The fire had burned low and he sat up, pushing the cat off his chest. He got to his feet, blinking, and turned on the lamps. Damn, he thought, I must have dropped off. I should have gone to the *alimentation*; there's no food here. I'll go over and see what Mum and Dad are doing, have supper with them perhaps, or borrow some eggs. He went upstairs, unpacked his bag and put *War and Peace* on his night-table. He hung his jacket on one of the wooden pegs on the back of the door, and pulled on his old grey sweater, crew-necked and comfortable. He turned down his bed, and thought about putting in a hot-water bottle. No, I won't bother, he said to himself, I'll do it when I go to bed if the house still feels cold. He went down-stairs and put more logs on the fire, arranging them carefully so that they could not roll out of the fire-basket. Then he opened one of the kitchen cupboards and took out a small tin of catfood. He emptied the contents into a saucer and put it on the floor. The cat, curled into a tight ball, slept on in front of the fire.

'Well, I'm off now,' he said. 'Supper's on the floor when you want it, daft old thing.'

He opened the door to the courtyard and stepped out into the cold, sparkling night. The sky was ablaze with stars, the air was silent and still and smelt of frost. Domenica's pots of box were already faintly rimed, each small green leaf edged with silver. It will be warm and sunny tomorrow, he said to himself as he crossed the courtyard, we must get on with the pruning. He opened the door to the presbytery kitchen and found Robert opening a bottle of Veuve Clicquot. 'Hello, Dad. What are you celebrating?'

'Hello, Giò. Nothing in particular; just cheering up the old girl.'

'Oh? What's up?'

'Anna phoned to say they're not coming down after all. I think your mother's a bit upset.'

'Poor old Mum. She'll have to make do with me, won't she?'

'Olly and Baz are here, too. They're staying in the cottage.'

'Of course they are, I forgot.'

Robert put another glass on the tray, and Giò carried it up to the salon, followed by his father. He put the tray down on the table, poured the wine and took a glass to Domenica.

'Hello, darling.' She took the proffered glass. 'Good heavens, bubbles! What's all this about?'

Giò bent down and kissed her. 'Don't you think the return of the prodigal is a good enough reason?'

Domenica lifted her hand and touched his cheek. 'Yes, of course I do,' she said, smiling at him.

'And when we've finished the bottle,' said Giò, 'we'll go to the café and have a steak.'

'Excellent idea,' said Robert, sitting down beside the fire. 'Especially as we appear to have run out of everything, totally.'

'We have three eggs,' said Domenica with dignity.

'At least, we haven't got a fridge full of leftovers,' said Robert.

'Very true, darling,' agreed Domenica. 'We've been *eating* them, remember? *Ad nauseam.*'

Giò looked from one to the other, shook his head, and laughed.

Olivia was making up the beds in the spare bedroom, ready for Tom and Max. They had got rid of the old matrimonial bed that had been part of the furniture when Olivia had inherited the little house, and replaced it with two rather hard divan beds, separated by a small chest. Olivia had done a deal with her grandmother and had exchanged the original large white provençal quilt with its flowered border for two single nineteenth-century ones in an unusual brilliant peacock blue, with a predominantly scarlet pattern of formal urns. They looked very cheerful in the small bare room, but Olivia regretted the loss of the more beautiful white *boutis*, the traditional bridal quilt of so long ago. She thought of her bedroom in the Sologne, big, beamed and spacious under the roof of the barn that she and Baz had bought two years ago, and were still converting, step by step. It was nothing like the pretty farmhouse in the Touraine that Basil had originally envisaged as their future home. It was a rather brutal, solid limestone building with an immensely deep roof, of brown lichen-blotched stone tiles, pierced along its length by the cat-slide roofs of small dormers. Mulberry trees grew against the walls, and ivy clung tenaciously where it could, doing its best to get under the tiles. At present, they did not have a proper garden, one simply walked out of the house and into the landscape. White ducks and a few malign-looking muscovies from the neighbouring farm marched past their windows at will, and frequently entered the house. Since their arrival, they had discovered other disadvantages to living in the Sologne, notably the ferocious mosquitoes that bred in the many lakes of the area, but it was their first proper home and they loved it.

Olivia did not mind being there on her own when Baz's career as a foreign correspondent took him away, as it frequently did. During these solitary periods, she got on with her own work, at the same time trying to complete a new piece of restoration on the house as a surprise for Baz on his return. If she got too lonely, or needed to go to Paris for any reason, it was quite a short drive to Orléans, where she took the train to the capital, seventy-five miles distant. In Paris she would stay with her mother and Patrick at Grands-Augustins, or with her mother-in-law on the Ile St-Louis. Her married life was one of peaks and troughs, though the troughs were not unhappy ones, just very different. She often thought that she would feel less alone if she had children, and was aware that Basil wished it more than anything, though he rarely spoke about it. But she was only twenty-four, she did not wish to interrupt the smooth progress of her career as a printmaker, and told herself that there was plenty of time for a family later. There was much to accomplish before then, at least one more exhibition, and even more importantly, finishing the house. Still, she said to herself as she checked that the drawers of the chest were empty and turned the radiator up a little, it'll be fun to have the two boys here for a few days, we must think of amusing things to do with them.

Down in the kitchen, Basil was roasting a chicken on the spit, suspended over the wood fire. He had set two places, and put bread, cheese and wine on the table. In the drip-tray under the bird he had arranged parboiled potatoes and baby turnips, and as he sat by the fire watching the spit turning, he basted the vegetables with the oil and juices that flowed from the little bird, fragrant with rosemary and garlic. He felt intensely happy, as he always did when he was alone with his wife, and especially when performing a ritual that seemed to him both romantic and primitive, like ploughing the earth, digging a well, or cooking on a spit over an open fire. In fact, he was quite aware that his thinking was rather bogus, and smiled at himself. Nevertheless, this clinical self-knowledge did not prevent him from indulging quite deliberately his capacity to enjoy these experiences as often as he could.

'That smells divine,' said Olivia, coming into the kitchen.

'Nearly ready,' said Baz. 'Pour the wine, darling, will you?'

After they had eaten, and washed the dishes, Olivia suggested going to the café to have a cognac and watch the news on the telly. 'We haven't read a paper or listened to the news for nearly a week,' she said. 'Aren't you suffering from withdrawal symptoms?'

'Not in the least,' said Basil. 'They know where I am if they need me, don't they? For the moment, it's total happiness to be here with you.'

'Is it really?' Olivia put her arms round his neck. 'Don't you find it a bit quiet?'

'It's heaven.' He kissed her, and they put on their coats and crossed the Place de l'Eglise to the café. As they came through the door, they saw Domenica, Robert and Giò seated at a table in the corner, eating their supper. Basil went to the bar, and Olivia threaded her way through the busy café, pulled up an extra chair and sat down at their table.

'Fancy seeing you here,' said Giò, kissing her.

'Fancy seeing you.' Olivia returned the kiss. 'Did you come on your own, Giò? When do the others get here?'

'They're not coming.'

'Not coming? Why?'

'Oh, it's too difficult to explain,' said Domenica, and then did exactly that. 'They're snowed up, and Philippe's lambs are all getting born prematurely, it seems, and Josh is staying there to help him, and Max wants to stay with Josh. You know how it is?'

'Well,' said Olivia cheerfully, 'never mind. *We're* all here, aren't we?'

'I just hope you like oysters and goose, that's all,' said Domenica dourly.

'I adore oysters and goose,' said Baz, overhearing this remark as he arrived with the cognac. 'Surely, that can't be a problem?'

'No, darling, it's not a problem.' Domenica emptied her glass. 'Is that cognac for me, Baz?'

'Who else?' said Basil, handing it over, and returning to the bar for reinforcements.

Chapter Eighteen

'Did you get him, then?' asked Mabel cheerfully, as she came back with the bottle of whisky, as well as the items she required to make macaroni cheese.

'No, there was no answer. He must be out.'

'You did *ring*, didn't you?' Mabel sounded suspicious. 'You didn't change your mind or anything? Lose your bottle?'

'No, of course not.' Dido looked at Mabel. 'I'll try again a bit later, he's probably gone out with Vassili and Heleni.'

'I thought he wasn't that social?'

'He's not, usually.'

'Oh.'

'Mabel, I promise you, there's no reply. I'll try again later, honestly.'

'Well, OK. As long as you do. Now, what about a drink? I'm parched.'

'Good idea.' Dido found glasses, and they turned on the telly and watched the Festival of Nine Lessons for a while.

'Bleedin' carols,' said Mabel glumly. 'They always make me blub.'

'Me too,' said Dido, and laughed.

'I'd rather 'ave a Morecombe and Wise repeat, meself.'

'That's on tomorrow, I should imagine,' said Dido, flicking through the stations.

'Well, better get me skates on if we're going to eat

324

before eight.' Mabel topped up her glass and went to the kitchen.

Dido looked at the telephone. It was more than an hour since she had last tried Guy's number, perhaps she should try again? She checked the number in her pocket-book yet again, and double-checked the codes in the directory. Then she picked up the phone and dialled the number. There was a pause, then the electronic clicks, another pause followed by the ringing tone. She listened, her heart beating fast, imagining the long room with its wooden ceiling, the big sofa with its warm sheepskins, the wide glowing fireplace and Guy's black leather chair with the stool for his legs. She saw the chair quite clearly, empty, with Guy's sticks lying on the floor beside it, as if he had suddenly got up and walked away, with no need of the sticks. She frowned uneasily, letting the phone continue to ring until it became increasingly obvious that there was no one there, either willing or able to answer it. She put the phone down reluctantly, feeling that she was breaking even the slender thread of contact that remained if she allowed it to go on ringing. She sighed, got up from the sofa and poked her head round the door of the galley kitchen. 'I'm just going on deck for a breath of air, Mabel, and try and get rid of this headache, OK?'

'Well, don't hang about up there, will you? The nosh'll be ready in ten minutes.' And indeed, a delicious and comforting smell of cheese sauce filled the little space.

'Smells lovely,' said Dido. 'I won't be long.'

She closed the kitchen door, put on her coat and went out onto the deck. She stood for a few minutes watching the quiet activities of the river at night, taking deep breaths of the faintly putrescent air, consciously trying to relax and calm her underlying anxiety. Don't be ridiculous, she told herself. He is a grown man; he is almost certainly out for the evening, there is no reason at all for him to stay at home on the off-chance that I might ring him. She sat down on a bollard, wrapping her coat tightly round her, and watched the moon rise through the electric orange haze that prevented the London sky from becoming completely dark. She remembered with sadness the velvety pitch-blackness of the sky at Koulari, the blaze of stars, the beautiful sickle moon rising over the mountains of Albania. What am I doing here? she asked herself unhappily. What have I done? Suddenly, down in the studio, the phone began to ring, shrill and insistent. Her heart in her mouth, Dido leapt to her feet. Thank God! It must be him she thought, half-falling down the steps in her hurry to reach the telephone. Trembling, she picked it up. 'Hello?'

'Dido?' It was Jake.

Disappointment and anguish flowed through Dido, followed by rage. 'What do you want?' she said through gritted teeth.

'Just thought I'd wish you a merry Christmas.'

'Thank you,' she said coldly.

'I thought perhaps you'd like to come out for a drink?'

'No, I wouldn't.'

'Oh, come on, darling. It's Christmas; let's not quarrel.'

'Jake, are you really so thick and conceited that you don't believe what I keep telling you? Everything is over between us, absolutely and completely.'

'You don't mean . . .'

'I bloody do!' She slammed down the phone and stood there shaking with fury and frustration, close to tears.

Mabel opened the galley door and came in, carrying

a tray. She began to set the table. 'Not 'im then, darlin'?' She glanced at Dido furtively as she stood there, her arms crossed, pale and tense, her lips in a straight tight line.

Dido looked at Mabel, tried to smile and shook her head. 'No, it wasn't him.'

'Well, give it another go, while I get out the dish, and then we'll eat.'

'I don't think there's much point,' began Dido.

'Do it!' said Mabel, closing the kitchen door behind her.

Without hope, Dido dialled the number. It was engaged. Her heart leapt with joy. He must be at home now! She waited a moment, and then dialled again, agitated, trembling. As before, the phone rang and rang, there was no answer. She hung up.

Mabel came in with the macaroni cheese, and they sat down together to eat it. Mabel did not ask whether Dido had had any luck; it was quite obvious that she had not.

After supper they washed the dishes, then made up Dido's old bed for Mabel. Dido found her some pyjamas and an old pair of her mother's slippers, of pink quilted satin.

'Cor,' said Mabel, 'aren't we posh?'

They watched the television news, then Dido said she thought she'd go to bed – it had been a long, exhausting day and she still had a headache.

'I'll watch the box for a bit,' said Mabel. 'Des O'Connor might be on. He's a laugh and no mistake; I like him.'

'Why not?' Dido agreed. 'And don't worry about me; just pop through to the bathroom when you want to.'

'Don't 'ave no choice, love, do I?'

Dido laughed. 'No, you don't.'

'You're not going to try him again, then?'

Dido looked at her watch: ten-past ten. 'It's ten-past twelve there,' she said, frowning. 'They'll either be out still, or gone to church, or in bed more likely.' She sighed. 'I'd better wait, and try again in the morning.'

Mabel looked at her sympathetically. 'I expect you know best, love. You try and get some kip, why don't you?'

'I will.' Dido bent down and gave Mabel a kiss. 'Thank you for coming, darling Mabel. You're an angel.'

In her bedroom, she kicked off her shoes and lay down for a moment, closing her eyes. In a way, she felt relieved that it was now after midnight in Corfu, and that it would therefore be rather antisocial of her to telephone at such a late hour, but a small inner voice told her that Guy might be lying there in bed, staring at the phone, willing it to ring. She put her hands over her eyes, feeling exhausted, feeble, and emotionally drained. I'll try again tomorrow she told herself, I'm sure that's best.

She felt uncomfortable lying flat on the bed, it seemed to make her headache worse, so she got up, went to the bathroom, had a wash and cleaned her teeth. Then she went back to the bedroom, piled her pillows into a high heap and leaned against them, massaging her stiff neck. On the night-table was a pile of books and she picked one up and opened it at random. The book was an anthology of English verse and she began to read from the top of the page.

What, you want, do you, to come unawares,
Sweeping the church up for first morning prayers,
And find a poor devil has ended his cares
At the foot of your rotten-runged, rat-riddled stairs.
Do I carry the moon in my pocket?

Dido read these lines three times, and an ice-cold sensation crept over her, a strong premonition that something terrible had happened to Guy. She lay for a moment, paralysed with fear, then picked up the extension phone and dialled his number, her heart hammering in her chest. The phone at the other end rang and rang and was not answered.

'Something has happened,' she said aloud. 'I must go to him at once.' Suddenly calm, she got off the bed, put on her shoes and went quickly to the studio, waking Mabel, who was quietly asleep in front of the telly. 'Sorry, Mabel, I need the phone book.'

Startled, Mabel sat up. 'What ever's up now?'

'It's Guy. I'm sure something has happened to him. I must get a flight tonight, if I can, and go to him.' She found the number and phoned the airport. She explained that she urgently needed to fly to Corfu, could they do anything?

'As it happens, you're in luck, madam. I've just this moment had a cancellation on the last flight out to Athens tonight. Then you could get a local flight to Corfu. How would that suit?'

'Brilliantly.'

'Can you get here by eleven-fifty?'

'I'll be there,' said Dido. She gave her Visa number and arranged to pick up the ticket at the desk.

'Blimey,' said Mabel, as Dido put down the phone, 'you're a fast worker and no mistake. What about packing?'

'I don't need anything except my cards and my passport.' She rang for a taxi, then put everything she needed into her bag, put on her coat and went out onto the quayside to wait for the cab. Mabel stood beside her, shivering.

'Don't wait,' said Dido, putting her arm round

Mabel's shoulder. 'You'll catch your death. Go on down, I'll phone you tomorrow, I promise.'

The lights of the taxi flashed as they came into view. Dido bent and kissed Mabel. 'Goodbye, darling. Have a happy Christmas.' She leapt into the cab and was gone.

'Chance'd be a fine thing,' said Mabel. She stepped gingerly over the gangplank, and down the steps to *The Maid of Wapping*.

Guy lay in his long black chair, his eyes closed, concentrating on the telephone, silently urging it to ring. He opened his eyes and looked at his watch: twenty-past eleven. He had been back from the taverna for about half an hour. It's only twenty-past nine in the UK, it's not too late for her to ring if she wants to. He felt his back slipping against the leather cushions, and pulled himself back to an upright position, determined not to fall asleep. He looked at the whisky bottle on the table at his side and was sorely tempted to pour himself a drink. No, he said to himself. I'll wait until midnight. If she hasn't phoned by then, I'll drink the whole bloody bottle and be done with it. His legs throbbed, rubbed and sore from the irons, and he tried to ease them inside the stiff cruel straps, but could not. Christ, he thought, why am I so useless and helpless, ugly and deformed? Why must I be in agony so much of the time? Why do I bother going on, is it worth it? Is it? Despising himself for his lack of spirit, but at the same time unable to prevent it, he slid deeper and deeper into his familiar state of intense self-pity and black loathing of his disfigured body. You'd better face it, Guy, he told himself coldly, she's backed off. She's realized the implications of spending the rest of her life with a cripple, and frankly, who could blame her?

He closed his eyes again, and tried extremely hard to relax, aware that his moods of anger and depression only made his physical suffering harder to endure. I wonder what it is about me that provokes so much hostility in others? he asked himself; even makes some of them want to destroy me? First of all Lavinia, and that was quite a surprise. As a boy, I absolutely worshipped her; it just shows how unreliable one's judgement can be. Then there had been the sneerers and bullies at school. He could not remember a single master or boy who had been supportive to him in his disadvantaged situation, or even kind. I suppose I must have been proud, aggressive and very unattractive myself as an adolescent, he told himself. He recognized that he had probably discouraged any attempts at friendliness, assuming it to be patronizing, and had become master of the sharp-tongued, abrasive riposte. He had been nicknamed The Jackal by some unremembered wit, though Guy had never understood the thinking behind this cruel taunt, which to this day made him squirm with shame. Though it wasn't particularly clever or original of them, he thought, I'm sure I could have dreamt up far more insulting and hurtful labels myself. In any case, he reminded himself sharply, annoyed at his continued capacity to feel hurt by the events of the distant past, I'm sure a lot of my unhappiness was entirely my own fault.

He had worked hard to get to Oxford and leave his schooldays behind him, hoping to find a more enlightened and intellectual approach to life at university, with less emphasis on physical excellence. But in the event, the change of scene had made very little difference, for several of his peers were at Oxford at the same time, and the word soon got round that Porteous was a pompous little cripple, and best avoided. He had found it virtually impossible to make a fresh set of friends. He had joined a couple of dining clubs, and for a few short weeks had participated in their competitive drinking bouts as a means of ingratiating himself into even such a brain-dead society as theirs. After a couple of disastrous episodes, involving brushes with the Bulldogs and a warning from his tutor, he had retreated from the field of battle, having no wish to be sent down. After that he had worked and lived in a fairly solitary state, keeping out of trouble. Girls had not figured in his life at all, and who could blame them? The young fear anything that is not the norm, it is instinctive for them to reject it, and he had understood their reluctance to become involved with him. Eventually, he had had the satisfaction of being called to the Bar, but the stares and half-concealed smiles of his fellows, as he fought to become a fully-paid-up member of the human race, were difficult to ignore, both at the time and in retrospect. And now it seemed that even Dido had rejected him. Poor girl, he thought. I wouldn't blame her. Why the hell should she be tied to a self-pitying wreck like me?

He looked at his watch: five-past twelve. He picked up the bottle of whisky, unscrewed the cap and took a long swig from the bottle. He replaced the cap and put the bottle back on the table, then he took a pad of paper from the lower shelf of the table and wrote a letter to Dido. He told her how much he loved her, how much happiness she had brought him and how much pain he was presently enduring without her. He hesitated for a moment, and then wrote: I imagine that by now you have decided to patch up your differences and return to Jacob Kroll who is, after all, your lover of so many years. I can perfectly understand that you would not really wish to end that relationship, and exchange the full and interesting life you led with him, for the narrow and parochial existence in this little island, which is all I can offer you. He signed the letter, blotted it carefully, folded it and put it in his jacket pocket. He swivelled round in his chair and lifted his legs to the ground. Then, grasping his two sticks firmly he stood up, and steadied himself. He turned off the lamp, then walked carefully to the garden door and let himself out. The full moon shone brilliantly overhead and the silvery leaves of the olives shimmered in the cold night air. The brightly-lit grove was quiet and still, not a leaf rustled, not a sound came from the taverna or from Vassili's cottage. Guy could not even hear the gentle rattle of the stones dragged by the tide on the shore. It was as if the world held its breath, and was waiting for something to happen. Slowly, he made his way across the moonlit ground, under the black-shadowed trees to the chapel, tall and ghostly pale under the moon. He pushed open the door and went in. He looked around him at the faded frescoes, at the stone seat round the walls, bespattered with swallow's droppings, remembering the coolness of the stone on his hot back as he sat there with Dido beside him, the scent of her bare arm round his neck and the softness of her lips on his cheek. He crossed the crumbling, moon-bleached stone floor to the foot of the rickety ladder. He looked up at the platform so far above, close to the roof, and checked that the letter was still in his pocket. Then, letting his sticks fall to the ground, he grasped the rungs of the ladder and hauled himself up, hand over hand, sweating with the exertion, until at last he reached the top of the scaffolding. With a final, lung-bursting effort, he heaved himself over the top of the ladder and dragged himself onto the platform. It was stinking with owls' detritus: soiled feathers, regurgitated pellets and shit.

For a few moments he lay there, gasping for breath, his heart pounding, his cheek resting in the evil-smelling filth. Then, painfully, he rolled onto his back and gazed at the painted vault above his head. The gold stars looked suprisingly large at such close quarters, and he could see that they were really quite crudely painted, their edges jagged on the rough-hewn blue-painted stones of the vault. If the smell wasn't so foul, he thought, and my bloody legs didn't hurt so much, it would actually feel rather peaceful and pleasant up here. He sat up and undid the straps of his leg-irons. He threw them over the edge of the platform and heard them crash to the floor below; I shan't be needing you again, fucking things, he thought. He lay down again, on his side, and gazed through the gaping hole in the wall, over the tops of the olive trees to the sea beyond. He felt sad, and extremely tired, but calm and strangely relieved, as if he had reached the end of a long, exhausting and apparently pointless journey. He looked at the moon silvering the tops of the olive trees, at the real stars thrown like a scarf of diamonds across the sky, and reflected in the glassy water of the sea. It's a beautiful world, he said to himself; it's a pity there's so little room in it for misfits like me.

The plane landed on time at Athens. As soon as she had cleared passport control Dido went as swiftly as she could to the West Terminal. At the Olympic Airways desk she booked a seat on the next flight to Corfu. She had to wait for nearly an hour before take-off, so she changed some money, found a telephone booth and tried once more to ring Guy's number, but the phone was dead, presumably out of order. Trying to remain calm, and not to allow her anxiety to turn to panic, Dido paced up and down impatiently until her flight was called in rather a casual manner, and she went out with three other passengers to the local plane. The passengers carried their luggage on board with them and stowed it wherever they wished, to Dido's surprise, used to the strict regulations of international airlines. As the little plane droned steadily northwards through the still cold air, she sat beside a window and watched the huge full moon slide slowly down the sky, shedding its light on mountain peaks and rippled silver seas. If I weren't so anxious and afraid, she thought, I expect I'd think this one of the loveliest things I'd ever seen. Once landed and disembarked at Corfu, she decided not to waste time by trying to telephone again. Instead, she ran as fast as she could to the few waiting taxis and in five minutes was speeding towards Koulari, desperate to get there but terrified of what she might find. The moon had long set as she stood in the dark olive grove and watched the lights of the taxi disappear up the winding track to the main road. The house was dark; there were no lights in Vassili's cottage; Guy's car was not in its usual place. As her eyes became accustomed to the darkness, she saw that the garden door to the sitting-room was open. She entered the house, crossed the familiar room in the dark and turned on the lamp beside Guy's chair. On the table was an almost full bottle of whisky, a writing pad and Guy's pen. A piece of white blotting paper lay under the pad and the word 'Guy' in reverse leapt out at her. Picking up the blotting paper, Dido could just decipher the preceding words: 'parochial life in this little island which is all I can offer you'. She drew a deep breath, replaced the blotting paper where she had found it and went swiftly round the house, checking all the rooms carefully. She took the big hunter torch from its hook and went out onto the dark terrace, flashing the light over the balustrade, searching the ground below. She went down the steps and walked slowly round the side of the house, the powerful beam of the lamp illuminating the surrounding trees and shrubs as she examined them inch by inch. Fearfully, she looked into the swimming pool, now empty and loosely covered for the winter. Turning, she shone the torch towards the parking area, and it was then that she saw that the door to the chapel was wide open. Oh God, she thought, that's where he'll be! What has he done? She began to run, stumbling over the rough ground while the beam of light from the torch bounced erratically in front of her. She went into the chapel, and saw at once Guy's sticks and his leg-irons, lying at the foot of the ladder. She walked across the floor and stared at them stupidly, then flashed the torch round the walls of the chapel and went fearfully to the rear of the scaffolding but could find nothing. She returned to the foot of the ladder and picked up one of the leg-irons. He must have taken them off himself, she thought; he can't have got far without them. Up in the roof, she heard a heavy dragging noise and looked up, startled, then shone the torch, lighting the platform so far above. 'Guy? Are you up there?'

Two hands gripped the edge of the platform, then Guy's face appeared, streaked with dirt. 'Hello, Dido.' He sounded angry in his effort not to lose control. 'Turn that bloody lamp off, for Christ's sake!'

Laughing with relief, Dido put down the torch and climbed swiftly up the ladder. 'Move over, Guy, I want to come up.' He moved aside, and she crawled onto the platform and lay down beside him, head to head. She took his dirty face in her hands and kissed him softly on the mouth, then looked at him severely, frowning. 'What the hell do you think you're doing up here, for heaven's sake?'

'What do you think? Taking a close look at the stars.'

Their eyes met, dark with apprehension. A goose walked over Dido's grave and the hair rose on her head. 'Can we go down now, and go to bed?' she asked quietly. 'It's terribly cold up here.'

'Why not? You go first, then if my hand slips, I can fall on you. On second thoughts, that's a lousy idea, I'll go first.' He manoeuvred himself over the edge of the platform and slid slowly down the ladder, gripping the rungs with alternate hands. Dido watched him, her heart in her mouth. 'OK,' he called, 'now you.'

She followed him down, then buckled on his leg-irons. They went slowly back to the house, and to bed. Lying together, too exhausted to talk, but clean and comfortable in each other's arms, longed-for sleep stole upon them. Once Guy opened his eyes, drowsily, and listened to his owls hooting in the olive grove. The sound no longer sounded unbearably sad to him, but beautiful and comforting. He turned his head and looked at the sleeping face of the woman he so dearly loved, and had so very nearly lost, then closed his eyes and drifted back to sleep.

He woke at dawn. The sky through the bedroom window was a pearly grey, and a few birds had already started to sing in the trees below the terrace. His left arm, still cradling Dido's head, had gone to sleep and he had severe pins and needles in his hand. In spite of the discomfort, he remained absolutely still, unwilling to disturb her. He gazed at the slowly lightening sky, light-headed with happiness and relief at finding that her presence beside him was not a dream. He watched as a local *caique*, its lights lit, came round the head-land and made its purposeful way towards Koulari harbour, perhaps bringing home a party who had been to the midnight service in Corfu Town?

'Hello.' Dido raised her head from Guy's arm. She leaned on her elbow, blinking at him sleepily. 'Didn't you sleep, darling?'

'I did,' said Guy. 'Like the dead.'

Dido winced and put her finger on his lips. 'Don't say that, please.'

'Sorry. It just slipped out.' He sat up abruptly, and shook his arm energetically to restore the circulation. Then he kissed her, and leaned back against the pillows. 'I don't suppose I have to tell you how desperately unhappy I've been without you, Dido. Promise me you'll never run away again?'

'I promise.' She smiled at him ruefully. 'It's my besetting sin, bunking off in the face of trouble. I always run, get the hell out of it all. I'll have to stop doing it now, won't I? The fare to Corfu is too expensive to allow for too many flits, isn't it?'

She got out of bed and put on Guy's dressing-gown, then sat on the end of the bed. 'I'm going to tell you exactly what happened with Jake, Guy, and then perhaps we can put it behind us, forget it ever happened.'

'Please don't,' said Guy. 'I really don't want to hear about it, and I'm sure you don't want to talk about it.'

'But I really need to tell you about it, Guy, if you feel you can endure it? It was stupid of me not to tell you at the time, I see that now. If I'd shared the whole ghastly thing with you then, it would have been painful, but we could have talked it through, and none of this would have happened, would it?'

'I suppose not.' He held out his hand. 'OK, tell me about it if you feel you must, but get back into bed, please.'

'Shall I make some tea first?'

'Dido, get back into bed!'

She got back into bed, and told him exactly what had happened, from the moment she had looked up from her bale of straw, until her battered exit from the stable, followed by her tepid bath in the house to cleanse herself of Jake, and finally her decision not to tell Guy about her ordeal, for what at the time seemed like good and proper reasons. Dido stopped talking, and there was a long silence.

'You make me feel ashamed,' said Guy at last. 'I don't deserve you, Dido. I should have been much more sensitive to the complexities of a relationship like yours and Kroll's; more able to take on board any kind of grey area that might still exist between you.'

'But it didn't exist,' said Dido. 'Not as far as I was concerned, at any rate.'

'I know that, now. The point is, if it *had* existed, I should have been able to deal with it, even sympathize with it, as well as understand it. But I didn't. I reacted like a child; I was angry, and jealous.'

'I don't mind that,' said Dido, smiling, and putting her arms round his neck.

'Don't mind what?'

'Your being jealous.'

'Oh.' He kissed her. 'Well, you may as well know, I *am* jealous, and possessive too.'

Dido laughed. 'No one's ever been jealous of me before, as far as I know, so it's rather a nice feeling.'

'I'm glad you think so. It's not a nice feeling *being* jealous, I have to tell you. It's absolute hell.'

'Yes,' said Dido seriously, 'I can imagine it would be.'

Guy looked at her intensely, as if he still couldn't really believe that his nightmare was over. 'What made you decide to come back so suddenly, Dido, without even phoning?'

'Without even *phoning*? You must be joking. I spent the entire evening trying to get through to you, and there was no reply. Where were you all that time, anyway? Surely not up there on that filthy platform?'

'No, I was at the taverna for quite a time.'

'At the taverna?'

He explained about the christening party for Katerina's baby. 'It was a shame you weren't here for it, they danced the *agiriótikos*; it was beautiful.'

'And I was having macaroni cheese with Mabel.'

'With Mabel?'

'Yes, and it's really on her account that I'm here at all. She made me understand what an idiot I'd been, and she helped me take all Jake's things out to Strand-on-the-Green and dump them by the dustbins.'

'How on earth did you manage that?'

'We took a taxi.'

'What else?' said Guy, and laughed. 'Then what happened?'

'Well, then I went to bed, meaning to start phoning again in the morning, and I picked up a book, and read this horrible poem about a corpse lying at the bottom of rotten-runged, rat-riddled stairs. It gave me the most ghastly fright, and in no time at all I was on my way to Athens. Poor Mabel, she was spinning! I mustn't forget to phone her.' She turned to Guy, and looked at him severely. 'And while we're on the subject, why the hell didn't *you* ring *me*, you brute?'

Guy looked back at her steadily. 'If you knew how much I wanted to, my darling; and how many times I very nearly did.'

'Well, why didn't you?'

'Because I knew that if we spoke, I would break down, and you would guess at once how terribly badly I needed you.'

'Would that have been a bad thing?'

'Yes, it would. I wanted you to come because *you* needed *me*, though you may find that hard to believe.'

'I don't find it hard to believe, because it's true. I do need you, Guy.'

'Do you really?'

'Yes, I do.'

There was a tap on the door, and Heleni came into the room carrying a breakfast tray. *'Kali mera'* she began, and then saw Dido lying in Guy's arms. She let out a loud scream and dropped the tray with a tremendous crash on the floor. She stood there, rooted to the spot, her hand over her mouth, staring at them. Guy and Dido began to laugh, as swift heavy footsteps sounded in the passage and Vassili appeared in the doorway, white-faced, expecting the worst. When he realized what had happened, he grabbed Heleni round the waist and twirled her round and round, while they exchanged a joyful torrent of Greek. Then Vassili ran across the room, took Dido's hand and kissed her wrist, at the same time showering them with excited good wishes. The only word that Dido understood was *efcharistó*, thank you. Heleni stood shyly in the doorway, nodding in agreement, smiling at them. Then order was restored, the tray and the broken china removed, and a cloth brought from the kitchen to wipe up the mess.

'Do you think we'll get another tray?' said Dido, after Vassili had gone, closing the door behind him. 'I'm absolutely starving, aren't you?'

'Now you come to mention it, yes, I am.'

In ten minutes there was another knock, and Heleni, suitably composed and serious, came in with a fresh tray. She put it carefully down on the table, at Dido's side of the bed.

'*Efcharistó*, Heleni.' Dido smiled at her.

'*Típota.*' Heleni made a little warm gesture with her hand, and departed, leaving them alone together.

'Never has coffee smelt so wonderful,' said Guy, as Dido poured him a cup and passed it to him.

'Or yoghurt looked so utterly delicious,' said Dido.

'Or toast so catastrophically burnt,' said Guy, and laughed.

On New Year's Eve Guy received a phone call from his lawyers in Dublin, informing him that his sister's body had been found in the river at Inniscarragh. A thorough search had not revealed a will, and it therefore appeared that in due course all her possessions would pass to Guy, her only surviving relative. McDonnell went on to suggest that if Guy decided to fly to Ireland for the funeral, it could be made to coincide with the completion of the sale of Inniscarragh, now imminent.

'Oh, darling, do we really have to go?'

'No, we don't. I never want to see the bloody place again. As for the completion, I've already signed all the necessary documents. If there's anything else, McDonnell can fly out here.'

'Poor old Lavinia,' said Dido. 'I wonder what happened?'

'No one seems to know. Evidently, she was wearing her overcoat and boots, so perhaps she was going for a walk. She fell through the old bridge, they think.'

'Poor thing, how sad.'

Guy said nothing. He had not told Dido about his last interview with his sister, and saw no point in doing so now.

In the late afternoon, they walked up to the chapel. They sat on the ledge that encircled the internal walls, just as they had done on Dido's first visit.

'There's something I need to know,' she said, 'and then we'll never speak of it again.'

'Yes?'

She looked up at the platform. 'What were you doing

up there, Guy?' She looked back at him. 'And why did you take off your leg-irons?'

'They were hurting me, and I didn't think I'd be needing them any more.'

'Were you planning to throw yourself off?'

'Yes. I was.'

'I'm very glad you didn't.'

'So am I.' He turned his head and looked at her. 'You got here just in time.'

'Thank God.'

'Amen to that.'

They sat together in the gathering dusk, soothed by the peaceful atmosphere of the little chapel.

'Dido, my love?'

'Mm?'

'I suppose we'll have to get married in town, in the official sense, but it would be nice to get the old priest to give us a blessing here afterwards, wouldn't it?'

'Yes, it would be lovely. But isn't the place too much of a ruin?'

'Well, we could restore it, couldn't we?'

'But that would cost a bomb, surely?'

'Probably, but it's only money, isn't it?'

Dido laughed. 'Yes, but we still have to be prudent, don't we? All these air fares must have made quite a hole in the exchequer, and now that I've asked Mabel to live in *The Maid of Wapping*, we haven't even got the money we would have had if I'd sold her.' She frowned, looking worried.

Guy took her hand and kissed it. 'Now is probably the appropriate time to tell you that we are going to be rather obscenely rich,' he said quietly, and told her the seemingly enormous sum he had been offered for Inniscarragh. 'And now we'll have Lavinia's assets on top of that, and knowing her, I'd guess she was pretty loaded. I'm just astonished she hasn't left it all to a cats' home, or something.'

'Perhaps she has,' said Dido darkly, 'and they just haven't found the will yet.'

'Perhaps she has,' he agreed, and laughed. 'In that case, we'll just have to give it all back, won't we?'

'I wouldn't care.'

'Neither would I.'

Postlude

At four-fifty Patrick and Anna got off the plane at Montpellier, hired a car at the airport, and drove to Souliac. As Patrick drove along the familiar *autoroute* towards Nîmes and Rémoulins, Anna watched the red ball of the sun dropping slowly down the sky towards the distant blue mountains, and could scarcely believe that they had been in the snow and ice of Normandy only that morning. The decision to come down had been swift and without problems. After supper the previous night, while Philippe, Josh and the two boys had gone out to check the ewes, Anna and Patrick had cleared away the dishes and washed up. 'What's the matter, darling?' Patrick had asked, quietly.

'Nothing's the matter; why should it be?'

'Come on, tell me. Is it Domenica?'

Anna looked at him, her dark eyes troubled. 'Yes, it is. I feel bad about crying off their *réveillon*. I could tell she was upset about it. It's not at all like her, really.'

'As a matter of fact,' said Patrick, 'I don't find it surprising at all. We haven't been down to stay with them for more than two years, if you think about it. We come here so often, it's like our second home. It's become a habit, hasn't it?'

'Well, Philippe needs us, doesn't he?'

'No more than Domenica, by the sound of things.'

'Oh, dear,' said Anna. 'Now I feel worse. You've muddled me.'

'Don't be silly, darling. We've made a mistake, that's

345

all. We'll fly down tomorrow and surprise them.'

'But what about the children?'

'What about them? Josh is here, and Marie-Claude; they'll be fine. They won't miss us at all. As a matter of fact, I wouldn't mind a few days without the children, just us.'

'But what about Mum and Dad, and the others?'

'That's different; they're not little boys. They don't hit each other, and quarrel all the time.'

'Are you being a reluctant father, my love?'

'I am, yes; on a temporary basis. Do you mind?'

'No, I don't,' said Anna. 'I don't mind at all.'

Just after half-past six they drove into the Place de l'Eglise and parked beside the green metal gates of the presbytery. The squat church tower and the naked branches of the plane trees were silhouetted against the velvety deep blue of the sky. The stars were already appearing, one by one.

'It's lovely to be back,' said Anna, looking around her at the familiar setting of her childhood, the dripping mossy fountain, the café, the *alimentation,* the *boulangerie* and the post office. 'I'm glad we came.'

'So am I.'

They got out of the car, and Patrick took their overnight bag from the back seat. Anna pushed open the iron gate, which uttered its customary complaining squeak. They crossed the courtyard to the big double doors to the kitchen. A crack of light was visible at the base of the door, and they could hear the voices of Robert and Olivia inside. Lifting the latch, and pushing open the heavy door, Anna went in. Her father, concentrating on stitching up his geese so that the stuffing would not escape during the roasting, looked up abstractedly.

'Anna! What are *you* doing here? I thought you weren't coming?'

'We changed our minds.'

Olivia, her hands wet from peeling potatoes, rushed from the sink and threw her arms round her mother. 'How *terrific* that you came! Domenica *will* be pleased! She was really pissed off when you chucked, wasn't she, Grandpa?' She flung her arms round Patrick and kissed him, too.

'Yes, she was a bit,' said Robert.

'Where is she now?'

'Upstairs. Having a rest in front of the fire.'

'Having a *rest*?' said Anna. 'That doesn't sound like Mum.'

'Oh, well,' said her father, mildly, 'we're all getting a bit past our sell-by dates, I suppose.'

Anna laughed, but she felt a distinct sensation of dismay, and a reluctant recognition of the inevitability of the passage of time. She took off her coat and hung it on the back of the kitchen door, then went upstairs to the *salon*. Domenica lay on the sofa, her eyes closed, her wild curly grey hair like a cloud against the burnt-orange velvet of the cushions. She wore a scarlet cashmere sweater, one that she had had for years, and mole-skin trousers. Her hands, blue-veined and knotted with arthritis, were folded on her stomach. For the first time, Anna realized that her mother was getting old. She sat down on a low walnut nursing-chair beside the fire and waited for her to wake.

'Hello, darling,' said Domenica, without opening her eyes. 'I thought I heard your voice.'

'Hello, Mum.' Anna got up, and knelt beside her. 'How are you?'

Domenica opened her eyes and smiled. 'I'm so glad you've come,' she said. 'I could do with a bit of female company.'

Anna laughed, and kissed her mother. 'What about Olly? Won't she do?'

'Too young,' said Domenica. 'Not enough water under the bridge. Is it too early for a drink?'

'Certainly not. I could do with one myself.' Anna got up and went to the table where a tray of bottles and glasses waited. She poured two small armagnacs and returned to the fireside. '*Salut*,' she said, raising her glass.

'*Salut*,' replied Domenica. 'Did you all come, darling?'

'No, just me and Patrick.'

'How lovely.' She looked at Anna, her grey-green eyes soft. 'You must phone them all, later.'

'I will,' said Anna.

THE END

The Golden Year
Elizabeth Falconer

One enchanted summer in Provence and its aftermath.

Summers, to Anna, had always meant the Presbytery, the mellow old stone house in Provence where her mother, the formidable Domenica, lived. Now that Anna's marriage to Jeffrey was all but over, she thought that she had herself well organized, dividing her time between her riverside home in London, her two teenage children and her career as a gilder and restorer of antiques. And then there were her summers in France – a chance to eat and drink magnificently, to sit in the sun and to recharge the batteries. She hardly realized how narrow and lonely her life had really become.

But one summer her brother Giò, an antiques dealer in Paris, brought down a new friend to the Presbytery. Patrick, a handsome television director, suddenly opened up Anna's life in a new and wonderful way, offering her a wholly unexpected chance of happiness. But she did not immediately see that others might not share her joy, and that her beloved brother Giò could have quite different ideas about Patrick and the future.

'A DELIGHTFUL EVOCATION OF THE SIGHTS, SOUNDS AND FLAVOURS OF LIFE IN PROVENCE'
Family Circle

0 552 99622 X

BLACK SWAN

The Love Of Women
Elizabeth Falconer

Nelly and Hugo lived a seemingly enviable life, with their three adorable little girls, their holidays at the beautiful family home in the Channel Islands, and their large, if disorganized, London house. Why, then, did Hugo feel increasingly inadequate? He began to wonder why Nelly had married him instead of Basil, their close ally from Cambridge days. Basil had instead become an indispensable family friend, and Nelly's demanding job as a hospital doctor seemed to overshadow Hugo's own successful but unremunerative career as a writer – Hugo felt as though his only function in Nelly's life nowadays was to babysit the children and keep an eye on the erratic au pair. One day, in a fit of rebellion, he packed his bags and went to stay with Basil's mother in her peaceful Paris flat on the lovely Ile St-Louis.

Basil, meanwhile, was facing an uncertain future. Tied by loyalty to Nelly and Hugo, and with a muddled and ambivalent series of past relationships, he was at first reluctant to commit himself when he met Olivia, the self-confident young English art student living in Paris who was interested in the work of Basil's late father, a much-admired Russian painter. While Hugo discovered how hard it was to escape from family ties, Basil was to find that friendship and love do not easily mingle.

'AN UNHURRIED, LUXURIOUS STORY OF RESOLUTION AND DISCOVERY . . . THE NOVEL'S CHARM LIES IN ITS UNPRETENTIOUSNESS AND THE AUTHOR'S AFFECTION FOR CHARACTERS'
Elizabeth Buchan, *Mail on Sunday*

0 552 99623 8

BLACK SWAN

A Mislaid Magic
Joyce Windsor

'I LOVED IT. I THOUGHT IT FRESH AND SHARP AND FUNNY,
WITH A MOST WONDERFULLY ECCENTRIC CHARM'
Joanna Trollope

All the beguiling charm of Dodie Smith's *I Capture the Castle*
combined with the witty view of Britain's upper classes portrayed in
Nancy Mitford's *Love in a Cold Climate*. A totally compelling first
novel which is funny, sad, and utterly delightful.

Lady Amity Savernake, neglected, rather plain, and youngest
daughter of the Earl of Osmington, was seven years old when her
stepmother (disparagingly referred to within the family as Soapy
Sonia) took her to London, bought her a fitted vicuna coat with a
velvet collar, and introduced her (at the Ritz) to Rudi Longmire, the
genie who was to change their lives.

It was Rudi's idea that there should be a midsummer Festival of Arts
at Gunville Place. The ugly Dorset pile, seat of the Savernakes, would
be transformed into a pastoral paradise; singers, actors, musicians
and exotic visitors – as well as the family – would bring enchantment
into their world. As Rudi, Master of Revels and Lord of Misrule,
drew each and every one of them into his exotic plans, so excitement
spilled out into the countryside. A dead may tree threw out leaves
and blossomed. The local white witch absentmindedly gave her pig a
love potion, and two village maidens were accosted in the woods by
a genuine Dorset Ooser.

And within the family it seemed the enchantment would solve their
various discontents. Soapy Sonia, Grandmother Mottesfont, even
Claudia, Amy's corrosive and rebellious sister, bloomed in the
midsummer revels. And young Amy watched and listened and for a
brief childhood span was given the magic of complete happiness – a
happiness she never forgot – not even in the disruptive aftermath of
that heady summer, or in the years that followed.

'IT HAS ALL THE INGREDIENTS OF A FAIRY TALE . . .
WHIMSICAL . . . SHARPLY FUNNY IN PARTS'
The Times

0 552 99591 6

BLACK SWAN

A SELECTED LIST OF FINE WRITING AVAILABLE FROM BLACK SWAN